PRAISE FOR *Willa's Grove*

"*Willa's Grove* is the book my heart needed...
It's a love letter to female friendships, to the power of
vulnerability, to the strength of community, and daring to
live authentically. An absolute must-read."

—JULIE BARTON, *New York Times* bestselling author of
Dog Medicine: How My Dog Saved Me from Myself

"This is the novel we need right now.
Willa's Grove is an affirmation of creativity,
sisterhood, and the power of belonging."

—CHELSEA CAIN, *New York Times* bestselling author of *Heartsick*

"*Willa's Grove* is just the midlife vacation read
every woman needs to spur her on and grab hold of
'So now what?' I didn't read this aching and inspiring
novel as much as wrapped myself up in it."

—V. C. CHICKERING, author of *Nookietown* and *Twisted Family Values*

"[A] stirring debut...*Willa's Grove* shows the insights,
comfort, and courage that women can find in community."

—JANET BENTON, author of *Lilli de Jong*

"Laura Munson has captured the magical safe haven of her
Haven Writing Retreats in the pages of this gripping novel."

—SUKEY FORBES, bestselling author of *The Angel in My Pocket: Love, Loss,
and Life after Death* and Haven Writing Retreat alum

"*Willa's Grove* is a novel, yes, but inherent in these pages is the stark truth about the inevitable magical highs and crushing lows of women's lives. It reminded me that we have to find our tribe, nurture it, and hang on."

—SHEILA HAMILTON, author, mental health journalist, and host of @BeyondWellWithSheilaHamilton.com

"Reading *Willa's Grove* is like going to a girls' weekend where everyone spills their guts and tells the truth about their apparently not-so-perfect lives. It's truthful, raw, and, well, totally fun."

—CATHY LAMB, author of *All About Evie*

"So what's next? That's the big question in the fiction debut from memoirist Munson…Readers will be able to relate to the themes of female friendship and personal growth."

—BOOKLIST

"This novel is intended to be an inspirational story, and it delivers. Many women readers will find themselves represented by one or more of the characters…They might come to understand the women in their own lives better, as well as find their own secret anxieties represented and tackled through the story… *Willa's Grove* offers a pathway to writing one's own new story."

—NEW YORK JOURNAL OF BOOKS

"*Willa's Grove* is an easy read with a captivating premise: what happens when four women, each in a mid-life crisis, gather for a week in rural Montana to ponder the answer to the question: so now what?"

—SAN FRANCISCO BOOK REVIEW

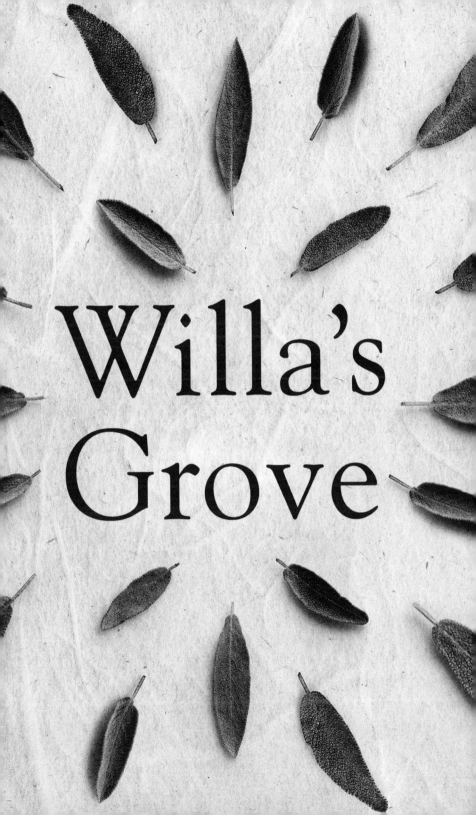

Willa's
Grove

Willa's Grove

Laura Munson

New York Times and internationally bestselling author

BLACK STONE
PUBLISHING

Printed in the United States of America
Originally published in hardcover by Blackstone Publishing in 2020

First paperback edition: 2021
ISBN 978-1-79995-638-9
Fiction / Women

1 3 5 7 9 10 8 6 4 2

CIP data for this book is available
from the Library of Congress

Blackstone Publishing
31 Mistletoe Rd.
Ashland, OR 97520

www.BlackstonePublishing.com

I dedicate this book to all of the brave people who have come on my Haven Writing Programs, found their essential voices in intimate community, and set them free. You inspired me to write this book so that people far and wide can see what happens when we gather in honor of self-expression, with kindness, honesty, and support ... especially in the woods of Montana.

I also dedicate this book to my children, for making room for me to write and to create this community, alongside my motherhood. I hope that you can find deep passion in your work, wherever your paths lead you! I believe in you with all my heart.

"We must be willing to get rid of the life we've planned, so as to have the life that is waiting for us."
—JOSEPH CAMPBELL

"Nearby is the country they call life."
—RAINER MARIA RILKE

The Women

On a typical day in their typical lives, three women went to their mailboxes and found—amid junk mail and bills and shiny flyers for unshiny things—an invitation, sealed with a bold *W* pressed into sage-green wax.

They had been waiting for this invitation. They longed for it as much as they feared it. Because to break this seal was to release a behemoth of a question—a question so impossible that they had almost stopped asking it.

Each hesitated, looked around, and in respective order, thought, *Sweet Jesus, What the hell, Here goes nothing,* and slid her finger under the seal, revealing a thick handmade note card, pressed with silvery leaves.

Words winked up at them. Words that might, if given the chance, change everything.

They swallowed hard and pulled out the card. Inside, nestled with a wild bird feather, were the following words:

You are invited to
the rest of your life.
You know you can't go on like this.
Not for one more day.
You need an interlude.

* * *

Imagine this:
You are in a farmhouse in Montana,
wrapped in a soft blanket, sitting
by a warm woodstove. There is a cup of tea
in your hand, just the way you like it.
There are women surrounding you
who need this just as badly as you do.
We all have the same question.
The question is:
So now what?
Come to Montana and find out ...

Love, Willa
(You don't have to do this alone.)

Each woman held the invitation to her heart, drew in a deep breath before letting out an exhausted sigh that echoed from Connecticut to Wisconsin to California and back to Montana, and went inside to call a dear friend.

The Invitation

Willa walked into the Mercantile, her plaid flannel pajama bottoms tucked into her mud boots, her duct-taped parka zipped up to her chin. It was a cold late-April morning and it had taken her all week to get the courage to take the steps she now took. Past Earl and Wink, the farrier brothers getting their coffee before rounds, past Tally Hansen setting out her Morning Buns on parchment paper atop the cracked glass counter, past Syd the Dog Man and his daily, "I can't resist," growling about his type 2 diabetes, and ending with Marilyn at the post office counter, admiring the latest stamps just in.

"Morning, Marilyn. I need some stamps, please," said Willa, her hands firmly in her pockets.

Marilyn eyed Willa like this was a test. "US Flag, Endangered Species, or Wild and Scenic Rivers?"

"Wild and Scenic Rivers, of course," said Willa, adding, "I hear the Upper Missouri is one of them. And the Flathead too. Read it in the *Great Falls Tribune*." This was a test she longed to pass. These days, she didn't have it in her to be any more misunderstood than she already was.

Marilyn glared over her reading glasses and pushed a pane of stamps forward.

Willa produced three envelopes of the handmade stationery she'd been saving, pressed with slivers of sage leaves from her garden, added a river stamp to each, and put her lips to the wax seal, sending them off with a kiss. *I hope I chose the right words*, she thought as she slid them into the slot marked NOT LOCAL. NOT LOCAL was used most often, LOCAL only seldomly, word of mouth and the Community Bulletin Board being what they were in Willa, Montana. Willa, Montana, with its very own zip code. Population: thirty-five. Well, thirty-three now that her sons were at college. Thirty-two since Jack's heart attack last September. And soon to be thirty-one.

"That'll be six dollars and sixty cents," said Marilyn, glancing over Willa's shoulder. "Hey, Earl."

"Hey, Marilyn."

Willa recognized the familiar leathery voice, but no *Hey, Willa* followed. There hadn't been any *Hey, Willa*s lately. There had been times in her life when she'd wished she was invisible. But as a forty-six-year-old widow in the rural Montana town she loved madly and deeply, and perhaps unreasonably, this wasn't one of them.

She gambled a smile at Earl, whom she'd never known not to be up for at least a morning headline or a carnal joke. He looked past her at Marilyn. Willa could feel Marilyn's scowl between her shoulder blades, as if she was branding NOT LOCAL into her skin. She put a ten on the counter and Marilyn pushed her change toward her like chess pieces.

Willa took the change and her stamps, pausing, waiting for some sort of peace offering, but none came. So she offered her own version and dropped the money into the spare-a-dime jar, and looked at Tally, who stared into her pastry display. *Even Tally*. Willa lingered, looking at her, trying to find words, but none came.

Then she went to the door she'd passed through a million

times with a million *Hey, Willa*s and stopped short, the sting of it too much. She turned and looked at each of them. Really looked, even if they wouldn't look at her.

"We never dreamed of leaving, you know." She fought back tears. "It's my home too." She didn't say, *I have no other choice.* Because Montanans found choices where most people couldn't fathom them. And stood by them.

The hard fact, as far as this beautiful adopted oddball family of hers knew—this pack which for decades had lived and breathed and grieved as an undeniable unified western front—as far as their Montana-ness could fathom: Willa Silvester was choosing to leave them for no good reason. Except for perhaps *grief.* And grief wasn't enough of a reason. She could barely admit the *real* reason, even to herself.

So, no. No one met her eye to eye, or even eye to boot.

Willa sighed. "Well, if you see some strangers here before too long, they're my friends."

Still nothing. Not even the cock of a head. That was the nail in the casket. Willa, Montana, loved its visitors.

Then Willa did what she'd been dreading for weeks: She pulled a cardboard sign out from under her parka. She found a lone tack on the Community Bulletin Board—full of its usual lost dogs and give-away puppies and fifth wheels for barter for chainsaws and snow tires and all the important currency of a town of thirty-five—and pushed it through the poster and into the old dry cork.

TOWN FOR AUCTION

WILLA, MONTANA (1 SQUARE MILE)

THE HOMESTEAD:

(HOUSE AND INN, BARN AND CORRAL, GARDEN,

ORCHARD, BEE BOXES, CHICKEN COOP)

THE MERCANTILE:
(POST OFFICE, STORE, BAKERY, SALOON,
GAS PUMP, PAY PHONE)

MAY 19, 3:00 P.M. IN THE MERCANTILE PARKING LOT
***LOCALS ONLY: GOODBYE PARTY TO FOLLOW
(UP AT WILLA'S)

There it was in writing on the Mercantile Community Bulletin Board, where everything she'd wanted to communicate with the town over the years had been attached by a tack into this exact cork— her twin boys' birth announcement, the annual Harvest Cider Party in the orchard, summer movie nights at the barn, the Fourth of July parade and fireworks down Main Street (the only street), town meetings at the Merc, new batches of microbrew and honey, forest-fire alerts, hand-me-downs, the Free Library, the Christmas Swap, Hunter Safety classes, Meals on Wheels (and hooves) for the ill, the old, the lonely. And there had been thank-you notes for any number of services offered in kind to the town by its denizens: knife sharpening, lawn mowing, hay hauling, fence mending, gun repair. And then her most recent posts: her boys' college announcements, Jack's memorial service, their horses and mules to give away.

In a matter of weeks, this twenty-year chapter of her life would be over. And she had absolutely no idea what she was going to do next. The only thing she *was* sure of was that she was leaving. And that her heart had splintered into too many pieces to count, never mind put back together. So now what? It was anybody's guess.

Willa couldn't bear to look at any of them then. Instead, she closed the old, time-tested door behind her and walked past the gas pump, wondering if it would go dry now. Whether the phone booth would get disconnected. The ECI cooler left empty. (Earl was dyslexic.) *They'll finally fix that*, Willa thought. *Or not.*

She stopped and stared out over the womanly foothills that rubbed up against the masculine mountains of the Lewis and Clark National Forest, the friction of the two holding this town in place. She had always thought if the hills didn't push back, those mountains would have swept the whole valley west, right into the Missouri River. She wasn't pushing anymore. She couldn't.

She picked up a rusty nail from the parking lot, rolling it between her fingers. Then she pressed it into her thumb, but not for blood, holding it there, imagining the invitation she really wanted—the invitation to return to everything that came before the desolate day last fall that had rewritten her history. *Pull yourself together, Willa. The women are coming.*

She pitched the rusty nail into the trash can, got in her truck, and drove home, trying not to look at the homemade signs attached to every single highway mile marker along the way:

PLEASE DON'T BUY OUR TOWN.

PLEASE DON'T BUY OUR TOWN.

PLEASE DON'T BUY OUR TOWN.

Willa, Montana, did sympathy to perfection. Change, not so well. Abandonment, not at all.

She pulled onto her road and cut the engine. She could hear his voice telling her for the hundredth time that the truck was a '74 Ford pickup—"F-100, Forest Service green, with the first SuperCab. For our family," beaming like an about-to-be father of twins. She caught herself smiling in the side mirror and imagined herself on the passenger side, pregnant, holding his hand, so proud of this land and how they cared for it. And this family of four that was about to be.

She looked at her meadow, cupped by the ridge behind it and Bison Butte in the close distance, and imagined it fractured.

House, house, house, house, house. Maybe a mill. Maybe a silver mine. Maybe shopping outlets. A cell phone tower. Natural gas rig mats. A power line slicing it right down the middle.

"I'm sorry, Jack," she whispered, and swiped the tears from her cheeks. But she was practical before she was romantic, and a mother first and foremost. Her boys needed her to move on, even though they didn't understand that yet. They'd swallowed it like the bitter pill that it was. "You gotta do what you gotta do," Sam had said. Ned had nodded and looked at Bison Butte.

Willa put her hands in her pockets and felt the thank-you note she'd toiled over. She hadn't had the guts to tack it to the Community Board. It could never say enough and it could never say it right. Because it wasn't enough and it wasn't right, and it never would be. She read it now:

Wherever we all end up, I wish us all love, peace, joy, and the beauty of this place to live in us always. Thank you for being who you have been to my family. And to Willa, MT. I am so sorry that I have to move on. I'll love you all forever. Willa.

She crumpled it up and put it back in her pocket.

To the white-tailed deer who grazed in the meadow, she said a stern, "Absolutely … *no* … woe … is … me." It might just be herself and three Not Local women in her home the night of the nineteenth, but at least there would be a proper *goodbye* to Willa Homestead. Willa, Montana, would be a vision in her rearview mirror on her way out of town on the road to So Now What.

Day One

Willa woke just before dawn, as was her custom, and walked the meadow. The women were coming … and she wasn't ready. On the outside, yes. The beds were made, the bread and soup prepared, lilies of the valley in a vase on each of the nightstands. But not ready in the way that really mattered. *Ready* meant that she was that much closer to *goodbye*.

Dawn wasn't any better at easing the pain. Dawn flashed, as it always did, and always would, relentless: the flash that couldn't take itself back, the birds already making their proclamations in the trees and sky, the deer standing at attention from their matted-grass nests.

This morning it was as if they were milking dawn into day, eager for this reception—like they'd met in the night and agreed to perch in particular places to greet the three women as they arrived in Montana. The creature world accepted its future without needing to know its parts. The creature world still said, *Hey, Willa.*

She reached her arms out to all of it. "You know how to end things. I've watched you lose fawns to trucks and ducklings to foxes. You mourn only for a second. And then you just go on so gracefully. I want to do this like you!"

And as the sun crested Bison Butte and floodlit the meadow, she saw her answer. She saw it in the duck couples out for a morning swim—mallards, mergansers, and goldeneyes. She saw it in the four young bucks grazing in the tall grass along the drive. In the red-winged blackbirds, alert as soldiers, *churring* in the cattails, and in the sandhill cranes strutting the fence line. Even a mountain bluebird, sunning itself on a tree snag, seemed to want Willa to know that she'd done the right thing by sending those invitations. The Homestead would hold her for one more week. And these women too.

"I really don't have to do this leaving … alone?" she whispered, taking heart in the fact that this meadow called upon you to rest. Linger. Stay awhile and be better for it, like so many wanderers had. She took in a deep breath of the sweet May air that smelled so much like her babies' heads—she'd never get over that smell. Maybe this week of women really *would* help. Willa wanted to believe it was possible.

She picked armfuls of lilacs to bring up to the house, dropped her nose into their tart domes, and remembered her best friend's words: "Willa. Simply put, you need help."

It was Bliss's idea—Willa's best friend from the second they met at summer camp on the Upper Peninsula of Michigan. Junior counselor to camper, it was a typical innocent girl crush. Even then, the younger Bliss was the advisor, and Willa the dreamer. Bliss had been as intrigued by Willa's Chicago as Willa had been by Bliss's Wisconsin, and they'd written each other weekly postcards through the years and never faltered. Bliss told tales from small-town America—of marching bands, church socials, girls who married young, parents who expected her to do-as-we-say-*and*-do (and Bliss had).

It felt grounding to Willa, who told tales of rallies, protests, museums, and once-banned books her professor parents expected her to read and understand. Bliss had been a mature thirteen, and sixteen-year-old Willa had been smitten with her first taste of rural steadiness. The two were attached at the hip and had remained so through the years—back and forth in postcards all the way until last month when Willa had sent one that read: *If you'd like one last visit, you better come quick. I'm selling Willa, MT. The Homestead, the Inn, the town. Everything. The auction is on May 19.*

A week later, the phone rang, and Bliss's velvet voice quelled the panic of packing boxes and slowly emptying rooms. "Willa Silvester. What on earth?"

"Bliss. I ..." Willa faltered, crying months of tears into the phone.

"I know, sweetheart. Let it out. You don't have to be strong with me."

"I can't ... do ... it, Bliss. I thought I could, but I can't." Willa stopped herself, but knowing her friend had her ear to her phone was too much. "I took a bad fall. Off the hayloft. I spent weeks in bed. I could barely move. I let the whole place ... go." She gasped between sobs, still feeling the ache in her back ribs. "I didn't harvest the potatoes. I let the apples fall and rot. I canned nothing. I closed up the Inn. I—I gave away the horses. And the chickens. There're mice running around everywhere." She gasped a breath again. "And I had to put Dash down. That ... was ... the last ... thing ... I ... could handle. The boys are gone. And Jack—"

"I know, honey."

"I thought I was so much ... *stronger*. I'm so *ashamed*."

"Oh, that's silly, my friend. I'll bet the whole town was up there at the Homestead clamoring to take care of you, if I know Willa, Montana."

Willa was quiet.

"You didn't tell them, did you? Just like you didn't tell me. Or your boys, I suspect."

Willa's face twisted with shame, relieved that her friend couldn't see her. Then she inhaled as deeply as she could so she could blast, "Word got out. And they tried to help! But I wouldn't let them. I told them I was fine." She swallowed hard. "And I repaid their kindness by giving up on the dream and calling an auctioneer." She shook her head. "Nobody has any idea why, and I can't tell them. And no one is talking to me. Why would they?" And with the last of it she said, "These are my *people*, Bliss."

"Willa. Why aren't they talking to you?"

"It's a long story. But suffice it to say ... even if I hadn't had the accident ..." She swallowed hard again and pushed herself. "I can't afford to stay. Our money is all gone. And I don't know why. But I have a pretty good feeling it had to do with Jack and how much he loved these people. And if I tell them that, they'll be more ashamed than angry. And I don't want that for them." She sniffed and threw her shoulders back. "I have to leave. This is not a one-woman show. Jack used to quote Emerson: *To be great is to be misunderstood.* I don't know if I'll ever be great. But I have learned this: sometimes you just have to let yourself be misunderstood."

"Willa, you've got the purest heart of anyone I know."

She didn't like compliments, but she forced herself to feel her friend's kindness. She'd missed kindness. Life in Willa, Montana, had always been so *kind*. "Bliss, I have no idea what I'm going to do with the rest of my life. And you know as well as anyone that it's *killing* me to pack it all up. There're half-empty boxes in every room. It's a mess. I'm a mess. I don't know this person I've become. I wake up in the morning and just feel this low ache in my chest. And I can't shake it. Every night I hope that when I wake up, it's going to be gone. But when I open my eyes in the morning—even *before* I open my eyes ... I know it's still there." She forced the next phrase. "You know how crazy about each other we were."

"It was truly rare," said Bliss.

Stop, Willa. No one wants to hear this. Not even Bliss, and especially not after what she's just been through. But the words rolled out anyway. "Sometimes I just sit on the floor and catch myself staring into space thinking: *I don't know what I'm supposed to do.* And I don't just mean with the rest of my life. I mean with the next *second.* I've never felt this way. I'm so ... *scared*, Bliss. *Scared* isn't something we *do* around here." She stopped herself. "Sorry. I just don't know how to do this."

"Keep going, sweetheart. Let it all out. You need to," said her friend.

"I don't have anyone to talk about it with, Bliss. Or anyone to help me figure out what to do. Or how to save this town. Everyone's broke. There's no local economy without us. But there is no *us* anymore. Shit!" She bore into her tears and tried to stop them. "I don't know where I *belong* anymore. It took me a long time to belong *here!*" She gasped, hating her self-pity. "And I miss my damn dog."

"Oh, sweetheart," said Bliss. "If you weren't scared, you wouldn't be human. And being human is a lot to admit to ... for you. Please take that as a compliment."

Willa got her tears under control. "I'm so sorry to burden you with this. You've gone through so much. We should talk more often. It's so nice to hear your voice. I've been really ... lonely. I didn't realize how completely *reliant* I was on Jack and the boys. I catch myself talking to him, like he's in the next room. Like he's still here. I feel so ... *pathetic.*"

Bliss let out a little hum like a prelude to a lullaby. "Willa. Listen to me. The last thing you are is pathetic. And if it helps any, I think that there are plenty of us out there who feel like you do. Especially at our age. We're right on the heels of everything our young lives made. Or didn't make."

Bliss paused, and Willa knew she was grieving all the miscarriages, the two failed adoptions, and now the divorce. "Our toes are on the shadows of what's next. And we're scared and we're suffering and we're lonely. And we don't know how to find one another. Or admit it. So we stiffen our upper lip and pretend we're okay. We are *not* okay. At least I'm not. And you're not."

"No. I am *not* okay." Willa wished Bliss was there to crawl into bed with, like they had as girls, and hide from the world. "How did we get this way, Bliss? I'm an island. Even when everyone was still talking to me … all winter, I've been a total recluse. I don't know how to call on my community, and it isn't calling on me anymore. Do you feel like an island too?"

"Completely."

They were both silent.

Bliss started to speak but stopped herself.

"What?"

"What if we opened up the Homestead—the Inn, the barn— all of it, and had a gathering of women? A small gathering of islands who maybe don't even realize how isolated they've become. And how badly they need a safe community. Even if it's temporary. Just a small group of us who are all trying to figure out what comes next. And who just need a *break* from life."

Willa cringed. "That sounds lovely. In theory. But I couldn't take care of a barn cat right now, never mind a community of women."

"You wouldn't have to. We'd take care of ourselves, just *together*. We'd put the Homestead to good use—what you created it for. I can't imagine Willa Silvester leaving her Homestead without letting it give its gift one last time. And it'll do you good."

Willa sighed. She knew it was true.

"What if you invite me, and I invite a dear friend who is looking down the barrel of So Now What, and she asks another friend who is too? Four friends of friends. And we come to each other at your beautiful Homestead. And we help you get your place packed up. Because that's what women do. Or used to do before we forgot how badly we need each other. And you don't have to host us or do anything. Just being away from our lives and in Montana and with each other … might help us find our answers."

"I think I'd like that."

"I'll take that as a *yes*." Bliss's voice rose a few notes like it did when a solid plan was in the making. "How about this: You write an invitation to make it official. You *are* the consummate hostess after all, and you've *always* had a way with words. I supply you with their addresses so all you have to do is send the invitations. I can just picture it, with that gorgeous paper you make with the herbs, and that beautiful wax seal you always use for your winter Solstice cards. They'll say *yes*, because of course they will. Their dear friend has already given them a good talking-to and made a *persuasive* case for their futures!" Willa could picture Bliss's stalwart, unbudgeable stare. "They get that invitation in the mail, and it calls to them with a force they haven't felt in years. And we all fly out there the week of the auction. *And* we help you pack. *And* we'll throw a *goodbye* party whether the town likes it or not. We'll put the Willa Homestead to bed with one last burst of celebration for its namesake!"

I was like that not too long ago, thought Willa. She couldn't imagine it now. "To be honest … I was going to sneak away the day after the auction. I can't imagine hosting a party, Bliss. No one would come, anyway."

"*We'll* be the party. You can't say a proper *goodbye* sneaking out the back door, Willa."

"I can't ask strangers to help me pack up my life."

"Why not?"

"What do I write on the invitation? I'm not my old self. At all."

"Just write: *You are invited to the rest of your life.*"

Now, Willa waited. Everything was ready. Woodstove creaking with heat. Early pea and mint soup bubbling on the stove. Her hard-crusted bread, just out of the oven, airy in the middle with her kitchen's wild yeast. Her signature strawberry rhubarb pie was cooling on the counter. She'd even put on her best wool shawl, teal blue, which fell over her best long linen skirt, instead of Jack's old hunting sweater and work pants, which she'd worn holes in all winter. She pulled the shawl up to her chin for a moment. Marilyn had made it for her birthday years ago. Maybe being with these women would feel like this shawl. Bliss's compass was something to trust. Her own ... not so much anymore.

The women had rented a car in Great Falls and were due any minute. Bliss, her simple, stern, God-fearing, long-distance best friend. Harriet, Bliss's childhood idol who'd taken Most Likely to Succeed so high up the ranks of self-help guru-dom, that she had pushed it over the edge and herself along with it. Jane, Harriet's best friend from their wild days as roommates in New York City, who was now living the perfect Christmas-card life in the suburbs of Connecticut, apparently *perfectly* miserable.

"Shit!" Willa shouted, throwing open the door and standing barefoot on her front porch. Panic swept around her like the blowing leaves she'd ignored all fall, still stuck in the porch corners. She suddenly didn't want strangers anywhere near her beloved land or her beloved house. Or her beloved ghosts. The house was alive to her and had been for two decades. It had taught her how to be the woman that she had become. And it had gotten her through the winter, demanding that she get out of bed and make tea and phone her boys. It called her out to its porches to see that winter was over and the apple trees were beginning to bud. It held her in its sturdy walls that Jack had built and she had painted. It showed her that she was alive when it let predawn through its windows and forced her to open her eyes. It winked at her when it creaked and cooled in the night air. *Life is still possible*, it promised her.

"Get yourself together," she said, in a voice that was more the house's than hers, and went inside, pulling the door shut. She stopped at the gate-legged table and ran her hand over the endless country dust. Adjusted the lilacs in the old blue spatterware vase. Leaned in toward the age-spotted mirror, which mottled her green eyes, or maybe this was just the way they looked now. She'd been ignoring mirrors all winter. It was like middle age had hit the minute Jack died, the grays salting her chocolate-brown hair in a coarse grind. She tucked her hair behind her ears. That was one thing she wasn't going to mourn: her youth. As Jack always said, "Willa was born old."

Then she turned to the front door, putting her hand on the sturdy weathered wood like it was Jack's back, and said, "There'll be four of us again for a few days. Do your magic. Please."

BUH *buh buh* BUH BUH ... *bum bum.*

Willa leaped back.

They were here.

Life would move now.

She took in a deep breath, whispered, "Here we go ..." and opened the door.

Bliss stood on the porch in her standard flower-print dress and old cardigan, her blunt ash bob and bangs, her arms wide open. And Willa folded into them as she always did, forgetting how a hug from Bliss was like a hug from the most loving, doting grandmother that ever lived.

Bliss gathered her by the shoulders and looked at her squarely. "I know I've said it to you on the phone, but I need to look you in the eye and say how sorry I am that I didn't come for the memorial. It's hard to leave Mother these days. But I still feel badly about it. I should have been here."

"That's okay. I didn't need another person to feel sorry for me. The whole town was a basket case. I just wanted to get it over with."

"And if I know you, Willa, you were the one holding the basket."

Willa shrugged.

"Well, you don't have to hold it anymore, my dear. Here we are!" Bliss's face could have held the entire state of Montana with its hope as she stepped aside and said, "Willa, meet Harriet and Jane."

A woman, with a map of hard road on her face, stepped forward wearing a long red cape with fringe and red suede knee-high boots. "Thank you for doing this, honey. I'm Harriet." She leaned in and kissed Willa once on each cheek and then stepped back as if she'd touched an electric fence. "Sorry. Not much of a hugger these days. But my, how your Montana is stunning! Such a little gem in the middle of nowhere with that Mercantile! We bought Morning Buns for breakfast tomorrow. People looked at us like we were Martians! I loved it! So freaking happy to be out of California!"

She leaned forward and whispered, "I fell for you the second I read your *fabulous* invitation!" Then she blurted, "That old-fashioned wax seal! Who *does* that these days! You all are too young to remember when it was a fad." She rolled her eyes. "And I loved your word choice, Willa. A much-needed interlude, indeed. In B-flat! B for *balls-if-I-know* what's up with the rest of my life!"

Willa hadn't heard so many notes come out of someone maybe ever. Somehow, they made chords and even more re-markably, a whole song. "Welcome, Harriet," she said, keeping her distance. She wasn't much of a hugger these days either. "My boys are in California at college. Hopefully they don't feel like Martians there. I wonder sometimes." But California was their big chance, especially with everything they were losing. And Willa promised herself once again that she would never, *ever*, dip into the money she and Jack had saved for their boys. *Thank God for their scholarships.* She caught Bliss peering under her bangs at her and Willa brought herself back to the women.

As if Harriet had picked up on her far-away place too, she said, "Well, California can take just about anything. Even me!" She rolled her eyes again. "I have definitely put that one to the—"

"Let's not go there," said Jane, stepping forward with her hand outstretched, as sharp and starched as her white, collared shirt, pressed jeans, cowboy boots, and turquoise jewelry. "So nice to meet you, Willa," she said, shaking her hand with aggression. "I'm Jane Bradford. Thank you so much for having us. I'm so looking forward to this week," she added, still shaking Willa's hand, her flawless blond ponytail bouncing along with it. "And your house is gorgeous. Just gorgeous!"

Willa held on hard. *Am I going to have to shake hands like this and give two-cheek kisses and talk in exclamation points wherever it is that I end up?*

Then Jane presented her with a heavy gift, wrapped in white paper and a pale pink satin bow, her eyes dancing like a little girl at a birthday party. "Just a tiny token of appreciation. From the city."

Willa fished for the right words. "Thank you, Jane." She met each of their eyes, trying for her most welcoming smile. "Come in, come in, you all! Just in time for tea."

"The groceries are in the car," said Bliss. "We got everything on the list."

"Thank you! I'll get them while you're unpacking. How much do I owe you?"

"Not a thing," said Jane.

"Our treat," said Harriet.

"You're giving us a priceless gift. It's the least we can do," said Bliss. "And we're ready to help you with those boxes!"

Willa hardly knew what to say. "Oh, don't you worry about those. I got a second wind and muscled through it last week," she lied, picturing all the boxes and stacks shoved into the spare room. "This is *your* time to get away from it all. Come on in. I'll show you around."

The three women rolled their luggage into the front hallway.

Jane exclaimed, "Lilacs! Ours are over with on the East Coast."

"Ours are just about done," said Bliss. "What growing zone are you here in Montana?"

"Zone four," said Willa. "But we had a scarily warm winter this year and the melt came early. My sump pump started working in early March."

By their silence, she figured none of them knew what a sump pump was.

Bliss said, "Isn't this place so special? I told you. It's like something from another time. You don't even have a TV, do you, Willa?"

"No, actually," said Willa. Was that a bad thing?

"For a long time, they didn't have electricity either. Or running water," said Bliss. "They were all about self-reliance."

Willa pictured herself falling off the hayloft, hitting the dirt, and hearing five solid cracks in her rib cage. She swept the image away. "It was just the way we chose to live."

Bliss ran her hand along the banister. "The first time I came out here was in the nineties, I think. I had never seen an outhouse before. I thought it was so *exotic*."

Willa looked at Jane, who was gripping her turquoise necklace. "Don't worry. We have electricity and indoor plumbing now." She smiled. "Let's get you all settled," and she walked into the kitchen, the women following her.

"I've always loved how the kitchen is in the middle of the house," said Bliss. "Like it holds it all together."

Bliss seemed so happy, and Willa was glad. She pictured her friend's world so bleak these days, alone with her mother who was forgetting her history, while Bliss couldn't stop remembering.

Jane's face took on preternatural wonder. "I feel like I'm in *Little House on the Prairie*," she said, and then whispered, "Dirty secret: sometimes when I'm having a bad day, when the kids are at school, I watch *Little House on the Prairie* reruns."

Harriet hacked a laugh. "Since when do you stop long enough to notice you're having a bad day, Janey?"

"You'd be surprised," said Jane, looking at Harriet like she was staring into the sun.

Willa had no patience for small talk, especially now. The Inn guests over the years had been so Montana-drunk upon arrival at the Homestead. This was going to take some doing. Especially with Jane. *Don't judge a book by its cover, Willa. You know better than that.*

"Welcome to the Homestead. This is the main house. You're staying in the Inn, which is through that hallway," she said, trying to locate her old innkeeping self, and set Jane's gift on the kitchen table.

"I love all the beadboard and wainscoting and crown molding," said Jane. "It's very Vermont."

"My husband was from Vermont." She assumed Bliss had filled them in about Jack.

And Jane confirmed. "I'm sorry for your loss."

"Gutting hell you've been through. And the dog too?" said Harriet.

"The dog too," said Willa, not knowing how to divert their pity. Those were just the facts.

Jane's jaw muscles clenched and released, like she was scanning her stockpile of appropriate things to say. "This must be a very hard place to leave."

"It is," said Willa, looking at Bliss for some sort of rescue, but Bliss seemed overtaken by her own memories of the Homestead, still holding on to the banister.

Jane practically lunged toward her gift then, with arms that looked like they'd worked cattle. "You should probably open this sooner rather than later."

Willa had never been good at receiving gifts, especially now when she was trying to purge. She found a distant smile. "Whatever it is, Jane, thank you," she said, bracing for some New York City thing—a break-the-bank candle or an assortment of clever cocktail napkins. She untied the beautiful bow, pulled the paper off, and lifted the lid, her nose stinging with the creamy citrus of gardenias. Real gardenias. Dozens of them on long stems lay in two parallel columns, flanking a bottle of champagne on each side.

Willa was floored. "I've never seen this many gardenias in my entire life ... and in one place! And I haven't had champagne in years. Thank you, Jane. This is too generous," she said, running the gardenias under Bliss's nose to wake her from her daze.

Bliss blinked and moved her hand from the banister to Willa's back. "They're lovely."

Jane smiled, satisfied. "Might as well start off with a bang!" And she pulled out her cell phone, raised it as high as she could, and snapped a photo of her gift and the women.

Harriet's hands were on the bottle like the mic she'd apparently held so skillfully on so many stages. "Hello, lover," she said to the champagne. "To hell with tea. Let's crack this bitch! May I do the honors, Willa?"

"Go ahead," said Willa. "I'm sure I'm the least qualified person in this room to open a good bottle of champagne. And I definitely don't have the right glasses for it. Unless it's okay to drink champagne out of a wine glass."

"Oh dear. I didn't think of that," said Jane, crossing her arms.

"It's chic if we say it's chic!" said Harriet, popping the cork like a pro.

"Let's save the wine glasses," said Bliss. "I know they're special," pulling four Mason jars from the cupboard.

Willa was grateful. They'd been her fifth anniversary gift from Jack. Hugh and Bliss had been there for it: candlelight, fresh venison from their hunt, expensive wine, everything so perfect. She knew she couldn't get anywhere close to it now, but she tried. She went to the pantry and took out her wedding crystal bowl and every other vessel she could find for the gardenias, arranging them as Harriet and Jane set the jars of champagne on the kitchen table.

It occurred to Willa that she might cry. In just minutes, her house had been steeped in beauty. Feminine beauty. No muddy boots and guns, no oil-slathered Carhartts, no strewn schoolbooks, sweat-drenched socks, baseball mitts on the counter where she was about to make bread.

But gardenias. Champagne. Women.

She took a jar and raised it. "Here's to So Now What," she said.

They raised their Mason jars, clinked them together, echoed, "To So Now What," and drank.

They were silent for a moment until Harriet said, "I almost didn't come, you know. Truth be told. I had to force myself into a cab this morning to go to the airport. I don't really *do* groups anymore. But I couldn't get over those words. *So Now What.* They haunted me until I finally just had to say *Boo* back. And here I am! Which you may all come to regret!" She downed the rest of her champagne.

Willa eyed Jane to see her reaction to this red blaze of a woman. But Jane ignored Harriet, put her nose into the crystal bowl of gardenias, and breathed deeply. "I almost didn't come either. *Because* of those exact words. *So Now What.*" She shivered. "I'm *allergic* to them. At least that's what my therapist tells me. My inner saboteur and I are thick as thieves." Jane took a small sip, then a big one, and shrugged her starched shoulders.

How were either of these women going to fit into her life here? But Willa reminded herself: it wasn't her life this week. This was the small sisterhood that Bliss promised they all needed.

Bliss's voice soothed, as it always did. "Even though I knew the invitation was on its way, and I'd booked my flights, it really threw me for a doozy. It was so *real*. I really *am* being invited to the rest of my life." She looked so sad, her big brown eyes blinking just under her bangs.

Willa looked into her Mason jar. "Since we're being honest … I can't tell you how many times I've wished I could take that invitation back. I wasn't sure how it would be to have people in the house again."

"But we're not just *people*," said Bliss. "We're dear ones of dear ones. Yet we're new to each other as a *group*. I think that's why we all said *yes*. We all deeply need safe people in our lives … but *new* people. Who *get* what we're going through."

Harriet clinked her empty Mason jar against Willa's full one. "I'm pretty sure Jane said *yes* because I told her I'd come to Connecticut and publicly embarrass her at her country club if she didn't." Her face broke out into a giant grin, and Jane placed a manicured middle finger on her cheek.

"I *would* have, you know," said Harriet, topping off their jars and pouring the rest of the bottle into hers.

"I'm well aware," said Jane.

"Key word: *safe*," said Bliss, eyeing Harriet.

Harriet held up her hand. "Honey, you knew what you were getting into when you invited me."

Bliss just blinked at her, and Harriet played with the tassel on her cape. "Safe. Promise."

Jane looked at Willa. "It was such a lovely invitation, Willa. With the sage woven into the paper, and that lovely matching seal. And I get a *lot* of invitations." She waited, as if for a reciprocal giggle. When none came, she continued, a little pink in the face. "Anyway, I loved the visual—sitting by a fire with tea and a blanket. I haven't sat down and had tea like that, without being at some board meeting or book club or God-knows-what … in *ages*."

Willa smiled. "Well, let's get you situated in your rooms, and then we'll go into the keeping room and have tea," she said, pointing to the little room off the kitchen, "and get to know each other."

"That sounds nice," said Bliss.

And then a whisper of an old voice came to Willa from somewhere deep in her mothering, her innkeeping, her townkeeping. A voice the keeping room knew well. "Why don't we have tea and tell each other our stories? So we can help each other. When's the last time someone asked you to do *that*?"

They all looked at her with variations of hunger and fear.

"Not in a long, long time," said Bliss.

Harriet lifted one eyebrow and held it, like she was trying to dare her demons.

"You mean the *real* story?" said Jane. "You mean … outside of *therapy*?" She crossed her arms and got a little pink again, in the cheeks.

"Yes," said Harriet. "The *real* story."

"Not that it'll be easy," said Bliss. "But the stakes are high. We have decisions to make. This is a time for truth."

Willa gave them her warmest smile. "Well …" She took in a deep breath. "I guess what there is to say then … is *welcome* … to the rest of our lives."

Things were already different. The Homestead was full again. The women were in their rooms, unpacking. A house full of women. Willa had longed for fullness all winter, but not exactly this. Men had been her world. And the people of her town. And then emptiness. Her fault. She'd turned them all away.

She suddenly needed the barn and she walked out into the grass toward it, barefoot.

The barn was the place she would miss most. The boys called it her *church* because at night it glowed like a cathedral. *What future of mine has a place like this in it?* she thought, taking in a deep breath as she slid back the heavy door, rusted and stubborn without Jack's springtime elbow grease.

Dust danced in the sweet stink of phantom hay and manure. She'd choose this smell over gardenias any day. Willa looked at the hayloft and went to the exact spot where she'd fallen. Where she'd forced herself to stand and get back to the house, knowing she had just minutes of adrenaline before the pain took over.

"Such a stupid mistake," she said. Just a split second when her mind had taken itself off the work and drifted out the window, looking at Bison Butte, thinking of Jack. Pain had become such a relative term. She'd given the farrier brothers the boys' mules after Jack's memorial, and his quarter horse, Pilgrim, to Syd the Dog Man, to help exercise his sled team in summer. But she'd kept Sook until that one moment of grief had caused another.

She went to the rope swing, looking high into the front truss where they always launched their flight, past the rafters covered in swallows' nests and bat guano, all the way to the back truss, where they'd land. Since her fall, she wouldn't think of climbing up there on those shaky ladder rungs, though she'd yearned for that feeling of flight, the upside-down stomach and the thrill in her throat. Instead, she took the rope from its place at the base of the ladder, climbed up just a few rungs, and jumped onto the big knot at the end, giving in as it gently bent her through the barn light.

"So now what," she whispered, holding on to the rope as it swung her through light shafts, rafter by rafter, light, dark, light, dark. "The rest of my life," she said, straightening her arms and leaning back, staring out the big window at Bison Butte.

She wanted to call to her future self, *You'll find new ways out there*, but nothing came from her mouth as she swung into the next light shaft, held in warmth for a second.

Then she jumped off before she was back in the grainy, gray barn light, and made her way to the stalls, the home of her best girl—the only girl she'd had as her own over the years: Sook.

Sook and Dash had kept her together after Jack's death. After the accident, she'd given her horse to Marilyn's granddaughter, Nel, whose mother was a meth head somewhere in Missoula, her father a Blackfoot that had tried to find her. But her mother refused to share. Refused and then left. No possible contact. If there was one human Willa wanted to save, it was Nel.

Nel was the only one Willa had let back onto the Homestead. Nel with her chestnut freckles, each one telling a different story that all ended up lost. She hadn't wanted anyone else seeing her so banged up, so needy, so disloyal, even though she'd tried desperately to find a good buyer who would keep everything as it was. The "good guy" developer over in Missoula who was famous for his devotion to conservation easements. The rich old-money mining family in Butte, still recovering their reputation. The eccentric wildlife biologist maven in Bozeman, known to take generous measures for raptor habitat.

No buyer. The auction, her last-ditch effort. And Dash gone too.

How had all the joy just drained away?

Now it was all women here. And it felt more strange than good.

She pictured Bliss, Harriet, and Jane settling in, laying their suitcases on the luggage racks, sitting alone on their beds, scanning walls covered in black-and-white photos her family had taken of their Montana moments. Of their horses and mules and dogs trekking through rivers and mountains. Of the meadow and Bison Butte in all hours of light, gaining and fading. And always the main house and Inn and its porches, caught on film through all four of their eyes, in frozen moments. She wanted these women to love it the way everyone loved the Homestead.

Trust yourself, as she'd told her boys so many times. But she couldn't feel it.

Where would she start? Why did all of her stories seem so sad when her life had been so happy? Maybe she would just tell them about the parties. She went into the tack room and ran her hand along the huge sheet she had sewn for movie nights, which was folded like a flag from a defunct country, the projector next to it. From June to September, every Friday night, six stitched-together king-size top sheets hung off the side of the barn, and the whole town, and whoever else was in Willa, sat on the hill and ate her famous popcorn (dusted with brewer's yeast) and watched whatever film Jack could find on his trips to the city.

Now she stared at the empty hay bins, the empty tack hooks—no saddles, no bridles or halters or reins, no brushes or curry combs, or grain pellets, or vet wrap. Not even fly spray. She'd given it all away. Except for the King saddle that Jack had given her for their wedding. She pulled back its cover and ran her hand over its gorgeous leatherwork.

She leaned against Sook's stall and let the scene play in her mind: how she'd hugged her horse's silky neck, whispering into her ear, "Take good care of this little broken girl," and thought, *From one broken girl to the next.*

And she'd braided her tail, forgetting about her ribs for a moment, then Nel's hair, both with matching red ribbons. "Ride on by, every so often," she'd told Nel. "I can show you some of her tricks once I heal up."

And Nel had. A few days a week, even on bitter-cold winter afternoons. She'd help with chores and bring homemade soup and biscuits from Marilyn, and even pie, as if her old friend was trying to say, *We miss you, Willa. Let us back in.* But Willa couldn't look the people of Willa, Montana, in the eye. She was betraying them all. It was hard enough to look at Nel, but she could because of Sook. It had been her peace offering.

After Willa's ribs had healed enough, sometimes Nel would say, "Why don't you take Sook for a ride? My grandma doesn't need me at home yet. There's always something that needs done around here."

Should Willa tell the women how fiercely she longed for that offer? And how when it came, she'd taken it like a thief, galloping up Bison Butte each time like it would be the last, stopping at the top where she'd pictured spreading Jack's ashes.

Maybe I'll bring them with me instead, she thought now. Was that the first step to her So Now What? Spreading his ashes? Could she do it without Sook?

Nel hadn't come by since the word got out about town being for sale.

Willa gritted out the words, "No *woe is me*," as she pulled the barn door shut and then walked into the orchard, admiring the blooming apple trees. This yard had been the town common. It held a perpetual memory of the Cider Press Party—bees feeding on the pile of spent cores and peels, kids playing in the trees, the parents drinking Jack's autumn Pissant Porter, the old-timey music Jack's beloved band, Grin and Bear It, would play under the cottonwoods.

The happy memories were so quickly eclipsed now, and she saw them all there at the memorial. They'd drained one of his last kegs and played dirges and sea shanties, and she'd smelled fear in the air rather than cider. Should she tell the women that afterward she'd hopped on Sook, bareback, while the boys and a few friends were passed out on home brew in the barn? She'd ridden up Bison Butte, fearing winter. Faking moxie. Thinking of what the doctors had told her: "His heart literally exploded." It was a condition he'd had and not known about his whole life. Thank God it wasn't hereditary.

No. This was not their burden. She'd keep that to herself.

Could she tell them about her twenty-ninth birthday, when Jack had saddled up the horses and said, "Follow me," until they got just a few yards from the Merc? They'd dismounted and left the horses to graze while he blindfolded her, spun her in a few circles, and led her by the hand. "Now, open your eyes." And there in front of her was a road sign. WILLA, MT, POPULATION: 35. Then he'd spun her around to the Merc, and a brand-new US POSTAL OFFICE sign on the front with its very own zip code. "We're a real town," he'd said with his Cheshire grin.

"Emilio and Maria would be proud," Willa had said, so honored, and a little shy that he'd named it after her and not his grandfather or grandmother, who'd homesteaded this land.

Now she stood staring at the house and the Inn, and said, "Where do I start with my beautiful life? Maybe I'll start here: I am a traitor to four generations and my one true love. So now what, indeed."

My story, thought Willa as she walked barefoot through the grass, eyeing the old familiar room lights in the Inn. *The rest of my life.*

She sighed as she ascended the steps to her front porch.

I suppose it begins with right now.

Willa set out the tea service in the keeping room, with her favorite Hu-Kwa smoky tea and homemade shortbread. She heard voices down the hallway and closed her eyes for one last second of solitude.

"I hope you're ready for us," called Harriet.

"I hope I am too," whispered Willa.

"Oh, I love a keeping room," said Jane, peering into the little room. "That's very New England. They've all been turned into monster kitchen additions these days." She held up her phone and took a photo. "So cozy!"

"My husband loved them too," said Willa. "Take a rocking chair. Pour yourself some tea. I hope you like smoky. And there's some shortbread for you. Help yourselves." She was quick to grab Jack's chair, with a view of Bison Butte.

There was a throw blanket on each chair, and the women wrapped themselves in theirs, poured tea, and sipped.

"It's so nice and dry here. My hair is very happy," said Jane.

"Mine too," said Bliss. "No frizz."

Then they were silent and Willa wondered how to break the ice.

Harriet said, "Oh for fuck's sake! We're not talking about houses, and weather, and we're not talking about *hair*! Let's *do* this! This isn't some damn tea party. No offense, Willa. We've got some serious shit to do."

Bliss snorted into her tea, shaking her head. "Harriet. Harriet. Harriet."

"Well, it's true, right? We're here to find some answers!" said Harriet, waving her hands at Bliss so that her bracelets jangled. "But before we get started, I would like to make a request."

Bliss smiled. "Go for it, Harriet. I've been following you off a cliff since you were my big bossy Wisconsin playmate."

Harriet blew her a kiss. "Okay. Here's what I propose: let's not push one button or stare at one screen this whole week." She shot a glance at Jane, who looked into her teacup.

"*Please*, let's not," said Bliss. "My mother watches *Golden Girls* reruns all day long. And I've stooped to the all-time low of playing solitaire on my cell phone. You probably don't even *have* a cell phone, do you, Willa?"

Willa shook her head, feeling like a misfit in her own home.

"I swear, all of this button-pushing is going to reverse our opposable thumbs," said Harriet, winking at Willa. "You and Jack had it right."

And Willa smiled at her, but not entirely.

Jane eyed her purse. "I've got to stay in touch with my kids. And you know how I love taking photos."

Harriet put out her hand. "Jane. Cough it up. Your iPhone, in its perfect little silver monogrammed case, needs to take a freaking *vacation*. Palmer's watching the kids. And you don't have to document absolutely everything you do. This is time for *living*. Give it."

Jane frowned. "Harriet … taking photos is how I stay *okay*. That and yoga. And therapy, I guess. Ugh—I'm *so* sick of therapy. Same thing over and over. Every week. At least photos make me feel like I have something *interesting* to show for my life."

Harriet narrowed her eyes and pointed at Jane with her shortbread. "Social media is the worst thing that ever happened to you, Jane Bradford. I challenge you not to take one posed photo for the next week. Only candids. Like you used to."

Jane put three fingers in the air. "Girl Scout's honor." Then she reached into her purse, sprang up, and said, "Candid, everyone!" and snapped a shot of them.

"Jane! You can't have a *posed* candid," said Harriet, grabbing for Jane's phone.

Jane shoved it in her purse, held her purse against her shirt, and said, "Harriet. Don't be so … damn … *controlling!*"

Harriet crumpled back into her rocking chair and pulled her blanket up to her chin. "I'm sorry. I'm just sick and tired of this cult of the *self* our society is addicted to. *Look at me. Look at me.*" She wiggled her hands on either side of her red tasseled earrings. "Frankly, I'm sick and tired of *everything*. I'm in Montana. I just want … the world to fucking *pause* for a week. I want that *interlude* on the invitation."

Jane looked at Harriet with something so sweet in her eyes. "I'm sorry, Harriet. I forget sometimes what you've been through. I just know you as my friend Harry. I'll be more careful."

And by the way that Harriet closed her eyes and tilted back

her head, Willa saw that despite her plugged-in personality, Harriet was not okay—not any more than the rest of them were.

Bliss said, "I think we need some rules. I vote that we all be as vulnerable as possible in these next few days, if we're really going to figure things out."

"I agree. Full frontal," said Harriet. "And we need to spill it. I mean ... have the conversations that women need to have. And that we're *not* having. Even with our best friends and family. We need *full reveal*. The nasty-wasty despicable true messes that we are." She cleared her throat. "I should speak for myself. But, ladies ... we need to *talk*."

Jane smiled a smile so tight it almost squeaked.

They all were silent, looking everywhere but into each other's eyes.

Willa rocked slowly, waiting for the women to settle—to give themselves to the keeping room, and for the keeping room to give itself to them.

"And no one tries to *fix* anyone," said Harriet. "I go into total rebel mode if anyone tries to *fix* me, and believe me ... you don't want that to happen. Let's just let it all hang out. No big frigging analysis about our lives. And no tying it all up in a perfect pink bow." She eyed Jane.

"How about in our free zone, we get rid of *I'm sorry* too," said Willa. "Unless we really owe someone an apology."

Harriet rocked hard in her chair. "I'm with Willa. Why do women say they're sorry just because they're expressing themselves? Or if they cry? Or if they sneeze? Or if their arm touches you when you're walking down the street together? It drives me crazy. I would *love* to get rid of *sorry* this week."

"*Sorry* is one of my top used and abused words," said Bliss. "Like I owe everybody an apology just because ... my life didn't pan out. It was supposed to go one way. And it didn't."

"Ditto," said Harriet. "That. Is. For. Shit. Sure."

Willa had run so far from self-pity, she didn't know how to touch this conversation.

Jane helped her. "Well on *paper*, my life looks the way it was supposed to look. But. Well." She sipped her tea. "I'm not sure if anyone ever did well by Supposed To."

Willa nodded and said, "I rewrote my Supposed To a long time ago. And then the Supposed To ended last fall. And here I am. Auctioning it all off."

Bliss leaned forward and looked at each of them, slowly, carefully, with that sure blink of hers. "Seems like life goes like that—in versions of what's Supposed To happen. And then what *actually* happens. And then it all leads to where we are now. Trying to find our So Now What."

They all nodded, rocking, almost in time, as these chairs had a tendency to do.

Then Willa stopped rocking. "I have an idea. Instead of the pressure of telling our whole life story to each other, why don't we tell each other how we thought our lives were *meant* to go. What was *supposed to* happen. And then why don't we tell each other what *actually* happened. Because it sounds like the two were very different for all of us. That way we'll get a sense of how to help each other find our So Now What."

Bliss's face widened to an adoring smile. "You have the best ideas, Willa. She homeschooled her boys, you know."

Jane and Harriet gave her blank stares and Willa hurdled them. "It's not like there were other options. Anyway, this might take the rest of the night. But like Harriet said, that's why we're here, right? It'll be a lot of talking tonight. And then tomorrow we'll get out into the woods."

"I need these woods," said Bliss. "They always change me for the better. But 'tis true that I could use some good old-fashioned jawing. I live with a woman who last week put her hearing aid batteries in her ears. Not in the actual hearing aid. In her *ears*. We had to go to the ER."

"Oh, Bliss. I'm so sorry. Bea was such a wise wonderful woman," said Willa.

"Yes, she was," said Harriet. "She was the one who told me I could leave Wisconsin. I'm not sure if I ever told you that, Bliss."

Bliss took a long sip of tea. "Doesn't surprise me. She'd be able to tell all of us what our So Now What is. But it's like she's died and there's this husk of a woman in her place. I'm really happy to be here. This is exactly what I need. Thank God for the neighbors. Their daughter is a nurse and she's looking after her this week."

"I don't talk about this stuff," said Jane, her tea to her nose. "As a rule."

Harriet nodded, but not altogether enthusiastically. "I'm pretty sick of hearing myself speak. But something tells me that you ladies won't tolerate any level of bullshit. So I'm all in. I can't stand another *drop* of BS."

Bliss said, "Willa and I came up with the idea for this gathering when we realized we'd both become islands."

"Oh, I'm an island, all right," said Harriet.

"Me too," said Jane. "You wouldn't know it from the outside."

"I think that's more common than people realize," said Willa to the women. "You ready?"

Jane slapped her hand on the table and said, "Hell no, but let's do this thing!" which made the rest of them giggle, coming from her frosty-pink-valentine lips.

"Oh, hell. I'll go first," said Harriet. "Get it over with. You'll all feel better about yourselves after you hear me yammer."

Harriet closed her eyes and rocked. "Supposed to Be. Supposed to Be. I *rebelled* against Supposed to Be. I never wanted to get married. I never wanted to have kids. I created my own Supposed to Be. I wanted to be rich. I wanted to be fabulous. I wanted to get out of Bucky Badger, Wisconsin—no offense, Bliss."

"No offense taken," said Bliss.

"According to my high school yearbook, I was the Most Likely to Succeed. I was *obsessed* with fame. I wanted success with a capital *S*. At least that's what I *thought* I wanted! And so what did I do? I used my looks and my smarts and my *ambition* … and I took a simple message and dressed it all up into ten easy steps, and I went out there and became the biggest hypocrite of a motivational speaker that ever walked the earth." She stood up and started pacing the room.

"You want to know what total bullshit is? Watch me up there on that stage, holding my hands *just so* at my navel, working a room full of upper-middle-class women who look like they're waiting for bread at a refugee camp. You want to *find yourself*? I'll tell you who you are. You *need* what I've got, because clearly I've got it all figured out—I've got the Beverly Hills blowout and the glow-in-the-dark bleached teeth to prove it." She flicked her hair and pretended to pose for a photo.

"Watch me say the word *empowerment* like I invented it. In fact, for twenty-four ninety-five, I'll sell you a T-shirt that says *empowered* in my very own empowered, red, all caps, Hard Ass *handwriting*."

She wrote her signature in the air and pierced it with a giant exclamation point. "Since *when* did women have to *pay* to be empowered? Women are by *nature* powerful, and we don't need some chick in a white pantsuit with a yoga ass telling us to remember that!"

"Actually," said Jane, raising her hand, "I do. I need someone to tell me I'm powerful. And I do yoga. Sorry. Oops. No *sorry*. Namaste." She lowered her head and put her palms together.

"Keep going, Harriet," said Willa. Women like this didn't

come to the Homestead. Was this what she would find out there in the world? And in the meantime, would Harriet find one thing about Willa, or Willa, Montana, interesting at all?

"Anyway. So what I *wanted* to have happen was to, yes, help women find their voices and follow their dreams … just like *I* had. But it was no small secret that I wanted to be rich and famous to boot. And I got it all. I was a grade-A famous, McMotivational speaker. Branded. Platformed. Bestselling books in airports with my airbrushed face slapped on the cover. Prancing around stages in fuck-me heels and making gobs of money preying on women's insecurities."

Harriet sat down and started rocking, hard. "My whole shtick was: Don't put up with anyone's bullshit! Be a Hard Ass and claim what you want! Kick guilt and shame and worry and apology to the curb. Go out there and get what you want and take no prisoners. And for fuck's sake—you nailed it, Willa—stop saying you're *sorry!*"

"In other words … be like a man," said Bliss.

"You got it! Leave it to you, Bliss, to cut to the chase. It's taken me *months* living like a hermit on Big Sur to figure out the collateral damage I've done in the name of Women's Empowerment. God, you're so crazy wise. Maybe I should have just stayed in Wisconsin."

"No, Harriet. You had to leave," Bliss murmured.

"I feel like my intentions were pure—*mostly* pure, at the beginning. But the train ran away with me. I couldn't stop. I was a full-blown attention junkie. I craved those standing O's and those tearful *thank-you-for-saving-my-life*s. Women loved my Hard Ass message and they loved the way I delivered it." She stopped rocking and leaned forward like a detective cracking a case.

"But there was a *problem*, you see. What about the power of *femininity?* The more I did all that cartoonish buffoonery, the more I realized that what I was really teaching was anti-*woman*, just like

Bliss said! But hell—I could never admit that's what my platform was really all about, or I'd be kicked off the stage. And who would I be without the *stage*? My parents called me Shittie Tinkie after all. Remember that, Blissful? Even though my mother tried her level best for those ringlets with those damn hot rollers … I wasn't quite Shirley Temple material."

Bliss cracked a smile, but a sad one. "They used to make her perform at all of their parties. You were good, Harriet. You know they thought you were good."

"Yeah, well … then out of the sides of their mouths, they'd call me a *show-off*. WTF?" Harriet swatted at the air. "Listen, I take full responsibility. It wasn't their fault. I loved every minute of it, are you kidding me!"

She closed her eyes like she was receiving the worst news of her life. "Until I didn't. One day—and I remember exactly where I was, lying in my underwear on my white leather chaise in my white house in Malibu—I had a good old-fashioned Wisconsin come-to-Jesus moment. I realized, lying there, that I was *exhausted*. Chasing success had turned me into this *caricature* of myself. This lie of a woman who was teaching other women to live in emphatics. At decibel ten all the time, all fire, quick to respond and quick to call *bullshit* … and it was just a *horrible* way to live! And my body went into these convulsions. And no white leather Mies *chaise longue* or white teeth or white pantsuit or midcentury Malibu mansion could stop them."

She opened her eyes. "I lay there like that for days, crying and moaning and thrashing around. It really, really, *really* scared me." She looked at Bliss.

"Why didn't you call?" said Bliss.

"Call? Hard Ass Harriet doesn't *call* anyone. Hard Ass Harriet is the one that *you* call when *your* life is in shambles. I don't mean *you* you, Bliss. I just mean the proverbial you."

Bliss blinked. "Well the proverbial me, and even the *me* me, might try to give it a go once in a while. The *calling for help* thing. But let's get back to you on the couch."

Harriet smiled at Bliss. "Blissy-pie, I haven't given myself a proper couch in *years*. It's more like a ten-thousand-dollar *dental* chair." She hooted. "I'm almost done. I promise. So ... lying there in my underwear with dried snot all over my face and an ocean of tears soaked into my zebra, yes *zebra* skin rug—nice, huh—I realized that I just wanted a life I can count on. With people I can count on. Kinda like life back home in Wisco, frankly."

Bliss shrugged.

Harriet shrugged too. "But I didn't know how to be that person. Not in the least. And so instead of doing what everyone else does, and like ... going to an ashram in India ... I completely shat all over my career. I kicked my ass off that stage. Hard Ass Harriet took her final bow. Jane, you mentioned your inner saboteur? Well, mine would eat yours for breakfast, lunch, dinner, dessert, cheese course, and coffee ... and still be famished." She paused and twirled her hair. "And I've got the viral video to prove it."

Jane's eyes darted from Harriet to the bookshelves, to the window, to her tea. "Seems like there's a way to get that video off the internet."

"Nope. Believe me. I've tried. It's there in *perpetuity*." Harriet rocked hard and then came to a sudden stop.

Willa was glad she hadn't seen this infamous video. And wouldn't.

The women were silent.

"So that's my Supposed to Be. It was *success*. And I got it. It actually happened. And in the thin-air altitude of it ... I realized it was all a myth. My version of success was a myth. And now I'm trying to find out what it is to live one honest moment. Because either I go public and admit my sins and get back in the game—cuz everyone loves a sinner ..." She shut her eyes tight. "Or that's it. I'm done for good. And I turn into a normal human being for the first time in my life. Whatever the hell that is."

Willa saw something of Jack in Harriet—the fierce way he had spoken of this land and how they would claim it and make it theirs. And sustain it. They shared the same sort of grit. The kind that gets you in trouble.

Harriet held her hair at the nape of her neck like she was trying to make it hurt. "I'm done. Mic drop. Tip your cocktail waitress. Don't drive home alone." She stood up, took a deep bow, and slumped back into her chair. "Is it time for wine yet?"

"Thank you, Harriet," said Willa. "Thank you for all of that. And for going first."

"PS, I'm intense," said Harriet, looking at Willa.

"Wine sounds like a good idea," said Jane. "In vino veritas. And I'll need some help with *veritas* if I'm going to do what Harriet just did. But there's *no way* I'm going next."

"We brought wine," said Bliss.

"They didn't have the greatest selection, though," said Jane, looking profoundly concerned.

Willa stood. "That's one thing Jack left me plenty of. He loved his wine. I'd like to go through his stash. I can't take it with me."

"What *can* you really take with you in the end?" said Harriet. "Hell if I know."

"Maybe my Herend bunny collection," said Jane with brooding in her brow.

Harriet rolled her eyes. "You and your little painted porcelain bunnies."

Without moving, Jane said, "At least I don't have a Steuben bowl filled with champagne corks from Nobu, Malibu. *Ticky-ticky-tacky!*"

Bliss jumped up like a referee. "You sit, Willa," she said. "I know where the wine is. And I'll go next," she added, walking fast out of the keeping room.

Willa knew what Bliss was doing. She was protecting her from having to go down to Jack's Cave and see his most treasured things. Willa hadn't been in the Cave since she'd typed the invitation on his old Remington.

"Thank you, Bliss," she called after her, sitting back in the rocker and covering herself in the throw blanket. "They don't make 'em like that anymore," she whispered.

"It's my utter pleasure," Bliss called back.

And Willa knew then what else Bliss was after, down there in the Cave: the Hugh that Jack loved, and that Willa did, too, when he was as good to Bliss as she deserved.

"What a fucking asshole," said Harriet. "She was always so much better than he'll ever be."

Willa looked at Harriet and whispered, "Let's not give him any more power than he deserves."

When Bliss returned, the women migrated to the kitchen, which always drew people to it. Willa took the good wine glasses from the cupboard, while Jane opened the bottle.

"Ah, Jack was a Rhône Ranger, I see," said Jane.

"A *what?*" Willa asked, wishing she'd come up with a more sophisticated response.

"Oh, just some tony thing my husband says. Côtes du Rhône fans are called Rhône Rangers where I live."

Don't judge a book by its cover, thought Willa again. She wanted to like Jane. What was under all that tight-lipped starch?

"Well, Jack always said he liked the wine from that region of France because the roots have to work so hard to get through the limey soil," said Willa.

"That's so Jack," said Bliss, and Willa tried her best to smile. If she was going to be in this circle of women, she'd have to learn to keep Jack out of it. But Jack had been a part of just about everything for her entire adult life. She muscled herself. *It's time.*

The women were here. This was the breathing room between her before and after. She took a long, deep breath.

Like Bliss could read her mind, she said, "The Homestead always makes me so hungry. Why don't we eat dinner."

"I'm *famished*," said Jane. "I couldn't sleep last night, I was so nervous. What can I do to help?"

Willa clicked into innkeeper mode with relief. "I keep it very informal around here. The soup is on the stove. Minted pea. The spoons are in the drawer under the bread box. There're napkins on the table. Help yourselves. And I'll warm up the bread."

The women served themselves, and Willa poured the wine and felt a wave of purpose. The careful hands on her china, the movement of food to table—it all felt so kind and right. Maybe this really was the proper way to close down the Homestead.

As they took their seats, she said, "I would love to offer our family grace. It's not religious. I guess it can be if you want it to be. It's just to honor the food and how it nourishes us. Is that okay with you all?" Willa swallowed hard because it was always Jack who said it. He'd learned it from a monk who'd stayed with them at the Inn.

They all nodded, though Bliss looked less eager for it.

Willa said, "Let's hold hands."

They did, and she began,

"This food is a gift from the whole universe.
The earth, the sky, and much hard work.
May we be mindful of our deeds as we receive this food.
May it transfer hatred, anger, and greed.
May it prevent illness and keep us well.
In gratitude, we receive this nourishment,
that we may seek the path of love, compassion, and wisdom."

"Are we supposed to say *Amen*?" said Bliss.

"If you want," said Willa.

"I like *shanti*," said Harriet. "It's Sanskrit for *peace*. I just love that."

They were still holding hands.

Bliss said a quick, "Amen." She looked at her soup, let her spoon hover over it, and took a sip. "There is a whole lifetime in this soup," she said, and took another sip. "And I miss it." Then tears spilled down her face like a dam had broken. "We had fun, didn't we?" Bliss brought her napkin to her face and dropped her head into it, sobbing, shoulders shaking.

The women looked at each other.

"It's okay, Bliss. Let it out," said Willa. "It's when we don't cry that's the problem."

Harriet said, "Crying means you're alive, honey."

Jane looked down at her soup like she'd dropped an earring into it, and her face went pink again.

Then Bliss's napkin came down to reveal her blotchy wet face. "I'm not really a drinker, but I feel like drinking a substantial amount of wine tonight. Here's to So Now What," she said as they raised their glasses.

"Look into each other's eyes!" Harriet said. "Otherwise we won't have sex for a year!"

They all quickly looked each other in the eye.

"I'm going to have *sex* again?" said Bliss, laughing through her tears. She took a big breath and blew it out so that her bangs lifted and parted. "I better go right now while I have the courage. Ready for nothing?"

"Ready for everything," said Harriet.

Bliss rolled her eyes. "I work at a church basement bookstore, for crying out loud. In rural Wisconsin! We tell each other *Jesus's* story. Not our *own*!"

Harriet slammed her hand on the table. "Hey—your story is important. Even if it's a hot mess. None of us came here to walk on eggshells. This is real and this is raw and this is *exactly* what we all need. Because life is fucking hard, and we fucking die at the end of it. I mean, *seriously*? It's a miracle that anyone can get out of bed in the morning." Her bracelets clanked as she swung her hands open. "We need *each other*! And we need *kindness*! We need a *lot* of kindness. And we need to stop walking around saying that we're *okay* when we're not. We're fucking *not* okay! Is anyone in this room *okay*? Speak now or forever hold your pea soup." She drilled a stare at each one of them.

No one said anything.

Harriet went back to her soup. "Sorry. I promise I'll try very hard not to do that again this week. And I don't know where I get off blabbing about community when I'm living as a confirmed hermit."

Bliss dotted her eyes with her napkin and smiled at her friend. "Well ... on *that* note. Hard act to follow. But I guess I'll go for it." Then her eyes twinkled for a second. "You know ... we're all fluent in this language. In the language of community. And yet we so rarely speak it. It really is our mother tongue."

Willa smiled at her friend. "Well said."

"I can barely wait to hear your story, Blissful," said Harriet. "I've always loved to hear you speak. It's like fresh air."

Bliss smirked. "Well I don't know about *that*. Let's see. What was *supposed* to happen ... Mine's not very complicated. I *didn't* leave home. I'm from Wisconsin ... I stayed in Wisconsin ... in the same little town near the university. Go Badgers."

She started to laugh but coughed instead. "I was charted to stay in Wisconsin. Get married. And have children. Traditional marriage: husband works, I stay at home with the kids. Church on Sunday. That was what I wanted. It's nice when what was Supposed to Be and what we *want* are the same thing."

Now Bliss's face got red and she took a sip of her wine. "Well, everything added up, all right. I married a handsome young man named Hugh who went to my church and worked at the bank. We bought a house not far from my folks. He was a good man and I loved him and he loved me. We were in our early twenties. We had everything going for us. People said we were the golden couple. And we were. We really were."

"You really were," said Willa.

"And I was lucky too. Golly, was I lucky. I had what I wanted. A big house—four bedrooms for the kids we'd have. I drove a nicer car than my parents ever could or would. I joined the garden club, which is pretty rinky-dink in our town, but it's what all the women who don't have to work *do* with their time. It's a status symbol. So is being on the altar guild, which I ran for years. I had friends, community, a prayer group, a loving husband, money. I wanted for nothing. Except children."

Bliss stopped and swallowed hard, in an obvious war with her tears. "Only the babies didn't come. They tried—some of them hung on longer than others. Years of infertility drugs. Injections. Procedures. Grapefruit-sized ovaries. Pregnancies with multiple fertilized eggs. Choices. Impossible choices. But we chose to keep them all. Six of them total. All of them, miscarriages. One of them late term. And finally, a hysterectomy." She paused, like she was trying to take a deep breath but couldn't get more than a shallow one.

"Do you really want to hear all this? I feel like I'm writing a depressing version of our Christmas card letter."

"Yes," said Willa and Harriet together.

Jane poured herself another glass of wine.

"Okay. It just feels so … indulgent. Sorry. I mean—ugh. It's a nervous habit."

"Anyway …" prompted Harriet.

"Anyway …" Bliss smiled at her friend. "Hugh didn't want

to adopt. No one we knew had adopted a child. So ... the extra bedrooms stayed empty. And I tried ... I really tried to live a childless life. I put all that energy into the church instead. I was a lay reader. I sang in the choir. I worked in the nursery. I ran the soup kitchen. I spearheaded the canned goods drive. I taught Sunday school and I directed the Christmas pageant, because secretly it was the closest way I could be with children."

Bliss looked at Willa.

Willa nodded at her.

Then Bliss let out a long, breathy sigh. "But *I* wanted to be in the PTA. *I* wanted to make a casserole for the football banquet. *I* wanted to be the carpool mom with the van full of kids, off to piano lessons, or ballet, or gymnastics. *I* wanted to sit in the front pew with my camera on a tripod documenting my beautiful daughter playing Mary, singing 'Silent Night.'"

She shook her head. "Instead, I was the one prompting the shepherds and donkeys to come in on cue. But they did give me a lovely plant every year as a thank-you. I have a sunporch full of Christmas cactuses. Cacti, I guess I should say. A whole sunporch full of Christmas cacti."

"It's not all it's cracked up to be," muttered Jane. "Especially when they're teenagers."

Harriet glared at her.

Jane shot her hand to her mouth. "Sorry. I didn't mean to say that. That was insensitive of me. I apologize."

"No *sorry*," said Bliss. "It's my cross to bear. So to speak."

Harriet said, "Bliss is right—we all have to be responsible for our feelings, especially in a gathering like this week. Believe me—I made a fortune off of women's emotions. And ... there's a high likelihood that a lot of emotions are gonna fly. And we have to feel permission to share. That should be one of the rules."

"Still, I'm sorry. Ugh, it's like a tic. I've got Sorry Tourette's," said Jane, swatting the air as if to rid herself of it. "Please. Go on." She dragged her thumb and forefinger across her mouth. "Zipping my lips."

Bliss said, "Well ... the truth is, Hugh would have probably been fine with it being just the two of us." She sighed and shook her head. "But I started in on the adoption talk again. 'God has put a child in this world for us to be its parents, Hugh. I feel it with all my heart.' But this time, I could feel him pulling away from me ... and I knew ... I was losing him. And it was probably my fault. Maybe I wanted children more than I wanted Hugh."

She looked at Willa and looked away.

And Willa knew that Bliss was feeling guilty that Hugh was at least alive. Willa supposed she could be feeling guilty that she had her boys. You could always find something to feel guilty for. "You've got this," Willa said, as if to say, *We are too close for guilt to ever drive its wedge*. She wondered how close Harriet and Jane were. Or Harriet and Bliss, for that matter. Or how close the people of Willa, Montana, would be to her once she left. They'd been family. She'd turned her back on them in guilt and shame. It occurred to her that feeling guilty that she was leaving wasn't helping any of them. "You know you've got this."

Bliss sighed. "Well, at that point I was desperate. I had to save my marriage and I didn't know how. People don't really get divorced in our town. At least not anybody that we knew. But he wouldn't talk about God with me anymore. Or pray with me. He started skipping church. We slept in separate beds and we blamed it on his snoring, but we both knew it was more than that. We became ... roommates, really. But I still loved him, you know?"

She passed her finger through her bangs. "Having a child felt like the *only* way to save our marriage at that point. Maybe he felt that way too, or maybe I just wore him out, because one day ... he finally agreed. But only to a private adoption. He insisted that we be completely in control of our choice of birth mother. I didn't care. I was ecstatic! And I have to admit, I really did believe it would heal our marriage. I felt God whispering in my ear. Everything was going to be okay. We were going to be a family after all."

Bliss paused and Willa knew she had to find a way through a heartbreaking string of words. "Well, I won't make a big to-do over it. We went through two private adoptions, and both mothers decided at birth to keep their baby."

"I didn't know that, Bliss!" said Harriet. "I'm so sorry. And that *sorry* is allowed!"

"Thanks, but I don't want sympathy, Harriet. That's why we didn't tell people. We told Jack and Willa. That was it."

Willa smiled at her. "I'm not sure that we helped. But we tried to."

"I get it," said Harriet. "But I wish I could have been there for you. Just for the record."

Bliss shrugged. "You were. In your own way. Whenever I needed a boost, I'd read one of your books, or watch you doing your thing on TV. A few times it was like you were speaking directly to me without really knowing what I was going through. You told me that I was *strong*. I could *handle anything*. I tried to convince myself. You have such a way of calling out our doubts and speaking to all that we can be. I can't tell you how many times I thought, *What would Harriet do?*"

Harriet rolled her eyes but said, "If my bullshit helped you, I'm glad."

Bliss sighed. "Anyway. I begged for us to try it one more time. That was in January. We picked yet another birth mother, and she accepted us, and we really felt that she would give us her baby because she was young and her parents were hiding it from people in their community, a few towns over. She's an adorable young girl, and she and I really connected. And Hugh thought it would be a good idea if I went away for a while instead of fixating on the pregnancy this time. I wanted to come out here and help you, Willa, but Hugh insisted that my mother and I deserved our *big trip*, he called it."

Jane groaned like she'd heard this story a hundred times and knew its ending.

Another breathy sigh from Bliss. "So he sent my mother and me off to Paris. One of our dreams. She'd been recently diagnosed with dementia, so we knew this would be a very special trip in every way. Our first ... and probably our last. Hugh was like a superhero, doing this for us, and we loved him for it and thanked him profusely, all the way to the airport. Two weeks, all expenses paid, in Paris."

Bliss's voice caught, and she looked at Willa. Then at Harriet, who put her hand on her hand and said, "*The truth will set you free*, or so you've always said to me."

"I'm taking too much of our time," said Bliss.

"You take as much time as you need," said Jane, like they were old friends.

"So, *anyway* ..." said Harriet, wiggling Bliss's hand.

Bliss dropped her head and dragged her fingers down her face. "Soooo ... anyway ... there we were, all the way in France, feeling like princesses, eating macarons and going to the Louvre and Notre-Dame and all the things we'd seen in movies but never dreamed we'd actually see in real life, sending Hugh photos of us to show to the birth mother and as a thank-you to Mr. Wonderful himself. And it felt like my heart might actually heal from all those years of *longing*. And that I could allow myself to hope again for that little baby I'd love with all my heart. Maybe I'd get my dream after all. And Hugh and I would be *happy* again. And he'd *love* me again, and love *God* again, and we'd be better than ever. And then, the morning of our last day, I got an email."

Jane gasped and put her napkin to her lips.

Bliss downed the rest of her wine and gave a smile that could bite right into her glass. "He was in love with someone else and had been for quite some time. He was divorcing me. And marrying her. When I got back, he'd be gone. And he was. Moved right in with this woman. This younger widow. Who has three small children—two girls and a boy. And that was the end of that. I didn't fight it. The divorce was final on April first. And I was the fool."

Harriet growled. "That motherfucker."

Bliss shrugged. "He tried to warn me. He didn't want to adopt in the first place. I put all my attention into it. I probably neglected his needs. It takes two. You know?"

"It does not take two to cheat and lie and hurt you like that," said Willa.

Jane poured herself another glass of wine.

Bliss leaned forward. "Get this. He announced his engagement the day after the divorce was final. On *Facebook*. He didn't even try to cover up that he'd been having an affair. Talk about breaking the norm."

"Oh, Bliss," Willa sighed. "If they'd told us in our bunk beds at camp what we were in store for, we might not have signed up for any of it."

"Yes, we would have," said Bliss. She dropped her head back, but the tears spilled down her face anyway. "I didn't want to cry. Sorry."

"No *sorry*," said Jane.

Bliss shook her head. "So that's pretty much it. We don't talk. It's like we were never married. It's like I don't exist for him. He puts pictures all over the internet of him with these children and writes, *I'm so blessed*. They're not his children to be blessed by! It's all about him. It's like he's gone *crazy*!"

She sniffed, her face deadpan. "So. Anyway. My mother moved in with me. Her Social Security pays our bills, and Hugh has to pay alimony. It's not much but it helps. So I took a job at the church bookstore, and I did manage to squirrel away some savings for my one-day children over the years—maybe to take that mother-daughter *big trip* to Paris. I'll be okay financially." She sniffed again, clearly willing back the tears.

"But I have no idea what the So Now What looks like. The biological family didn't sign up to give the baby to a single mother. And I doubt they ever would. I'm waiting to find out. Plus, I'm forty-three. That's pushing it enough as it is."

Harriet said, "Plenty of women have children when they're your age. Brush that one out of your mind."

Bliss took a long sip of wine. "And that's it. That's my story. I go to church with my seventy-year-old mother who may soon not remember my name, never mind the Lord's. My ex-husband is the picture of happiness with his ready-made family—thank God they don't go to my church. My friends are all busy with their kids. Some of my older friends are empty-nesters and are traveling with their husbands, waiting for their grandchildren."

That one stung, even though Willa knew Bliss didn't mean anything by it. Still, she stared over Bliss's shoulder, at the front door for ballast. She and Jack had always talked about following bird migrations when the boys were grown up.

Then Bliss let out a sharp, "Hah!" and leaned forward on her elbows like she was gossiping. "The *real* truth is … my friends aren't really showing up. At all. And it hasn't been too friendly at church, either, if I'm being utterly honest. I quit the choir. The alto section felt like a high school slumber party. It's like everyone thinks adultery and divorce are *diseases* and I'm contagious! I keep trying to look at it like, *Oh they're just busy.* Or, *They don't know what to say.* Or, *They must think I have a support system.* But I don't. Except for you, Willa. And Harriet. You've been great."

"Not really," said Harriet. "I've been so consumed with my own shit, I haven't really been there for you, and you know it. I call from time to time. So what? I should have flown there and held your hand during the divorce. And I should have told Hugh where to put it. And I should have come to church with you and taken Communion with you and stood next to you and guarded you during coffee hour. And helped with Bea. And shown those small-town cowards that you have people, and that *they* are your people, and that they need to show up for their people, *especially* when life gets hairy. Not just when it's sunshine and lollipops and freaking Lumberjack Days!"

"But maybe that's exactly why they're acting this way, Harriet. Maybe I'm the living example of what can happen. Even when you do everything you're supposed to do."

Harriet groaned. "*Supposed to* should be abolished from the English language. That's what got us all into trouble to begin with."

"You poor lamb," said Jane, swanning her neck toward Bliss.

"Please don't feel sorry for me. I joined a community ensemble and I like the sound of my voice blending with new people. They're not really my friends, but when I'm singing with them, I feel like I'm a part of something. That's the one thing that makes me happy these days. But everything else feels like I'm just going through the motions." She took a long sip of wine.

Willa watched her hold her breath and caught herself trying to breathe for her friend.

Finally, Bliss let it out. "And while I'm being completely honest, I haven't been going to church lately. Bea doesn't seem to notice. I can't handle the way people look at me! Or don't look at me! During the week, I sneak in and do my job at the bookstore, but I just haven't been able to get myself there on Sundays. And so lately, with the whole day free ... I've got to thinking. And ... I'm ashamed to say it, but I'm not sure *what* I believe anymore."

Bliss paused and looked into Willa's eyes, deep and wide. "I asked Bea once, when her mind was still strong, why she went to church. You know what she said? She said, *Because it's the right thing*

to do. I don't want to go to church for that reason. I want to go because I believe what I was taught to believe—that the creator of this
universe, a force that could make a place like Montana ... loves me."

Willa thought about all the boys' big questions and all Jack's
big answers. If Jack was at this table, he would say, *God doesn't
love. God IS love. You don't need church to merge with the divine.
Go walk in the woods.* The woods had been the closest Willa had
known of church.

Jane said, "I don't mean to offend in any way, and I'm more
of an Easter and Christmas type of Christian these days ... I
mean, do you know what Palmer and I gave up for Lent this year?
Tanqueray. Not *all* gin. Just Tanqueray. *Please.*"

Harriet snort-laughed.

"But I'm just wondering," Jane continued, "don't we *all* lose
our faith at some point in our lives ... in *whatever* it is that we
believe in?" She took a sip of wine. "What do I know?"

Willa couldn't help but think that Jane knew a lot more than
she let on. *Honestly, when is the last time I took a walk in the woods?*

Bliss took in a deep sigh. "I guess. But I wasn't *supposed* to
lose my faith. And God wasn't *supposed* to turn his back on me.
The divorce was the last straw. But before I throw in the towel
altogether, I want to find one prayer that I believe God will hear.
Because maybe it's been my fault. Maybe my prayers have been all
wrong. I mean ... I pray for parking places."

"I do too," said Jane, twisting her ponytail. "If we're being
honest."

"I've totally prayed for a parking place," said Harriet. "But I
mean ... it *is* LA."

Now Bliss smiled. "Are you three ready for this?" She paused
and Willa nodded. "I already want to take these words back. But I
have a decision to make. And if I don't make it in Montana, when
will I make it, never mind find a prayer for it?"

She poured herself a glass of wine like it was contraband. "I didn't quite speak the whole truth before. I'm not waiting on the birth mother to make her decision. I actually … haven't told her."

"Uh-oh," said Harriet.

"Yep. There's a sixteen-year-old girl in Wisconsin who thinks that her baby is going to a nice Christian couple, and I don't know how to break the news to her. I have *got* to break the news to her even though I can't *imagine* her still wanting me to be the mother. A forty-three-year-old single mother who's questioning her faith in *everything*? And do I even dare tell her about that part of it? It wouldn't be fair if I didn't."

"None of that would be a problem in California," said Harriet.

"Well, it is where *I* live. You know that very well, Harriet Cassidy, whose real name is Harriet Rud," said Bliss sharply. "I've always had such a strong faith that God would take care of me no matter what. And even he's abandoned me. If I keep getting abandoned, then maybe the truth is—I shouldn't be a mother after all."

She needs to go outside, thought Willa. *We all do.* "Would this be easier for you, Bliss, if we got some fresh air? The birds all change their songs at dusk."

"Yes. I would love that. I would love to sit on your front porch, like we used to," said Bliss.

They stood up, all of them looking at Willa like lost children.

"Bring your throw blankets," she said, leading the way. "It cools off fast once the sun goes down."

Side by side on Adirondack chairs, they took their seats. Willa looked down into the meadow like it had been a week since this morning's dawn. The robins were singing their nighttime arias, and she hoped it would call Bliss out of herself. The smell of gardenias floated in from the open front door, and she breathed deeply. "Where's Jane?"

"Trying to get cell service. See her over by the barn?" Harriet pointed. "It's going to take a while for her to let down. She said she had to call her kids. But I bet you anything she's taking a landscape shot and cyber-slathering it. She's totally addicted. Every single picture she takes looks like it belongs on her living room mantel. Perfect, perfect, perfect."

"Sorry," said Jane, calling to them as she jogged toward the porch. "You all look so lovely there." She held up her camera. "Say *money*. It gives you a much better smile than *cheese*."

"Case in point," said Harriet.

No one said a thing as Jane took the photo and looked at her phone. "Oh, one more. Harriet, you look mean." She snapped another photo. "Good one." She took her place in the fourth Adirondack chair, next to Harriet.

"Where were we, Bliss?" said Willa.

"I don't want to talk about my faith anymore," said Bliss. "I have a decision to make. That's my So Now What." She let out a loud sigh. "And there is something else that no one on earth knows about. But it breaks my heart every day. And I have to figure out what to do with it."

Willa recognized the taut sound in her friend's throat before tears. "It's okay. Say what you need to say, Bliss."

And maybe it was because none of them looked at each other, but instead into the meadow, losing its long shadows, Bliss said, low, "I call to them in my sleep. They were alive to me, even though they were never born. All six of them. They were *alive* inside me. I grieve them. More than losing Hugh. Isn't that twisted?"

Tears streamed down her face. "I wanted to have ceremonies. I wanted to name them." She choked on her words. "But he refused to participate. And I didn't have the guts to do it alone. So I never did."

Jane slapped her hand on the arm of the chair. "I'm sorry, but what an asshole! He doesn't deserve you!"

"They rarely do," said Harriet.

"I have absolutely no idea what comes next. And I'll leave it at that. Thank you for listening," said Bliss, wiping her face with her sleeve.

"Thank you," said Harriet. "For keeping it real. You show us how."

Willa said, "Yes, thank you, Bliss. Sometimes it has to hurt worse before it gets better, I think." But she thought, *Does Bliss believe that the only way her God will show its love to her is by giving her a baby?* How brutal an equation. But then she put the mirror back on herself without Jack. Not that he was her God. But it raised a damn good question: *How contingent is our essential sense of love … on another?*

They were silent, the light fading fast, the North Star bright, next to the sliver of moon.

"It's so quiet here," said Jane, "that it's *loud*."

"Remember that time we went ice fishing and Jack lit luminarias all around us?" Bliss said. "That was the first time I heard this silence. And you're right, Jane … it *is* loud. Like drumming."

"I can hear my heart beating in my ears," said Harriet. "Unless I'm channeling the natives."

"Are you ever scared here, Willa?" said Jane.

"No. I feel safe here. I've never locked the door. I don't even own a key to my house. Jack didn't believe in it. And he convinced the city girl in me to let it go."

"You don't lock the *door*? Even at *night*?" said Jane.

"No."

The last birds sang and the frogs began their mating calls in the marsh.

"Maybe we ought to save my turn for breakfast," said Jane.

"No way. You're not getting out of this, Janey," said Harriet. "Plus, we have pie."

"Do you know what I'd love?" said Bliss. "Scotch. Do you have any scotch, Willa?"

Willa thought of Jack's last bottle of Lagavulin sitting on his bookshelf in his Cave, the mossy Scottish peat behind some of the best kisses of her life. She thought back to typing the invitation on his old Remington, holding the bottle to her lips but not drinking. "I don't think so," she said. "But I have more wine."

Harriet and Jane raised their hands, and Bliss went into the house and returned with a fresh bottle.

"You'll *need* wine for my story," said Jane.

"It's the first night," said Bliss. "I think it's okay to get a little socially lubricated," she said, pouring wine into their glasses. Willa smiled at how her friend's Midwestern accent came out when she drank.

"Do you see the northern lights here?" said Jane. "I've always wanted to see the northern lights."

"Sometimes," said Willa, thinking of so many nights with her family of four lying on sleeping bags in the grass. The boys falling asleep. Jack holding her hand in the dark. Sometimes the emerald-green tornadoes would come. But that wasn't really why they were there. It was just being together, the four of them. She lit the candles along the railing and smiled as they illuminated the women's faces, lined up on her front porch.

Bliss broke the silence. "Pie sounds like a good plan. You won't be the same after you taste Willa's pie." She stood.

"Please, Bliss. Let me get this. You all enjoy the quiet." Willa went to the kitchen, cut up her pie, and placed slices on the Limoges dessert plates—her mother's wedding gift. Even though they hadn't had a proper wedding. It had been a peace offering for leaving her city Supposed To.

The frog sounds were at their fullest. She didn't have the

sounds of family in this place anymore. But she had this. And tonight, three women on her front porch.

Willa smiled, pulling four forks from the drawer that knew her hands so well. How had life become this moment of these women in this place on earth? She felt the house wondering too, as she put the plates of pie on a tray. And as she went back to the porch, she tried not to think of all the times she'd laid Jack's clothes out on his chair and sat down into them, trying to feel him.

"Strawberry rhubarb," announced Willa.

"Oh, yum," said Bliss. "I love your strawberry rhubarb pie the most."

Willa served them and settled back into her chair. "Okay. Jane's story."

Jane cleared her throat. "Jane's story ..." She took a bite of pie. "I've never tasted strawberry rhubarb like this before. There's something secret in it."

"Apple cider vinegar," said Willa. "In my crust."

"Apple cider vinegar!" said Jane. "Tell me more."

"We used to make the cider vinegar from our apples and sell it at the Merc. Jack started his morning with a spoonful of it. He swore by it." *Drop the Jack talk, Willa.*

"Can I be you when I grow up?" said Jane.

"Willa, you're one of those people who makes me feel guilty about my life," said Harriet.

"This is just the way we are," said Willa. "We make things." She caught herself. "Made." She was glad for the night air. Maybe it would help Jane tell her story. Her real story.

"Time to blow your wad, Jane," said Harriet.

"Oh God," groaned Jane. "Well, I should preface this with something Bliss said earlier: I'm excited for tomorrow too. I'm an open-the-window and fling-back-the-door kind of a girl. Well, it's how I used to be, anyway. I'm *dying* to explore Montana and see what everyone's talking about back home. Plus, I'm not a real fan of navel-gazing, so … I have to admit … this sitting here talking like this is *excruciating* for me."

"Not me," said Harriet. "I've done enough of flinging things back. Hole me up, baby! I'd be happy not to leave the house for the next week."

"I promise we're going to take a deep dive into Montana tomorrow," said Willa.

Jane took a long sip of her wine. "Well, I apologize in advance. I'm sure my story isn't really that interesting. Or sympathetic. And I'm sure you're going to judge me."

Harriet shushed her. "No judgment. And no *sorry.*"

"You're safe here, Jane," Willa whispered, watching her face flicker in candlelight.

Jane crossed her arms and looked at the black night, twinkling with stars. "I know it sounds silly with that huge sky over my head, but I'm feeling sort of … *trapped.* Full disclosure, I'm prone to exit strategies. I hardly know what to do with no cab to call. No airport within miles. No concierge to bail me out. I'm not used to this. At all."

Willa tried to conjure words that would help. "Jane. Instead of feeling trapped, why don't you think of this week as an exit from your *life.* Like *this* is your safe place. A lot of people have come here for that exact reason."

"Huh." Jane pulled her blanket up to her chin. "*This* is my exit. Okay. Thank you, Willa. I like it. I bet you were a very good innkeeper. And mother."

Willa could see Jane's white-toothed smile in the candlelight.

"Okay. Here goes nothing. My story. What was *supposed* to have been, and what *actually* happened. And So Now What by Sunday." She took a deep breath. "My Supposed to Be can be traced back generations, all the way to the *Mayflower*: Perfect marriage. Perfect kids. Perfect family. Perfect social calendar. Perfect legacy. Harriet was right—I don't stop. I have a checklist a mile long, and I'll never get to the end of it. And quite frankly, I *like* it that way. I can look at my list in the morning and see that my day has a design to it, with purpose, and people, and places. And at the end of the day, I look at it and I see all of it crossed off, and I know I did a good job. I don't know what I'd do without my list. These days the kids are so busy that I have a list for each of them, on *top* of my master list. The sports uniforms, the award ceremonies, piano recitals, SSAT and SAT tutors, decorating committees, school applications. My husband says that on my dying day I'll write *Die* on my list, cross it off, and slip into the great hereafter." She forced a laugh.

Harriet said, "I've seen her lists. With a giant pink *J* on the top. They belong in the Smithsonian."

"It's more of a periwinkle blue now, actually," whispered Jane, pulling her legs underneath her. Still in a whisper, "Here's something I've never told anyone. Sometimes ... when I've *really* got it bad ..." Her voice rose. "Oh, you're going to think I'm *crackers* ... but I might as well be brutally honest if I'm all the way out here in Montana. Sometimes I do *extra* things and I write them down *after* the fact. And then I cross *them* off too!" She dropped her head back and laughed.

"Oh. That *is* crackers," said Harriet.

"Harriet! You said this was safe!" Jane whacked her on the arm. "Anyway. I can't see the future. And that's because ... well, the long and short of it is that I don't necessarily *want* to see the future. Who is that woman going to *be* without her four kids and their busy, busy lives? I can't even really *remember* myself before I was a mother. I'm pretty sure it was all about the city and the job and the little black dress and being courted by fabulous men." She sipped her wine. "This is probably the wine talking, and I know I sound like I'm complaining, but ..."

"Just go for it, Janey," said Harriet.

Jane threw her hands in the air. "Well, I really *miss* that little black dress. It was like I turned around and I was up to my ears in diapers, living in the suburbs. And a lot of those years are just a *blur*. I mean, who *was* that girl with just one list, and what did she *do* with her day? I know that she was curious. Wildly curious. And she paid attention to things that other people weren't paying attention to. And she could see things that I've lost the ability to see."

Harriet said, "You should have seen her photos. What did you call them, Janey?"

"Stolen Moments. People sitting on the subway. Having a cigarette break. A lot of shots through windows. I used to walk the streets at night and photograph people. People in in-between moments. Sitting alone watching TV. Or on the phone. I have a lot of shots of people gazing out their windows, so lonely. Those were my favorite."

"The interlude," said Bliss.

"Yes," said Jane. "The interlude. I used to know how to take it."

"Where are all those photos, Janey?" said Harriet.

Jane's face released from its grip. "I really don't know, Harriet. Lost somewhere along with that little black dress and my Leica camera. And I never lose anything."

"You were talking about an empty nest," said Bliss.

"I was? Ugh." Jane threw up her hands again. "And Palmer. God. *Palmer*. A future with *just* Palmer and me? What would that even *begin* to look like? When the kids are all gone away at boarding school and college in a few years, I'm supposed to do what everyone else does, of course: travel. Hit the golden road. Check off every Relais & Châteaux from Berlin to Bangladesh."

"Pretty sure there's no Relais & Châteaux in Bangladesh," said Harriet.

Jane ignored her and looked at Willa. "I don't mean to be

insensitive to your situation, Willa. Please forgive me if my suburban froufrou first world problems are upsetting."

Willa said, "Please. We're here to let it all out. No one ever really knows what it is to walk in someone else's shoes, even if it looks one way on the outside." But she couldn't help thinking how lucky in love she'd been with Jack. Even with an empty nest, their life would have been so full.

"Let it rip, Jane. Gag order off!" said Harriet.

Jane held on to her ponytail like it was a sturdy rope. "Well, my kids are, you know, *teenagers*. And they're not necessarily *nice* to me, which I know is par for the course. But that's a story for another day." She paused, her head dropping to one side.

"I know it's terrible of me, but part of me is looking *forward* to an empty nest. The first one will be off to college next year. The next one will be a junior in boarding school. The one after that is gearing up for his freshman year in boarding school. And then in two years, all four will have fledged. So Now What? I want to see the *world*. But Palmer will only do it if there's a golf course involved. Again, first world drivel. But the *old* Jane? She wants to spend her days *wandering* again. You know? Getting a little *lost*."

"Looking through windows," said Harriet.

Jane looked into the night sky. "Yeah. Looking through windows. Not chasing a little white ball. And I'll tell you right now, Palmer has *no* interest in that. I heard it straight from his mouth at a party a few weeks ago. Our friends are going to China, and I heard Palmer ask why. The husband said, *To get it over with*, and Palmer gave him a good pat on the back and said, *Exactly. Which is why you'll see me at Pebble instead.*"

"Why don't you go wandering on your *own*?" said Harriet. "Being alone is *dreamy*. You can do whatever you want. And with *your* pocketbook, dear, you *can* actually do whatever you want."

Jane fidgeted. "Whatever *I* want? When's the last time I

thought about what *I* want? Well, I guess coming *here*. But prior to that? What if I get to my exotic place, and I'm afraid to leave the hotel room. I've become so *timid*."

"Oh, you're not timid!" Harriet shrieked. "You used to have New York City hanging on every syllable that came out of your mouth. People would actually wait for Jane to plan *her* weekend before they planned theirs. Jane *invented* the little black dress! She walked into that PR firm the first day, and even though she was the newbie, I wanted what *she* had. Why do you think I asked you to be my roommate, Miss Thing?"

Jane groaned. "Anyway, that's that. I'm done. Willa, your turn." She practically dove into her glass of wine.

"Why *did* you come here, Jane?" said Harriet. "And don't say it had anything to do with the possibility of me publicly shaming you, honey."

Jane crossed her arms even tighter. "I honestly don't know. I was lying in bed last night with my suitcase all packed, dreaming up all the reasons why I didn't want to come. Thinking that the So Now What question doesn't have to be that hard to answer. *Why do I have to go all the way to Montana?* And I thought, *When the kids are all off to school, whether or not I get to travel, I'll just redo the kitchen like everybody else.* And then the craziest thought came to me, but it was so real and so loud. And it frightened me. Are you ready for this?"

They all nodded.

"It said, *Jane, if you redo your kitchen, you're going to get cancer.*" She took a sip of her wine. "It sounds *ridiculous*. But the long and short of it is: One of the women in our tennis group got cancer and died this year. She was the picture of health. I mean she had *every*thing—*did* everything so … *perfectly*. It just *floored* us all. And then this dark cloud set in. This *doom*. And I knew I had to take that interlude you wrote about on the invitation, Willa. I had to break that lovely seal." She smiled so sweetly. "I *had* to. Or I'll keep living like this. And if I keep living like this … well. It's hard to explain."

"I don't mean to be dense, but why would you get cancer from redoing your kitchen?" asked Bliss gently.

"I'm not sure I understand either. It was just what came into my mind. And now it's taken full occupancy and I'm running scared. Maybe it's that I don't *know* what I want. I *thought* I knew, but I'm not sure I really ever did. I have all the things I'm *supposed* to want. I have what a lot of people would *love* to have. But I don't really want any of it. And at this age, I'm completely unemployable. Except for charity work. And God, I shudder at the thought of playing bridge at the club for the rest of my life. Or waiting for grandchildren." She devoured a few bites of her pie.

With her mouth oddly full, she said, "And I tell myself that I want to travel—that I'll be relieved when they're all off at school—but I think the truest truth is … all I really know *how* to want is my kids. And like I said, soon they're not going to need me. So, I keep us all busy-busy-busy so I don't have to think about any of it." She swallowed her bite and gazed up at the stars again. "I bet there are a lot of shooting stars here."

"Wait," said Harriet. "You want your kids to leave home so you can travel, and yet you don't want your kids to leave because … wait, why? You'll be stuck with Palmer? And so you're just going to remodel the kitchen. And that's going to give you *cancer*? I'm so confused."

"Obviously, Harriet, I know that cancer doesn't come from remodeling a kitchen. I'm just trying to be honest. I think my friend's death gave me a sense of *urgency*. What if we have less time than we think? I don't want my only accomplishment outside of motherhood to be the Carrara marble countertops and light fixtures in my damn kitchen! Oh God. Shut *up*, Jane! I sound like such an *idiot*."

"Maybe the quest for perfection is its own kind of cancer," said Harriet.

Jane played with her wedding ring. "That's the sort of thing I would underline in one of your books, Harriet. Do you know that all my friends have every single one of them? You need to be easier on yourself," she said, with a generosity that Willa was glad to know Jane possessed.

"You mean they didn't burn them in the village square?" Harriet laughed.

"No. They didn't. You're still their hero," said Jane.

Harriet leaned in. "Thanks, but nice try, Jane. Come on. You're all the way out here in the middle of nowhere Montana. In candlelight. With a captive audience. Staring at the biggest sky you've ever seen. We want to hear your story. Your *real* story."

Jane picked up her wine and swirled it in the glass. "I *told* my story. I don't really want to go deeper into it, if that's okay. Maybe tomorrow."

"You want *me* to tell it?" said Harriet, poker-faced.

Jane looked at her with the same poker face. "I don't know why I always let you do this to me, Harriet."

Harriet said to Bliss and Willa, "You know there's an actual Hard Ass high five? Come on, Janey." She stood up, swatted her butt, fist-bumped the air, and opened her hand like a traffic cop.

Jane made an attempt at high-fiving Harriet's palm, missed, and said, slurring a little, "Ooops. I might be a wee bit over-served!"

Harriet smiled and sat back in her Adirondack chair. "Good, Jane. Let your hair down for once. You don't have to take care of anyone this week but yourself."

"Yeah. That's what I'm scared of." She sipped on a mostly empty glass and seemed not to notice.

"Tell the rest of your story, Jane. It's just us, and some coyotes," said Bliss.

"Coyotes?" said Jane.

"Classic case of fogging," said Harriet. "Focus, Janey."

"God, my therapist calls me on that all the time. Fine. Time to put on what Harriet would call my *big girl panties*. She's got every woman in Connecticut putting on their big girl panties. And none of them admitting it to each other, unless they've had too much chardonnay at book club."

"Fogging," sang Harriet.

"Okay, fine!" Jane yelled. "Here goes nothing. I'm going to do this fast and get it over with." She crossed her arms in front of her and tightened her jaw. "I followed the Supposed to Be rules as if I invented them myself. I come from the *land* of Supposed to Be. I come from Seen and Not Heard. I come from Don't Ask. And Don't Tell." She lost steam and ate a bite of pie. "Willa, this pie is divine! I'm going to gain ten pounds this week."

"Fogging," whispered Harriet.

"Fine. Harriet said that I invented the little black dress. Well, if that's true, then I now have a whole closet of their more matronly versions. And they rotate with the benefit du jour. And whatever purse you're supposed to have but not brag about. And men in velvet dancing pumps and freaking needlepoint cummerbunds. Don't ask. And maids who come and clean dustless surfaces, and vacuum dirtless floors and rugs."

Jane gazed at the stars. "I'm like a paper doll. Just cut out my outfits on the dotted line, and fold them over my shoulders, and I'll do whatever you want—be your tennis partner, cook your dinner, follow your lead on the dance floor, remind your child not to end a sentence with a preposition and how to say *please* and *thank you*, tour boarding schools and ask just the right questions, all in the perfect cashmere twin set."

She threw her hands in the sky and said, "In other words, you *hate* me."

"Nobody hates you, Jane," said Harriet. "Do I have to come over there and grab your face and kiss you on the lips? Because I know how much you love that. Keep going!"

"Ugh! Fine. The Supposed to Be faded into What Actually Happened without me even noticing it. And now I'm passing all of it on to my four children. In dancing school and French lessons and handshakes and table manners and debutante balls. And lacrosse and field hockey and squash and tennis and paddle tennis. *God*, how many racquet sports can there *be* to master? And I worry. I worry so *much*, that they will crumble under it all. Or *worse* ... do it all as well as *I* have." She let her wince go slack.

"I mean, we have a river that runs through our property. And we've never once been in it. Or canoed on it. But we have the mother-*you-know-what*-ing vintage wooden canoe featured on the back lawn, because we're hearty WASPs, of course. And we like our good, clean, ruddy fun. And none of us *ever* has to be told the rules to Charades. We *all* know the rules to Charades."

She stopped herself but more words flooded out. "It's like the British say when they fire someone—they've become *redundant*. That's what I'll be when my kids leave. Redundant. And sometimes, to be perfectly honest, I just want to walk away from the whole thing." She put her hand over her mouth. "I can't believe I just said that out loud."

"There. You did it. That's what I wanted to hear you say. Sometimes you just want to walk away from the whole thing. Don't we all," said Harriet. "Good job, Janey."

They were all silent, like if anyone said anything, Jane might run for her exit.

She gave a blousy laugh. "And if I have to give or get one more *fucking* candle or *fucking* picture frame or *fucking* scented room infuser for one more *fucking* hostess gift ... I'm going to go *Looney Tunes*! I'm over it! Especially the fucking *candles*!"

They all went into hysterics, each in their own way, but loud and with percussion.

"What's so *funny*?" said Jane.

Harriet said, "I'm just glad you're not over gardenias and champers!"

Jane looked deflated. "I'm sure it's hard to understand because I have so *much*." Then her head fell back onto the chair. "They say you can't really love anyone until you love yourself. I hate that saying. Because I have no idea what it really means."

"Those are the most honest words I've ever heard come out of your mouth, Jane Bradford," said Harriet. "Nice work."

"I'd like to stop there. Or I might throw up. Actually, I *am* going to throw up." Jane got up and leaned over the railing.

"No, you're not going to throw up," said Harriet. "Just take a deep breath. You're fine. Hearty WASP constitution, and all that."

"This would *not* be happening at home," moaned Jane, dry-heaving. "Sorry," she said.

"No *sorry*," they all said at the same time.

"Is she okay?" Willa whispered to Harriet.

Jane dry-heaved again. "I'm okay," she said, holding both hands to the starry sky.

"Yes, you are," said Harriet. She stood up and put one arm under Jane's. "You're more okay than I've ever seen you. I just hope you remember it tomorrow." And Willa heard Harriet mumble in Jane's ear, "But if you're anything like me, it'll be better if you don't."

Bliss stood and took their plates. "Let's go into the great room in the Inn and stretch out. Those comfy couches are calling me."

"Fabulous idea," said Harriet. "It's Willa's turn now," and she and Jane led the way back into the house.

Willa stopped and waited as the women filed into the house, and then lifted her face to the sky. "Why does it feel like I'm betraying you to tell them about us? Don't worry, I'm not going to tell them all of it. Not the part where you left us broke. Was it some sort of mistake, Jack? Did you loan out some money and mean to pay it back? Did you hide it all somewhere in one of your crazy conspiracy fits? I can't miss you this much and be this mad at you at the same time." The anger was something she was only now realizing had grown in her all winter.

"Come on, Willa," called Bliss from inside.

And she left Jack in the dark, to go to the women. *What's it going to take for him to finally go?*

Ten minutes later, changed into their sleepwear and slippers, the women were lounging around the inn's great room. Willa put another log in the woodstove. She'd decided to keep it short. It was late. They'd all come a long way. That would be her excuse.

"Your turn, Willa," said Bliss, lying on the sofa with her feet on Harriet's lap. Jane lay in one of the large leather chairs, yawning in her pink chenille bathrobe, her matching slippers on the ottoman.

Willa took her favorite roost in the window seat, surrounded by pillows that smelled like wood smoke and resting heads. "Well, you already know most of my story. You said that you have to love yourself before you can love others, Jane. I'm not sure that's true for me. And I'm sure, Harriet, that your Hard Ass brand doesn't agree. But honestly, I don't think that I would have ever found real love for myself if it wasn't for Jack showing me how. It's like my life is comprised of before I met Jack and after." She paused to feel that warmth she always got in her belly when Jack walked in the room. *Keep Jack out of this room, Willa.*

"I have to say," said Harriet, "as much as I don't *want* that to be true, I think I can wrap my mind around it. I can *imagine* it's true that sometimes we need others to show us how to love. And *that* doesn't have to make us weak. Do I have any experience in this department? Hell no."

"Willa is the last thing from weak," said Bliss. "Tell them

about your upbringing. I always thought it was so fascinating."

Willa tucked deeper into the pillows. "Well, I had a perfectly happy upbringing. My parents were professors. I was charted for a career in academia—to live in a place where people quote dead poets and consider a breach in loyalty to the Oxford comma a sin. Though, to your point, Jane, I gotta say, when your truck skids off the road in the middle of January, *where's the winch at?* is music to your ears." Willa thought of all the times her mother and father had visited and looked down their noses at the Montana locals. It had driven its wedge and she'd picked Jack.

"Anyway, I met Jack backpacking around Europe as a student. I was reading Emerson's *Self-Reliance* on a mostly empty train in Andalusia. We locked eyes and he dug into his backpack and pulled out the same book. I mean the same exact book. Torn and old, that I'd picked up in my parents' study, who loved the Arts and Crafts movement and collected Roycroft books. And somehow, this young man from Vermont had picked up the exact copy at a used bookstore in Boston! I will never forget that smile when he pulled out his book. Like we'd made each other up—to be sitting exactly there at exactly that moment in our lives, with that exact book. Then he opened it and said, *You read the first paragraph, and I'll read the next.*" Willa looked at Bliss to steady herself. "We read the whole essay that way."

"That's so you and Jack." Bliss smiled.

Willa took a deep breath. "This is a lot harder than I thought it was going to be. I haven't talked this much in a long time."

She also didn't want to admit that she hadn't been able to bear looking at their Emerson books side by side on the keeping room bookshelf. Nor was she willing to admit that in one of her dark nights of the soul this winter, too deep into Jack's wine stash, she'd hidden them. And hadn't been able to find them since. She thought of their beautiful antique covers with the publisher, Elbert

Hubbard's quote: "*The love you give away is the only love you keep.*"

"It's the perfect quote for the essay," Jack had said. "The only way a truly *self-reliant* human can love. Giving it freely, not hoarding it. Not waiting around for it to come back to you. But knowing, truly, that to love is the most important act of all. That's what we keep. That's what fills a person's soul. That's why I bought this book." When he'd said that, she'd fallen in love for the first, and probably the last, time. Another reason they had called it the keeping room.

Willa must have shown it all on her face because Bliss mouthed, *You can do this.*

And Willa knew she meant that she should tell the *whole* story. About the money. But she didn't want to. It made Jack look bad or wrong or like he wasn't the best man she had ever met.

Willa sighed again. "Well … it was all so beautiful. He had this dream to come to Montana, where his father had been born and where they still had some land in the middle of nowhere. He called it *the middle of everywhere.* He wanted to live off the land like his grandfather Emilio, who was the original homesteader here. I was mesmerized by his vision. My parents named me after Willa Cather, and I'd always wanted to live a life like in *My Antonia*, on the wide-open frontier, not in a stuffy classroom. I wanted to create my own Supposed to Be too, Harriet. I just didn't know I could actually pull it off until I met Jack." She didn't say, *But that was a lie, wasn't it. I couldn't pull it off* without *Jack.*

Like Bliss could read her mind, she said, "I remember him telling us about his legacy with so much pride. What was that quote he loved?"

"It was his father who loved it and he passed it down to Jack. And Jack couldn't get it out of his head. After a while, neither could I. I'm sure I'm paraphrasing Thoreau, but this is how I memorized it:

Go confidently in the direction of your dreams. Live the life you have imagined.

It's not what you look at that matters, it's what you see.

Our life is frittered away by detail ... Simplify, simplify."

"Not redo your kitchen?" Jane groaned.

"I want to know more about Emilio," said Harriet.

"Well, Jack came from a long line of visionaries. Dreamers, really. The Silvestri family—they changed their name when they emigrated, to Silvester. Emilio was an immigrant Italian coal miner. He wanted to be a hay farmer, but so much of Montana was full of trees. So every day, he stashed one stick of dynamite from the mine in his lunchbox, until he had an arsenal to blow the stumps out of whatever Montana earth he could acquire one day." Willa loved to tell this story and it was nice to have it fall on new ears. It had wooed guests at the Inn for years.

"Then a horrible mining accident happened. The worst in Montana history, down at Bearcreek. And Emilio and his wife, Maria, were forced to either leave Montana or find some land. So he took the dynamite, came north to this part of the woods, found this land, cut down trees. But he loved the forest, so he just carved himself enough of a field to hay. And bombed out the stumps to make the fields you passed on your way up the hill. He bragged that his surname means *woodland*. And he grew hay and they had a baby boy. And they did all right, until he was drafted for World War II. And he had to leave his dream and go fight against his own people."

"Can you imagine? After all that?" said Bliss.

"Don't tell me that his wife and baby had to leave too," said Jane.

Willa felt a defense rise in her. "How was she supposed to hay the fields alone with a baby? And they didn't have any money, of course. So she and her baby went back East to live with relatives who'd also emigrated. She had no other choice." Willa felt like she was talking about herself, and slowly shook her head. "And they didn't treat Italians well during World War II. She was constantly afraid of being sent to an internment camp."

"I'd forgotten that story," said Bliss. "It's amazing. One stick of dynamite a day in his lunchbox. So resourceful."

"I bet it was *her* idea," said Harriet.

"I've often wondered what that journey back was like for her—physically, mentally, emotionally. To leave the land where she'd started a family and built a life she thought she'd have forever?" Willa thought of her mother sitting in this very room after the memorial, saying, "Well, you can have your old room back. And the boys can come to Chicago for vacations now. They'll like the city. It'll be good for them. I don't think they'll last long in Southern California. They're awfully intelligent." Just like all the times her mother had undermined Jack and Willa's dream, she had let the comment slide. *I am not going back like Maria. I'm going somewhere else. Somewhere new.*

Willa tucked deeper into the pillows. "Emilio didn't come back from the war. And Jack's father grew up and married a Yankee from Vermont farm stock. And so Jack grew up working the land. But his father and his grandmother were always talking about Emilio and Montana, so Jack never felt like he quite belonged in the East."

"Isn't that what so many of us crave: *belonging*?" said Bliss.

"I think you're right, Bliss. Which is another reason why it's so hard for me to leave. Jack was obsessed with Emilio's dream. He desperately felt that he needed to go back to the old ways and live in harmony with the land, in the wilds of Montana, where he felt this fierce calling. And it became my dream too. This is where I've belonged for my entire adult life."

Harriet said, "Now I get why it's so hard for you to leave. You feel like you're letting down a whole legacy of dreamers."

Willa made a weak attempt at a smile. "I can feel them here sometimes. That's pretty much my story. I'm breaking ghosts' hearts." She did not say, *Especially Jack's.*

"I can't imagine being that brave," said Jane. "To leave everything you knew and to come all the way out here. Just to adopt his dream would be hard enough. But to *live* it. I could never be that brave."

Willa sighed. "Brave? I've never felt *brave.* Maybe more ... stubborn. Or idealistic. Or unrealistic. We told each other that we would change the world in our own small way. He'd do it by example, truly loving this land and his neighbors. I'd *mother* it into a better place, because I *knew* I wanted to be a mother. I wanted a house bursting with activity and life, unlike the one I was raised in. He wanted that too. So we dropped out of college, bought a Volkswagen camper, and drove across the country until we identified the land from the county plat room in Great Falls, and claimed it. Jack's father had held the deed and we had it in our hands and they didn't balk. It was one of the proudest moments of Jack's life." Willa closed her eyes to picture that glorious day.

"I'll never forget the look on his face when we drove into the fields his grandfather had farmed and saw the original cabin that they lived in. It was unlivable, but we used some of the wood to build the barn. He was so sorry his father hadn't lived to see it."

"I bet," said Bliss.

"Your parents must have had a *fit!*" said Jane.

"My father never got over it. We didn't really talk. He passed a few years ago. My mother has been more forgiving, even though she can't relate to our life at all. She wants me to come back to Chicago and live with her. I can't imagine that being the answer to my So Now What. Please, no. I'm just not a city girl anymore. Even that prince of a city that I still consider home in some ways."

Willa paused. This was a time for truth. "I actually haven't told her that I'm selling Willa, Montana. She'll want to know why. And I'll have to tell her the truth. And it's a no-win. If I tell her I can't handle the lifestyle on my own, I'll get a giant *I told you so*, but it will be to the tune of one lethal throat-clearing. Sadly, she's the only real security I have. And she's a widow, living off a professor's pension."

"Is there more to the story, Willa?" Bliss smiled kindly.

Willa nodded at her friend. She knew she had to let it out if she was going to move forward with her life. "Well, the truth is … Jack left me with not much except this place and its value. And I really can't tell my mother that part or she'll go off on Jack. Even in his death, she judges him. I am her only child and she made it so that my choosing Jack was a way of not choosing her. She's never really forgiven me. If the town sells for a decent amount of money, I'm going to move close to my boys. If it doesn't, I guess Plan B is to go back to Chicago until I can get on my feet. My mother and me living in that hot apartment with all her retired professor friends visiting constantly, with their heads so far up their asses … I can't imagine it. I don't know. Maybe it would be good for us. I'd have to learn to play mah-jongg."

"That's a horrible idea," said Bliss. "I can't picture you in Chicago at all. You belong in nature. Out West. At least California is the West."

"*Wait*, wait-wait-wait-wait. How much is *not much*? Did Jack leave you with *nothing*?" said Harriet.

Willa gazed out the window at the center of the Big Dipper and imagined Jack's face. "I'd rather not talk about it. I'd rather talk about how fabulous he was. He took after his Yankee mother, but he had his father's Italian olive skin. He was so gorgeous to look at. He had coal black hair and a square chin with a little dimple in it. And these Arctic blue eyes like a husky. His whole self just *pulsed* with possibility. And virility. And curiosity. Jack had some money from his mother's mother and we bought tools to build our home and milled our own trees for wood. And we built our house and had our boys and lived off the land. And lived the dream." Her throat caught, and she looked at Bliss. "We did it. We really did."

Bliss nodded. "You did it so well, Willa."

She needed a break. Telling her story was like talking about a life on another planet that she couldn't return to. And not knowing where the money had gone made it worse.

Jane held the pillow to her chest like it was for protection, and said, "You built your own *house*? Your*selves*? You actually hammered the *nails*? No *architect*? No *contractor*? Jesus, where I live, it's a coup if someone chooses their own throw pillows. But you ... you actually hammered the *nails*?" She held her pillow even closer.

Willa refrained from the customary Locals' eyeball roll to Not Locals' comments like this. "Yep. We sure did. Jack was a handy Vermonter and he was patient with me. He taught me how to use a chainsaw, power tools, to be a steward of the forest. Before we knew it, our boys were running around, we had a beautiful vegetable garden, a full-to-the-brim root cellar, and productive fruit trees. Horses. Bees. Eventually it grew into a town and an inn and we were suddenly the owners of Willa, Montana, with our very own zip code."

A barred owl hooted and she smiled. "I've always loved that call. Sounds just like *Who cooks for you*, doesn't it? Whenever we'd hear it, Jack would say, *Willa does*." She waited and it hooted again.

"What a life you've got out here," said Jane. "I don't think I'd know what to do with it."

"Believe me, I wasn't always so comfortable here. At all. When we got to this valley, all they had was an old Quonset hut they called the Inconvenience Store, which maybe, on a lucky day, had warm beer, bait, and canned beans. They had no place to get supplies, no firefighter outpost, no place to have a beer, no Friday movie night, nowhere for the community to gather."

Willa looked at the woodstove. "This is so hard. I sound like I'm bragging."

"You get to," said Bliss.

"Anyway, those were the glory days of my life. And they seemed to just go on and on. I'm lucky I had them, aren't I?"

"I don't know if I'd call it *luck*," said Harriet. "Sounds like a life of serious intention to me."

Willa tucked another pillow under her head. "Life was beautiful, you know? We were the cornerstone of this community. And then when we added the Inn to the Homestead, people started coming to us from all over the *world*. And we never had to leave. And we liked it that way."

She smiled, looking at the Inn logs on the bookshelves. "I loved every minute of it. So many wayward wanderers—wondering what to do with their lives. A lot like us all those years before."

Bliss said, "Willa would sit here for hours listening to them, giving them advice. Jack called her *Dr. Willa, Esq.* I love that he made you a doctor *and* a lawyer."

Willa smiled, thinking of Jack's bellowing voice. "It made my parents furious. Since I didn't have any letters after my name at all." Her smile faded and she pushed herself to get to the finish. "I thought it would never end. It was beautiful until it wasn't. Jack dropped dead of a heart condition he didn't know he had last fall. And I learned the real meaning of self-reliance."

She laughed, because suddenly, the whole thing seemed absurd. "And somehow, I'm a forty-six-year-old widow who owns a town in Montana. And has to leave."

There was more to tell, but Willa wanted to be quiet now. She was telling on ghosts, on top of betraying them. Still, she felt she owed the women a glimpse of the truth since they were baring their own. "The long and short of it is, like most things in Montana, it comes down to money."

"But Montana is *all* the rage right now," said Harriet. "You stand to make some serious money at the auction. Don't you?"

"Plenty of our visitors wanted to move to Montana. One man from Texas offered us two million—was ready to write a check. But we turned him down. This was our place. It wasn't for sale. No matter what. But now ... I don't see any other way. I called around. Didn't get any real leads. Resorted to an auction. They handle all the advertising. And that's why you see those signs on the mile markers. Word got out. But, I doubt it'll sell for much. There's no local economy here." Willa realized she was biting off every nail on her left hand. Her fingers stung and words escaped her mouth. "I'm just so mad at myself that I didn't keep better track of our finances."

Jane sunk deeper into the leather chair. "I'm not sure what your situation is, Willa, and I don't mean to make assumptions, or be horribly offensive. And I'm sure this is the wine talking. But for what it's worth, I think there are more married women who know *zero* about their finances than they would ever admit. No matter how educated we are. I think so many of us trust that things are being taken *care* of. We have the house and the kids and everything *that* entails on our shoulders. And the man provides." Jane pulled her robe up over her mouth. "Sorry. It *is* the wine talking. I'll shut up."

But then she pulled back her robe and shot her hands up in the air. "Call the PC cops, but at least that's *my* marital agreement. It's *very* traditional. But who knows? If Palmer died, or left me ... I might be totally *screwed.* I have *no* clue what our finances are. And of *course*, I know better. But I'm just being honest. Harriet, no judging. It's the way Palmer *loves* us. If I took over the career and the managing of finances ... what would be left for him? Golf? *Providing* for us is Palmer's *love* language."

Harriet groaned and said, "Fuck that, Jane. You need to know what shape your finances are in. *Always*. You need to have your own bank account too, frankly."

"Easy, Harriet," Bliss said. "No one needs to be laid out in lavender. I'm probably the most practical person you know, right?"

"Yes," said Harriet. "You put the T in teetotaler! *Usually!* Montana Bliss is going to be a new adventure."

Bliss ignored her. "Well, I didn't know anything about our finances either. I intentionally stuck my head in the sand. I know exactly what Jane's talking about. What's wrong with wanting to be taken care of?"

"Hard Harriet wants to Hard Ass high-five you until you wake the fuck up." Harriet shrank into the couch and rubbed Bliss's feet. "But the soft part of me wants to wrap you in my arms and tell you that there's nothing wrong with wanting to be taken care of."

Bliss said, "Willa, we're interrupting. You haven't finished."

"That's fine. It's hell to hash it all over." Willa wasn't ready to tell them about the fall, and she hoped Bliss would keep it to herself. "But I think I'll skip to the miserable fact that I gave away our horses and mules, and then our dear golden retriever, Dash, got cancer and I had to put him down this February. And announce the auction. And tell my boys that I'm selling." She laughed again, which was better than crying she supposed. "In short, it's been a shit show here since the day Jack died."

"Jesus, Willa, you have every right to at least a *little* self-pity," said Harriet. "Jesus." She looked at Bliss. "Sorry."

Bliss shrugged. "No offense taken. You and Jesus can duke it out. He and I are on hiatus."

"If this place sells for what developers have offered us in the past, I could have enough money to get a good start in a new place. But what are the townspeople going to do? This is all they have. Like I said, there's no real local economy. People scrape by, and we all depend on each other, and on the people who come to Willa to see our little slice of heaven, thanks to the press we get from time to time. One write-up in particular in the *New York Times*. That one put us on the map. But it's not enough to make a real living. You have to live off the land if you're going to live in Willa, Montana."

"What's going to happen to it?" said Harriet, with real worry in her face.

Willa sighed. "That's why everyone is so mad at me. We all know that the new owner won't keep it as it is. They'll probably hack the whole thing up into bits and sell it off to snowbirds who want a piece of the Montana dream but who rarely come to actually *live* it. And the houses will be huge and empty. And where is everyone supposed to go? A lot of them have been in this valley for generations."

The women were silent until Harriet said, "Well, do they know you've got financial issues?"

"No. And they can't know. It's a long story and I actually don't know most of it." Willa started to tear up.

Bliss said, "You're doing your best, Willa. And that's all that counts. Remember what you said to me on the phone? Sometimes we have to let ourselves be misunderstood."

Willa sifted out all the things she didn't feel like saying and found this: "Truth be told … if my boys didn't need me, I'd be a wanderer. Like the people who come to the Inn."

She went to the shelf where the Inn journals were kept. "These are the logs from all of our years of guests. They didn't just write down things like, *Great pie*, or *Thank you for your hospitality*. They're full of incredible stories and artwork and poems and heartbreak and wonder and *life*. It became a tradition."

She opened a book and held it up, flipping past the colorful images, sketches, and handwritten passages, each one a different style—some tiny and tight, some long and loopy. Then she held up another and did the same. "A lot of people would return annually just to revisit what they wrote the year before, as a measure of where they were in their lives. When the *New York Times* article was written about us, of all the things they could choose to feature about this place, they spotlighted these books. Read through them when you have a quiet moment. Maybe you'll find inspiration in these pages." She closed the books and smiled like she was holding her twins on each hip. Just simple black artist sketchbooks she'd ordered in bulk that had come alive in her home. "I'll take these books with me wherever I go."

Jane yawned. "What a lovely legacy. Thank you for sharing it with us," she said. "Sorry." She yawned again, bigger. "I woke up at four o'clock this morning, and you know how it is on the night before travel. I never sleep."

"God, I'm *wired*," said Harriet. "I think I'll stay up and read through those journals."

The women sat in silence, staring at the fire, until they heard a gentle snore. They looked over at Jane, whose head was tilted back, her mouth open just a bit, her hands on the pillow pressed against her chest.

"Poor thing," said Harriet. "She just needs to collapse. You should see what her life is like. She takes care of everything and everyone. She never comes up for air. Not for one second. Let her sleep right there. She has insomnia, so we shouldn't move her."

"Are you sure?" said Willa. "I'd hate to have her wake up in the middle of the night and not know where she is."

"I'll leave the light on in her room. She'll find her way." Harriet took a few of the journals and said, "I'm going to immerse myself in all things Homestead. Thanks for a stellar first night, Willa."

Willa smiled at her, so strange to see those journals in the hands of someone like Harriet.

"I'm hitting the hay," said Bliss. "Do you need any help shutting things down, Willa?"

"Nope. There's nothing to shut down anymore, really. No

animals. That's the strangest part of all. There's always been at least a dog."

"Poor Dash," said Bliss. "He was such a good boy."

"He really was," said Willa, but she wasn't thinking about Dash. She was thinking of all of them, all the beating hearts, all the way back to Emilio and Maria. She gave Bliss a hug and Harriet a quick kiss on the cheek, and then went back to the house.

She'd trained herself to go out on the front porch to feel the night air and had rarely missed this nighttime vigil in all these years.

Tonight the marsh was in full frog cacophony and she stood there, looking at her favorite constellation, Delphinus, the one you could barely see, but could sometimes *only* see once it claimed you. It was where she looked for Jack. He had shown it to her the first year they came to Montana.

"Come to me, my love, and tell me that I am doing the right thing. Or at least forgive me. Or at the very least … tell me: Why did you spend all our money? Did you really believe we would always find a way to be okay? Because I have absolutely no faith in that right now. None. I'm sorry. I'm not as strong as you."

She waited for the decrescendo until there was one frog, maybe looking at Delphinus too. And then it stopped. And Willa went inside to sleep.

Day Two

Willa woke but did not open her eyes, as was her new habit. It could be any day in her life, and it could be one of the good ones. Maybe the boys were little, playing with their feet in their cribs, cooing and singing to each other, not quite yet needing her breast milk. And maybe Jack was asleep next to her in a gentle snore, a repose before a day of mettle. Maybe there would be a jam session tonight with Grin and Bear It, and maybe the whole town was coming over for soup, bread, and pie in celebration of whatever they'd made up to celebrate this time—Tally Hansen's win at the Great Falls bake-off for her Morning Buns, the quilters guild monthly meeting, which for some reason was attended by the whole town, or just the raw fact that they'd made it through to spring. With closed morning eyes, any time in her life was near enough to step into and live again. All she had to do was choose.

Widow's prerogative, she reasoned, keeping her eyes closed just a few more beats to hold herself in emotional traction. But this morning there was a feeling buzzing in her ribs like she'd had when the twins would move in her womb and she'd remember that life was happening inside her. This morning she had the deftest sense that life was happening in her *home*, and it was good. But she couldn't quite place it.

Jack? Then she smelled gardenias. And felt the slightest gnaw of a wine headache.

No. Not Jack.

The women.

Then she heard the crisp ping of plates and a moan in the floorboards, the oven squeaking open and closed.

She sat up in bed. Were they awake? Were they making breakfast? What time was it? Odd for her to sleep in after all those years of making homemade scones and sausages for her Inn guests. She threw on her robe and tied it as she bounded down the stairs, the scent of gardenia getting thicker and thicker.

"I dreamed there were elves in my kitchen!" she sang, turning the corner. "It's true!"

"One elf," said Jane, smiling and drying her hands on Willa's favorite apron, the one with MONTANA MAMA emblazoned across the top. "The rest are still getting their beauty sleep. I hope I didn't wake you up. I just wanted you not to have to lift a finger. Good morning! Coffee?"

"Coffee sounds delicious," she said, taking a steaming mug from Jane. "Thank you. I can't remember the last time someone made me coffee." It was disorienting being dormant in her own kitchen, especially with Jane in charge, the least likely of the women to understand how her life worked.

"It's my pleasure. And you deserve it." Jane smiled. "Cream or sugar?"

"Black. I have a wee headache. I don't really drink these days."

"I have a wee headache too. I'm afraid we were over-served. Blame it on the waiter!"

They both chuckled, but Willa wondered if Jane remembered last night. She hoped she did.

"We thought we should let you sleep. I hope you didn't wake up in the middle of the night in a state of panic, wondering where you were."

Jane took the Morning Buns out of the oven and set them on Willa's favorite Blue Willow tray like it had belonged to her own grandmother, not Jack's. "Between the Montana air, travel, a *lot* of talking, and wine, I was dead to the world until I woke up ready to go at six o'clock. I'm an early riser, so that was sleeping in, East Coast time." Jane looked down. "I *have* to get one of these aprons. I need to be more of a Montana Mama. I'm more like the Queen of Quotidian."

"My boys gave that to me years ago for my birthday," Willa said. "I can't believe I slept in. I was going to get up early and make scones. Some hostess! What time is it?"

"It's only eight o'clock. I couldn't go back to sleep, so I've spent the morning reading through the Inn journals. Naked Frisbee golf in the orchard! Sordid sex in the meadow between wayward strangers! Full moon bison bone scavenger hunts! I can see why the *Times* called this place, and those journals, *iconic*!" She looked lovely standing there with her blond hair pulled back in a tight ponytail, her eyes the blue of the china tray. "We have a guest log at our beach house. But the most risqué the entries get are an errant limerick! It helps that we summer on Nantucket." She giggled.

Willa pretended to get it. "They're pretty remarkable, aren't they? Wherever I end up going, I'm taking them with me. They're the closest thing I have to … proof. You know?"

Jane nodded, but not convincingly.

"Shall we sit in the keeping room?" said Willa.

"Yes. It's so cozy."

Willa put a few logs in the woodstove, which still had hot coals from the night before, and took Jack's rocker, letting the coffee steam fill her nose. "Thank you, Jane. This is so nice of you. Really. Thanks. I've missed those Morning Buns. And someone to share them with."

"Of *course*. This is what I *do*. *You're* a mother. *You* get it," Jane said. She put a bun on a plate, passed it to Willa, and sat in a rocker with her coffee.

"I like your style," said Willa, biting into the buttery cinnamon flakes. "My sons refuse to use plates. Crumbs everywhere, always. I miss those crumbs sometimes. Funny what you miss."

Jane smiled. "I'm sure I will too, one day."

They were silent, sipping their coffee.

"What's the plan for today?" Jane looked aggressive and competitive and scared.

Willa held back a smile. "I was thinking we'd go foraging for mushrooms in the woods. To earn our dinner!" *Tone down the damn self-reliance*, thought Willa. "But I guess it depends on what everyone wants to do."

Jane's face lit up. "Oh, I *love* foraging! We go blueberry picking on Nantucket. *Used* to go. The kids don't want to anymore. They say it's *boring*. I bet your boys never used *that* word a day in their lives, living here."

Willa didn't want to seem self-righteous, so she said, "Well, that's only because we ate off the land, and they knew that there wouldn't be dinner if they balked."

Then Jane said, "Your life here is so *authentic*. Mine is such a *sham* in comparison."

Willa didn't know what to say to that. They sipped their coffee in silence again, except for the nesting mewing of red-naped sapsuckers, and she thought it was probably good for them both to be out of their mother roles, though she envied Jane for still being knee-deep in hers. Certainly Jane's motherhood wasn't a sham. Motherhood didn't allow for it. Willa wondered what part of Jane's life she was referring to.

Then Jane looked Willa straight in the face. "What you created last night, Willa ... I've never had a night like that. *Ever.* We don't really *do* that sort of thing where I live. Maybe in our toasts at bridal dinners. We're *good* at toasting. Like we're good at Charades. I think I mentioned that last night in my wine haze." She laughed. "You just can't *buy* a night like that."

Was *that* it? Did everything in Jane's life have a price tag? Is that how the world worked outside of Willa, Montana? What if she couldn't fit back into mainstream society?

"Not that Supposed to Be and all that was *easy.* At *all.*" Jane blew a puff of air through her frosted pink lips.

"I'm a firm believer in storytelling," said Willa. "Our stories change, you know? And I think we forget that. I think we lock into a certain time in our lives and memorize it and live by it. But when we tell our stories out loud, we can hear what's true. That was a large part of how we raised our boys. *You think life is unfair? Tell us the story that had you arrive at this opinion.* And they'd tell it, and life would be fair again. Usually. I miss hearing all about their escapades."

"I know what you mean, at least with my first. He's so independent. He rarely even speaks to me unless he needs something. Usually *money.* I can barely get a mumble out of any of my kids these days. They used to just go on and on forever about their stories and I remember it driving me crazy half the time." Jane rocked, lost in reverie. "I'd give *any*thing to have those stories back in their sweet little voices. They can be so ... *mean* to me."

Willa couldn't relate. Her boys had never been those teens people talk about.

Jane said a stoic, "Maybe that's why the four of us are here. To unmemorize our stories."

"Or at least to write new ones," said Willa.

They rocked, sipping their coffee.

Willa watched a gentle wind in the apple trees and a robin hopping from branch to branch—nests made, eggs laid, mother keeping them safe and warm, father nearby just in case. "It's nice having this place full again."

She looked at Jane, so out of her usual world. It must have taken some serious courage to accept the invitation. "I know you're itching to get out and explore Montana. I wish I still had my horses. We'd go for a morning ride. Something tells me you know your way around horses."

"Hah. The Queen of Quotidian has forgotten how to ride and is probably too practical to take the risk. She'd be left in the dust even if she got the guts." Jane stood and admired a photo of Willa and Sook in golden autumn light, Willa's hair long and chocolate brown. "You're both bays," she said, putting down the photo and sitting back in the rocker. "I showed in the hunters and jumpers as a child. What happened to *that* girl? I miss horses. I was always … not sure how to say it. I was always *true* on a horse."

"*True.* That's the perfect way to say it. I gave my mare to a lovely girl who hasn't had an easy life." She took a sip of coffee, trying not to think that she might not ever see Sook again, holding back tears.

"I'm sorry, Willa. Your story is just *heart*-wrenching. Isn't there any way that you can keep the town and this place? And get your horse back? It's so magical here."

Willa didn't want whatever kind of pity comes from rich guilt. "It *was* magical. But one person can't summon the magic. It takes a lot of hard work. And resources."

Jane swept invisible crumbs off her khakis and sniffed. "I have nothing to complain about. I was born with a silver spoon in my mouth. I *literally* have the spoon. So *I* suck."

"We're born into what we're born into. It's nothing to feel bad about," said Willa, mother to mother. "Sometimes I felt guilty raising my sons here when I was raised with all the advantages of the big city. I moved here by *choice*. They were stuck with it. I think that as much as they loved it, they were restless. I doubt they'll come back to Montana to live, now that they've had a taste of California."

Jane's face turned pink and she clenched her jaw in contortions of composure. Then something gave. "I know that restlessness and I know that guilt. Instead of the requisite grace I was supposed to glean from those heaping silver spoonfuls…I ingested pure guilt. I *majored* in guilt in college. I was *supposed* to major in the men at Harvard, Yale, and Princeton! You know—my M-R-S degree. But from the start, I didn't *want* to. And there was *hell* to pay." She sniffed again. "And I wasn't brave enough to pay it."

"I think you nailed it last night when you said that *supposed to* never really served anyone."

They rocked and took bites of their cinnamon buns and sips of their coffee.

Jane said, "It's not like I wasn't *grateful*. I was *very* grateful. Even though I got *called* ungrateful. I'm sorry. I just wanted *more*. But I didn't have what it took to rebel. Unlike Harriet. Unlike you." She cocked her head at Willa like the robin in the apple tree. "I traded the little black dress and the Stolen Moments for a white Volvo station wagon. And, yes—monogrammed in periwinkle blue. JPB. The P stands for my maiden name. But my friends joke that the P is for Perfect. Hah. They have no idea what's going on inside of me."

Willa didn't know what to say. She had never sold out a day in her life. But there was a strong chance that she was now. It churned in her gut.

Jane cocked her head even more. "And Lord knows I've spent my life trying to make up for my restlessness, or as my mother called it *contrariness*, by being Miss Volunteer par excellence. Like there's this ungrateful gremlin constantly at my back, chasing me down. And I run. Boy, do I *run!*"

"I think we all have some sort of monster on our back," said Willa.

Jane straightened her head and slanted her eyes. "Willa, you don't seem like you do. You seem like you don't care *what* people think. I mean, in a good way."

Willa trod carefully. "I do care what people think. I'm devastated that this town thinks I don't care about them. But it's true ... Montana taught me to choose where I care and where I don't a long time ago. It's been my best teacher. It's hard to explain—life has its own rhythm here, and you can't speed it up or slow it down. It makes you pay attention to what really matters. And, I suppose, who you really are. And what you really want."

"Who I *really* am? What I really *want*? Huh." Jane clenched her jaw again. "I wish I knew how to even *ask* myself those questions. I just know that what you wrote on the invitation is true—I *can't* keep going on day after day in this same *routine*. It's like I'm *sleep*walking. I *try* to break out of it. I really do. I see a therapist. I go to yoga. I write in a journal—but I always feel like I'm just *swirling* in this vortex of *woe* in those pages. It's just the same damn thing every time. I don't *get* anywhere. I think the journaling actually makes it *worse!*"

She bit her lip as if to keep her mouth shut, but words leaked through. "I wonder if I'm depressed. I asked my therapist if she thinks I am. Because, believe me, if there are drugs for this, I'd run straight to my doctor and beg for them." She sipped her coffee. "Do you know what she said?"

Willa shook her head.

"She said that I'm not depressed. Ready for this? She said I'm *ungrateful*. Her *too*! I wanted to throw the box of Kleenex at her and run out the door and never go back. *Ungrateful?* I said to her. *I've spent my life trying to prove that I'm grateful! I'm the best thank-you note writer on the Eastern Seaboard.* But she said, *Jane.*

Gratitude—real gratitude—isn't meant for other people or things. Gratitude is meant for you. Well, *that* seems selfish!"

It hit Willa straight in the heart. Maybe that's what the town thought about her. That she was ungrateful. "What else did she say? We don't have any therapists in Willa, Montana. Not officially, anyway."

"Well, she told me to get rid of my regular journal and instead, to keep a *gratitude* journal. She had me write what brings me happiness, and peace, and *contentment*. Hah! But I gave it the good old-fashioned college try. Let me tell you—it was a *wash*. I listed all the things I have to be grateful for. My children. Lovely home. Another lovely home. Health. Et cetera, et cetera. With only my so-called gratitude staring me in the face, I realized that I didn't really *feel* grateful for any of it. With the exception of my children, of course. But everything *else*? *Nothing.* Zilch. I just wrote what I *thought* I should be grateful for. And my therapist called me on that *too*! How am I supposed to get rid of the restlessness if I can't even feel *gratitude*? Even my *gratitude* journal is a fake!"

Willa wished she could just send Jane out to dig in the garden all day. "I think that if you *know* something is inauthentic in your life, it's usually that your truth is right around the bend. I mean, it seems like you're trying, Jane. Really hard. With all that yoga, and journaling, and therapy. And you feel that authenticity with your children. I mean … there are people who don't even feel *that*. The girl I gave my mare to—her mother chose meth over her own daughter."

"That's awful." Jane ran her hand down her ponytail. "Don't tell anyone this. But my therapist is the only one who knows that I'm here. I told Palmer that I'm at Canyon Ranch—get this—at a gratitude retreat. I made that up, but it's probably a *thing* these days. It used to be a bunch of little old biddies sneaking in *gin* and pretending to do *water* aerobics. I sort of miss that." She giggled and then her face dropped. "God. Who am I kidding? Even

Palmer calls me ungrateful. Maybe I really *am* ungrateful. Like I said: my life is a sham. I'd day-drink if it weren't for the calories. I wonder if they day-drink at gratitude retreats. I know I would!"

"Spoiler alert! Gratitude retreats are overrated," said Harriet, bombing into the keeping room in a red silk bathrobe, furry red slippers leading the way. Her voice was an octave lower than the night before. "You shouldn't have to try that hard. Take a walk on the beach, for fuck's sake. Sit on a park bench. Pet a dog."

Dig in the garden, thought Willa.

"Oh look—it's the Red Devil herself. Coffee?" said Jane, smiling at Harriet, but through a clenched jaw.

"Morning, Harriet," said Willa, wondering if she knew the extent of Jane's darkness.

Harriet gave Jane a kiss on the forehead and poured herself a mug of coffee. "Sorry, but that stuff gets my hackles up. I once spoke at a gratitude *convention*. Yep, you heard me—a gratitude *convention*." She looped an imaginary noose around her neck and pulled. "I got paid fifty thousand dollars to lead a room of five thousand women in silence for an hour. And every three minutes, I banged a gong and asked, *What are you grateful for?*" She pulled the imaginary rope tighter, stuck out her tongue, and made a croaking sound.

Bliss appeared in the doorway. "What did I miss?"

"We were talking about how grateful we are that we're going *mushroom* picking today!" said Jane.

Willa couldn't tell if she was being sarcastic or serious, and she prided herself on being able to read people. She'd never met anyone like Jane.

"Morning, Bliss," said Willa. "There's coffee and Morning Buns, thanks to Jane, our early bird."

"Is that a freaking Lanz nightgown, Bliss?" Harriet shouted. "I'm making you burn that thing or you really *will* never have sex again."

Bliss pulled the sides of the bulky flannel nightgown out as far as they would go and did a deep curtsy. "Nobody messes with my Lanz." Then she turned to Jane. "Did you sleep okay out on the chair, Jane? I didn't hear you in the night."

"I was in the arms of Morpheus," said Jane with a contented sigh.

"And you, Willa?" said Bliss.

Willa said, "Oh, I always sleep well. My problem is not wanting to wake up." She looked out at the robin in the apple tree. *Or get out of bed. But I can't do that anymore. I have to make the most of these last days here.* She forced herself out of her mind and into this room of women. "Thank you for listening to my story last night. I know it was probably too long, and it was late, especially after a day of travel."

"Are you *kidding*?" said Harriet. "It was *fascinating*. And it makes me want to shake the people of Willa, Montana, awake! It's their town to fight for too!"

"I feel the same way," said Jane. "Isn't there something we can do? I once gave a friend an actual olive branch. I ordered it from a florist. I don't suppose you have a florist in town. Do olive trees grow here?"

Even Bliss rolled her eyes under her bangs.

Harriet said, "Because this is such a Mediterranean climate."

"Be nice," said Jane.

Willa tried to save her. "Even if there were, would *I* pass me an olive branch right now? Probably not."

"You're awfully hard on yourself, Willa," said Jane. "You're just doing what you have to do."

"That's what I tell myself, anyway," said Willa.

Bliss leaned forward in her gentle way. "Willa. If you could say what you want to say to the people of Willa, Montana, what would it be?"

Willa pictured the thank-you note she'd written and then

stuffed into the pocket of her parka. She rocked until she heard the creak that made her feel like Jack was near. "I just want to tell them that I care about them. And that I don't want to leave. But I don't know how to stay. And I want to tell them that I believe in this town. And that no matter who takes it over, it will be strong because of its people. And that they have to pull together. And that they don't need Jack or me in order to be a community."

The women stared out the window at the spring morning, a chickadee doing its *myyyyy treeeee* song in the aspen grove along the marsh.

No one spoke.

"Do you know what that sound is?" said Willa. "It's the chickadee. The bad-ass chickadee who winters over while all his buddies are down in Arizona and New Mexico and even Central and South America, and now he's staking his claim. That high-low song is saying, *I made it through a Montana winter and I get first licks on my tree. This is my tree. My nest. This is where my mate and I will have our babies. This is where they'll launch from when I teach them to fly … and come back to when they're tired. This is where their mother and I will bring them their food. This is where they'll be safe from wind and hawks. This is where they will leave from one day. My tree.*" Willa swallowed against tears.

"It's a lot to lose," said Bliss.

"It certainly is," said Jane.

Willa sipped her lukewarm coffee and looked out at the chickadees flitting around in the aspens.

Jane passed the Morning Buns around. "You know, Willa, in one way, I envy your position. Think of all that freedom you have. To do whatever you want to do, on new horizons. I feel *anything* but free." She paused and rocked. "I was telling Willa earlier that I feel so *stuck* these days and so … full of this horrible and unjustified and confusing *doom*. I can't seem to shake it. And

I don't know how to talk about it. Not even with my therapist, really. I don't have the words."

Harriet finished her Morning Bun and wiped the cinnamon sugar on her bathrobe. "I think a lot of women feel that way. They just don't admit it. We women take on too much and it's eating us alive. And in so many cases, we *choose* to do it, so we don't really have an excuse. And then we feel STUCK! And then we feel *guilty* about feeling stuck. Which gets us even *more* stuck! And we don't *talk* about it! So it just *ferments* in us."

"I'm so screwed," said Jane.

"Used to be at this age, women were looking at their twilight years," Bliss said. "Now people live to be ninety plus. That's half a lifetime from where we are right now. What's it going to look like? How do we muster the courage and the stamina for our future if we can't express the truth about the way we feel right now in our present?"

"Which is that we need HELP!" Harriet power-surged, the morning sun in her mouth. "And that's NOT a weakness! We all hauled our asses out here to Montana to HELP each other and to GET help, and that's POWERFUL!"

"Harry, don't scream. I have a wee *mal de tête*." Jane played with her ponytail, and then pulled out the elastic, so that her hair fell feral down the sides of her face. "I'll tell you one thing. If I don't do something about this ... I'm gonna *blow*. Tectonic plates. Yellowstone." Her eyes widened. "I've *never* said that out loud. And there's no way on God's green Earth that I'd admit that to *any* of the people in my normal life."

Bliss said, "I know exactly what you mean, Jane. If I said what I really want to say to the people in my regular life, I think that—" She buried her face in coffee steam.

"That what?" said Harriet.

Bliss shook her head. "That ... I don't know, Harriet. I'm just so *hurt* inside. I used to confide in Hugh. He was my person." She shrugged and sipped her coffee. "And my lifelong confidant has always been my mother, and now when I tell her how I feel, it's such a gamble. Every so often she has something to say that helps. But more and more, I just get a completely vacant stare. So I keep it in. Is that how you feel, Jane? Like you just have to keep it all inside?"

"Oh believe me—I've *stuffed* it all down my whole life. Stuffing is what I *do*. I'm *terrified* of that place inside me that is molten hot. I'm a walking volcanic *antacid*! And I do everything I can to push it down. I can't really describe it. I don't hear the bird you're talking about, Willa. It's like I'm wearing white-noise headphones all the time. And I have to force myself to listen through them. And to put *words* to what I hear or what I *feel*? God. Growing up in my family, we were *punished* for speaking when we weren't spoken to. It's no wonder that I haven't really said what I want to say my entire life. I mean, do I even *know* what I really want to say?"

Harriet put her red-slippered feet up on the table and groaned. "I think a big part of the problem is that we don't know what *conversation* we really want to be having. It's either small talk or we're one-upping each other with who's more fabulous or who's more miserable. Women need to start being *real* with each other. *Severely* real. We need to say what we really *want* and *need* and *have* to say!"

She shot to her feet and pointed with her coffee mug. "And that means we need to talk about *money*! And *sex*! And the way we feel about our *bodies*! And what keeps us up at night, and what does or *doesn't* get us out of bed in the morning. *All* of it! Instead of running around trying to pretend that we're not freaking catastrophic *basket* cases inside!"

"Shhhhh …" said Jane. "You're *shouting*."

Without thinking, Willa said, "It's because we need to be tough. No one's gonna help someone who can't help themselves."

"But that's just not true!" flared Harriet. "No one can help anyone if they don't admit they need help! People can't read our hearts, never mind our brains. We have to *ask*!"

"I don't mean to be hard on you, but … how are *you* asking, Harriet?" said Jane.

Harriet plopped back in her chair, the light draining out of her. "I'm *not*. Women are *mean*. They freak me out."

"Well, *we're* not mean," said Willa. "And you, in your words, *hauled your ass* here from California. So that's something." She smiled at Harriet. She'd never met anyone like her either. Willa wondered what she'd been missing living here all these years. Maybe life out there was going to be full of surprises.

Bliss chimed in. "Why are women so often our worst enemies? Even the church mice have gone lethal. If Hugh had *died*, they'd be over every day with a new casserole. Divorced people don't get casseroles."

Harriet whispered, "PS, never trust a woman with a casserole in her hands," and then said aloud, "Didn't anyone get the message on the playground? Women run the world! We need to unite! No mean girls!"

"I never knew what to do with those girls," said Willa.

"They're just scared," said Bliss. "Not that it makes it okay."

"I'm pretty sure I *was* the mean girl," said Jane.

They all sat silent, rocking.

Jane threw up her hands. "Oh hell. I'm *still* the mean girl! I *have* to be the mean girl to keep my—*God* this is going to sound so perfectly shitty—but to keep my *position*. I mean, I'm *nice* and everything. I'm a very *nice* mean girl. If I stop being the mean girl, then I have to … I have to … Oh, hell if I know. But I *do* know that there's *no* way I could say *any* of this or *be* the way I'm being *here* … at home."

Bliss chimed in. "I think it takes something like this—something far away from our normal lives. None of us have really logged miles together as adults. We don't take each other person-ally. You know?"

"Spot on, Bliss. As usual," said Harriet.

Jane said, "I like the fact that this is temporary. I mean, no offense, but I think it's better that we don't live in the same place. I think I might be able to be my true self with you all. At least, that's what I'm going for."

"Ah, your true self," said Harriet. "Who is she, anyway? When you find out, let me know so I can give it a whirl."

Bliss sighed. "I'm liking this so much. This skipping small talk. This being so honest. Do you know what I hate the most? Grocery store conversation."

"Fuck grocery stores," said Harriet. "We should create a T-shirt that says BACK OFF, BITCHES."

"How about NO THYME TO TALK," said Bliss, giggling.

"How about just I'M NOT IN THE MOOD FOR YOU," said Willa.

"Wait—you do your own grocery shopping, Harriet?" said Jane. "I thought you had people who did that for you."

"I *did*!" said Harriet. "But not any longer. Now I just eat whatever I can find at the gas station. Not kidding."

"Tell me that's not true," said Bliss, passing her another Morning Bun. "You are way too skinny! You need some good old-fashioned Midwestern meat on your bones."

"Fine." Harriet took another Morning Bun and devoured it. "Fuck my image. Fuck needing to be skinny to be a powerful woman. Pack it on, baby!"

"That's definitely one place I can't afford to be my true self—at the grocery store!" said Jane. "I know that sounds horrible, but there's too much at stake. We all *belong* to our town and our *reputations*. You know what I mean?"

Willa knew exactly what she meant but didn't say a thing.

"We're all deeply identified with something," Harriet continued.

"Or someone. Or some place. I heard it in our stories last night. What is the *true* us and what is the *us* that is defined by our identity? Yes, Jane, you're a mother. That is *of* you. But that's not *you*. That's where I got into trouble. My brand and its message was *of* me. But it wasn't *me*, like I thought it was. There's a big difference."

"I think that's what's so hard about leaving this place," said Willa. "Even more than my motherhood, I feel deeply identified by this place on earth." She let her eyes gaze out the window, looking for a moving creature. A pileated woodpecker hacked at a tree snag by the marsh. The thought came to her, *Wherever I go, I hope there will at least be birds.*

Jane stood up and stretched like she was getting ready for calisthenics. "*My* true self is getting *truly* stir *crazy* with all this *soul*-searching! Let's go mushroom picking!"

"You know what I'd like?" said Bliss. "One of those hot sausage and sauerkraut sandwiches from the Merc. With the sweet mustard and butter pickles and American cheese. Do they still make those?"

"They do. People drive miles for those sandwiches. I've been craving one for weeks," said Willa. "But I'm persona non grata in there, as you know."

"Well, *we* can go in there," said Jane.

"I'm sure there's mail I need to pick up. Maybe something about the auction. Maybe something on the Community Bulletin Board I need to know about," said Willa. "I wish I wasn't so scared to face them all."

"What's so scary about it?" said Bliss. "I mean, really. What's the worst thing that could happen?"

Willa rocked. "That I'll see the pain in their eyes. That I'll see how we failed them."

"Well, we'll look into their faces for you," said Bliss. "Why don't we get dressed? We'll swing by the Merc for sandwiches. And we'll march in there and get your mail too. We'll take our rental car so they don't recognize it. And you can hide in the back seat if you want, because it's okay to be a chicken sometimes, damn it. And then we'll go mushroom picking. How about that?"

"Thank you." Willa smiled. "You know what I really want to say right now? I feel something I haven't felt since Jack died. I feel secure, having you all here. Really. Thank you."

They all smiled at her.

"You make it easy," said Bliss.

Jane let out a little squeal as she raced out of the room. "Mushroom picking!"

Harriet rolled her eyes and followed her.

And Bliss looked out the window, blinking at chickadees. Not saying anything at all.

Town looked different, the way anything does that you are about to leave. Willa saw every stitch of it, slumped down in the back seat of the shiny red midsize SUV, a billboard flashing: WILLA'S FRIENDS. People wouldn't come within twenty feet of a rig like this, and that was fine by her. She pictured the women in the Merc, getting the silent treatment from people who really only knew how to be polite as a rule.

From her new-leather, no-rust, no-crack-in-the-windshield perspective, she thought, *It really is a dump.* Had it always looked this way and she'd just worn rose-colored glasses? Or like her, had it let itself go without Jack there to be its constant champion? It didn't matter. The Merc roof was drooping. The siding was rotten in parts. The red paint on the sign was worn off the *M* and much of the *T* and the *L*. The gas pump had seen better days—she wondered who'd backed into it, likely drunk, leaving the Saloon. And the Saloon— it looked about as tired as its day-drinkers. Willa and Jack weren't there to say, *Hey, we need some help up at the Homestead.* And instead of ordering another round, they'd be in Willa's garden, weeding the beet rows with her, in return for armloads of fresh vegetables.

She noticed a new table in front with an overflowing ashtray, a few old chairs with the foam coming out of their seat cushions. Jack wouldn't have allowed that on his watch. That was no kind of welcome to Willa, Montana. Where had the picnic tables gone? She suspected there wouldn't be hanging baskets later this spring when it warmed up enough—her job, and she'd be long gone. The post office sign, which had always been so official and even sterile, looked a little embarrassed to be in this company. "Somebody needs to take care of this place," she whispered.

She pictured that somebody. Maybe it wouldn't be a developer after all—maybe a young couple with big dreams and a nest egg. Whoever it was, hopefully the new owner would give her at least a month to tie everything up. Maybe they'd let her store some things in the barn until she found a place. More and more she was considering selling her house furnished and only taking her most cherished belongings, like the Blue Willow platter, some of their books—definitely Jack's Thoreau and their Emersons, if she could ever find them. And the Inn journals, the guitar. She'd load her truck with just the very basics, but she'd keep their bird migration atlas close. And once she got herself on her feet, if she lived frugally enough, maybe in a few years she'd find a way to actually go on that bird migration that she and Jack always talked about. For now, the question was where to go next.

I just can't go back to Chicago, she thought. It all depended on how much the town sold for. She hated that fact.

Where would I go if I didn't have any responsibilities? Willa stared at the Merc and tried to lose herself in images of Costa Rica, Belize, toucans and howler monkeys, the Georgia O'Keeffe landscapes of the Southwest—of being a woman, on her own, in places so new and unknown. Like the Calliope hummingbird, no bigger than a june bug, who migrated alone. One had gotten its beak caught in the kitchen window screen last summer and died there, and she'd shown it to Jack, cupping the iridescent green tiny thing with the violet bow tie at its neck.

He'd said, "To hold something this mighty, this beautiful and brave, that we were never meant to … in the palms of our hands."

She'd said, "It's like an offering. We need to honor it. Let's freeze it. So we can have it just like this to remember." Almost as if she'd known that theirs was a grace period that would have to end.

So they'd put it in a small jewelry box, on a cotton pillow, and tucked it on the top shelf of the kitchen freezer. Willa looked at the Calliope every so often. Its color was always just the same. She hadn't looked all winter.

She sighed. She'd need to release it to decay soon. Maybe she'd fling it over Bison Butte along with her husband's and dog's ashes. Seemed heartless to launch a bird from a cliff when you knew it could no longer fly. Maybe she'd follow a Calliope hummingbird out of town and just keep following it.

She shook the migration fantasy out of her mind and imagined the moment at hand—the women in the Merc being stared up and down by the people of Willa, Montana, mainly Marilyn. She could hear their minds ticking—especially when it came to Jane. They'd consider Jane proof of what they'd always suspected Willa was ultimately made of: *city folk*.

Willa sunk down in the back seat and stared at the flaxen May sun. "I don't belong anywhere without Jack and Sam and Ned," she whispered, wishing she still snuck a cigarette from time to time. "Maybe I'll start smoking again," she said and laughed.

Syd the Dog Man, and fiddle player in Jack's band, appeared in front of the Saloon then. He was riding Pilgrim. Willa slumped down a few more inches and put her face up against the window to get a good view. "Pilgrim looks skinny," she said. "Is he not feeding him? His dogs better not be getting first choice."

Syd tied Pilgrim up to Jack's old hitching post and went into the Saloon. He'd be in there for at least three beers and a few goes at the gaming machines.

Willa looked around. Town was quiet. The women would be chatting in the Merc, either out of fascination or as spies, and someone would be chatting back for the same reasons.

I just want to touch Pilgrim. Only a few steps and she could be at his side, nose in his mane and thick, proud-cut neck—always a stallion, that horse.

Leaving the car door open, she made a beeline for Pilgrim and dropped her head into his chestnut mane. He turned his nose to her and gave her a long sniff.

"It's me, boy. Good boy. It's me." She kissed his neck and put her hand on his muzzle to feel the velvet. "Can you believe he's gone?" she said low. "I hope you're happy with all the dogs. Is Syd taking care of you? Is he playing you music like Jack used to? He's as close as I could get, since Earl has too many horses already." She checked under his belly to see if the flies were eating him alive like they always did, but either it was too early or Syd was doing his job.

Then the Saloon door opened and she heard not Syd, but other Willa, Montanans, whose voices she recognized, yet whose faces she couldn't attach to their timbre, warped by alcohol. Jack was the one who kept track of daytime at the Merc. She got the Inn guests and the afternoon wanderers and Jack's musician buddies after work, wanting to jam.

"Well, no one's buying my house, that's for damn sure. I own it. It's been in our family three generations. I wouldn't live in one of them hippie cabins if you paid me and I'm glad I didn't fall for it. He came in like Jesus Christ himself. And now what are those families supposed to do?"

"To my way of thinking, Jack made plenty of money off the renters. I wouldn't be surprised if he was getting some sort of money from Uncle Sam too for having those low rent houses. And without him here to run the place, she doesn't care if the whole town gets mowed down. She'll just go back East. I hear they both come from money."

"She don't care if some rich Californian kicks them all out."

"Or slumlords 'em."

"Whoever it is, they'll probably put up one of them gates and shut us all out."

"Anymore, you can't trust anyone with deep pockets. And she's running out of town with her tail between her legs and all the money. You going to the party?"

"I'm not gonna lie. I'll miss that woman. She's not bad to look at neither. And you can't match her soup and pie. And especially her bread. And Jack's beer. They still have a few kegs at the Saloon. I've been rationing myself all winter. That man could make beer."

"Yeah, well, you can say *goodbye* to the Saloon too. Nobody's gonna keep that place running. I think Jack built it just so he had himself his own watering hole."

Willa heard the men coming around to their trucks. Pilgrim sidestepped so that she was up against the hitching post and could get a better view. It was as she thought—the two biggest assholes in town. The *only* assholes in town, really. And people forgave them because they'd been two kids who'd never stood a chance in hell with the fathers they'd had. But Willa was shaken. How could they think she and Jack would possibly do *any* of those things? Was this what *everybody* thought?

They gunned their jacked-up trucks and peeled out of the parking lot as Pilgrim's ears pinned back and Willa said, "Easy, boy." She felt utterly sucker punched.

The dust parted then, and Bliss, Harriet, and Jane emerged

from the Merc—women with plans. She waited for them to get to the SUV and took one more deep sniff of Pilgrim's neck. She knew she was being melodramatic and she didn't care. She whispered, "Wherever I go, I'll take you with me in my heart." Maybe that was the only thank-you note she owed. And she beelined it back to the car, this time to the driver's seat, her heart in her stomach.

"That place is a lost boon!" said Harriet, getting into the back seat with a large paper bag. "It's like a movie set! I love it!"

"More like boon*docks*," said Jane, getting in next to Harriet. "I felt like they were all looking at me like I was one of those middle-aged women in the Sundance catalogue."

Harriet cackled. "You bought your entire wardrobe for this week in that catalogue and you know it. Earrings and all."

"At least I didn't fall for the five-hundred-dollar wearable horse blanket," Jane winked.

Bliss got into the passenger seat and passed Willa a stack of mail. "Here you go," she said. "No one said much to us. They knew exactly who we were, though. The woman behind the counter barely looked at us and we ordered all of her sandwiches and eight Morning Buns. Were those your preserves for sale on the shelves?"

Willa's heart sank even lower when she saw Jack's name on one of the envelopes, the rest junk mail. She opened it slowly. *Time to report your livestock.* She'd missed the deadline, anyway. She tried to smile. "Yep. Apple plum butter. And my canned rhubarb and strawberries for pie. They've also got pounds of frozen huckleberries in their freezer that I picked last August with Jack and the boys. He knew where all the best patches were." *You just have to be everywhere, don't you, Jack.* Would he follow her out of town too? Down deep, Willa knew it was her choice.

Jane passed Willa her cell phone. "I took these photos for you."

It was just as she'd said. Stolen moments. There was Marilyn sitting at the post office desk, doing her crossword puzzle. And Tally wiping down the counters with a smile on her face but still looking like she might cry. And the back of Earl, drinking coffee at the table, alone, wishing Tally would finally pay some attention to him.

"These are perfect portraits," she said to Jane.

Jane smiled, but with purpose. "Did you see the photo of the rows of your apple cider vinegar? I love the packaging. I'm a sucker for old typewriter print. Same as on the invitation."

Willa swiped to the next photo and there they were, Jack's pride, and the labels typed in his Remington best: A TEASPOON A DAY. She smiled. "He loved that typewriter. It was Emilio's. His own handwriting was illegible."

Bliss said, "You didn't take a profit for any of it, did you, Willa?"

Willa felt like she needed to defend themselves, after what the young men had just spewed. "Not for things *we* made. The other local goods sold in there are on consignment. We took a small income from the *other* goods sold, and the gas, and whatnot. And then a cut goes into the town coffer which keeps up the Merc and pays the employees." She didn't say that that was almost empty too. There was just enough to pay the employees their last check before the auction.

"Did you get a shot of the bulletin board?" said Willa.

None of them said anything.

Finally, Bliss said, "There was a big sign over your auction sign that said PLEASE DON'T BUY OUR TOWN. We didn't think you needed the visual."

"We took it down," said Harriet in a quiet voice.

Jane said, "What are they thinking? If you're leaving, and they can't afford it, they're digging their own grave. I mean, they should be *ashamed* of themselves."

How did we ever become the bad guys? Willa thought as she pulled out of the parking lot. "You know, it was never us versus them. It was always, *always* us-us. We had each other's backs and we showed up for each other. It hurts, the way they're acting." She didn't want to have to admit her fall. But she didn't want the women to judge the townspeople either. She swallowed hard. "What are they supposed to do? They're desperate."

"I get it. When I quit the altar guild, I got the same cold shoulder." Bliss cleared her throat. Willa could hear the *buck up* in it. "I recognized one man in the Merc. With the gray moustache. He used to be in Jack's band. Guitar player. He smiled at me. I think it was a message for you, actually."

"Earl," said Willa, smiling. "At Jack's memorial, he played one of his favorites. 'Shenandoah.' And started bawling so hard I had to put him to bed like a little boy. Jack loved Earl the most."

"It looked like he wanted to say something to us," said Bliss. "But it was like he knew his place. I did see that Grin and Bear It is playing tomorrow night at the Saloon. I can't imagine them without Jack," said Bliss.

She knew her friend meant well, but still she was startled. Life had gone on. "I wonder who's playing the mandolin," she said. "Maybe they just have a fiddle, guitar, and bass now." So many memories. Where to put them now? The woods would help. She pulled off onto the dirt road that led to the burn where the morels would hopefully be plentiful.

"You know what I smelled in that mercantile?" said Harriet. "Fear. With a capital *F*." Willa knew that smell. Just not in the Mercantile.

"Listen, Willa. They know they've been lucky to have you and Jack. And they need a scapegoat. Believe me. I know all about it. You being the bad guy makes them the victims and people *love* being victims. Because God forbid they take a good look in the mirror."

"What's there to look at?" asked Willa, feeling defensive. "Their hearts are breaking. This town saved them. And I'm packing it all up right underneath their feet."

"How did this town save them?" asked Harriet.

"That's the *long* part of the story," said Willa.

"You know," said Jane, "you might be doing them all a *favor*. Maybe the next owner will be in a better position to create more jobs."

"That's what they're all afraid of. They don't want change. And they insist on respect. And they know they won't get it from an outsider."

She took a deep breath. "And no one will keep it the way we did. It's a lose-lose for everyone, because whoever buys it will be totally rejected if they change one thing," said Willa. "I mean, they lost what held it all together when Jack died. And I just … couldn't be Jack."

She caught Bliss's eyes. She hoped she hadn't told the women about her fall. Either way, she added, "And for the record … they tried to help me this winter. In their own way they tried. I just needed to be alone. And I think I needed to see that they could carry on without us."

"Life doesn't let you have it both ways," said Bliss, eyeing Willa back.

"Bitter pill," said Harriet.

Bliss said, "I might be overstepping. But now could be the time to tell the long part of the story, Willa. That way, we can help you."

Willa felt her face flush. She knew Bliss wanted her to talk money. Not broken ribs. "It's hard to talk about it, you know?"

"I know," said Bliss. "But you might as well. We're here for you."

Willa gripped the steering wheel, and then let her mind go with the well-worn ruts in the road. *Washboards*, they called them, after the old way of washing, hand to metal—the way they had washed for years. Would these women understand her life? Would they judge Jack like they were judging the townspeople? *Might as well*, she thought. *But not the fall. Not yet, if at all.* She couldn't give up totally on her self-reliance.

"Well, I didn't want to go into this last night. But it's a real mess. Half the town owns their homes outside the city limits. The other half pays rent to us. A long time ago, Jack wanted to help people who were living disenfranchised lives in the middle of the woods—many of them in horrible conditions, some of them old and sick, desperately needing a community around them. And so he built cabins on our land, over near the Mercantile, and rented them out for very little—really, just enough to cover basic costs. Montana houses take a beating and they require a *lot* of upkeep. Most of the renters are on Medicaid or collect Social Security, and really relied on us. Well, they relied on *Jack*. He was always over at the renters' houses fixing things and helping them out." Willa slowed for a pothole.

"What I *suspect* happened—and especially after what I heard today outside of the Merc, which explains a *lot*—was that some of our renters couldn't even afford to pay the low-income rent. And I wouldn't be at all surprised if my dear, starry-eyed Jack, was floating them. Like family." She gripped the steering wheel harder. "Thinking that somehow we'd be okay, financially, with the income from the Mercantile and what we managed to put in our savings. And certainly not thinking he'd drop *dead*." She shook her head. "That savings was our nest egg. And it's gone. Thank God we were smart enough to put away money for the boys. But I would never touch that. It might be all they have."

"Can't you get government subsidies for low-income housing in Montana?" asked Bliss.

"Jack never wanted to get mixed up with the government. He wanted to keep it simple and I did too. Plus, I don't think our cabins would even qualify. They're very basic and at this point, pretty worn in. People in Willa, Montana, lead simple lives. I mean, Bliss you know this: Jack and the boys and I have lived mostly off the land. What's in my meat freezer, or root cellar, or put up in cans in the pantry, or foraged, or growing in the garden, or taken from the chicken coop ... that's what's on the kitchen table." She took in a swift breath. "And I can't do it alone. I have to sell. That's the bottom line."

But before she could feel the sting of those words, a doe leapt out of the woods in front of the truck.

Jane screamed and Willa slammed on the brakes, saying, "Love, love, love, love, love," honking with each *love*, holding the steering wheel steady, just in time for a fawn to prance out behind her mother, stop, and stare at the truck. They both stood there, like sculptures, not even blinking.

"That could have been bad," said Bliss.

"Look at them," said Harriet. "We must look like monsters to them."

It had been like this all winter. Every time she started to really fret, some creature would show up at close range. "I'm sorry I slammed on the brakes," said Willa, staring into the doe's wide eyes. "My nerves aren't what they used to be."

"Are you *kidding*, Willa?" said Jane. "You're so calm. I would have swerved off the road and hit a tree!"

Then the doe leapt into the woods and her fawn followed.

Like they'd released her, Willa felt her Montana-ness return. "*Never* swerve. Especially on the highway. We've lost too many people to swerving and head-ons. And never slam on your brakes either, unless you're *positive* that no one's behind you." She started driving again. "You have to be willing to hit them. I hate that. But you have to be."

"We have deer in Connecticut," said Jane. "But we're more worried about them eating our roses than hitting them. Oh, and Lyme disease. Do you have Lyme disease here?"

"Not yet, thank God." Then Willa said, "Do you know, in all these years, I've never hit a deer. Jack used to say that I had a magical pact with them."

"Was that what the *love, love, love* message was all about?" said Harriet.

"I've just always said *love, love, love* when a deer crosses the road in front of me. The kids started it."

Bliss leaned forward so that her voice was loud in Willa's ear, on purpose, she assumed. "Willa. With all due respect to the deer, and to Connecticut, and to love incarnate … you've got a whale of a problem. And I think it's mighty damn mysterious. I mean, do you really think that Jack would have drained all of your money?" There was shock in her voice, and Willa's nerves frayed again, hearing this tone from her sturdy friend. "I just … I can't *imagine* that he'd leave you in a lurch like this! He was such a provider for you and the boys."

Willa hadn't let her mind go there until now. "You think someone *stole* our money, Bliss?"

"I know Jack. And he might have been a dreamer. But he wasn't irresponsible."

Willa's mind reeled as the truck bumped over the muddy potholes. "I mean … yes, it's true—even the town coffer is almost empty. But I can't *imagine* anyone taking money out of it. He was the only one who had access to it. Or knew where it was in the Merc. I'm pretty sure. Besides me."

"Wait, he kept a bunch of cash in the Merc? Does that place even have a lock? Who knows? Maybe he had a little sidekick who helped him with your accounting?" said Harriet. "Who might have done a little light shaving off the top so that he didn't really notice? And then when Jack died, he just drained it altogether?"

Willa hated hearing them accuse the people of Willa, Montana, of being thieves. She opened her window to smell the May air, not sure how to even imagine such a thing. Even with the assholes in the parking lot. They weren't *wicked*. Just lost.

No one spoke until Jane finally said, "Well, can't you look

in your bank statements and see who was paying what? I'm sure there's some sort of paper trail."

Silence. Washboards.

It forced her to consider something even Bliss didn't know about. She toyed with telling them for a moment, but thought, *It'll just complicate things.* Because the truth was: Willa and Jack didn't actually *keep* money in a bank account for long. Except for the boys' accounts. He didn't trust banks and neither had his father or Emilio. He had an account for any incoming checks and to pay bills, but he didn't keep much money in it. He kept money in socks. Drawers. Mattresses. It maddened her, but she had so many other things to deal with, and she'd always chosen to brush it off. And true, there was a side of her that loved Jack for it. So independent. So much his own man. She tried to shake away the memory of the night that winter when she'd rummaged through all the usual places, desperate to find their hidden cash. And she'd come up with nothing. Not one dollar. That was when she'd realized something was seriously wrong with their finances.

But Willa didn't want the women to know it. It didn't bode well for Jack. Or her, especially after what Harriet had said to them about women needing to be financially independent. Never mind the whole self-reliance thing.

"However this happened, I know it stemmed from Jack's loving heart. It has something to do with the renters. That's the only thing that makes sense. He believed deeply that the love you keep is the love you give away."

The road turned a switchback and pitched them far to the right, then far to the left, and Jane clutched the armrests.

Willa laughed bitterly. "You should know that around here, we mostly pay in cash. Bartering. And kindness. And people trust each other." She paused for emphasis, and then added, "Any way you play it, I can't let the town know that I'm broke, or someone's gonna feel *real* guilty. Because if I know Jack, he protected everyone from the truth. Maybe they thought we had money. Maybe they thought we liked charity cases. Maybe we did. But I can promise you that whoever it is doesn't have the means to pay me back. And I don't want to start asking around, because I don't want to expose whoever that someone *is*. I could never do that. And honestly—it could be *any*body. Or a few people. And whoever they are, they're probably my *friends*. Or *were* my friends. We all raised our kids together. We've survived dozens of winters together."

Maybe the women could help her with *this*, however. "Here's what I snag on: If he wasn't charging them rent, he must have made some sort of *arrangement* with them. He must have had a plan for them to pay us back. Like Bliss said, he wasn't irresponsible."

She put her hand out the window to feel the wind. "But what I just heard in the parking lot—is what I *really* can't believe and I just want to be *sick*! There's a strong potential that at least a handful of them think I've concocted some diabolical scheme to leave town with all their money! *God!* I just need to go into the woods and clear my head. Because you're right, Bliss … I've got serious *shit* to figure out! And I need to focus on my exit. I've got my boys to think about!"

Willa accelerated and splashed the car through the springtime puddles along Teakettle Creek, turning toward the mountain where the forest fire had burned ten thousand acres last summer. She fought back tears thinking of what would happen to them all, especially Nel and Marilyn and their family, and what would happen to Sook.

Then mud streaked the front windshield like the truth that was in her face: Those die-hard Montanans would find a way to stay. Even if they had no money at all.

"We're Montanans," Willa said. "We find ways to stay." And tears flooded her vision and rolled down her cheeks.

They were all silent. People had never been good with Willa's tears on the rare occasion they came.

She swiped them off. "Let's not worry about all of this," she said. "Let's eat those sandwiches and go find dinner. We're getting a late start, but we have plenty of daylight this time of year." Usually the light was so welcome after the dark of winter. Willa wondered if she was ready for all this light.

The forest got darker and denser as they climbed the switchbacks to the burn. Willa pictured a forest of morels and tried to smile. The green forest gave way to black tree snags and charred forest bottom, and Harriet said, "My God! This looks like Armageddon. Do they just let these forests burn?"

Willa could remember asking the same thing long ago. "They do unless structures are endangered. Fires are part of the natural cycle of things. Some trees, like lodgepole pines, can't reproduce without the heat of fire to open their cones. This one was close enough to town for them to put some manpower on it. The fire outpost was at the Homestead and they all camped in our yard and we fed them. I loved having them with us, even though the sky was black and you could barely go outside. It was one of the worst ones around here in years," she said, pulling off the road. "This is a good place to start."

They got out of the car and Willa looked into the sharp fingernails of the burned snags. "They call these *widow-makers*," she said. "Their roots are burned out. So even in a light wind, they can fall over."

"Lucky it's not windy," said Jane, looking over her shoulder.

Willa took the woods seriously and wanted the women to as well. There was a conversation happening—between tree root systems and birds and four-legged creatures and wind and so much more. And she'd learned to hear it—maybe even speak it. She wanted the women to at least hear it too.

"So, not to freak you out ... but we're in grizzly bear country." This was usually Jack's speech, and Willa tried to reproduce it. "If we see one, and the likelihood is small, but just in case, the main thing to remember is *not* to run. They'll outrun you. Just stand still. If they rear up, they're just looking around. It's not a warning. Don't make eye contact, though. Show them you're not a threat by speaking to them in calm low tones. Slowly back up. Give it its space."

Harriet said, "Uhhhh ... what *is* a warning?"

Willa never liked to sell fear. She loved grizzly bears. You just couldn't walk these woods without honoring the fact that you were sharing oxygen with one of the most powerful creatures on earth. Teaching people about them felt like a deep honoring of them. "If it starts wagging its head and making coughing sounds and drooling with loose lips ... *that's* a serious warning. Or if it paws at the ground. Whatever you do, don't look it in the eye, don't scream, and *don't* run."

"*Excuse* me?" said Jane.

Bliss said, "Jack and Hugh saw a griz once, turkey hunting. I'll never forget the look on his face when they got back to the house. It was the only time I've seen Hugh *totally* humbled."

Willa remembered what it had felt like when they'd first moved to Montana—the fear she'd felt every time they went into the woods. She still felt it. But it was seasoned fear, like she had an agreement with the bears, like they knew she was *of* the forest, just like them. "You really can't worry about it. It's more dangerous to do most of the things people do every day in the city, like drive, or take the subway, or cross a busy street."

"I don't take the subway," said Jane. "Full disclosure."

"You can't worry about it. I have bear spray in my backpack, just in case. Black bears don't really pose a threat. This time of year, it's the griz mamas and their cubs, especially if they're newborn, that you don't want to run into. But really, it's so rare. Just better to be informed." Willa tried to find her biggest smile before she delivered the most important lesson. "And if she charges at you, that's when you get down into a small ball and play dead. She might swat at you or claw you, but she'll probably decide that you're no threat at all and leave you alone."

"Or not," said Jane.

"Listen—I've lived here for decades and I've only seen grizzlies at a distance. They're omnivores. Very happy on berries and a ground squirrel or two. They don't want anything to do with humans. They just don't like to be surprised by us." Willa checked which way the wind was blowing to keep track around dense brush and blind spots.

Jane zipped up her pink parka to her chin. "Widow-makers. Grizzly bears. And didn't the Unabomber live in Montana? Would I be a total failure if I stayed in the car? This isn't exactly blueberry picking on Nantucket."

"A little good old-fashioned fear might be good for you," said Harriet.

"Just stay close together." She thought of Jack telling her and the boys to get into "a family huddle" if they were ever charged. She felt a sad pang and opened her backpack, taking out her guidebook to divert their attention. "Let's talk mushrooms. These are the ones we're looking for. With these dark brown brain-like hats. But you have to check to see if the heads are attached to the stems, and if they're hollow inside. If not, then those are false morels, which are poisonous. We'll check them all at the end to be safe." She gave each of them a steady smile. "Ready?"

Jane looked like a little girl trying to talk herself into a haunted house. "Poisonous mushrooms too?"

Willa linked arms with her. "This is going to be a good thing, I promise. The forest has lessons. And we need them."

I*t feels good to be in the expert role,* Willa thought as she led the way into the blackened woods, breathing in the charred forest air to inspire Jane to do the same. "I'll make sure we find the safe ones. I know my mushrooms. I have patches all over the woods, especially in the fall when the white chanterelles bloom."

"I don't mean to be a terrible bore," said Jane, clinging to Willa. "But are there mountain lions in these woods too?"

"I remember Jack telling us that you won't know a mountain lion has you until you feel its teeth on your neck," said Bliss. "So you might as well not worry about it."

"Bliss is right. You really can't worry about it," said Willa. She hadn't been around Not Locals in a long time. She'd forgotten how much there was to fear here. Fearing the forest felt trifling now, compared to what lay ahead of her.

Harriet moved to Willa's other side and linked arms. "Are there rattlesnakes?" she asked. "That's the one thing I'm truly terrified of. Rattlesnakes. Especially *mindful* rattlesnakes. They're everywhere! And they wear such nice blouses and give such long hugs."

"No rattlesnakes up here in the woods," said Willa. "Don't worry."

Bliss linked arms with Harriet. "Church basements are full of them."

Jane added, "We have *all* kinds of predators in Connecticut. But they're dropping off their kids in Range Rovers and comparing their Fitbit steps," loosening her grip a bit.

"We'll just make a little noise so we don't surprise a bear," said Willa. And she thought of the story Marilyn told of the Piegan Blackfeet tribeswomen, Nel's ancestors, who, when coming across a sow griz and her cub, dropped to their knees and revealed their breasts, to say, *I am a mother too. I am your sister.* Maybe it was no mistake that she'd lost the women in her life. When was the last time she had called her mother?

"I've never felt more afraid," said Jane, gripping Willa harder.

"I'll take bears over the Ladies Who Lunch, thank you very much," said Harriet.

Willa felt like she was talking to her boys when they were little. "Here's the way to think of it: there's plenty of Montana for all of us to be in our natural element."

None of them looked altogether confident.

Willa stopped, unlinked arms, and faced the women. "Isn't this why we're here? To face our fears? Isn't this ultimately what's in the way of the So Now What? Everything is a grizzly bear if you look at it that way. But grizzly bears don't just attack for no reason. Unlike life. So this is good practice. And believe me, I may seem braver than you, but I'm not—not by much." Now she looked into the trees, listening. "Ladies. Let the forest give itself to you."

"Like Paris," Jane said. "That's how I look at Paris every time I go. I don't *do* Paris. I let Paris *give* itself to me. Don't tell anyone, but once I went there to see one sculpture, and to have one cup of tea and a macaron. And to get my hair done. Don't judge."

"What was the sculpture?" said Bliss.

Jane sighed. "*The Age of Maturity* by Rodin's assistant Camille Claudel. I'm obsessed with her. She was better than he was, and he tortured her for it, and she loved him anyway, and she ended up in the streets. It's supposedly a sculpture about youth being taken by age. But when I see it ... it's so obvious to me that the young figure is really Camille, reaching for Rodin, who is being taken away by another woman! Camille's face ... just *craving* him. I can't get over it. It's the very portrait of anguish."

Which was what Willa had seen in Jane's face in the keeping room this morning. *That woman has secrets too*, she thought.

"Shit—what was the tea?" Harriet asked. "Poet's Tears? Goddess Blood?"

Jane sighed. "The Casablanca, from Mariage Frères."

"And the macaron?" said Willa.

"Ladurée," said Jane, blushing. "Orange blossom."

"I would do anything to be that person," said Bliss. "All the way to Paris for a few indulgences. When I went, it felt like I had to take in the entire history of France in one visit. I doubt I'll go back again. Not after Notre Dame."

"So horrible," said Jane.

"But they will rebuild," said Bliss.

"Yes, they will," said Jane.

And Willa could hear Bliss's heart saying, *Will I?*

"I know it sounds terrible," said Jane. "But to me, my little extravagances are not really *overindulgences*. They're about tradition. And art. And perfection." She held herself by the elbows. "They're what's left of the last time I liked myself."

"Holy shit, woman," said Harriet. "You need to find your inner Paris."

Willa pushed just a bit. "So think of it this way, Jane: you're here in these woods to find one mushroom." She put her best mud boot forward and Bliss did the same. "We're going to look in the burn first, but I also want to pick arnica for a salve we can make together, so we'll go into the green forest over there a little later." Willa pointed.

"My homeopath swears by arnica," said Jane.

"You have a homeopath?" said Harriet.

"I have a whole posse," said Jane. "You name it. A therapist; an OB-GYN; an ear, nose, and throat guy for my thyroid; a GI guy for my irritable bowel; a homeopath for my gluten and dairy allergies; an acupuncturist for my hay fever ... blah, blah, blah. It takes a village, believe me."

"That's some posse," said Harriet. "I used to have all of that too. Plus a medium and a tarot card reader. Now I have not even a modicum of woo-woo wack-wonkery."

"*Wack-wonkery*. That's my new favorite word," said Jane.

"You can have it. A little spice for your next dinner party."

"Huh," said Jane. "I just realized … I haven't had any problems at *all* in Montana. I've been eating whatever I want. And I feel just *fine*."

"Of course you do," said Harriet. "This whole gluten-free, dairy-free, nama-fucking-ste up-your-asana cult of the self is just *oblivion*, signed sealed and delivered by the McMindfulness machine. It's out of control. Piggyback *mindfulness* onto *empowerment* and we're all fucked. Gag me with a yoga strap."

Jane looked like she was going to cry. "I don't know what I'd do without my mindfulness meditation. And yoga. Don't take mindfulness and yoga away from me." Then she swallowed and looked at Harriet. "When did you become so *cynical*, Harriet?"

"Hah! Am I cynical? Or have I just seen the purity of too many good messages be corrupted and sold to … no offense … people just like you, Jane. And it sickens me."

"But if it helps me, what's the harm? So what if I pay for it?" Now Jane *did* have tears in her eyes.

Harriet sighed and said, "I'm an ass and I know it. Maybe it's just that I'm not at all convinced that there's this *village* everybody talks about. Seems like at the end of the day, everyone's out for themselves. I speak from experience."

Willa recognized this banter as discomfort. "Well, this is our village for now, and it's a good one," she said, looking up at the circle of ponderosas that towered over them. Ponderosa pine forests were her favorite, the long brown needle bundles carpeting the forest floor. Burned branches had scattered like pick-up sticks, and it required high steps as she moved through. "Be careful," she said. "These are knee busters. But first, put your nose in the crack of the bark and take a deep breath."

Harriet did it first. "Ooo. Vanilla!"

Jane followed, and then Bliss.

They picked their way through the broken and burned forest, the women stopping every so often to put their noses in the bark.

Jane stepped onto a fallen tree, balancing on it in her tennis shoes. "See this log? This is what life is like for everyone I know. We walk along it, so carefully … and we *think* our feet are on the ground, but they're *not*. And then something *bad* happens and we're off the log and we don't know what the hell to do!" She jumped off the log. "Most of the people I know … they're still on the log. But it's coming. I feel it coming. Do you know what I mean?"

Harriet said, "I get 'em when the shit hits the fan. Before that, most of them were like you said, *on the log*. Love that. So true."

"I've tried really hard to walk on terra firma," said Willa. "The log sounds dangerous."

Bliss said, "Oh, I know exactly what you mean, Jane. I am an *expert* log-walker. That's why I'm such a mess. I thought I was on solid ground all these years. But I wasn't."

Harriet spoke sweetly, "Blissful, didn't you have any idea that Hugh had an asshole feature to him? An *ink*ling?"

Bliss shook her head. "I don't know what's true anymore."

Jane hopped on the log, and then off again, standing tall. "Well, whether we jump, fall, or get pushed off the log, I'm just glad to have my feet on the ground, at least for right now. And to be with you all. I never dreamed I would like you all this much." She marched ahead and the three of them smiled at each other and followed her.

They came to a clearing and Willa said, "Hear that whirring sound? That's the song of the varied thrush."

The thrush went to its next octave.

"It's one of my favorites," she said. "Every so often we hear them in the marsh."

The thrush stopped, never the type to go on and on. Then a high pitch pierced the treetops.

"That's the golden-crowned kinglet. Just a hair bigger than a hummingbird. You'll never see them. And older people usually can't hear them. Marilyn still can, but not her husband. She prides herself on that," Willa said, missing her old leathery friend.

"I just hear one big forest of birds," said Jane. "Is there something wrong with me? I'm in the woods. I'm pausing. I'm smelling. I'm listening. I'm off the log. Taking an interlude. Aren't I?"

"Just keep listening," said Bliss. "You'll hear them one by one. These woods do something to you. I feel so alive here!" Her face was flushed and bright. "And no ex-husband and his new *family* to run into. I'll take grizzlies and mountain lions and widow-makers and poisonous mushrooms any day."

Willa hoped that the woods would help Bliss find her God again. Or at least her prayer. She'd always had such a nonnegotiable faith. Willa didn't share it, but when they were in the woods, it was like it was the same entity they loved and worshipped. Bliss without her God was unsettling. Like Jack without Bison Butte.

"Jack used to call mushroom picking *a walk in the woods*. If he found mushrooms, that was gravy." And just as she said it, she stopped. A little brown brain on a beige thumb.

Willa knelt. She pulled out her pocket knife and severed the mushroom from the ground, then sliced it in half. "See how it's hollow? That's how you can tell."

"I want to find one!" said Jane.

"My boys used to say they looked like trolls giving a thumbs-up from underground." Willa smiled.

"Divide and conquer," said Harriet. "This is like hunting jade on Big Sur. Patience, diligence, and dumb luck."

Not dumb luck, thought Willa. *Never dumb luck.* "Just remember to stay close to each other. Within seeing distance."

Bliss was quiet and methodical, so easily in her own world.

Willa had forgotten how the mystery of the woods worked its magic. She'd only had the stomach for the meadow since Jack's death. She flashed back to their family tradition of going morel hunting on Mother's Day and smiled, though sadly. Those days were gone. What would it take for her to accept that?

There was a pace to morel picking, different from chanterelles. You walked a few steps, looked, maybe found one, walked a few more steps. Maybe not. But here in this burned-out forest, they were everywhere.

"I can't believe how many there are," exclaimed Willa, her hands black with char. "And so big!"

Stepping over burned branches and felled trunks, she imagined the fire and the flight of creatures to safe ground, the cries of those who knew they had to leave, and the cries of those who knew they were going to die there. Morel by morel, she thought, *Life was like this for so long. One lovely thing after another, all there for the picking and swallowing whole.* If only she could swallow her new self whole.

Then Willa had a sudden longing to be in the dense forest, in a patch of sun and moss. Out of the ashes. She held up her bag—half full. "I have enough for the soup," she said. "Are you all having luck?"

They held up their bags.

"Good grief—we have enough for each of you to dry and bring back home! This is incredible!"

Jane let out a squeal. "Who needs Whole Foods?"

"*Seriously*, Jane?" Harriet rolled her eyes.

"Sorry," said Jane.

"No *sorry* this week," said Bliss.

Willa led them into the lush forest, groves of aspen just greening. "Do you know that an aspen grove is all one organism?" she asked. "All of these are sprouts of a central base called the Mother

Tree. She only lives a hundred years or so, so she's likely dead. But her spawn's roots wrap around her. I love that. And see the yellow flowers everywhere? That's arnica. Just pick the flowers, not the roots." She passed them new bags.

"What are those flowers?" said Jane.

"Oregon grape," said Willa. "You can boil their roots and make yellow dye."

Jane pointed. "Oh, I recognize those! Those are wild strawberries, aren't they? *Fraisier*. My absolute favorite thing."

"They are indeed," said Willa.

As if the puppeteer dropped the strings, the women folded to their knees, picking the yellow arnica blossoms. They were silent and systematic, like they'd been waiting for this exact excuse to finally pause and feel their way, their moment, their fingertips ... blossom to blossom to blossom.

Willa thought how nice it was to be lost in the forage rather than in the future or in fear, for a change.

"Now *this* is fun," sighed Jane, reaching far to get a single blossom, like a wide tennis shot.

"I'd love to live off the land," said Bliss, moving to another patch of arnica. "I think I'd be good at it."

"Well, today you're a hunter-gatherer," said Willa, her fingers yellow and sticky, filling her bag. This was what she should be doing to move through her grief. Picking things. Life in one little thing by one little thing. She remembered Jack saying to her once, "Willa, you have everything you need ... right here." They were building their outhouse, and she'd gotten frustrated with her limited skills. He was pointing to the tools. But she knew he was referring to much more.

Willa, you have everything you need, right here, in this moment, she told herself, but she still heard it in Jack's voice.

Now she was in a stand of grand fir, running her fingers through the flat, fanning needles, like a mother playing with her child's hair. The stand of trees was thick, and she ducked under spiderwebs, scanning the ground for her sons' favorite Calypso orchids—little magenta star heads with yellow, spotted white purses. Willa crawled farther under its shady skirts until she knelt at the base of one of the sap-spotted trunks. "Ladies, you must be good-luck charms! Come here! Morels, and *now* look." She pulled back a branch to reveal the magenta gems growing in the forest floor.

"They're like orchids!" exclaimed Jane, crawling in. "How could something this delicate grow from this woody ground?"

"They *are* orchids. Calypso orchids. Or fairy slippers. My boys used to truly believe that fairies danced in them by moonlight," said Willa. "They'd beg to walk through the forest this time of year at night, sure they'd catch a glimpse of it."

"Let me guess. You obliged," said Harriet.

Willa smiled. Of course she did.

Jane reached forward to pick one, and Willa grabbed her hand. "These, we don't pick."

"Oh, I'm so sorry!" said Jane, blushing. "I guess I'm getting *too* comfortable. Did I pick too many mushrooms? Should I have left some for the wildlife?"

"There's been a lot of rain," said Willa. "The forest is full of food."

Bliss and Harriet joined them under the fir trees and looked at each other like they'd found themselves on the other side of a pixie portal.

"Let's just sit here for a while," said Willa. All this arnica, and the mushrooms, and Calypso orchids … Was this Mother Nature beckoning her to stay in Montana? Was it Jack?

"I feel like we're in a fort," said Bliss. "And we're little girls, getting away with something."

"Oh, we're definitely getting away with something," said Jane. "I'm just not sure what."

"I've felt that way every single day for the last two decades," said Willa. "Like I'm a little girl getting away with something I'm going to get in trouble for, and I don't care. It's worth it. I'm so glad you all get it."

"I used to feel this way at church," said Bliss.

"If I even knew it was *possible* to feel this way, I wouldn't have torpedoed my career," said Harriet.

Jane was silent, looking around, and Willa wondered what she was holding back. It was more than restlessness or guilt or ingratitude. It was a primordial longing. Maybe Jane would truly let the forest give itself to her, as she had started to in the keeping room.

They sat there in silence. A musky breeze parted the boughs, and she welcomed it as Jack. She imagined him taking a swirl around their circle, lingering at the back of her neck, kissing it, and blowing away through the woods. Willa touched her neck.

A Swainson's thrush sang its upward allegro and she smiled. "That's another one of our favorites," she said. "Did you hear that, Jane?"

"Maybe," said Jane.

Willa willed the thrush to sing.

But the forest was quiet.

Then, that upward billowing song.

"There! Did you hear that?" said Willa.

"I *did*!" said Jane. "It was *beautiful*! I really heard it!"

Willa smiled, and lay on her back looking up at the trees— one eye in shadow, the other in piercing sunlight. The others did the same and she wondered where their minds were taking them. Especially Harriet and Jane. There was an undercurrent between those two that Willa hoped wouldn't go tsunami, especially given Jane's tectonic warning. Hopefully now that she was listening for birds, she'd start to unwind.

She figured Bliss was trying to pray.

But they were silent. Maybe they were thinking about their futures. Or maybe they were thinking about mushrooms. Or nothing at all. The point was: They were together. Not islands. And Willa knew for sure that she had made the right decision inviting them here, no matter how the rest of their days together unfolded.

Suddenly, Willa noticed the top of a larch tree swaying. Then a branch snapped and fell to the ground. Jane let out a cry and all three of them peered through the tree skirts.

"What was *that*?" whispered Harriet, in an honorable attempt at calm. "Do you think that was a bear? And, Jane, shrieking doesn't help!"

"I think it was a mountain lion," whispered Jane. "I saw something leap."

"I think I saw a human face," whispered Bliss. "Maybe it was a hunter?"

"Oh great. Bigfoot," whispered Harriet.

"Be very still," Willa said. "Remember ... whatever it is, it wants nothing to do with us." She looked in the direction of the fallen branch and didn't see anything. Her heart raced. "It might be an owl that flushed. Just be still for a few minutes, in case. Then whatever it is will be long gone." And she added, "Huddle together."

She pictured Jack with his trusty can of bear spray dangling from a carabiner on his belt loop, and quietly opened her pack. She always chose to carry hers in the top pocket, which he'd warned against too many times to count. "I want to meet the wilderness on its terms, not mine," was always her response. But now she realized she'd taken for granted having a partner always at-the-ready. Because Willa's hand came up empty.

She'd never not had bear spray in that pocket. And then she remembered. She'd heard noises one night in January and had taken it out of her pack and put it under her bed, just in case. And forgotten about it. She pictured it lying there behind her dust ruffle, like a lost toy.

"I'm not used to being on the food chain," whispered Jane. "Can we call someone?"

Harriet whispered, "This isn't a game show, Jane!"

The women were still. The woods were still. Willa waited. She wished she was on Sook. Sook could smell a bear a mile away and always warned them in another direction.

"Stay here. Don't move. Huddle." Willa crawled out from the stand of fir and took a few steps into the thicket where the branch had fallen. A beam of sunlight illuminated the forest floor. Still steaming, a few feet in front of her, was a giant pile of bear scat full of seeds. But also full of bones. Likely … grizzly.

She looked into the mud for tracks. Plain as day: a mama and her cub. Now, by the length of the claws, for certain—griz.

"Holy—" She didn't get out the *shit*. Not twenty yards ahead of her, higher on the trail, was a light brown cub. No mama. Which meant that the mama was watching them both and that the wind had switched, blowing their scents up the mountainside— surprise guests. It would be just like Jack to bring in a wind like that and call her out into this thicket to face her fears. *On your own terms, indeed, my Willa.*

"Bliss," she called quietly, almost in a child's song. "You all go very … very … slowly back to the burn. Very … slowly. And stay close together."

She heard Bliss call, "Okay," in the same song. "Shouldn't you come with us?"

Willa knew she should stay with the women. Safety in numbers. But there was a force holding her in place. "I'll be … right there."

She thought she could just make out the words *Please, God* coming from Bliss's direction.

Then Willa heard the sound of breaking branches up ahead of her, closer than the cub. And then a grunt. A grunt was bad.

She breathed deep and said low, "Good bear. We don't mean any harm. Good bear. Nice bear." She heard Jack's voice: "Only get down if she charges. And if she does, ball up to protect your gut. Protect the back of your head with your hands. She has her cub—she'll go for the kill." Then he'd smile in a maniacal way, and say, "And if she takes you out ... it'd be a good death."

A good death? Willa stared at the ground. All she could think of were Ned and Sam looking at her while she'd held their dying father, trying CPR, failing, losing him. Failing them.

"I'm a mother too," she whispered.

She took shallow breaths.

The cub rolled in the underbrush.

She didn't dare move. Her heart thundered in her chest.

Then the sow came out of the woods and stood in front of her cub.

Everything stopped.

And Willa looked into that bear's eyes the way she'd looked into her beloved's as he took his last breath. They were steady, dark as marbles, the eyes of a mother who would do anything for her child. Those eyes locked Willa in their sights and did not let go, and Willa surrendered herself totally to them.

It was the bear's choice now. And as much as she knew that she should look away, she couldn't.

This is it, was all she could think. *This is it. Everything will be different now.* And like the Piegan women, she slowly lifted her shirt, and bared her breasts. "I am a mother too," she said again.

The sow lowered her head and popped her jaw. Her fur raised and pileated. Then she started wagging her head and coughing.

Look away, Willa.

Jack.

But her eyes stayed locked on the sow's.

"I'm your sister," she said, low.

Then the bear came at her.

Willa dropped to the mud, put her hands behind her head, forehead to the ground, and tucked in her knees as tightly as she could.

"Please," said Willa. *"Please,"* her voice rattled. And then she added, "Make it end."

All sound stopped, except for the birdcalls. She could still hear the birds.

She waited.

Her ears pealed in a high-pitched din, and her thundering heart went mute. Now not even the birds.

She waited in that deafening silence.

And waited.

She held her breath, feeling that bear sizing her up as foe. Mother. Sister.

Willa pressed her forehead deeper into the mud. She all but bit into it, trying to slow her tattered breathing.

"Jack," she whispered.

And for one sure moment, she felt him all around her, pushing her into the earth. Covering her, protecting her.

"Don't let me die," she whispered. "Please."

Then, only gravity was pinning her to the ground. The forest had emptied. And she knew she was alone.

She looked to the side, her cheek in the mud now. Arnica and Oregon grape forever. The sound of the thrushes. Her heart thundering once more.

She waited, then unfurled herself and knelt in the mud, shaking. Had she dreamed the bears? They had felt just as real as Jack's presence.

She stood and was relieved to see the scat. She grabbed a stick, her hands unsteady, and poked at a bone, pushing it into a muddy puddle, and then leaned down and wrapped it in a mountain maple leaf, and put it in her pocket. Then she said, "No scat more beautiful than grizzly scat. The whole story of the forest in it." Jack's line. But in her voice now.

"You were here. Weren't you," she said.

"Willa," she heard Bliss call.

"I'm here. I'm coming," she called back.

He's gone. The mother bear took him from me. I can't feel him.

She stood there for a moment, getting ready for panic. But it didn't come. And then she said, "Thank you," because she could feel herself there. Her feet on the ground. Her hand clasped around the bone in her pocket.

Willa shook her head and went to the women.

When she got to them, they were at the edge of the burn, standing close to one another as if in prayer. "What was it? Did you see anything?" asked Harriet.

"No," said Willa, her heart still pounding. "I didn't see anything."

Then her hands started shaking and she clasped them together and held tight. "I think we have enough mushrooms and arnica. Let's get home and make dinner."

"You are the bravest person I have ever met," said Jane.

A raven cackled in a tree somewhere. And she remembered Nel telling her, "Raven: shapeshifter, signifying change."

Willa thought she might be sick and she breathed through it. "We'll go back this way. It's more open." Their scent was known now, and the sow and her cub would move far away from them.

The women were silent as they recessed along the thin deer paths on the edge of the forest that led to the old logging road.

When they got back to the car, in a muddy pothole that still held their tire tread marks, were the prints of a grizzly bear sow and her cub. And two giant piles of scat. Bones and all.

"Holy shit, it *was* a bear!" exclaimed Harriet. "Get thee into the red, steel SUV!"

Three of them jumped into the car and slammed the doors shut. But Willa stood there, looking at the scat. And she wondered if the bear wasn't quite done with her yet. She looked into the woods. And she wondered what this "it" was that she had begged of the sow. Make *what* end? Jack's soul spinning around this place all winter? Her pain? Was he really gone for good? Did she want him to be gone?

"Willa, are you crazy? Get in the car!" shouted Harriet.

Willa took one last look into the woods and nodded. Maybe "it" was winter. No … "it" was everything before ten minutes ago. The mother bear hadn't just taken Jack. She'd taken from Willa what she could no longer use but hadn't known to surrender.

She got into the driver's seat and looked at the others. She tried to be light, but her words were heavy and low. "Well, you've just had yourselves a Montana adventure!"

"You can't get *that* at the school board fundraiser!" said Jane from the passenger seat. "Did that scare the hell out of you, Willa? Or are you really that brave? You have mud on your forehead and cheek, by the way."

Willa looked into the rearview mirror at the mud on her face, leaving it there—Piegan.

Bliss said, "Do you really think it was a bear that we heard? Or was the scat separate?"

"Oh, it was a bear, all right. Wasn't it, Willa?" said Jane, almost proud.

Harriet said, "I'm not gonna lie. If I'd have seen a bear … I would have run. No offense. I know we're trying to be the proverbial *village* and all that. But I would have run. I'm not wired to sit still when danger is near."

Jane grabbed Willa's arm and peered at her with her Blue

Willow eyes. "I get it. The wilderness isn't *supposed* to be safe."

Willa tried to smile, but her face was numb. "It's not trying to be anything other than what it is. It's just wild. That's all."

"Huh," said Jane, crossing her arms and leaning against the car door.

"Maybe the whole reason we're here is to have the hell scared out of us," said Harriet.

Willa wanted to say, *If a noise and a pile of scat scared the hell out of you, you haven't roamed around in the woods enough.* But she could not shake the image of that sow's eyes. And she knew she needed to go into the woods a lot more before she left Montana.

Bliss's eyes danced in the rearview mirror. "What I really want to say is … I just prayed one good prayer," she said. "And for now, it was to the forest. The forest can hold it all for me, at least until Sunday. I can look it in the eye. And see it looking back at me."

Willa thought, *Maybe that's what just happened to me.*

"What I really want to say is that I'm scared as fuck of my So Now What," said Harriet. "I don't think I really knew that until fifteen minutes ago."

"What I really want to say is … for some reason, I'm feeling happier than I've felt in a long time," said Jane. "Even though, my God, it's almost ten o'clock in Connecticut! I can't believe that the sun is just now setting! I'm suddenly famished!"

"I can't believe you lost track of time," said Harriet. "Nicely done, Janey."

"What I really want to say," said Willa, starting the car, "is … I could use a beer and a burger at the Saloon."

Harriet hooted. "I could definitely use a good belly up to the bar!"

"I wouldn't mind some of Jack's beer," said Bliss.

"What about the mushroom soup?" asked Jane, like she'd just lost a balloon to the wind.

"We can make mushroom soup tomorrow night." Willa wiped the mud from her face with her sleeve. "If the band is playing tomorrow, then the Saloon will be mostly empty tonight. And I think I can handle the regulars. This time of day, they're pretty harmless."

Bliss said, "Sweetheart, nothing that could happen in that bar is half as scary as what could have just happened in the woods."

You have no idea, thought Willa.

They jiggled over the rutted washboards and bounced over the deep potholes, this time none of them seeming to care, as if they had inner shock absorbers now. On the main road, Willa took in the rusted farming implements, deer carcasses being picked at by bald eagles, bullet-pocked road signs, as if she was seeing it all for the first time. It helped wash the adrenaline out of her.

"*Please don't buy our town*," said Jane. "That's so sad. If they only knew what you're up against."

Willa slowed at the entrance to the Saloon. The parking lot was packed. "Shit," she said. "What's going on?" Whatever the reason, it was a deliberate celebration, and she hadn't been invited.

"I thought it said Grin and Bear It is playing *tomorrow*. I'm so sorry that I didn't read the sign more closely," said Bliss.

"No *sorry*," said Willa, slowing down even more. "Shit. Everyone in town is in there! That's not just for the band. That's a *goodbye* party. I don't have it in me."

"Oh, come on, Willa. We'll protect you from grizzly bears on bar stools," said Harriet. "I would never run from one of those!" She growled.

Willa parked and said, "Why don't you all go in. I'll stay out here. Maybe you can order me a take-out burger and bring me a beer."

"You sure?" said Bliss. "Harriet's right. You have us to support you. Might be a good thing."

Jane said, "Maybe you could open a conversation with someone who might see things your way."

"I can't expose anyone. It's not my style. Let them think I'm a thief. So be it. You go in. I'm happy to wait out here."

"Do what you need to do," said Bliss, putting her hand on Willa's shoulder.

"Thank you," said Willa. "Swiss and mushroom burger. Medium rare. Extra fries. I'm hungry. I'll pay you back."

Bliss nodded and Willa watched the women walk into the Saloon like locals. *Must have been the woods.* And then she thought of the sow griz popping her jaw, and the feeling of being so close to what could have been her end. *Make it end.* She was sure then, that the "it" in question referred to Jack's presence on this planet, not hers.

Uncontrollable tears jettisoned from her, because when they opened the Saloon door, she heard the familiar old-timey sound of Grin and Bear It picking away at one of her favorites: "Ripple." As if Jack was singing it directly to her. As if the bear hadn't taken him. "*If I knew the way ... I would take you home.*"

She sang along, missing his voice. Trying to make up for it with her own.

She couldn't stand it. They were having a *goodbye* party without her, and that meant they wouldn't be coming up to her house after the auction. Willa, Montana, did things once and for all.

She heard the fiddle solo then, and she opened the car door to listen. She didn't think she heard a mandolin, but she had to see for herself. As far as she knew, the band hadn't gotten together since Jack's memorial. "*Dah duh dah dah dah,*" she sang and went around the side of the parking lot. Then she bolted behind the Saloon, near the dumpster, and peered in through the back window.

They were all in there. The band—Syd on fiddle, Earl on guitar, and Wink on stand-up bass. No one on mandolin. Marilyn and her husband, Vic, were sitting at a table in front. Vic was holding his trumpet in case he wanted to play a riff or two, his oxygen tank close by. Nel, Tally, everyone. She looked for the women. Harriet was sitting on a bar stool. Jane was right behind her, arms crossed. Bliss was next to her, swaying.

Then the band stopped playing, the back door swung open, and she smelled cigarette smoke. She pulled back behind the dumpster, wishing it was dark and not dusk. It was Earl.

"Earl," she said, coming out of hiding. "Hey."

"Oh, hey, Willa," he said, looking at the bruise-colored clouds. "Saw your friends in there."

"Yeah." She got a *Hey, Willa*. She wanted to hug him.

Earl took a drag and blew it into the sky. "Some of us still smoke in the back. Did you see that table up in front? Jack'd never okay that."

"That's for sure."

"You can come in, Willa. It's not like you're not allowed. There's been a sign on the Merc board all week about tonight. But you don't come down much anymore."

"Yeah. Well. You know." She paused. "Miss you, Earl. Miss you all up at the house jamming."

"Yeah. Well, Syd's not too happy, being a renter and all. New owners'll probably raise their rent and run 'em all out of town. So ..."

"Yeah. I get it. You don't have to explain. It's a mess." What words could she find to get to the truth—that wouldn't somehow incriminate anyone, including Jack? None came.

They both looked at the sky.

"Can I bum a smoke?" she said.

"Sure." He pulled out a bag of Drum tobacco and rolled one for her. Then he passed her the cigarette and held up his lighter so that his face shined in the flame. It was such a good face, with heartbreak spelled forward and backward all over it. She took a mental photograph of it, then leaned against the dumpster and took a long drag.

"Earl, did Jack tell you anything? About the renters?"

He shook his head and blew out smoke. "He didn't like to talk about that whole situation. He didn't like to separate himself out from everyone. You know?"

"Yeah."

"How are the boys holding up?" he said.

"College is a good distraction. And California, I suppose."

"I suppose," said Earl. He wasn't good at being aloof. He was probably the kindest man, next to Jack, she'd ever met.

Willa took another drag, feeling the nicotine buzz she'd long ago abandoned. "Saw a sow griz and her cub today up Teakettle Creek. By the burn." She pronounced it *crick*, as she had for years, to fit in.

"Yeah. They're out," said Earl. "Got into Petersons' shed. Jed opened the door and practically shat his pants. And Jed's not scared of nuthin'!" He had the laugh of a young woman, for his hulking body, and Willa couldn't help but laugh along with him. "Musta scared your ladies pretty good."

"Yeah. Well. I didn't tell them. I didn't want to get them too riled up." Willa took a drag and watched the smoke until it blended with Earl's. "And like a dumb shit, I didn't have my bear spray. Jack never went into the woods without it. What was I thinking?"

Earl picked tobacco out of his teeth and shook his head. "Aw—that stuff's overrated. I think it's more like dinner seasoning." He smiled. "Too spendy, anyway."

She knew what he was getting at. Even Earl. She wished she could say it. *Earl. I'm broke. Jack spent all our money. And in case you thought that we were rich East Coast people ... for the record ... we're not! Maybe you can get to the bottom of it. Ask Syd.* But she stopped herself. Better to leave them with at least their dignity and a good story about how they were lied to and cheated and ridden hard and put away wet.

"Well, you didn't get *eht*, anyway," said Earl, taking a drag off his cigarette.

"Yeah. But it was really strange, Earl. I was just standing there for a while, looking at the cub. Then the mama came out and I knew I wasn't supposed to look her in the eyes, but I couldn't help it."

They smoked while a logging truck jake-braked down the highway.

The hammering sound of it broke something in Willa then, and she let the words pour out. "It was like her eyes grabbed me and wouldn't let go. And they asked me if I wanted to live or not. You know? Without Jack. And I wasn't sure. 'Cuz it's been a pretty bleak winter, Earl. Not gonna lie."

Willa took another long drag.

"And then she bluff-charged me, Earl. She freaking *bluff-charged* me! But I broke free from those eyes and dropped to the ground. And she left."

"Did you shit your pants?" said Earl, perfectly serious.

"Can't believe I didn't." Willa took a step closer to Earl and looked into his eyes. "You know what I think? I think your mando player was taking one last lap."

He grunted and flicked his butt into the dumpster. "He'd do something like that, wouldn't he?"

"Yeah. He would." She took a long drag. "I think she took him with her. I think he's gone for good."

The instruments were tuning up, and Earl turned for the door. "I better go back. You should come in, Willa."

"Earl?"

"Yeah?"

"He come to you in a dream or anything?"

"Nah. But Syd said he was riding Pilgrim up Raven Canyon, and the horse started acting funny by Jack's old hunting tree stand. But that's probably the weed talking, if it's Syd."

"Yeah." Willa ground her feet into the gravel.

"Hey," said Earl, stopping at the door. "Strange year for snow geese, huh?"

"I missed 'em this year. Couldn't take it."

"Did you hear that they're back? They came through like always, but we had that cold snap and the lake was still frozen, so they circled back. And they're here now. Strangest thing."

"Climate change," said Willa, trying to look away. But she couldn't help imploring that face of his. "Remember that year you came with us?"

Earl smiled and nodded. "That damn swirl we got caught in? Never seen anything like it. Been meaning to go on over and see 'em before they go up to Canada." He eyed her and she knew exactly what he was getting at.

"Yeah. Well. My heart can't handle it, Earl. It dogged me all April. I'm over it." She looked into the clouds and the mountains going black. "We were going to go with them this time. Did you know that, Earl? Follow the migration up to Canada for the summer. Shut down the Inn. Take a break. Then come back down with them in the fall."

"Yeah. He told us."

She could feel him working into his next words. She let him. She needed to hear them the way she'd needed to hold Jack's ashes to realize he was finally dead. All of him in four pounds of white ash.

"Maybe it's a good way to say *goodbye*, Willa." He paused. "I'd go with you, if you wanted."

"No. No, Earl. You'd have the whole town hating you for consorting with the enemy. But thanks."

"Well. I'm just sayin'. I think it would do you good. They

don't come back a second time. I've never seen that." Earl opened
the door so that the sounds of the Saloon coated the night sky.
"I saw some flying over the other day. Not far from your place."
Then his moustache spread wide across his face. "Maybe your
mando player really was taking another lap."

"Or maybe the world is just full of things that don't add up."
She didn't mean to sound so bitter, especially not to Earl. "That's
really nice of you, Earl. To offer. Really." She tried to smile at him.

"Bye, Willa. Say *hey* to the boys. Tell 'em we miss 'em."

Earl pulled the door closed behind him, and Willa stood
there, not knowing where to go. Wishing she'd said, *Come on by
the Homestead after the auction. Bring the band.* But it wasn't fair to
pressure him. This was their *goodbye* party. And she didn't have the
courage to go in, even with his invitation.

So she walked forward, toward the road sign that said WILLA,
MT, POPULATION 35. "Sometimes you just have to let yourself be
misunderstood," she said, not at all convinced.

She put her palms flat on the cold metal and pressed her weight
into it. She wanted to be in the Saloon. She didn't realize how much
she'd missed being an insider. Not knowing that the geese had flown
over and were back? That would have been news impossible to miss
if she'd had the guts to be a member of her own town these last
months. And that was *before* she announced the auction. How was
she any different from Harriet, really? A holed-up hermit.

Allowed? Who did the allowing around here now?

She slapped her hands on the sign. Maybe just for a beer and a
burger. She'd show them she could. She'd hide herself in the women.

Willa wiped off whatever mud was left on her face, went back
to the Saloon, and looked in the window. Huck Carlson was buying shots for the whole bar. Must be Social Security check day.
And Harriet was holding one up over her head, seemingly in a
group toast. Jane's arms were still crossed. Bliss had a red cup in

her hand and was headed toward the door. The band was tuning up, and Marilyn was helping Vic up on the stage with his trumpet and his oxygen tank. Nel was behind the bar, doing a Shake-a-Day with Tally, who was clearly losing but laughing anyway, blowing on her dice.

She felt the crumpled thank-you note in her parka. Maybe she'd write a new one and sneak into the Merc and post it after all. "I love you people. And I always will," she said, memorizing the scene through the dirty broken windowpane. "And I know you love me too. And that you're just afraid. Like Bliss said. I forgive you, even if you can't forgive me." Then she snuck around to the car and met Bliss there, holding the beer. "Thanks. How is it in there?" she asked, taking a long sip of Jack's beloved beer, rolling it over her tongue before she swallowed. "Damn, I've missed that."

"It's civil. You should come in. I think Harriet might be making you your friends back. She bought shots for the whole bar and now they're on a roll."

"Do I still have mud on my face?" she said.

Bliss whisked Willa's forehead with her soft fingers, cupping her cheek. "Come on." And she led Willa in a way that she'd only known with horses.

Inside, the band was loud into a lick that she hadn't heard before, Wink bawling into his harmonica.

Harriet was sitting backward at the bar and lit up when she saw Willa, patting the stool next to her.

Jane moved to the other side of the stool, as if to hold her place, and Bliss closed the circle as Willa sat.

"I see you have your Pissant Porter, my dear," said Harriet. "How about a shot too?"

"Yeah. Jameson," said Willa. She looked at the women, not over their shoulders or heads, but into their eyes as they flanked her, and mouthed, *Thank you.*

Harriet motioned for the bartender and Willa shrank into her stool. She couldn't look at Nel. Nel was the one she was letting down the most, and giving her Sook wasn't enough.

Harriet passed her the whiskey and Willa shot it back.

"You're doing great," said Harriet, trading the shot glass for Willa's beer. "Liquid courage." She smiled.

Jane darted her head over her shoulder toward the band.

What? mouthed Willa.

Jane's whole face furrowed. "Call me crazy, but I think I just heard that man bragging about making mountain lion broth. He says it's good for the gut!" She looked back at Willa. "He looks like he wants to chop that woman into little pieces and eat her with fava beans and a nice Chianti."

"Is he wearing a vintage Griz letterman jacket and sort of looks like Warren Beatty?" said Willa.

"Maybe Warren Beatty's bum brother! I'm pretty sure he just said that he has turtle broth too. And the woman speaking with him looks like she thinks it's a pickup line." Jane leaned in and mouthed, *And she* likes *it!*

"Oh, that's Adele and Poe. They do that. It's their little spring mating dance. He tries to shock her and she tries to prove that she's unshockable. He gives it his best effort all winter long, but she'll only give in this time of year—before she starts leading her pack string. And he'll get lucky again in the fall when she comes back from the high country."

Willa peered past the women to the man they were gawking at. "Poe. Jack gave him that name. Short for *poet laureate*. He used to be a genius. Before his fall." She pulled back into the circle the women had made around her and thought of the circle of ponderosas which had held them earlier in the woods.

"I should give him one of Jack's coats. That coat he wears must be thirty years old. And it couldn't be warm. I don't think he'll ever get over his glory days at the U of M. You wouldn't know it, but he's originally from New Jersey. Played ball here and never left." Willa shook her head. "So many ways to hide around here," she said. And suddenly she was standing.

Bliss and Jane stepped to the side, and now Willa had a full view of the Saloon … and it of her.

Each person took a turn looking her up and down.

The band was playing a light instrumental jam and she caught a glimpse of Earl looking at her too.

"We can leave," whispered Jane in her ear.

But Willa went to Poe.

"Willa," he said, shifting his shoulders from Adele to her. He smiled, his top lip doing its best job to hide his missing teeth. "Been a while."

"Heard you gave your girl away to Nel," said Adele, but Willa wasn't looking at her. She could get mean after a few rounds, and she was clearly well into the pitcher next to her. "Beer?"

"Got one. Over there. But thanks." She still looked only at Poe. Of all of them, he was the one she could handle in this moment. She looked at him, knowing exactly what he wanted to say to her. He'd said the same thing to her for twenty years. So she said it for him.

"Write me a poem, Poe?"

The music was softer, like the band was listening for his answer too. All eyes were on Willa and Poe.

He opened his mouth, showing his jagged, yellow, twisted teeth. And closed his lips over them. Then he looked away in a hard snub that she didn't believe one bit until he spoke: "I don't have one in me. Not for you, Willa."

Even the poetry had run out of Poe.

She looked at Adele, horsewoman to horsewoman, and Adele looked away, topping off her pint.

The bell from the grill rang twice and she heard a loud "order up!" from Nel.

Willa went back to the bar to look her last hope in the eye: Nel. But the assholes from earlier in the parking lot were on bar stools, and they blocked her from the grill.

"Excuse me," she said.

They didn't budge, and now Marilyn was at the bar. "You ordered all of these *to go*, right?" she asked, giving Willa a grimace.

Willa felt Harriet rub up against her like a hungry cat. "No," Harriet said. "We ordered them *for here*."

Marilyn stared just over Harriet's red hair. "One was *to go*."

"They're all *for here* now," Harriet said.

Marilyn looked at Willa and called, "Nel. They're all *for here* now. They changed their minds."

Willa held Marilyn's stare the way she had with the sow. "No," she called to Nel. "Mine is still *to go*."

Nel came out from behind the grill with a box. "Here you go, Willa," she said, doing her best to avoid looking at her. *Even Nel.*

"Come by on Sook sometime," said Willa. "While I'm still around. I haven't shown you her best trick."

For an instant, Nel's eyes, and even her freckles, brightened. Then faded. And she went back to the grill.

"Why don't we take *all* of them *to go*?" Bliss called after her, closing in on Willa's other side, Jane close behind her.

"Ketchup, mustard, mayo, relish?" asked Marilyn, staring at her, now deadpan.

"No thanks," said Willa, holding her gaze. "Tell Nel to stop on by. I have something for her."

Marilyn leaned in. "Willa. Don't you think that girl has had enough people leave her?"

Willa pulled back like she'd been gun-kicked in the chest. No poem from Poe. And now she was as good as a meth addict to her dear Nel. She couldn't have gotten to the door faster.

In the car, Jane stewed. "I've never seen anyone treat a widow like that. How dare they!"

"They're acting like *babies*," said Harriet. "Classic abandonment issues."

"It's so strange. They've always been the definition of salt of the earth," said Bliss.

"Clearly they envy you," said Jane. "You're on to bigger things. They're just jealous that you're shaking off this one-horse town and moving on! And *they're* stuck here, going nowhere ... *slowly*. And they *know* it. And they're *punishing* you for it."

As Willa pulled onto the highway, the yellow eyes of deer on both sides, she felt an acute kinship with this town and its people. They were nothing if not misunderstood. Who knew how to be abandoned, after so much love?

She found great irony in saying to Jane, "Don't judge a book by its cover."

Jane was silent.

Willa added, a little heat under her words, "Do you know what the crime rate of Willa, Montana, is? Zero. The worst that happens here ... is people talk behind your back."

"And leave," said Harriet.

"And leave," said Willa.

They were silent again. "Did they talk shit about me before I walked into the Saloon? Actually, I don't want to know."

They were silent.

"Great. They talked shit about me." Willa drove in silence to Homestead Lane, stopped the car, and cut the engine.

Like her words had poured out to Earl, they poured out now. "We were going to follow the snow goose migration. Last month. North for the summer. Hundreds of thousands of them stop over on a lake not far from here. And then head north to Canada to breed. It was Jack's gift to me for getting the boys homeschooled and off to college with free rides, thank God. I tried to go see the birds at the lake. But I couldn't make myself do it. And now I find out that they didn't come in April. The lake was frozen. They're here now."

"You have to see them," said Bliss.

"You *have* to," said Jane. "We'll hold your hand."

"Let's go tomorrow," said Harriet.

Willa looked at each of their outlines and said, "What I really want to say ... Willa, Montana ..." But she stopped. There was nothing to say that would heal any of this.

Then she turned to the endless dark sky. "What I really want to say, to you women, is ... I didn't know how to ask for you. And when I did, you came. Thank you. I've needed you."

"Thank *you*, Willa," they each said.

She started the car and drove slowly, methodically, up to the house.

"That was a *lot* for this cowgirl," said Jane, yawning on the front porch. "Mushrooms and bears and bar fights, oh my."

"That was not your mama's mundane," said Harriet.

"Even for Willa, Montana, that was a doozy," said Bliss. She sat down on the front porch and passed out the burgers.

They sat there, eating in silence until Willa felt a sudden pull to Jack's Thoreau collection. Words were what she needed now, more than money. "Can I read something to you? As a sort of 'Taps' to our day?"

"Please," said Bliss.

Willa got the Thoreau book from the keeping room shelf, trying not to notice the empty spaces for their Emerson twins. She went back to the front stoop and opened the book to a well-worn page. "This quote sums up everything that Jack put into Willa, Montana. Whenever I wondered if I could live this life or second-guessed all our work running it all, he'd read this to me. It's perfect for the four of us and what we're doing together this week."

She readied herself for these sacred words, in her own voice now:

"How sweet it would be to treat men and things, for an hour, for just what they are! [...] When we are weary with travel, we lay down our load and rest by the wayside. So, when we are weary with the burden of life, why do we not lay down this load of falsehoods which we have volunteered to sustain, and be refreshed as never mortal was? Let the beautiful laws prevail. Let us not weary ourselves by resisting them. When we would rest our bodies we cease to support them; we recline on the lap of the earth. So, when we would rest our spirits, we must recline on the Great Spirit. Let things alone; let them weigh what they will; let them soar or fall."

"For just what they are," said Jane.
"Lay down this load of falsehoods," said Harriet.
"Recline on the Great Spirit," said Bliss.
"Let them soar or fall," said Willa, and thought, *The snow geese.*

They all gave each other loose, long, tired hugs. Even Harriet, who seemed to have forgotten her aversion to hugging.

As they moved inside the house, Bliss smiled with a certain brand of romance that Willa knew was Montana-spun, and she stopped to put her nose in a vase of gardenias. "If grace had a scent, it would be this."

"Let's all get a good night's sleep," said Willa. "Wait until you see the snow geese tomorrow. The swirl and roar of it will erase most things. At least for a good solid hour or so. I hope they're still there. I need to soar."

But she wondered if this time, she had fallen too far.

Day Three

Willa woke not knowing where she was. She'd had a dream. She closed her eyes to remember. It had been a good dream and she'd felt safe in it.

Something about a house. Something about sun and a red door.

She remembered. It was a dream about a new home. She couldn't remember one detail other than the red door, but it had felt like she belonged. *What would that look like? Belonging somewhere besides Willa, Montana.*

She took a deep breath and let her mind wander. *Open land close by … for walks.* She couldn't imagine driving somewhere to take a walk.

And there would have to be a little town. Something simple, but not as simple as Willa—at least a café, and a grocery store, and a bookstore. And a hardware store. You could judge a town by its hardware store.

This didn't feel bad, thinking about a place from the safety of her bed, eyes closed. She tried a little harder.

And a farmer's market would be nice.

And a library.

And maybe a music series that comes through on a regular basis so I could get the culture I've missed all these years in Willa. A classical music series would be nice. She smiled. "Bach," she said. "And Mozart. And maybe some choral music. Maybe some requiem." She'd spent all winter blasting requiem from the rafters, letting the death knell ring.

Jack never could understand her love of choral music. What else wasn't he a fan of that she could indulge in now? She forced herself to flirt with the idea. He thought beauty was always second to function. She had privately disagreed for years, even though she thought everything they created was somehow beautiful. So maybe a companion garden with flowers and vegetables living symbiotic, not in rows, and with minimal weeding. Heavy on roses. Hollyhocks and delphinium next to garlic and carrots. *And it would be nice to have chickens again. Just a few, for eggs. A sunny kitchen with a good woodstove. Or a fireplace in the living room. A real fireplace, not one of those horrible gas ones with the fake logs and the switch to flick.* A real fireplace was probably illegal in California, which was where she figured she'd go. To be close to her boys. She kicked the covers off. She couldn't imagine a home without a hearth in it.

"I can't leave this house!" she cried, her eyes wide open in the beginnings of dawn.

A stern inner voice interrupted her. *Willa. Fear isn't going to get you anywhere. Your thinking is all wrong. Think the freer thought instead.* And it wasn't Jack's voice. It was another voice that she recognized. It was her mother's voice. She had always been a staunch believer in freedom, especially for women. Which was another reason her rejection of Willa's life hurt her so much— what was freer than living in the wild?

The freer thought.

Well, what if the town sells for a lot of money? Maybe I'll be okay after all. Maybe I can *give the boys a nest egg. And maybe I can even travel. Be the girl who took trains all over Europe. Like Jane said about horses—find* that *girl again.*

But what if Willa doesn't sell for much? And I end up in some depressing apartment somewhere with some job that I hate? Nobody has any land in the city. I won't have a garden. I'll have a few tired herbs in a window somewhere. And a mountain of bills to pay. And the boys won't have any respect for me anymore. I'll never be this Montana Mama again. Shit—should I go back to school at age forty-six? I'm going to be getting letters from AARP in a few years! What the fuck have I done with my life?

Willa. Think the freer thought.

She took a deep breath, forcing herself to count to five.

I am a survivor. I lived through this winter. I can live through anything. Maybe I can have one of those reality TV shows Marilyn's always talking about. City-girl-turned-country-girl-turned-city-girl. God, am I fucked!

She leapt out of bed. *Make it stop!*

Think the freer thought.

She looked at Jack's closet. She had to get rid of it all and she hadn't started. The boys had put what they wanted into boxes in their closets, to be shipped to them. She'd parted with a few things, mostly given to the band. Jack's mandolin and albums to Earl. His tack to Syd. To Wink, his sheet music. And she couldn't even think about his Cave in the basement.

The freer thought?

She dropped onto her window seat and tried, really tried, to open to it, staring out over her dark yard and fallow garden.

What if the future could be ... good?

And she actually smiled. Just for a second before it faded. But it was a real smile.

Robins sang and dawn gained, and her yard showed itself in dark green now. She wished she could freeze dawn's fleet—an old wish. Maybe she should stop wanting to freeze time.

She looked at Bison Butte. It was glowing, the sun pouring

like honey over its crown and down its gullies. It had been her own private view for months now. By summer Solstice, this town would be sold, there would be someone else in this room, maybe watching dawn. And she would be somewhere else, either rich, poor, or somewhere in between.

She had a sudden aching need for a dawn walk. But the snow geese would be enough of Montana for one day. Especially after the griz. And the Saloon. She should savor what was left of her time in this room.

As she watched her yard swell in long shadows, a robin landed on her roof, just below her window. It looked in her direction, opened its yellow beak, and strutted toward her, out for blood. She knew what it was doing and she slapped the windowpane.

It hurled itself at the window anyway, fanning out its wings. Then it swooped around and came at the window again. *Thwack!*

Willa jumped back. "Stop!" she yelled. This happened every few springs—a robin overdosed on instinct, protecting its territory from ... *itself.* The symbolism of this was not lost on her, and she opened the window to remove the reflection. The robin landed on the roof line, cocked its head at her. His hard work was done. His instincts, suicidal. He stared, his beak still open and angry.

Willa couldn't stand it. "You're fighting yourself!" she cried.

The ineffable smell of gardenias crept under her door, as if to say, *Go now.* And she knew it was the house calling her out, down the stairs to her mud boots and parka, and out to the meadow at dawn, as it had for years. Perhaps she'd make it up the butte. She hadn't been there yet this spring and she knew she needed to stare it down.

Halfway down the drive, she heard Harriet's hurried voice calling after her. "Hey! Willa! Wait up!"

Willa didn't want to share dawn. Not this one. She stopped and watched the morning glow light up Harriet's hair like a torch coming at her as fast as the robin. And perhaps just as angry.

Harriet huffed. "I saw you. In my window. You walk like a horse in the snow. Long-legged and aware of everything around you. Do you do this every morning?" She stopped at Willa's side, catching her breath. "I used to be a morning person. It's nice being up before you owe the day anything."

Willa wasn't sure what to say. She was always silent on her dawn walks. "Morning, Harriet." She turned toward Bison Butte, which seemed to have moved a hundred yards closer to the house than yesterday, coming for her since she would not go to it.

"I've never seen a snow goose. What do they look like?"

Willa wanted nothing more than to be silent. "Like white ducks. With black wing tips." She walked a little faster.

Harriet was wearing her red cape and Willa couldn't help thinking that she looked like Little Red Riding Hood, only in flip-flops with a red pedicure.

Looking at the flip-flops, Willa said, "I was going to go up the butte. But we can stay on the road if you'd like."

"I don't want to hold you back," said Harriet.

"It's okay. That place is haunted anyway. I thought it might be good for me to go up there. Before the snow geese. It was Jack's place."

Harriet skipped a few steps forward to catch up to her. "Can I ask what the ghosts sound like? Do they talk to you? Mine all sound like drugged porn stars."

Willa smiled. "There isn't much that shocks you, or scares you, Harriet. Is there?"

Harriet lifted her face to the sky and flung out her arms, wide-handed. "Just me! I'm the scariest thing I know!"

"I met a bird like that a few minutes ago."

Harriet was quiet, like a girl at a campfire waiting for the ghost story to begin.

Willa didn't want to tell it, which was why she knew she

needed to. "Bison Butte—that hill over there past the meadow, with the sharp cliff at the end ... that was used as a buffalo jump."

"What's a buffalo jump?"

She could hear Jack's voice explaining it to their boys. She tried it in her own words. "They're all around the West. Some of them are older than the pyramids of Egypt or Stonehenge. The long and the short of it is that the natives would round up a herd of bison and drive it up a butte ... and off the cliff. But in truth, it was an elaborate ruse."

"Oh, I love an elaborate ruse! Tell me more!" said Harriet, out of breath.

Willa imagined what she hated to imagine. "They'd build piles of rocks with aspen saplings to create borders, like lanes, up to the top of the ridge. And there would be people hiding and waiting there holding blankets and hides ready to wave at the herd to keep it in the funnel. Then, from up the hill, one of the young men would make a bison calf distress call. The herd would start moving in that direction, to surround it and protect it from whatever was causing it harm. Three or four men dressed in wolf or coyote skins would move toward the herd from below, and the herd would travel away from them, going to the calf sounds, up and up as the young man called to them."

"So they were following their instincts," said Harriet. "But *tricked* by their instincts," as if she'd been in Willa's head earlier that morning.

"Yes. Tricked by their instincts. I hate that most of all," said Willa. "But the natives had to live. They did this for thousands of years."

Harriet started walking backward so they could see eye to eye. "And I bet they'd run like hell toward that calf. To save it."

"Yes. The bison runners would gallop behind them, stampeding them right over the ridge. And then the rest of the tribe would be waiting below to butcher and dry the meat and turn it into pemmican. They used every part of the animal." Willa pointed. "There are layers and layers of bones and arrowheads and tools all resting at the bottom of the butte. My sons would spend all day there looking for arrowheads."

She looked at Harriet to see if there was any shock in her. There wasn't. More like a tepid flirt with consternation.

Harriet moved back to Willa's side and synced their steps.

Willa went on. "But the worst part is that as the bison charged away from danger toward what they believed was safety, at the last moment the lead bison would realize they were about to fall to their death … and they'd turn *back* into their herd … only to be stampeded over the cliff."

She looked at Harriet and continued. "Jack said he could hear their cries. But when I go up there, I can only hear their thunder. That's what my ghosts sound like."

Harriet's lips parted, dry and honest without her lipstick.

"And I have to go up there. Soon. To spread his ashes."

"What are you afraid of?"

"That part of me will go over the edge with him."

"I'll go up there with you, Willa. I'm not afraid of ghosts." She offered a small smile and sang, "*These flip-flops were made for walkin'* …"

Willa shook her head. "No. I have to go alone. The snow geese will be … well. Will be … a step."

They came to the meadow and Willa longed to walk in the aspens, just greening, but she looked at Harriet's feet. The rugosa roses would claw at them, no matter what she said, so she stayed on the road.

"I think I'm trying to fall out of love with this place, you know?" Willa began. "Were you like that when you sold your house and moved to Big Sur?"

"I was running away," said Harriet. "And home became my hiding place. It's like the bison. That's what I felt like in my career. Running and running, thinking I was getting somewhere. And then when I realized I was dying, and ran back, it was like my past—my years of ambition addiction—just stampeded me over anyway. Maybe we should stop trying so hard to be what we think we should be, and just accept who we are."

Willa felt a flash of kinship with Harriet. She looked at her red toes. "Can you handle some tall grass and maybe some thistle?"

"Of course," said Harriet.

Willa walked into the meadow, past the old spring, until she found the corner logs she'd stood on every May but this one. She stood on them now.

"This was Emilio and Maria's homestead. What's left of it." She walked along the rough-hewn wood to the next corner.

"And see that lilac tree? Maria planted it, so the story goes. Lilacs aren't native to Montana. So she must have brought in a cutting. Maybe she brought it all the way from Italy on the boat. We'll never know. But I prune it every spring, after the blooms die. And I think of Maria. And I wonder if she was to Emilio as I was to Jack." Willa paused and looked at the old wood. "Jack had a lot more to him than what he let people see."

Harriet walked along the foundation on the other side, balancing herself with wide open arms. "Keep going, Willa. Something tells me that you've never told this part of the story."

She pushed herself forward. Because it was true. No one on earth knew this. Not even Bliss. "Do you really want to know, Harriet? I mean, do you *really* want to know? Because look at me—I'm literally *on the log* here, and I've walked this wood too long. I need to step off and go."

"Yes. Of course. That's *exactly* why I really want to know."

Willa cocked her head like the robin, territorial. "Jack's father was hard on him. And he had a side of him that never got over it. A *very* dark side."

This felt like pure sacrilege, but she pushed herself to keep talking. "He wanted to be loved so *badly*. But he didn't really know how to let people in. It felt like my work to show him how."

She balanced along the wood, her arms out like Harriet. "Every one of those community parties? I made those happen. The band? He would have kept playing alone on the front porch, telling himself he was perfectly fine. That band became one of the happiest things in his life! Same with the garden. And the Inn and all its wayward travelers. And the Merc. And even the Saloon. My ideas. My prodding. My curating. His joy. Our joy."

Willa stopped, sick with something she didn't recognize deep in her throat and went over to the lilacs to smell their tart blooms. "And like I said … I loved every minute of it. And he learned to. Just like how I learned to love his dream and make it my own. And that's why it worked so well. For so long."

Willa snapped off a bloom and put it in her braid. "But there was one missing piece." She turned to the whole meadow, facing Harriet. "As much as he worked and worked to gain his father's acceptance by saving the family legacy, it was never enough. Even after his father was gone, he just couldn't stop trying to please everybody. Everyone around here already *adored* him. I told him so over and over. But he could never quite believe that he was lovable. It's the only reason I can possibly think of why he did what he did. He knew he had my love—that I truly accepted all of him. And that I didn't need saving. It was everyone else he was trying to save."

"In order to save himself," said Harriet.

Willa looked at Harriet, standing on Emilio and Maria's foundation, and nodded slowly. "And he couldn't. And I think it literally broke his heart."

"And that's why you're trying to fall out of love with this place. You're trying to end the cycle. For your boys."

"I want them to be free of it. Like you said about your ambition, Harriet. It's not healthy to be addicted to a place either. It'll stampede you right off the cliff if you're not careful."

"But you love it with all your heart."

"Yeah."

"So ... you're Maria."

Willa smelled the lilac and nodded. "It was her dream too."

"Maybe she was the first to dream it. Not Emilio."

"Either way, she had to leave it."

They were silent.

Then Harriet came over, put her nose in the lilacs, and said, "I'm sick of being strong."

"Me too," said Willa. "Do you really think you want to go back to your career, Harriet?"

Harriet just stared into the trees.

Four white-tailed deer ambled out of the woods then and fed on the new grass.

"I just want to know who I am, Willa. I've lived my life by *I'm not this, I'm not this, I'm not this.* And then, for a long time, I thought I'd found who I am. But I'm not that either. Who am I? I honestly don't know."

Willa pulled a lilac bloom off the tree and put it behind Harriet's ear. And Harriet closed her eyes and smiled like a child being bathed, letting out a long loud sigh.

The deer's tails went up. They looked at the women. And then went back to eating.

"Fear us!" Willa shouted at the deer, waving the lilac branches. "Whoever's coming next won't protect you like we have. Go!" She shooed the deer and they sprang off across the meadow, and it hurt her heart. Red-faced, Willa took one more sniff of the lilacs and went back to the road. "We only took one buck a year. And used every part of it we could."

"Seems to me that living here would teach you absolutely everything a person needs to really know," said Harriet. "If you let it."

They both fell silent.

Willa picked up her step. "We have a bit of a drive ahead of us. We should go up and make some sandwiches to take. There's nothing between here and the lake but the most beautiful river I know—the Smith."

They walked back to the house in silence and Willa could tell that Harriet was holding back her usual bravado, trying to let silence guide her for a change.

Willa didn't concern herself with it. She had thousands of forward-roaring birds to say *hello* and *goodbye* to, all at once.

After an hour and a half of driving in the old Ford, Jane and Bliss stuffed in the back seats because they all said that the rental wasn't "Montana enough," they stood on the shores of Freezeout Lake in that exact forward roar of birds.

"Well I never!" shouted Bliss.

"They call this a *swirl*," shouted Willa.

"It's like they're bringing down the clouds with them!" screamed Jane. "And spinning them all around us! Like cotton candy!"

"Clouds with black edges," yelled Harriet. "But no rain."

And for the next half hour, Willa didn't think of Jack or the boys or the auction or money or packing up her house or where she was going next. It was the mind-stopping, migrational, perfect pandemonium she remembered and had grown to count on for the So Now What that each spring demanded, whether you were ready for it or not. This year, it had waited for her to come to it.

Some of the geese flew around the lake in undulating S's, practicing their flight patterns. Hordes of them landed and splashed and skimmed. They quieted for a beat or two, then lifted and swirled again around them.

Willa had brought her binoculars as usual, but for some reason could not lift them to her eyes.

Jane was turning in slow circles with her mouth open and her head to the sky, like she was in a snow globe.

"Here," she hollered to Jane. "Take these. Try to follow one bird."

Jane pressed the binoculars to her eyes with such intensity that Willa laughed out loud, muted by the roaring geese. "One bird," Jane shouted above the din. "One bird!" She walked along the lakeshore in one direction, then in another.

Willa watched Jane the way she'd watched her boys play this game. The three of them had spent many homeschool mornings this way, each of them following one bird. She'd forgotten it until now. Could you follow a bird in a city and not hit up against a building or someone else's property?

"Damn it. I lost it!" shouted Jane, casting the binoculars skyward to choose another. Then she walked the other direction, pointing them straight to the sky, and then down to the lake. "Damn. Lost that one too." Pretty soon Jane was around the bend, out of sight.

Willa turned to say something to Bliss and Harriet about Jane's adventure, but they were out of sight too. She was glad then to be alone with the birds.

Willa sat in the sand with her legs crossed and her head to the sky, dizzied by the frenetic orchestra of the geese. She looked out at a peninsula, and pictured herself standing there, just last year, with Jack and the boys. At the time, she'd imagined it might be the last migration they'd all experience together for the next four years. She didn't know it would be the last in their history.

She pictured them there. It was dawn, and they'd camped out

the night before. She'd woken them just before sunrise to go out on the peninsula and watch as the reverberation of hundreds of thousands of geese had risen at once, like the lake rising to the sky, to feed on the spent grain in the farmers' fields. And they'd waited, walking along the relatively quiet water, watching the silvery tundra swans and diving northern pintails take temporary control of the waters, until the snow geese swirled back, just like Jane said, like clouds spinning around them and dropping to water.

There was no one on the peninsula now.

Willa walked to it and stood just shy of where her family had stood, looking at the emptiness of it, which was now her truth.

Then she saw something at her feet, and she stepped backward. A dead goose. White neck twisted back in a sort of ruthless half knot. A broken wing. And one red spot on its chest.

She looked closer. It wasn't blood. It was its actual heart. Someone, or something, had made a small incision and pulled out the heart, and left it. She thought of the story the Lakota told about Custer, how in his vainglorious and murderous and reckless death, the women twisted knives in his ears … *so he could hear in the next life*. Who had held such a knife to this heart? A wildlife biologist? A hunter? An animal? Another grief-ridden widow?

She went in closer. No footprints. No prints of any kind. She sat down next to the bird and watched the world around it. Even though the creature world endured its loss so expeditiously, she'd also heard that birds mourned, and even drowned themselves after the death of a mother or mate. Would she be that kind of bird?

She looked around for some sign of grief in this goose's world, but none of the others seemed to notice, or know, or care.

She pulled one feather from the broken wing, white with a smudge of black at its tip, and twisted it in her fingers. He'd stood here with her. He'd kissed her on the lips while the boys explored the lake. It had been a deep, lingering kiss, and she'd leaned back into his arms, and he'd lowered her, steadily and strongly, onto the ground, where he'd kissed her with his full weight, like he was engraving himself into her. Right where she now sat.

So she lay back and stretched out her arms, closing her eyes and imagining his weight and his kiss. But it did not feel free. And so she opened her eyes. But there was no freer thought there either. So she stared straight at the sky tide of snow geese, ebbing and flowing, and thought:

Let them soar or fall …

Until they soared her to sleep.

She woke like she was late for something she couldn't remember and sat up to see the women lying in a line to her right. All of them with their arms outstretched. She looked to her left, at the goose. At its ruby of a heart and stained red feathers.

"How did it die?" asked Jane.

"Sometimes they fall from the sky," said Bliss. "Or they get caught in a hailstorm. Could be anything."

"That's the reddest thing I've ever seen," said Harriet. "Is that its heart?"

"Yes," said Willa.

None of them wondered out loud and she was glad that they were quiet. They'd had enough words.

But then Jane said, "Is Montana always so … *Montana?*"

Willa took a long time to respond. "It's like after birth. And after death. Only all the time. If you're paying attention."

Bliss said, plain and simple, "Well, its holy shows today."

Willa crouched by the goose and spread its wing feathers. "Pick a feather. Here. The smaller white feathers, with just a bit of black at the tip. To remind you."

On the way back, just south of Great Falls and the Missouri River, Willa stopped the truck along the Smith River.

"They're threatening to build a mine over here. It would bring in a lot of jobs. Good chance it'll poison the river with acid. This is the only part of the road that shows the river. But further on it just gets more and more beautiful—walls of limestone and so pristine. Fifty-nine miles of it. No towns or public access. We used to take the raft and go camping with the boys on it when we were lucky enough to get a permit. Takes four days. Unrivaled fishing. Montana needs to fight for it."

She felt sick, then, that she was trading her loyalty for money. "No matter what your politics or religion or opinions are, the one thing we all have in common around here is our love for the land. And our commitment to our wandering rights."

"Wandering rights. I love that," said Jane, leaning into the front seat.

"The stakes are so high here," said Bliss. "That's why I love it. It reminds me how truly small I am every single time. And how wild is the base of the natural world."

"It's so rugged and masculine here," said Harriet. "And yet, there's a softness to it."

Willa tried to find the right words. "The natives had it right. They were in harmony with it all." The thunder of stampeding bison flashed in her mind, reminding her of another loss. "Last year, right after Jack died, the geese went the wrong way on their way back down south. And they landed in an old open copper mining pit in Butte. It's acid water. Thousands died."

"How horrible," said Jane.

They were all silent.

"They say there's copper in these hills. In my nightmares I can already see the site pillaged and contaminated. Why can't we leave it all alone? It's naive of me to think so highly of humans. But still, why can't we learn? Montana owes us nothing and yet it gives so much. I wish we could reverse what feels like the inevitable."

"I'm sure Palmer would have something to say about it. He's

not much for nature," said Jane. "He throws a *fit* on Nantucket when they close the beaches for the piping plovers. He put a bumper sticker on our island truck that said PIPING PLOVER TASTES JUST LIKE CHICKEN. I made him take it off." She continued, "But not because I really care about the birds. I'll be honest. I just didn't want people to think we're somehow … *backward.* The truth is, I've never paid as much attention to birds as I have this week. I haven't really paid attention to birds at all."

Bliss laughed. "If you think about it, the four of us aren't so different."

"Yeah, Bliss. When I watched those birds take off," said Harriet, leaning into the front seat too, "I thought *migration is what we're all doing.* We'll find our next stop." She put her hand on Willa's shoulder. "And you will too, Willa."

Willa laughed. "I'll likely be heading west in this old truck. This thing'll run longer than I do."

They fell silent again, cruising down the two-lane highway in wide-open big sky country, chasing the daylight home.

The morels were spread out on the kitchen table and Willa was wiping them off with a pastry brush. She'd thawed one of the last containers of her chicken stock as well as the chanterelles she had frozen in butter last fall. Jane was cutting leeks and Harriet was putting them into a water bath. Bliss was stoking the fire and humming what sounded like a hymn.

Willa kept shaking her head, wondering what to do with all this help. Even the boys didn't help her with the weekly soup and bread. Not like this. This felt like something akin to childbirth, with the midwives and doula holding her, moving her, speaking in low, calming words, the women from town busy in her kitchen.

Tally. Marilyn. Adele. Nel's mother, before the meth got hold of her. Toddlers playing at their feet. She'd missed the community of women so dearly.

Willa thought about the soup instead.

It needed something. Sage. Fresh garden sage—not dried from her pantry.

She was ashamed to face the garden. It was a world of rot—decaying squash and beheaded sunflower stalks and sad starts. But the sage might have wintered over. It sometimes surprised her, though it was unlikely. It would make the soup sing. Willa wanted to believe that it had lived against the odds.

She put on her mud boots and went around to the side of the house, prepared to meet the garden eye to eye and break the news: *You're on your own now.*

But some things were stubborn if not outlandishly hearty, and she smiled when she saw the silver-green leaves on the old wintered-over wood.

"Thank you," she said, rubbing the leaves, smelling the sage. She took three sprigs and went back to the house, smiling at the window to see her kitchen filled with women, chatting, enjoying her home, creating something together. And it struck her then that the house would be just fine without her. It would accept new people, new smells, new comings and goings. Willa swallowed hard. It felt like part betrayal, part permission to leave.

Just then, a buzzing being flitted past her and she looked around for what she knew was the first hummingbird. It hovered in the air, close enough for her to make out its variety. Her favorite. The Calliope. It felt important to honor it aloud. "The smallest hummingbird. The one who migrates alone."

The bird buzzed away, and Willa's eyes darted with it, tracking its jigs and jags until it stopped in a holding pattern in front of her open door.

"No," warned Willa, thinking of the dead bird in her freezer. But it flew into the house anyway.

Willa snuck up the steps and gently joined it at the window where its wings buffeted the glass. "Stay still. I'll let you out." This had happened to her once before, many years ago, and she remembered her fear of this tiny buzzing trapped thing.

Now she made a soft cage with her hands, cornering the bird in the window frame.

It didn't fight.

She felt a tickle on the palms of her hands, like she was holding a quick summer squall. She closed her palms and brought the bird to the front porch, where she held it for a moment. Held its flight and its future … and let it go.

"Thank you," she said. *To hold something this mighty, this beautiful and brave, that we were never meant to … in the palms of our hands.* Only, with the sage on her fingers, it was in Willa's voice now.

Then she went back to the kitchen, and directly to the freezer. The small cardboard jewelry box was where it had been for years, on the top shelf, behind the ice trays. And she pulled it out and lifted the lid with hope and fear in equal measures. But there it was—still green-backed, the magenta bow tie stain at its throat.

"What's that?" said Jane.

Willa put the lid back on the box. "Oh, just something I was wondering about."

"What? A frozen bracelet?" said Jane, smiling. "I'd recognize a jewelry box anywhere. Inquiring minds …"

"Well," said Willa, stalling, not wanting to see shock in someone's eyes when they looked upon her little treasure. But a frozen bird in a Montana house wasn't such a far reach. And they'd already seen the dead snow goose today.

"You don't have to," said Jane. "If it's personal. I don't mean to pry. My mother keeps her will in her freezer, for Lord's sake."

Willa looked at Jane, standing there in her pink twin set and pressed jeans, blond ponytail, and wide Montana-kissed blue eyes.

"It's just something I found one summer and didn't want to let go of. So I froze it."

She looked at Jane again, and then at Bliss and Harriet who drew closer to her. "All right, fine. It's a hummingbird. The smallest one. The Calliope." And she pulled off the lid and held the box in her palm for them to see, hoping that they wouldn't be repulsed. "It migrates alone."

Jane cooed, not gasped. Harriet and Bliss joined her.

"Gorgeous little wonder," said Bliss, gazing into the cotton nest and its sparkling jewel. "We want to freeze time, don't we?" She looked up at all of them and none of them, as if she was speaking to herself. "But everything must move."

"Yes," said Willa, putting the lid on the box and placing it back in the freezer.

And the women went back to their soup preparation.

Over a mound of chopped morels, Jane said, "I love that you make your own chicken broth, Willa. I wouldn't know where to begin. I'm too impatient anyway."

"Uh … I'm pretty sure you begin with a chicken," said Harriet, straining the leeks from the muddy water bath.

Willa rolled the sage leaves together and cut them in thin slices, making a chiffonade that would brown nicely in the butter. "Chicken stock isn't hard. You just freeze all the stuff you don't use—the old carrots, the parsley stalks and outer leek greens and tough celery stalks—and then when you roast a chicken, you throw the carcass into some water with the frozen vegetables you've saved, and a few cloves of garlic, salt, peppercorns. A bay leaf. Fresh thyme if you have it. And a dash of apple cider vinegar. The trick is to bring it to a boil, and then turn it down to a low simmer. You don't have to have patience. Just a peasant's mentality."

She caught herself wanting to add, *Like Jack taught me*, but she remembered her plea to the bear.

Jane laughed. "Operative words: *when you roast a chicken*. We live on Whole Foods prepared meals. Don't judge. You saw the extent of my cooking yesterday morning. I can warm up anything and make it look pretty on a plate."

Harriet laughed. "Pretty on a Plate. That should be your porn star name."

Jane swatted Harriet on her butt with the wooden spoon.

Willa smiled, putting butter in the stockpot—one of her favorite things, browning butter. "In your words, Jane, I think you're *awfully* hard on yourself. You can only do so much," she said, watching the butter as it foamed. "And there's no right way to do life, anyway."

"Amen," said Bliss. "And I'm sure that with four kids, you are nothing short of a full-time magician, Jane."

Jane paused, knife in midair. "Yeah, well I have this new habit and the kids hate it. I've started being fifteen minutes late for everything."

"That screams passive-aggressive," said Harriet. "Just so you know."

"I think it's my way of finding time for myself. Nobody can touch me in that fifteen minutes. I'll stay just a few more minutes in the shower or run for just one more block. I don't know why I do it, really." She washed her hands with vigor. "Maybe it's my way of showing everyone that I'm not perfect."

"Maybe it's your way of building in an interlude," said Bliss, smiling. "Laying down your load, and *resting by the wayside*, Thoreau-style."

"Maybe. I don't know, I really don't. It started when my friend died of cancer. Like I said, it just floored me. She was so young. And she did *everything* right. And I sat there at that funeral, looking at her kids and her husband, bawling my eyes out for them ... and thinking that if her death was worth anything, it was worth showing all of these hard-wired, driven, *perfect* people that ... it can all just go away in an instant. *Poof.* And what did it matter that you went to all the right schools and belonged to all the right clubs and had the perfect home and were in perfect shape?" Her hands implored them all.

"And this is going to sound so *horrible*, but I imagined it being my *own* funeral. And I just felt this question burning in me: What's the point?" She turned to Willa. "*You* know this better than anyone here. What's it all *for*? You might as well just not try at *all*. You might as well be *late* for things, and let yourself *go*, and eat a lot of *chocolate* and ... oh, I sound like an *idiot*."

"You mean you might as well let yourself be *happy*?" said Harriet.

Willa nodded. "I was lying in bed this morning, and my mind was doing somersaults dreading my next chapter. And this thought occurred to me: *Think the freer thought.* I tried it. It felt good. Sort of. It felt like a relief anyway."

She looked at Jane. "When your mind goes to that place, is there a way to ask yourself what the freer thought would be?" She added the sage to the browned butter, giving it a stir with her wooden spatula.

"Hmmm ..." said Jane, grabbing her phone and taking photos of the chopped mushrooms and the women, one by one and without overture. "Well, maybe Harriet's right. Maybe these little fifteen-minute life grabs are my way of finding some sort of happiness in all of this *push push push* your way to perfect. I'm just so *sick* of it. Do any of you know what I mean? I mean, what am I pushing *against*? Death? My own *death*?"

Bliss said, "I go to a lot of funerals, since I'm on the altar guild. *Was* on the altar guild. I sometimes stand in the back, especially when it's someone I didn't know very well, and I do what you did, Jane. I imagine my own funeral. And I picture Hugh in the back row. Feeling so guilty. Like he did this to me by leaving me. That's so self-indulgent. Fantasizing my own death as payback to Hugh. Ugh." Bliss grabbed a sponge and started scrubbing the kitchen counter. Her face had never looked so sad to Willa.

"So what's the freer thought, Bliss?" Willa said, motioning to Jane to drop in the leeks.

"I honestly have no idea," said Bliss.

"How about that Hugh's a puny piece of shit and wouldn't have the guts to go to your funeral in the first place," said Harriet.

Bliss laughed. "Oh no. Believe me. He'd go. And put on a big act about how much grief he's in—right there, with this woman and her fake tears, and all her kids around them with practiced sad faces. They can't resist an opportunity to look like they're good people. When everyone knows they're both bad eggs." She looked out the window. "He didn't used to be a bad egg. Did he, Willa?"

"He had his moments," said Willa.

"He was a *stealth* bad egg," said Harriet. "I saw it in his eyes from the start."

Willa pointed toward a head of garlic. "We need a few cloves of garlic too."

"On it," said Harriet, giving two cloves of garlic a good *whack* with the side of a knife.

Willa continued, "Bliss, what if the freer thought is that you've been spared being married to a bad egg? I mean why would you want to be married to someone who is so good at causing you pain?"

Bliss looked at Jane. "Jane. *You* get it, right? I mean, doesn't your husband cause you pain? Marriage is filled with pain. I mean"—now she looked at Willa—"not everyone can have what you and Jack had."

Jane put her cell phone in her pocket and didn't quite look

back up. "If anything, *I'm* the one who causes *Palmer* pain. He *adores* me. The *idea* of me, anyway. He'd *never* leave me." She forced a smile at Bliss. "I'm with Harriet. Sounds like you have a fresh new start ahead of you! Just like Willa. I'm *jealous*, frankly. Or as my kids say, I'm *jelly*."

Bliss didn't look convinced.

Harriet launched in, "Oh, the suffering that comes from the mind. I like your *freer thought*, Willa. You could market that and make some bank. I'm not kidding. And unlike me ... you're probably uncorruptible."

"If you can come up with an idea for how I can make a decent living being who I already know how to be, I'll give you fifteen percent." Willa smiled and winked.

"I don't need fifteen percent. But you better believe that you can make a living off of who you already are, Willa. I tell women all the time, *Don't wait until the rug gets ripped out from under you to figure out what your passions are.* You can absolutely monetize your passions. Absolutely!"

"Yeah, well, I'm glad that my passions are in a row then. Even if my ducks aren't," said Willa, motioning for Harriet to add the garlic. "But I don't suppose you can make a living off foraging. Or making soup. Or riding horses in the woods. Or giving advice."

Jane pointed at her with her knife. "You could become a life coach, Willa! Everybody's doing it where I live."

"A life *coach*? What's a *life* coach?" Willa said, stirring the sage and leeks.

"It's like being a therapist. Only you don't need to get a degree," said Harriet as she ran her finger down the knife, releasing the garlic into the pot. "And you don't really dredge up the past." She paused. "And notice, Jane, that I'm not saying anything *cynical* about it."

"Noted," said Jane.

"I'm in no shape to be anybody's therapist," said Willa,

laughing. "But I could show 'em how to use a chainsaw. Or build an outhouse. Or drive a backhoe. Or make freaking apple cider vinegar." She laughed harder.

"I think you've got something there, actually," said Jane. "You could teach women how to be self-sufficient. How to be independent and badass like you."

"I don't feel very badass. I actually—" She looked at Bliss, who nodded at her. "Well, the truth is … I actually really hurt myself getting ready for winter. I took a bad fall off my hayloft in the barn." She could still feel the ache in her side. "And if I'd fallen differently, and couldn't have moved, I would have lain there for days. Who knows when someone would have found me. I wouldn't call that very *independent*."

"Oh, that's terrible!" said Jane. "I'm so sorry. You poor *thing*."

"It was such a stupid mistake. I got distracted. I know better than to get distracted on a hayloft." She put the lid on the soup and cocked it with the wooden spoon.

"I know what you mean, though, Willa. I've thought that before too," said Harriet. "No one witnesses my life unless I go into town. I had an exterminator for a while. I actually looked forward to him coming. Even though it seemed reasonably probable that there was a chopped-up grandmother in his truck."

Willa sighed. "Well, I guess I should admit that after I hurt myself, Nel is the only one I'd let near me. The young girl in the Saloon grill from last night. I gave my horse to her. I think I wanted to save her somehow. She's had a hard life. But I also wanted her to save me. That's part of why it's all so messed up. I just had to see who I was without Jack and the boys. And it turned out … I wasn't much. Not without Nel. And I couldn't save either of us."

"Why do we think that we have to go it alone in order to be strong? And why do we think we need to save anyone but ourselves?" said Bliss. "Why do we think we have to be so independent? Or that needing someone makes you codependent? Harriet, you use that word in your books and speeches like it's a swear word. I've always thought that life is better with others to depend on. That's what I miss about church, since it gave me the cold shoulder and I gave it back. We need community. Like I said, we are fluent in that language. But we don't speak it enough."

Bliss put away the pot she'd been drying and sat at the kitchen table. "And that's because, if you ask me … and you didn't … sometimes our regular community is too hard. And we hide from it like all of us have been doing in our own way. I think that every so often, when things get *really* rough, we need *this*. Friends of friends. In a new circle of trust."

Jane sat down next to her. "I couldn't agree more. Like we said yesterday, we sometimes need people who *haven't* logged hours with us in our day-to-day with all that *history* and all those scars and *expectations*. People who don't take our choices personally. Who aren't in our regular circles. Do you realize what a *gift* this is, ladies?"

Harriet gave Bliss a hard look. "I'm beginning to. And PS, never listen to half the shit that comes out of my mouth. Especially on the stage."

Willa smiled. "I feel like I *fit* with you women. I didn't at first, to be honest. But I do now. We've shared so much, just in a few days. I've missed that and I didn't even know it. I've missed … you." She brought a plate of grapes to the table. "I wonder if I'll fit in wherever I go. California seems so *shiny*, if that's where I end up. I'm not very shiny anymore. I never really was to begin with."

"What's the freer thought, Willa?" said Bliss, popping a grape into her mouth.

Willa put her hand to her heart and took a deep breath. "Well, that I have to focus on the next step. And that's to prepare for departure. And I have to believe that you can belong anywhere. As long as you belong to yourself."

"I think that it helps to have friends who don't judge you," said Bliss. "And you do."

And Willa smiled freely.

All four of them sighed over their empty soup bowls.

Harriet kissed Willa on the cheek. "That was delicious, my dear. Too bad we don't have any *digestivo*. I could murder a grappa right now."

"I'm in the mood for tea," said Bliss. "I'd love some of what we had yesterday. It tasted exotic."

"It's Mark Wendell's Hu-Kwa, isn't it? Yankee standard," said Jane.

"It ran through Jack's mother's veins," said Willa, taking out the black tin and passing it to Bliss. "I'd love some tea too."

Bliss opened the tin and took a deep sniff. "I need to feel more exotic. I'm the one who is *always* on time. I'd love to have some excuse for coming into a meeting late." She took down Willa's pink transferware teapot. "I've always loved this," she said.

"It's yours," said Willa. "I'd be happy to know it was alive and well and loved in a house in Wisconsin. By you and Bea."

Bliss held it to her heart. "Thank you, my friend. I would love to have this teapot. I will take good care of it. In my boring life where teapots never break."

Harriet gave Bliss a wild-abandon of a hug. "You're not boring, Bliss. You're *steadfast*."

Bliss blushed and scooped a few teaspoons of the loose tea into the teapot and poured hot water over it. Then she set the teapot on a tray along with cups and saucers, honey and milk, and teaspoons. Something about watching a woman make a proper tea service. Willa smiled at her friend, so methodical and hard-working. And they sat down in the keeping room, waiting for the tea to steep.

"Bliss, you have to live your life. You're only forty-three," said Harriet. "Have you considered getting a caregiver for your mother?"

"It's so expensive. I don't know if it's worth it. I'm happy at home with her. At least for now." Bliss sighed. "Who am I kidding? I don't think I'll ever really know what happiness is again, if I'm being frank."

"Aw, happiness is a Disney myth," said Harriet. "I'd be okay with just some real common garden-variety *contentment*."

"I wonder how old you have to be to finally give yourself to yourself," mused Willa.

"What do you mean?" asked Jane.

"I mean," said Willa, "just when do we become enough of ourselves so that we can accept ourselves for exactly who we are? And stop caring what our parents think—or anyone, for that matter."

"You mean stop kicking the shit out of ourselves?" asked Harriet.

"Yeah. When do we give ourselves that big break? And finally meet ourselves right where we are? Outside of the Supposed to Be. Without the shame over what didn't happen. Like I was saying before: When do we finally belong to ourselves?"

Jane let out a loud "*Ugh*. Never," pouring the tea into the cups. "I don't *deserve* a break. I signed up for everything I am. I'm ashamed that I don't do *more*."

Bliss sipped her tea. "My shame is everywhere I look, even in my mother's eyes. I should be taking her out more often. I think I use her as an excuse to stay home so I don't have to run into *them*. With her children! In places that used to be *our* places. It's such a small town. I pull onto Main Street and scan the cars to make sure they're nowhere near. Same with the grocery store, the post office, the bank. I'd be safe at church, if I *went* to church." Her eyes darkened.

Willa nodded. "So, Bliss. Humor me. What's the freer thought?"

Bliss blew out a long breath. "Well, I hate to even utter these words, but at some point, you're right, Harriet. I'm going to need help. And it's true. Every so often, I fantasize about hiring a nurse of some sort. Like my neighbor. Only dementia isn't in her field. Thank God for her this week!"

"Oh, honey," said Harriet. "You're too good. You should be looking into assisted living centers. You have a life to live! You can't just rot away!"

"Do you know how much those places *cost*? Plus, I can't do that to her. After everything she's given to me? My mother would be *miserable* in one of those places. And she has such lucid moments. Last week, I took her to the gym because they say it helps the brain to use eye-hand coordination. And she was dribbling a ball. I didn't know she could dribble a ball. Then all of a sudden, she lifted her leg and passed it under and kept right on dribbling— didn't miss a beat. And then she did the same thing with the other leg! She's going to outlive me!" Bliss paused, stirring honey into her tea. "And it gives me someone to take care of. You know? That's all I really love to do, since we're being honest."

"But who takes care of *you*, Bliss?" said Jane.

Bliss gave Jane a hollow stare.

Willa said, "I completely understand what you mean, Bliss. If we're taking care of someone, we feel connection. But don't we also want to be cared *for*? And I don't mean financially. I mean having someone in our lives who really thinks of us. Who's really *for* us."

"You had that in Jack, that is *for* sure," said Bliss.

Willa nodded. "I was very lucky."

"I haven't really had that," Bliss said. "I'd *like* it. Maybe that's why I want to be a mother. Is that messed up? I dream of my child loving me and thinking of me and yes, even caring for me the way I'm caring for Mother and how she cared for me. I want that legacy of love that I see people having. Especially with mothers and daughters."

They were all silent.

Finally Bliss said, "Let's not talk about all this anymore. Let's talk about Willa's honey. You can smell the apple blossoms in it. It's sublime. Let's talk about what's next for Willa. Your So Now What is the most pressing out of the four of us."

There was something up with Bliss. Willa looked into her eyes, which were now sunken and dark.

Jane said, "Please don't take this the wrong way, Willa, but like I said, I *envy* your freedom. Doesn't it feel at all … *spacious?* I mean, oh the *possibilities!*"

"That's the way to look at it, isn't it? Freedom," said Willa, still eyeing Bliss.

"You're going to be okay, Willa," said Bliss. "Wherever you go. You're that sort of person. I can see you living three totally different chapters of your life. Or more. You've lived two so far. I'm afraid I'm a one-chapter sort of gal."

"Come to Big Sur and live with me for a while," said Harriet. "You could be closer to your boys. I have an extra room."

Willa said, "Thanks, Harriet. Wherever I go, I'm pretty sure I have to do it alone. It's going to take a lot to shake this shame that I'm giving up on the dream."

"Why do we think we have to do everything hard *alone?*" said Bliss. "Is it because we think that no one else can relate to our shame? Or tolerate it? Or will love us despite it?" She stared at Willa, and then past her.

Harriet said, "Willa and Bliss, it's not like you did anything *wrong*. And as my grandmother used to say, *today's news lines the birdcage tomorrow.* Unless you actually *want* it to ruin your life. Which is its own sort of dealio." She downed her tea.

Bliss leaned forward, and said, sharp, "Harriet—my big-shot career might not be in the crapper. But in my little world, which you know *all* about, my problems are just as huge. I couldn't keep my husband. I couldn't make a baby, and so far, no one will give me theirs. I'm a religious flunkie. I'm a failure." She held up the teapot. "Another cup of tea, anyone?"

"You okay, Bliss?" said Willa.

Bliss just stared at her like she imagined Bea must stare at Bliss.

"Shame," sighed Jane. "My therapist says I'm riddled with it. I'm still trying to wrap my head around that one."

"Shame," sighed Harriet. "The driving force behind why we suffer."

Bliss just sighed.

"Shame that I can't do this life here alone," sighed Willa. Maybe this admission would help Bliss with whatever was going on, but Bliss just stared out the window.

Harriet put her fist in the air. "Shame should be kicked in the ass. Forgive me for going motivational speaker right now, but what if we went around the room and just got out everything we're ashamed of, once and for all? Kaput. Done. *Finito*. You game?"

Phrases careened around the keeping room table from everyone except Bliss.

"Shame that I'm rich and didn't work for a penny of it."

"Shame that I'm afraid to be alone."

"Shame that I'm a hermit."

"Shame that I'm broke."

"Shame that my kids are ungrateful."

"Shame that I'm afraid to let go of my house."

"Shame that I let ambition ruin my life."

"Shame that *I'm* ungrateful."

"Shame that I will go down in history as the McMotivational speaker Antichrist."

Jane and Willa caught their breath, looked at Harriet, and started howling.

Harriet banged the arms of her rocking chair with widespread palms. "That's the spirit, ladies!"

"Damn," said Jane. "That was *so* much better than therapy!"

They all looked at Bliss. Who blinked, blew into her bangs, and, staring out the window, said, "Shame that I'm not a mother. Shame that I couldn't hold on to my husband. Shame that I can't pray to my God."

"Bliss," said Harriet. "We're not done with you yet. What's your freer thought? Imagine a new story. What would it look like?"

Jane smiled. "Come on, Bliss. You're safe. Just like you said. Friends of friends. Who are now ... *friends*."

Bliss blew out a mile-long sigh and looked at her hands, opening them and closing them.

"Dream a little, Bliss," Willa urged. "You might as well."

Bliss stuffed her hands in the pockets of her denim jumper. "Well, if I *have* to ... I mean ... it might look like this." She closed her eyes and leaned back in her rocker. "I'm walking down Main Street."

She got lost for a minute, her eyes tracking back and forth under their lids.

The women were quiet. No one moved.

Bliss brought her teacup to her chest, her eyes still shut tight. "And I'm ... one of those women I see all the time. You know ... the ones with a small dog on a leash. A small, well-behaved, dapper little dog trotting along next to me."

She took a sip of her tea. "And my dog's leash is on my wrist, because my hands ... are ... you know ..." She smiled like it hurt, eyes still closed. "Pushing a baby stroller. And it would be a carriage ... you know ... the old kind, like a pram where you could look down and see the baby. Because ... you know ... the baby would be brand new. And it would be peacefully sleeping."

This time her smile looked like crying. But she kept with it, straining her voice louder. "And I'd want to make sure it was covered in blankets. Because it gets cold in Wisconsin. Even in June."

Bliss opened her eyes and looked up and pulled her head back like she'd been walking in the dark and hit a wall. Then a wide, soft, *real* smile spread across her face. "It would be a pink blanket. And she'd open her eyes and look up at me from underneath it, and she'd do that little stretch that babies do, and make a little gurgling sound, and go back to sleep."

She looked at them all, tears rolling down her cheeks. "And I'd know she was okay."

They held still. And Bliss looked down at nothing.

Finally, Harriet said, "Sounds like you need to get a small dog, and quick!" wiping the tears from her cheeks.

Bliss left her tears to fall. "What if she doesn't want me the way I am?"

Harriet stood up. "Well, there's only one way to find out. What time is it in Wisconsin?"

"Oh, it's way too late," said Bliss.

"It's only seven o'clock," said Willa. "That's eight in Wisconsin."

Bliss looked at them all.

Jane nodded at her. "We can hold your hand. Like we did with Willa. You don't have to do this alone. Just like the invitation says."

Now Bliss wiped her tears. She closed her eyes and Willa knew that she was trying to pray.

Willa said, "Bliss, you shouldn't feel pressured into this. On your own time."

Bliss stood up. "No. They're right. I'm like cement waiting to set. It's eating me alive and I need to do something about it." She looked at Jane. "Jane, I've known you just a few days. But I think that precisely *because* of that, you're the one for the job. Will you sit in the great room while I make the call from my room? I think

I need privacy. But not too much privacy. And no offense, ladies, but all three of you is *a lot*."

"It would be my honor," said Jane, her face pinking.

"Wait," said Bliss, sitting back down. "Be honest with me. Please. Do I even *want* to be a mother, Willa?" She looked at Jane. "*Do* I, Jane?"

Jane nodded and smiled. "It's a wonderful thing. Even when it's not wonderful."

Bliss looked at Willa. "*Do* I, Willa?"

"For me ... it's been a wonderful thing. Every bit of it. But I can't answer that for you, sweetheart. It's your choice."

"But *alone*?" said Bliss.

Harriet grabbed her friend by the waist. "Listen to me, Bliss. You have wanted to be a mother since you were a little girl! And you're finally here!"

"But when I tell her about Hugh and me, and if she still wants me to be the mother, what if something happens? Like with the other ones? What if she has the baby and wants to keep it?"

"Didn't you say that her parents wouldn't let her?" said Willa.

"Yeah. But what if her parents change their minds and won't let her give the baby to me? What if I'm not enough all on my own?"

"Hey, at the risk of sounding like every other motivational speaker out there—you are enough. Okay? Stop with the *enough*. God forbid a woman suffered from a case of *too much*. It's simple: No one is *enough* and no one is *too much*. You're exactly who you are, and let that be a good thing, and shit—of *course* they'll choose you!" Harriet almost shook her.

Bliss broke free, her face anguished. "But, Harriet. You know where we come from. And these people specifically want this baby to go to a good solid *Christian home*." Her eyes filled with tears. "Even if they're okay with me raising the child on my own, I'm not sure that I can give that baby a good solid Christian home.

I'm not even going to church right now. And I can't lie to her." Her tears fell into the creases of her pained face. "So now it's motherhood versus *faith*?"

Harriet cupped her shoulders. "Bliss. You're the living embodiment of Christianity if I know anything about it. Since when did it become a morality game? Let's hear your definition of a good solid Christian home. Bring it. Right now. Go on."

Bliss closed her eyes. "I don't know anymore. I don't know the difference between faith and religion. I'm so confused."

"Bliss," said Willa. "What does it mean to *you*? Not to anyone else. What does a Christian home mean to *you*?"

"To me?" Bliss said in a child's whimper.

"Yes. To you," said Willa. "Come on. You can do this."

Bliss's face let it all go. "It just means that it would be a loving home. No matter what. A loving and forgiving home. Where you could ask questions about God, and any question would be okay. And you could *doubt* God. And you could be *angry* with God. But you would *always* find love for the people in that house. No matter what. And they would find love for you. And you could *count* on it. Like the house I grew up in. Like the Jesus I've believed in. Whether we go to church or not."

"That's your *answer*," said Harriet. "You can throw in the religion later. But that's what it boils down to for you. And that's all that matters. Because this child will be *your* child. Not the birth mother's anymore. Or her parents'."

Bliss looked at Harriet with courage. "That's what it boils down to. For me. That kind of love."

Harriet nodded.

"And that's the definition of *enough*," said Willa. It was as if Bliss had just described the home in which she'd raised her boys. And she finally understood her friend's Jesus.

Bliss looked at her like only an old friend can. "Is it?" she asked.

None of them answered.

Then Bliss looked at Jane and nodded and they both stood. "Say a prayer," said Bliss, "if you're the praying sort." And the two of them left for the Inn.

"Please, God!" Harriet called after her. She looked at Willa and bit her nails. "I wish she'd chosen one of us. I know that town. And I am not at all confident that our Bliss is going to get that girl's baby. The single mother thing doesn't exactly play well in rural Wisconsin."

"She knows we're here for her." Willa cleared the tea service and Harriet helped her. "I'm glad she chose Jane. She probably needs the space from us."

The women stood side by side at the sink, washing and drying the teacups and saucers.

"When did she get like this?" said Harriet. "She was always into God. But when did she get so *churchy*?"

"I think it was her way of dealing with Hugh through all of their struggles. It seemed like he never really *got* her. She didn't really have his support. Did you know him well?"

"I met him once. At their wedding. Were you there? I don't remember meeting you if you were."

"I was too pregnant to travel. I felt bad about missing it. What was it like?"

"It was scarily Stepford. When she vowed to *honor and obey*, I think she really meant it and I think he really expected her to. I have a hard time going back there. She's been out to LA a few times over the years, but mostly Bliss and I talk on the phone. Truth is, she listens to me more than she shares with me. It's just sort of our dynamic. I wonder who listens to Bliss."

"We don't talk on the phone much," said Willa. "But when she visits, we stay up late into the night and she tells me how she feels. It's like she comes alive out here."

"She's told me many times that she never feels happier than when she's out here." Harriet sparked like sap in a fire. "God! They better give her that baby! What if the girl says *no*? If she could just spend some time really getting to know Bliss, she'd know just what Bliss said—her baby would be going to the most loving and forgiving and whatever *Christian* really means these days ... *mother* I can imagine."

Willa passed Harriet the teapot to dry.

"Do you think Hugh really loved her, Willa?"

"I never was sure. When they'd come visit, it seemed like it. But Jack always said, *Hugh is all about Hugh*. She was definitely *for* him. But like she said, I don't think he was ever really *for* Bliss."

Harriet dried the tray. "She's better off without him. There is *no* doubt in my mind that she can raise that child on her own. I mean, *who* is more capable than Bliss?"

"She's born for it. I just wish her town had her back."

"You know," said Harriet, "it may be a small town with a small-town attitude, but they will wrap themselves around her if she has a baby, church or no church. They're probably all confused about what to do with Hugh and this woman gallivanting around. But the moment Bliss has that baby she's always wanted, they'll know *exactly* what to do. It's not that they're shunning her. It's just that they're out of their comfort zone. Do you think that's what's going on here with you, Willa?"

Willa paused and listened to the frogs croaking in the marsh. "Who knows. Like Jane said, *isn't it amazing how people take each other so personally?*"

"I meant that about coming to Big Sur," said Harriet. "If you need a place to hide out for a while and be close to your boys. You could get a feel for a *new* place where *you'd* be new in it. And you wouldn't have to go back to Chicago with your tail between your legs. That would be going backward, Willa. You need to go *forward*!"

"Thanks, Harriet." Willa gave her a hug, a long one, and then pulled back, looking into her green eyes. "Harriet, we have the same color eyes. I'm just now noticing that."

"We do, don't we," said Harriet.

"I can say this to you, and probably only you." Willa paused. "I thought I'd lost my confidence. But really, since I've met you and listened to you speak, and after being in the woods again, and with the geese … and with you wonderful *women* … I think that what I've really lost is my *intuition*. Emerson called it: *untaught sallies of the spirit*. I always loved that. My spirit has forgotten how to *sally*."

"Willa, *you* know, I'm *sure* you know: You can't really lose your intuition. You just lose your *faith* in it."

Willa couldn't hold her green gaze any longer and she turned to the window, Bison Butte in gaining starlit silhouette. "How could I not know he was sick? That's what I don't understand. I could feel a cold coming on in my boys, just by the way their eyes looked. I can smell *snow* coming. How could I not have sensed that Jack's heart was failing him?"

"Maybe you didn't want to," said Harriet, pulling her back in for a hug. "Just like you don't want to leave this place."

"*Want to* and *have to* are two very different things. And I thought you didn't like hugs?"

"Working on the trust thing," said Harriet. "And you are a swell place to start."

Jane came down the hallway first, Bliss right behind her.

They both stood at the entranceway to the kitchen, Bliss's face neutral, Jane's face worried.

"They're going to think about it," said Bliss.

"They?" echoed Harriet.

"I didn't get to speak to the birth mother," said Bliss. "Just her parents."

"Did you tell them *everything*?" asked Harriet.

"I just told them that I would love that baby. With all my heart. The way I want to believe Jesus loves me." Bliss looked at her feet. "Even if I'm her only parent."

Willa went to her and hugged her.

"They just need a few days to think it over. They said out of all of the adoptive mothers, they liked me the most from the start."

"You seem crazily calm," said Harriet.

Jane chimed in. "You should have seen the look on her face when she came out of her room. I've never seen such poise under fire."

Bliss nodded. "It's out of my hands. Like everything else. And it's sort of a new feeling. To be considered for such an important job, just me."

"Well, you did your part, Bliss. Good for you!" said Willa.

They sat back down in the keeping room, mostly quiet, rocking, listening to a sudden late spring hailstorm on the metal roof.

"I love this," said Bliss. "Clear sky. Then hail. So Montana. Weather comes and goes so fast and furiously here."

"Like life, I guess," said Harriet.

"What adventure do you have in store for us tomorrow?" asked Jane.

"It's a surprise," Willa said, over the hail.

"So far, your surprises freak me out," said Jane. "But in a good way."

"Bring it on," said Harriet. "I want to know now so I can dream about it."

"No. Keep it a secret," said Bliss. "I have too much in my brain already."

Willa glazed over, thinking of the most sacred place she knew. She still wasn't sure if she had the nerve to go there. What if they didn't *get* it?

"I'm bushed," said Jane. "Good night, ladies." She kissed each one on the cheek. "You okay, Bliss?"

Bliss nodded. "I have never been more emotionally exhausted." She smiled. "But I'm okay. Thank you all so much."

Willa could see her crying as she followed Jane to the Inn.

Harriet stayed in her rocking chair. "Mind if I just sit here?"

"Not at all," said Willa.

"That's rain now. Not hail. Right?" said Harriet.

"Right," said Willa. "A hard rain like this always takes something with it."

Then she felt a stirring in her belly that she hadn't felt in a long time. *The sallies of the spirit.* She kissed Harriet on the forehead like an old friend, went to the freezer, and took the small box containing the Calliope hummingbird. Barefoot, she went out into the rain to the boulder at the edge of the yard. Rain dripping down her face, she opened the box and poured the little frozen bird into her palm. "Everything must move now." And she placed it on the boulder. An offering.

"Good night, sweet prince," she said.

And Willa went back into the house, dropped the small box in the garbage, ran a tea towel over her face and feet, and went to bed, listening to the rain on the roof and the rumbling of thunder. Or bison. She couldn't be sure.

Day Four

Willa woke feeling something new. Something like *calm*, she guessed. The women were helping. The storm had passed and the sky was that spring powder blue.

She went to her window seat and looked down at the boulder. The bird was gone. She nodded to the boulder and then to Bison Butte in the not-so-distance, as if it had blown in during the storm and taken her offering so that life would move forward now.

Now she was sure: they were going to the hot springs. After these last few days, they would have a reverence for her most sacred Montana place and would honor it the way she needed. So many *goodbyes*.

She went down to the kitchen and made the coffee and scones, cooked the last of the sausages from her kitchen freezer. She'd have to go to the garage freezer for more, but that's where the hunt was stored, and, like Jack's Cave, she'd been ignoring it for most of the winter, taking from it sparingly—a duck breast here, a piece of venison there. There wasn't much left.

She heard voices on the porch, and Bliss and Jane came through the front door holding walking sticks.

"Oh good! You got a nice morning walk," said Willa, so happy the land was being loved, especially now. "And you found some good sticks, I see."

Jane brought a sturdy straight aspen branch into the kitchen. "It was just lying there on the path. Must have broken off in the storm. I'm going to take it home with me. Is that okay? It fits perfectly in my hand."

"My boys used to shave off the bark, sand them down, and sell them at the Merc. You should definitely take it home to navigate those Connecticut carpool lines you've told us about." Willa smiled.

"This is for me and for me only. I'm going to put it in my bedroom, as a reminder that I can walk with bears." Jane smiled so big and pure that it gave Willa goosebumps. "*And*," she said, beaming even brighter, "see this skinny branch that vees off? This is what it's like to be here in Montana. I feel like I'm out on the skinny branches. Holding on in the wind. But it's not a storm like last night. It's a gentle spring breeze. And guess what?"

"What?" said Willa.

"I don't fall," said Jane. "Like in Thoreau's quote you read us." She smiled brighter. "So I guess I soar! Now to find out what that might look like." Her eyes were so wide.

Willa loved that Jane had put their favorite family quote to good use. "Main thing is to let it happen. Like Thoreau said. Allow, rather than resist."

"I love that." Jane smiled. "Allow."

Bliss leaned her stick up against the wall. "We were thinking about what you said, Willa. About an aspen grove being one organism. That's so beautiful to think of," she said, giving Willa a kiss on her cheek. "Good morning, my friend. It smells incredible in here."

"Can I do anything to help?" asked Jane, kissing Willa's other cheek.

"*You* get to be served this morning," said Willa, pouring out a few mugs of coffee and putting them on the kitchen table, along with a plate of scones, butter and honey, the elk sausages, and a bowl of ripe plums that the women had picked up in Great Falls.

"Where's Harriet?" said Jane.

"I heard her late last night when I went to the bathroom. She was bawling her eyes out," said Bliss.

"I heard her too, through the wall. It woke me up. She was yelling at someone, but I don't think she was on the phone," said Jane. "She was just bumping around in her room, *ranting*. I couldn't make out one word except for *fucking*-this and *fucking*-that. Do you think we need to worry about her? I mean … after what she *did*? I don't mean to be *indelicate*."

"I definitely worry about her all alone down on Big Sur," said Bliss. "She's never really had a group of friends or a community that she's not somehow in charge of. Even when she was a little girl, she was always the ringleader. And then she just got so busy pushing her way to the top. I think she's entirely at a loss for how to live her life now."

Willa imagined Harriet with her nose in the lilacs yesterday saying, "I'm sick of being strong." But was she intentionally trying to make herself weak by cutting herself off from the world? And was Willa doing the same thing? How could this red blaze of a woman and her have so much in common?

"Even when we were roommates, it took us a long time to be friends," said Jane. "I idolized her. And I guess she saw something in me. But there was one night when she'd had a big deal fall through at work, and some jerky guy she was dating had cheated on her—she was always dating the biggest *jerks*! And she came home and just *collapsed* in my lap on the couch. Like she was crying a whole *lifetime* of tears. I don't think she'd ever come undone with anyone *quite* like that. It scared me.

Those were the exact same sounds I heard last night coming from her room."

Bliss said, "I'm glad she had you then, Jane. She pulled away from everyone at home. Even me for a while. She's like the wall of Jericho. And I'm worried that she's going to come tumbling down. And that we haven't even seen the beginning of it." She looked at Jane with nervous eyes. "Not even on that video."

"If she's anything like me," said Willa, "she just has to learn how to be everything for herself now. And that might mean some dark nights of the soul. Believe me, I've had plenty. If this house could talk ..."

"Really?" said Jane. "I know I should probably agree. But I've been thinking about what Bliss was saying yesterday when we were making the soup—about community. I'm beginning to see that we need people to help us navigate this whole mess. I come *alive* when I'm around people. Whether I like it or not. I can be exhausted, but if I walk into a room of people, I feel this magnetic pull and suddenly I'm working that room. Palmer's the same way. We go to a party and don't see each other until the end and we love that about each other. We compare notes in the car on the way back home. It's probably our primary conversation, actually, outside of the kids. Talking about people at parties." Jane looked sad. She took a long sip of coffee. "Well anyway, I just think that people need people. Like the song says."

Harriet slid into the kitchen in her slippers, singing in her best Barbra Streisand, "*People who need people ...*" she kept singing, "*is the most codependent song ... on ... earth.*" Her eyes were puffy and mascara stained her lower lids. "Good morning," she said, going straight for the coffee. She sat down at the table and declared, "Well, it's official. I hate myself. I'm going to start a new twelve-step group—Self-Loathers Anonymous. And yes, Bliss, I do use the word *codependence* like it's a swear word. How about *inter-*

dependence instead? But still, if you can't stand yourself, how can you enter into any sort of *inter*?"

"Well … good morning, Harriet!" said Bliss.

Harriet shrugged. "I'd say *I'm sorry*, but we're not allowed to." She reached for a scone, slathering it with butter and honey.

"Do you want me to say it *for* you? But not to *us*. To *you*?" asked Jane, not entirely joking, passing her the bowl of plums. "You owe yourself an apology!"

"I think self-love is really hard," said Bliss. "Can't we shoot for self-*acceptance* instead?"

"Sure. I accept that I'm the worst person on the planet," said Harriet. "I tried writing what I really want to say in the little red journal I brought with me. Nothin'. Not anything that was remotely *nice*, I mean. I was just out for blood. God, I'm so *wicked*! I wouldn't treat my worst enemy the way I talk to myself in my own mind! And so then I tried the freer thought thingy."

"Did it work? Did you feel at least a *little* freer?" said Willa, sitting down at the table.

"Not … one … fig," said Harriet.

Bliss took a long sip of her coffee. She was like a different person this morning—something had lifted. "You know, this might seem off topic, but I think it applies. I remembered it last night just before I went to sleep. When my father was in the hospital dying, we had a lot of time alone together because I took the night shift. And one night, I was reading the Bible to him—he loved the Psalms. When I finished he looked at me—this man who went to church every single Sunday of his life, and sometimes during the week just to receive Communion—and he said to me, this godly man who loved Jesus so much he cried like a baby every year on Good Friday, *Bliss*, he said. *I'll be surprised if there's anything on the other side.* And I looked at him in utter shock, like he was ripping the world out from under me. And I said, *What have you been doing in church all these years then, Dad?* And he smiled and winked at me—he wasn't much of a winker, especially where the Lord was concerned—and he smiled the most holy smile I think I'll ever see in my life, and he said, *It's the only place I feel truly at home.*"

Bliss's eyes were wide again, and her cheeks the color of the flesh of the plum on her plate. "It wasn't Heaven that he was waiting for. *Church* was his home! And at the time it just leveled me. My *father*—this faithless man? How could that be true? *Heaven* was our ultimate home. With Jesus. And the Holy Spirit. *Seated at the right hand of the Father.* Not *church!*"

She took a bite of her plum and chewed, nodding her head like she was hearing a song. "And yet ... look at my life! I've made church my home too. Church is my Supposed to Be. Just like my mother said. But is the *right thing* such a bad thing? If it feels right to you? We were talking about *belonging* on the first night. Well ... I *belong* there. Even if the people currently aren't being so great. It's where I've shown up. Even if I'm doing it all wrong. I've still shown up."

Bliss wiped plum juice from her chin. "And you know ... to your point, Harriet ... I think that's what he was saying. The same thing you're saying. He accepted that maybe he didn't really have the faith he wished he had. And even so, he showed up all his life in this way that he felt was important. And that he loved. And that brought him purpose. Like my mother too. And like me."

Then she drilled Harriet with her eyes. "And like you have too, Harriet. Your whole career isn't a *sham!* You showed up for your messages and whether or not you think you were full of *shit,* you know full *well* that you believed in what you had to say. You were teaching women to be powerful, even if it got all tangled up in money or whatever you got tangled up in. But still ... you showed up! In a huge way! And you should *love* yourself for that!"

Bliss looked at each of them, one at a time, until each of them looked away.

"Like you've showed up for this *town*, Willa! And like you've shown up for your *kids*, Jane! Even and especially when what you love rejects you." Bliss looked sad then, but she found a smile. "And maybe that's all this thing called *life* is—just showing up. And doing your *best*. Even if it's not *perfect*. *Especially* if it's not perfect." Then she smiled, so fully absorbed. "And instead of hating that about yourself, Harriet ... how 'bout you *accept* that about yourself."

Bliss took another bite of the plum, chewed for a moment, and swallowed. "Maybe find *love* for yourself, despite it all."

Harriet grabbed a plum. "Well, if that's true, then these days ... I'm showing up being my worst! I mean, *mediocre* would suffice, right? But I'm finding that being your *worst* isn't that much different from being your *best*. It's all just a colossal chase trying to be something or someone or some *way*! And it's exhausting. And delusional. And I can't take it anymore." She took a big juicy bite for punctuation. "At the risk of sounding like a bumper sticker, I just want to be *me*. But I have no idea what that really is."

"But maybe that's enough," said Bliss. "Maybe your best is your *worst* right now. And rather than fighting it, maybe just accept it." She passed the bowl to Jane. "Or maybe your best is showing up for *yourself* for once, Harriet. And no one else. Even if it doesn't look that great. Maybe that's true for all of us. And why we're here. Showing up for *ourselves*, together. Outside of our Supposed to Bes. In whatever shipwrecked shape we're in."

Harriet didn't look convinced. She put her thumb and forefinger together like a yogi, closed her eyes, and chanted, "I aspire to be mediocre. I aspire to be mediocre."

Jane cupped a plum in her hand like a baby bird. "My mother always said, *Never let anyone off the hook for saying they're doing their best. Because what if their best isn't good enough?*" She looked up. "I hear that in my head all the time." Then she took a giant bite which burst juice all over her chin, and let out a loud unexpected slurp, grabbing for her napkin. "God, I'm a slob sometimes."

Willa thought of Nel and the Piegan father she could not know. And said, "Nel is part native and she owns it even though no one owns it for her. She knows herself by trees. Lakes. Rivers. Mountains." Willa didn't look at any of them. She wished Nel would come by for one more ride.

"Nel told me this Piegan prayer once:

> *"Honor the earth and all that exists.*
> *Be strong in this belief and practice it*
> *throughout your life*
> *because it makes for a world of kindness*
> *that binds all the good things of life*
> *together in a circle of harmony."*

"*A world of kindness*," said Bliss.

"*A circle of harmony*," said Harriet.

Jane said, "Yes."

Words leapt from Willa's mouth then. "I have no idea what my larger community is. But I know what *this* is. This circle. This circle within a circle." She smiled at each of them. "And I like it. A *lot*."

"Me too," said Jane. "We're like a *coven* or something." She smiled naughtily.

"No!" said Bliss. "I don't *do* witch stuff. We're more like nomads, not knowing where we're going next."

"I think it's more commune-esque. Circa 1972," said Harriet.

Jane crossed her arms in front of her sweater. "I don't do hippie," she said. "And probably not nomad either."

"You're both boring." Harriet yawned and put her hand on Willa's. "You know, my dear. You have really made me think about something I try very hard not to think about: *belonging* to something. I don't belong to *any*thing. I never even belonged to my own *brand*. It belonged to *me*."

"Where I live, that's what it's all about. Belonging," said Jane. "And it's everywhere you look. On the back of your car. On your boat. Your cocktail glasses. Palmer actually has our son make him cocktails in the family Yale lowball glasses. *Fill it to the bottom of the Y, son. Good practice for later!* Ugh. The last three Palmers have gone to Yale. Talk about *belonging*. Little Palmer is the *fourth*. Up until a few years ago, we actually called him *Four*. I finally put my foot down on that one." Jane ran her finger down the crease in her pants. "I just want to say to my kids, *You know … it's okay if you do it differently. It's okay not to belong.* You said it so well yesterday, Willa. I guess you can't really belong to anything with any level of authenticity if you don't belong to yourself."

"Well, when you figure out how to do that, let me know," said Harriet. "I used to have the women in my audience write themselves a love letter. Don't roll your eyes. It's cheesy, but they *loved* it! They ate it up. They told me over and over that it was the best thing they'd ever done for themselves. And that was before self-care was a *thing*." Harriet rubbed her whole face like it hurt. "Gawd. A *love* letter to yourself. I'm surprised I didn't get shot."

"Where I come from, it's considered *selfish* to take care of yourself, unless it falls under what we call *maintenance*." Jane mimed a mock injection into her frown lines.

"I come from farm stock," said Bliss. "We don't have time for self-care."

"Don't walk into the Saloon talking about self-care. Around here, people are just trying to get through the day," said Willa.

"Holy crap!" shouted Bliss, standing up. "I have the perfect thing for us to do right now. The *perfect* thing. I'll be right back. Don't go anywhere!"

The women smiled at each other as Bliss raced off to the Inn.

"She's like the little girl she was at summer camp," said Willa. "She comes alive in the woods."

"She was that way when we were little too," said Harriet. "When we'd go to the lake."

Bliss bounded into the room, out of breath, holding something behind her back. "I wasn't sure why I brought these. But I've had them for a long, long time. I was just going to write something special to each of you at the end of our time together and slip it into your suitcases. But I have a much better idea!"

She produced a bundle of postcards tied with a thin velvet robin's-egg-blue ribbon. "I collect antique Valentine postcards. I've been collecting them for years. I'm fascinated by the way people used to write, so formally and in such an elegant slant. On beautiful paper like Willa's invitation. Back before we had buttons to push. Only buttons to sew."

"I've always thought there were two kinds of people," said Harriet. "The ones who save the buttons that come with new clothes. And the ones who don't."

"But even if you save them, do you really ever *use* those buttons?" said Jane, like this topic was something she regularly tried to sort out.

"That's a whole different breed altogether—the ones who actually use the buttons," said Harriet.

"I use the buttons," said Jane.

Bliss cleared her throat. "Ladies! We can talk about buttons later!" She fanned out the cards on the table. "These are all blank. Never been written on. Never been mailed."

They admired the Valentines—their plump cherubs and swooning women with rosy lips, and long flowing dresses. The faded ribbon and old-fashioned glitter.

"Pity. They just don't make things with this quality anymore," said Jane. "Unlike your gorgeous invitation, Willa."

"I love that something on paper outlives a person. Our society is so disposable now," said Willa.

"Okay," said Bliss, rubbing her hands together. "Pick one. The one that speaks to you. And then we're going to do something with it."

Each one picked a card.

"So …" Bliss smiled, her face blushing. "Now … we're going to write ourselves a love note. Not a long letter. Just a note, postcard-length. Because when it comes down to it, what we really have to say is short and sweet. And like we've been discovering … if we can't say what we really want to say to ourselves … then how are we ever going to be able to say what we really want to say to others?"

Harriet groaned. "It has to be a love letter, huh. It can't be a *loathe* letter?"

"No. It can't be a loathe letter, my friend." Bliss smiled, playing up her Midwestern accent. "And you know as well as I do that loathing is really *fear* talking. Maybe the reason we're having such a hard time figuring out what to do next in our lives is because we're starting with fear instead of love." Her smile widened and brimmed over so big that it parted her bangs. "I have always believed that fear is the opposite of love. And lately, when I can't find my Jesus … I can find that. There's always something or someone to love, even if you can't love yourself."

"I've never thought of that before," said Jane. "But it's probably true. The opposite of love probably *is* fear. Not hate. Because hate is really just … fear. Huh."

Bliss smiled as big as she probably knew how. "And love is greater than anything."

"Jesus. You sound like a frigging *Christian* or something," said Harriet, winking.

Bliss was unstoppable. She didn't blink or flinch or react at all.

Willa smiled at her friend. "I only know how to write post-cards to *you*!"

Bliss laughed. "Mine wallpapered the walls of your outhouse! I used to sit in there forever, reading through our past in those postcards."

They were all silent for a moment.

Then Jane groaned. "I know I probably need to do this, huh?" She groaned again.

Harriet just stared out the window.

Bliss said, "Don't look so miserable! After we do this, we're going to have another Montana adventure. And if I know Willa, it'll be a doozy."

Willa smiled. "Just you wait."

"A simple postcard, old as the hills," said Bliss. "And then we're going to mail them."

"Oh *God*!" shrieked Jane. "Palmer will think I've gone cuckoo for Cocoa Puffs."

"You'll be home before the postcard gets there," said Willa. "Takes a week from our post office. At least."

"Yeah, well what if I don't *go* home?" Jane said.

"Ditto that," said Harriet. "What if we protest the auction, camp out here at the Homestead, and throw grenades at the new owner? Or freak him out with Tibetan prayer flags flying all over the place."

Willa looked out at Bison Butte. The thought that they would fight for this place made her feel like she was an even worse betrayer.

Bliss said, "Oh come on, ladies! Have a little fun. It'll be a lovely thing to get in our mailboxes when we're back home, feeling like all this was a dream."

"If I had anything to do with this," said Harriet, "I am sorry. That's what I get for talking about shit like self-care."

"No *sorry*," said Bliss.

"Harriet, *stop* being so *cynical*. Think *self-care*," said Jane. "*Some* of us *need* to do things like this. Some of us have never done *anything* like this *ever*. And never *would* in our normal lives. Even if it's *cheesy*. No offense, Bliss."

"None taken," said Bliss, smiling at her postcard like it was a baby.

Harriet scowled. "I *have* become a terrible cynic, haven't I? I don't know when it happened. It's a *lovely* exercise, Bliss. I owe you an apology. I'm just not used to being on the other side of this sort of thing."

"Is there a certain something that needs to be *in* the love letter?" asked Jane.

"You're not trying to get into Wellesley," said Harriet. "It's for *you*."

Bliss ignored them, and with a quiet countenance said, "Okay, so flip over your postcard and write yourself a love letter."

"All I can think of are brand slogans," said Harriet. "Kill me now."

"This is going to be harder than sitting in the woods with a bear in the bushes," said Jane.

"Let's be silent, in fact," said Bliss.

A love letter to myself, thought Willa. *Not from Jack.* He was such a romantic. Flowers for no reason in small jars on her nightstand. Notes on little pieces of paper where he knew she'd find them— the garden trowel, the compost pile, the chicken coop. And always written on his old typewriter. He said he liked to push the periods hard so that the little holes looked like constellations when you lifted them to the sky. *Not from Jack*, she promised herself. She looked out the window at Bison Butte again, as if there would be a message written in the sky in smoke. What would she say to herself if she were meeting herself for the first time—love at first sight, the way it had been for them?

She watched the other women, staring out the window, at

the bookshelves, at their postcards, at their pens. Not writing anything yet.

Willa didn't know how to begin. Jack always addressed her as *My love*. But this was another chance to part from him and she knew she should take it. Still … what words could replace his?

She looked at the insides of her hands, then at her thumb. She took her pen and began covering it until it was wet with black ink. Then she pressed it in the center of the postcard and pulled back.

Look at that. She smiled. She'd never looked at her thumbprint. She looked closer. It had a perfect circle in the center, with rings in ripples all around it. And it occurred to Willa: *I've been making ripples in this place for years. It's just the circle in the center that I'd forgotten about.*

And it was to that center that she wrote these words, in rings around her thumbprint:

I love you, Willa. I love you for the way you care for people. I love the way you cook and garden and love animals. I love the way you know your flora and fauna, season by season, especially your birds. I love how loyal you are. Your ripples will keep rippling wherever you go. I love you for that most of all.

But she didn't write *Love, Willa* as she had on the invitation. Because it could be any of them loving her—the town, her boys, Jack, these women, even her parents. And she needed to feel that too.

Then she looked at the right side of the postcard and wrote, *Please forward to Willa Silvester. The middle of another everywhere.* And added Bliss's address, just to be safe.

Jane slapped her knee and said, "Aha!" and put pen to postcard.

Harriet was writing in big loopy letters and ended with what was clearly a giant exclamation point.

"I think it would be nice to read these out loud to each other," said Bliss.

"Ugh," said Harriet.

"Double ugh," said Jane. "Mine only makes sense to me. I wrote it in a sort of ... code."

"I'll go first," said Bliss. "I've always loved this one the most." She held it up—hearts and birds fluttering around a cherub baby lying in a nest, all set by pale blue glitter. "Mine just says, *I forgive you. All of you. Even you, Bliss.*" She blinked and shrugged. "Forgiveness is the first step."

Willa tried to give her the best knowing nod she could conjure. "I'll go next," she said, holding up the card to show her thumbprint. "I've never noticed that I have a perfect circle in the center of my thumb." And then she read hers out loud.

"Lovely," said Bliss. "You *will* keep rippling, Willa. And if it arrives in my mailbox, I'll keep it safe. I promise."

"I know. Thank you," said Willa.

Jane beamed. "*This* is a perfect circle. Us. And I don't mean *perfect* perfect, like my periwinkle blue, mock middle name. But *this* sort of perfect. Kind. Loving. Real."

Willa smiled and looked at her thumb.

"Brilliant! I'll go next," said Harriet, clearing her throat. "*Hard Harriet—it's time to find what there is to love about yourself. If you would let me in, I can hold you close while you figure it out. Love, Soft Harriet.*" She looked up with solemn eyes. "And then I wrote, *love letter love letter love letter* until in my head it sounded like *let her love.* And so that's what I wrote at the end. In what I wish was red pen, but I will say: cursive is way more fun than all caps! *LET ... HER ... LOVE!*"

"I love that," said Bliss, smiling at her. "Out of the box, as expected."

They all looked up at Jane, who blushed.

"Uh ... well ... mine is a little ... *delicate.*" Then her face went crimson. "Are these hot flashes?" she asked Harriet. "I think I'm perimenopausal."

Harriet groaned. "Oh thank *God*, I'm done with *that* hell. I had *atomic* hot flashes. But, honey, something tells me that you're actually *blush*ing, not hot-flashing. One shade past pink, for once. Good for you, Janey."

Jane's face got even redder, and she tore off her cardigan. Her hands were shaking. "So mine just says, *I don't know how to love you. And I don't know how to* not *love you.*" She looked up. "And that's not necessarily just to me. It's to ... a few people." She looked down at her postcard, which had a giant heart on it with two arrows through it. Then she looked up. Gave a little hapless laugh. And said, "Makes sense that I got this postcard. Two arrows. Because that's what I'm shooting with." She looked down again. "But I don't want to talk about it."

They all stared at Jane, who looked at her postcard.

Willa shot a glance at Harriet who scrunched up her mouth and said, "Anyone else feel like they just wrote a *fake it 'til ya make it?*"

"Yes," said Jane, not looking up, her face still crimson.

"A bit," said Willa, trying not to stare at Jane. "But it felt like a step in the right direction. Thank you, Bliss."

Jane giggled, like her blush was bubbling over.

"What's funny?" said Harriet.

Jane looked up then. "I don't know. It's the strangest thing. I feel like I need to do cartwheels."

"I couldn't do a cartwheel if my life depended on it," said Harriet.

"I think I might have one in me, actually," said Bliss.

"Not me," said Willa. "I've been lying around all winter. I'm totally out of shape."

"Let's try!" said Jane, jumping up and running out the front door.

The others looked at each other, one impish grin after the next.

Jane was already cartwheeling and squealing, "Yippee!" when they got to the front porch.

"I swear, she's getting younger by the hour," said Harriet. "She's going to be a baby by Sunday and we'll have to stroll her back to Connecticut in diapers."

Bliss stepped onto the lawn and watched Jane's wheeling body, like a cat watching a goldfish. Then she said, "Here goes nothing," took a few running steps, and flung herself hand-to-grass, her legs following, bent at the knees, in what was more of a flat tire than anything else. She landed on her back, laughing and making a V for victory sign. "Nine point nine from the Canadian judge!"

Harriet screamed, "Harriet, you competitive nincompoop!" as she hurled herself onto her palms, her red nightgown falling over her, revealing a red thong and a perfectly sculpted rear that landed bare on the grass. "That was *fun!*" she shouted, pulling her nightgown back over her knees. Then she stood up and hurled herself back into the air, screaming, "Hard ass! Soft heart!"

Willa laughed and anchored herself against a porch post.

Lying on her back on the lawn, Jane shouted to them, "I hereby announce that I'm going to get fat. In case anyone wants to know. I'm through with maintenance. I'm going to let myself go. So suck it, Connecticut!"

"Whoot!" Harriet gave her the Hard Ass high five.

"Congratulations," said Bliss, lying next to her. "You know what they say—*fat and happy.*"

"Willa, your turn," said Jane, beaming. "Will-uh ... Will-uh ... Will-uh!"

"No way," said Willa, gripping the post. "After the hayloft incident, my back's not really capable of cartwheels."

"Oh, come on," said Bliss. "You can hardly call what I just did a cartwheel. Just give it what you've got. It's freeing. Pretend you're at summer camp. I remember that girl, and she can do a cartwheel!"

Willa looked at the grass like a clean palette. As if pushed from behind by a gentle wind, she let go of the post, jogged down the steps, flung her hands toward the ground, and lifted her legs over her head skyward. Time slowed as she felt herself circling through the air, her hands supporting her weight, her braid sweeping the grass—no thoughts, just the knowledge that when she landed, she'd be further across the yard than where she started.

Time flashed again, and she found herself landing squarely on her feet. She held the moment to her heart, keeping her gaze soft, then focused to see the women sitting around her, smiling and clapping.

"Heck *yeah*, you can still do a cartwheel!" shouted Bliss.

"That was *impressive!*" Jane cried, revealing every tooth in her mouth.

"Atta girl!" said Harriet. "Atta girl, Willa!"

Willa did a deep curtsey and sat in the grass with the rest of them, smiling.

Bliss stood. "And now we're going into town to mail the love letters."

It was so nice to have someone else in charge. Willa hoped that today Montana would give as much as it had yesterday and the day before.

"Go get your sturdiest hiking shoes, and, Bliss and Jane, you might want to bring your walking sticks. The terrain can be slippery where we're going this time of year. Harriet, there's a grove of aspens down along the meadow where they found theirs this morning. Or I have one you can use."

"I'd love my own walking stick," Harriet said, heading for the door.

Willa called after her. "Let's all meet in the truck in half an hour. Unless you're more comfortable in the rental."

"The truck!" they all called back.

She smiled. It was like there was a family living in this house again. "Okay. I'll pack water and the supplies we need." She and Jack had discovered the hot springs together and she hadn't been able to muster the courage to go since his death. Even though she'd needed to so many times. If they were going to find their So Now What, she knew no better way than to take the waters of Maria Hot Springs.

She went up to her bed and pulled back the dust ruffle. There it was, where she'd left it that night in January. She held the bear spray in her hand, thinking of the canisters in the Inn for the guests to use. "They can carry their own bear spray. I'm going the way of the Piegan," she said, putting the can back under her bed, and her hand to her breast.

They made a quick stop at the Merc for Bliss to mail the postcards, and Willa felt fairly strong waiting in the parking lot, held by the familiar old Ford, Jane and Harriet in the back seat, all of them on their way to her most sacred place on earth.

It wasn't a long drive, but it was a muddy one and when they got to the trailhead, they were happy to be on foot.

"Follow me," said Willa, cutting into the forest, feeling her blooming confidence, her third Montana adventure in three days.

The women used their walking sticks to navigate the muddy trail, hiking through the lodgepole pine and Douglas fir forest bottom. Willa had never used a walking stick. Nor had Jack. The creek was swollen with runoff from the melting snowpack high in the mountains, and much of the trail was underwater. A walking stick wouldn't be such a bad thing. Damn self-reliance. Maybe walking sticks were in her future. Maybe *reliance* was in her future.

Over the years, Willa and Jack had stacked small stone cairns, marking the places where you had to boulder-hop across the creek to the higher, drier trail on the other side. Like every year, the winter snows had knocked them over, and like every year, Willa set the stones on top of each other again, cairn by cairn, as they hiked and crossed, hiked and crossed.

There were four crossings, and since few people knew about the springs, it was all very remote, even for a local. She was happy to see the women handling the terrain like pros, jumping from rock to rock over the rushing creek.

"Where are you taking us, Sacagawea?" asked Harriet.

"Trust," said Willa. "Be careful, everyone. Step by step."

The women were quiet, placing their feet carefully on the rocks and balancing with their walking sticks, until they arrived at what was left of the last cairn.

Willa found the stones and restacked them, smiling—his hands, their marker in so many ways for so many years. Now her hands.

"We're almost there. The hard part's over."

Willa took them into the woods now, on a thin trail that cut up the south side of the creek and ended at a series of steaming thermal pools that she and Jack had barricaded off years ago with large rocks. The hotter pool was on top and flowed into the bottom pool, which was usually just the right temperature this time of year.

"Here we are!" she said. "The Maria Hot Springs. We're going to take the waters. These are healing mineral baths that the natives have been using for hundreds of years. Sioux. Crow. Blackfeet. I can think of no better way for us to find our So Now What."

Bliss stared into the pools and smiled.

Harriet leaned her stick up against a tree and flung off her clothes. Jane asked, "Do we have towels?"

"Yes. Plenty of towels and water. Don't worry. No one comes up here. We're alone, I promise," said Willa.

"I'm sort of a prude when it comes to being naked. Surprise, surprise," said Jane.

"Oh, Janey! No one cares! Get in the water!" shouted Harriet, sliding in from the smooth rocks which had launched Willa and Jack into these waters so many times. "It's LOVELY!" she shouted, dipping her head back into the water so that her breasts floated.

She's a natural Montanan, thought Willa.

"Yeah. That's exactly what I was afraid of," said Jane, looking at Harriet's breasts.

Bliss slid in without overture and draped her arms across a few rocks, looking over the creek, her bony back so pale after a long Wisconsin winter.

Willa had the sudden urge to touch it. No one touched your bare back except your lover. The waters would do that for both of them. She slipped in next, hoping that Jane would be less self-conscious if they left her alone.

"Oh. It's perfect!" said Willa, floating on her back, weightless. "It's heaven, really."

"Maybe it is," said Bliss, her back still to them.

"Don't think I'm a total twit, but I'm keeping my underwear on," said Jane, sitting on the rock with her arm over her breasts.

"Good Jesus, Jane. Get over yourself. You're going to have wet underwear the whole way back. Nobody *cares*!" said Harriet.

"Well I care, you ... crazy *bitch*," said Jane, without a hint of humor.

"Yo," said Harriet. "I'll give you *crazy*. But I ain't no *bitch*." And she swam over to the rock where Jane was perched, grabbed her leg, and pulled her in.

Jane went in over her head and came up splashing. "God! You are such a *bully* and you always *have* been!" she shouted at Harriet.

"Oh, lighten up," said Harriet, markedly nonplussed.

And then Jane came at her, grabbing her wet hair, her teeth clenched, and her eyes shut tight.

Harriet grabbed Jane's hair right back and they stood there

pulling at each other in what was the most hilarious yet disturbing match of wills Willa had ever seen.

She looked at Bliss, thinking she'd get a wink, but Bliss looked horrified.

"Hey, break it up, ladies," shouted Bliss.

Willa held back and thought, *They probably don't do it like that in prayer group.*

"Ladies!" shouted Bliss. "Stop!"

Jane and Harriet kept pulling, making strange straining sounds, not unlike childbirth.

Bliss waded over to them and put her hands on each of their shoulders, trying to pull them apart.

Harriet swatted her away and Bliss fell back against the rocks with true fear in her eyes.

"Dirty secret, Harriet. Sometimes I don't like you. At all," said Bliss.

"Yeah," grunted Jane, pulling harder on Harriet's hair. "Dirty secret: me neither! I sometimes can't *stand* you, Harriet!"

This was not what Willa had in mind, but motherhood had taught her that these things needed to work themselves out. She thought about Jane's tectonic plates. Thermal pools were Mother Nature's release. Maybe they were helping.

Then Harriet broke free and lunged at Jane, who squirmed and screamed until Harriet's hand emerged from the water, clasping Jane's underwear.

She shouted, "Dirty secret. I don't always like your cashmere-covered self either, Jane." She lassoed Jane's underwear in the air and shouted, "Fly! Be free!"

Jane retreated to the opposite side of the pool. "I don't know who you think you are sometimes! Once a diva. Always a diva!"

"I am *not* a diva!" said Harriet, throwing Jane's underwear at her and leaning back against the rocks.

Jane went to a full decibel shrill. "I heard you last night! You were watching that damn video over and over and ranting and raving. When are you going to forgive yourself? You fucked up. Move on! Stop feeling sorry for yourself and get back in the game. The world needs you! You're being *selfish* hiding in that beach shack!"

Harriet just stared at her with the vacant look of the sucker punched. "I'm not hiding because I'm *selfish*, Jane."

"Well, why *are* you hiding?" asked Jane, splashing water at her. "Tell us. Don't you *trust* us?"

Harriet's eyes were empty tombs.

"I heard you too. What were you raging against last night, Harriet? Tell us," said Bliss, earnest.

"It's worse than you think." Harriet shrank into the water down to her chin and said, "I'm hiding ... because I don't know how *not* to want it back. And I'm truly scared of it. My ego is begging for it like a vampire wanting blood. And I know that if I go back, it'll kill me. And I'll let it. No exaggeration."

"Jesus, Harriet," said Jane, putting her wet underwear back on. "You're not *serious*, are you? You're the most powerful person I know! And I know a lot of powerful people! Wake up! Don't you *know* how powerful you are? You've changed countless women's *lives*!"

"I've never been more serious in my life, Jane. Dirty secret," Harriet said, now with a haunted hollowness. "I have a dark cloud over me. It's always been there and it never leaves. I've just kept myself so busy that I've been able to ... lie. And now, alone, on Big Sur, I have to feel it. And I'm not doing well. At *all*. I've released this beast." Her face split into a grin, but she wasn't laughing.

"And if I go back to my career, it will follow me. And I won't be able to outrun it this time. I've let it settle too strongly inside me now. When I run, it gets wilder. When I'm quiet ... it's more ... tame." Then she slipped all the way under the water while the others looked at each other, and then at the water where her head should be emerging.

Bliss dove down and brought her up again.

Harriet was laughing but almost maniacally. "Blissful. Did you think I was trying to *drown* myself? Here in the Maria Hot Springs? With you lovely women? I'm not that much of an asshole! Even though you just admitted you don't like me."

"I didn't say I don't *love* you," said Bliss. "I just don't *like* you sometimes."

"That's what I meant too," said Jane. "I'll always love you. Even if you aren't on a stage." Then she groaned and sunk into the pool. "God, are we all *depressed*, do you think? Do we all need to go on anti*depressants*? I mean, if *Harriet's* depressed, then we're all *doomed*."

Willa sunk into the water, up to her chin. "Dirty secret: Since Jack died, sometimes I lie in bed and hold my breath and think that I could just go out that way. My boys would be fine. I wouldn't have to suffer anymore. I lie in bed with my hands on my chest the way they lie you in a coffin. Even though I want to be cremated." She looked at Harriet. "But I'm not *truly* suicidal. Are *you*, Harriet? I mean, really? *Are* you?"

Harriet looked at them all, somber and serious. "If I go back to my career, I don't know, Willa. I really don't know."

Jane splashed water at both of them. "How about you both *live*? *Okay?* How about all of us live! We have beautiful lives ahead of us! We have so much to be grateful for! And there's help out there if we need it! And there's ... *us*! Our perfect circle!"

Harriet looked at Bliss, who had a sharpness in her jaw. "Don't worry, Blissful. I'm not going to off myself." She let out a loud, "Hah! I'll tell you what's taming the beast for now! Dirty little secret that my critics would love to get their hands on: California weed. It's my new thing. Can you imagine? Me? A *stoner*? Jane's fifteen minutes late? I'm losing whole *days*, sitting alone in my pajamas, baked out of my mind, the beast sleeping on a dog bed in the corner. And I don't need a lecture. It's just a phase and it's helping me for now. What I *do* need … is a friend."

"We're your friends, Harry," said Jane.

Then Bliss said to Harriet, "You haven't really *had* friends, have you? Not since you became famous. I mean *real* friends. Besides Jane. And me. Have you?"

Harriet shook her head, blinking back tears, biting her lip. "No. That's my dirtiest secret of all."

They were silent, steeped in the thermal water, two little yellow butterflies dancing in the steam. Willa thought of Nel. How when she'd admitted her sleepless nights, Nel had given her a watercolor of a yellow butterfly and said, "This is to help you sleep and have good dreams." Willa wanted to hold them in her hands and give them to Harriet. And she was glad when they moved her way.

Willa said, "Well, Harriet. If you're having one of those dark nights of the soul … you can always call me. I'm no motivational speaker, but at least I can relate in my own way."

"Thanks," said Harriet.

And Willa felt it by the way Harriet looked at her, without flourish.

"I'd just like to know how to not be Hard Harriet. I'd like to be … *Harriet*. As far as I know … she might be very small. And quiet. And soft."

"You can be those things with us," said Jane.

Harriet smiled. "I know. But you're not in my daily life. What's it going to be like when I get back? That shadow is going to be waiting for me." She splashed the hot water on her face and dipped her head back to her forehead. "I don't know if I can beat it. I don't trust myself anymore."

"Of course you can beat it," said Jane. "You can beat anything."

Willa didn't know what to say, because she couldn't really trust herself alone either, if last winter was any indication.

"You better not off yourself, Harriet," Bliss said. "And you better learn how to get out of bed, Willa. Because if I get this baby, it's going to need all three of its godmothers." She sat up straight and serious.

"Oh, Blissful," said Harriet. "I'd be honored."

"Me too," said Willa.

Jane's smile spread over her face. "I'd love that, Bliss. I'm not *anyone's* godmother. And I would be a good one."

"Thank *you*, Jane," said Bliss, but her face went from grateful to gray. "I have a dirty secret too. Would now be the time to admit it? I've got a *really* dirty secret," she said. "And there isn't anyone alive besides you three that I'd trust with it. I'd like to tell it. I *need* to tell it. Especially given what's going on in my life right now. But you cannot tell a soul. You promise?"

All three of them held up their flat palms.

"I don't think I'm going to have an honest answer in the So Now What department if I don't admit this." Bliss floated on her back, making V's with her arms.

The women leaned against the rocks, surrounding her, giving her room.

"I had an abortion," said Bliss. "A long time ago. It was the very first time Hugh and I had sex. The first time either of us had sex with anyone. It was the summer between high school and college. My mother took me to the abortion clinic. I never told him." She floated there, gazing into the sky like it was her true confessor. "And I've never forgiven myself for it. I aborted our baby. That's what I need to forgive most of all. Not Hugh. Me." Her face was emotionless, like it had tried the whole spectrum and had exhausted it all. "I tried today. In the postcard. But like you said, Harriet, I faked it. And in no way did I make it. That's *my* shadow. That's what's chased me for the last few decades."

They were all silent, shrouded in steam and the dull smell of sulfur.

"You think you're being punished, don't you, Bliss?" asked Jane.

"Yes," said Bliss. "All of my prayers somehow have that penance in them. And no amount of penance seems to work."

Jane proceeded carefully. "But isn't forgiveness the whole point of Christianity? That's the message I've always heard."

"It's not Jesus that's the problem," said Bliss. "It's me."

Harriet swatted the water with both hands, clearly agitated. "The thing I got the most fan mail for was this very simple idea. I used to say, *If you're struggling to forgive, whether yourself or others ... then maybe stop trying ... and instead, try to love yourself.* Easier to say this to you than to myself, but maybe forgiveness is just too hard for where you are in your life. Maybe instead ... start with a little *love* for yourself. Like you were asking us to do this morning. A little tiny bit. Why don't you forget trying to forgive Hugh or yourself? Or God? And just give yourself a freaking *break*! Forget everybody else! And just start to give yourself a little love." Harriet's whole face blazed. "Maybe it'll make room for true forgiveness."

Bliss's face sank. "I may have said it this morning, but if I'm being honest, I really have no idea what you're talking about, Harriet," she said, looking so entirely alone. "When there has been wrongdoing, there can't be love without forgiveness first. It doesn't work that way."

"Of course it does!" hollered Harriet.

Willa went over and put her hand under Bliss's back, and Bliss released her weight into it so that Willa was floating her. She hoped the water would do its work because there weren't any words that could do this moment justice. She tried anyway. "It's hard not to try to fix things for the people we love, isn't it?"

"Very hard," said Jane.

"I don't want to be fixed. I just wanted to be heard. And not judged," said Bliss. "Thank you for that."

All four of them gazed up into the trees, floating, silent.

Then Bliss added, "Of course, with a baby, there's nothing to forgive."

And Willa held the silence for her too. Harriet and Jane followed suit.

Then Willa said with as much hunger as reluctance, "I have a dirty secret too. Can I share it? Just to be heard ... and not judged too."

"Please," said Bliss, letting herself stand. "Why don't I float you now?"

Willa fell back, letting her chest rise and the rest of her body float against Bliss's hand. Her ears were underwater and her voice sounded far away. "When the boys were about seven, I went through this ... *breakdown*, I guess you'd call it. I was homeschooling them, and they needed me every second, and Jack was always down at the Mercantile or working on some project for the town that we used to do together ... and I was so housebound with these little boys ... and I just couldn't take it any longer. I wanted to leave Montana and Jack and maybe even my boys. I didn't know where I wanted to go. I just felt completely claustrophobic. Like a bird in a cage in this place where everybody knew my business. I was still so young, and I felt like I'd given my life away and that I was just ... *stuck* here. I felt like I was suffocating. The whole self-reliance dream felt like a nightmare."

She let Bliss guide her around the pool, weightless and warm. "And it was no help that my parents were completely opposed to the life I'd chosen. To them, it was one thing to read about it, academically. And another thing entirely to *live* it. They felt that I was wasting my education, and as my father put it, my *life*, and so I'd pulled myself away from them and told myself that it was better that way. But I still felt their judgment. And to make it worse ... I was beginning to agree with them. But I couldn't let them know it. And of course, not Jack. So I kept it all inside."

Willa felt herself bracing, and Bliss steadied her with both hands now, floating her through the hot, healing water.

"And there was a week that spring when Jack and the boys went on an early-season fishing trip. And this man came by the Inn to stay. He was a screenwriter. From New York. He was handsome and sophisticated and complicated and exotic. And we sat up in the Inn which was strangely empty that week. He wanted to take a long pack trip into the wilderness to do research for a movie he was writing, and he wanted to look at maps. He liked his tequila and we drank a lot of it. I knew I was as exotic to him as he was to me."

Willa swallowed and let her ears rise above the water so she could hear her complete voice. "We spent the week together ... swept up in each other in every way. By the end of it, I was ready to go off with him. I honestly almost did. It was like I was crazed. Totally lost in my lust or whatever it was for this man and all that he represented. The only thing that kept me here was my mare. She colicked that last night. And he stayed up with me, rubbing her belly, tending to her, all night. And in the morning, she was fine. And I knew I had to stay. She had been my Montana teacher—other than Jack. I needed an other-than-Jack to put me back on earth as I knew it. And Sook healed, and the screenwriter left. And Jack came back with the boys. And I got to live out the best years of my life. I can't imagine there being anything better than those years."

She stood up and waded back to the rocks. "I saw the movie he made. It's an indie film that I went to see in Missoula. There's a character in it who owns a country inn. And loves a horse. And, ultimately, her family. And her Montana. Which is part of why it is crushing me to leave in this way."

They were all silent, and Willa looked into the trees and then at Jane. "So I know how you feel, Jane. And you too, Harriet. I had everything. And wanted out. But I was saved by my horse." Then she added, "That was the only time I came to Maria Hot Springs solo. I needed to take these waters to bring me back to myself. And that's why I brought us here today."

Then she looked at Harriet, hoping to drive home the case for living. "It was right here that I decided to stay. And fall back in love with my life. And life was beautiful again for a long time, and I was lucky and probably didn't deserve any of it. But I gave it everything I had. And then ... they all left. And now even Willa, Montana, has left me." Willa laughed bitterly. "So it's a fine bit of irony, really. We don't want what we have, and then it's *all* we want."

They were all silent.

Jane let out a long moan and slowly submerged herself to her chin. "Thank you for sharing that, Willa. Because if you can admit *that*, then I have to admit *this*." Her face puckered and she blew out a long puff of air. "I'm having an affair!"

"Of course you are!" said Harriet. "Good for you! It's all over your face."

"*What?*" Jane stood. "How did you know? And what do you mean, *good*, Harriet!? It's *horrible*! And I've got to stop. Or leave Palmer. And I have to decide by Sunday! And I have no idea what to do. It would ruin my kids' lives! I'd lose *everything*."

"Spill it," said Harriet. "What's his name? What's he like? Is he married? Is he golf-obsessed? Is he *you*-obsessed? Please tell me that he's *you*-obsessed."

Jane looked at Bliss. "Please don't hate me. He's married. With kids."

Bliss shook her head. "I won't." But the lines in her forehead, usually covered by her bangs, suggested otherwise.

Jane looked at the sky, her mouth melting into a satisfied grin. "Charles. Every Thursday. In the city." She dunked her head farther back and said to the sky, "It's the one time each week that I feel seen and paid attention to and *alive*. I don't know what I'd do without it. It's *how* I can be married to Palmer." She addressed them all. "And it's a *total* mess."

"I understand," said Willa. "I bet you never thought I'd be the one understanding. It's a manic feeling. And it's addictive. It took me about three months to bring myself back to earth after that. I couldn't stand my life. I was even mad at my horse for colicking. Everyone and every*thing* was in my way. I wanted that feeling again. Older love isn't the same. It doesn't have that … *craving*."

Bliss was quiet and Willa suspected she was holding back her anger at Hugh and Jane and herself and infidelity incarnate and a God that created a human race that would ever cheat on love. But instead Bliss said, "Do we ever escape all of this *wanting* in our lifetimes? Wanting. Wanting. Wanting."

"That's where all the hell lives," said Harriet, leaning back and sinking into the water.

"I'm sorry I called you a *bitch*," said Jane.

"A *crazy* bitch to be exact. I deserve it. I *am* a crazy bitch," said Harriet. "I'm sorry I made fun of you and pulled your hair."

"It was kind of funny, actually," said Jane.

"*Yeah*, it was," said Willa.

"*No*, it wasn't," said Bliss.

"I bet you let Charles see you naked," said Harriet.

"I'm like a different person with Charles," said Jane. "I did a striptease for him once." She dove underwater and came up laughing, holding her underwear, flinging it in circles in the air. "There's got to be some way for me to feel the way I feel with Charles in my normal life. There's *got* to be."

"You know," said Bliss. "I gotta say … it's so nice to just sit in our stuff *together*. And let the water support us. And no proselytizing. Thank you."

"Ditto," said Harriet.

"You sure you don't hate me, Bliss?" said Jane.

Bliss's forehead lines let go. "Jane. All of us have done something we're ashamed of. Do you hate me because you have four children and I had an abortion and now want a baby?"

"Of course not," said Jane.

Bliss added, "We can't walk around pointing the finger at everyone for our own messed-up life. We need to turn the mirror on ourselves. But kindly." She looked at Harriet and Jane. "And no more fighting, you two. I can't handle it. I need this to feel safe."

Harriet and Jane looked at each other and did an air pinkie-swear.

"I think it's healthy to get angry when we need to," said Willa. "I think we're all angry about something. And we're not supposed to admit it. Or we quickly turn it into pain. I'd just like to get angry and blow. Like you said, Jane. Like Old Faithful."

"Men do it all the time," said Harriet. "Women tamp it down. That's what my Hard Ass brand was trying to do. Get that shit *out*! Let that shit *go*!"

"What are you angry about, Willa?" asked Bliss. "Is it Jack? Or moving? Or is there more?"

Willa skimmed the water with her hand. "It's the *future*. I don't *want* to do it alone. *No* one will ever care about those boys the way Jack and I did together. We were so *strong* together. You know?"

"Yes," said Bliss. "You were."

Willa lowered herself back into the water. "And college graduation. And weddings. And grandchildren." She dipped her head back and let her tears fall into the water. "I don't *want* to do it alone."

Harriet asked, "Are you saying that you can see a future with another man in it, Willa? Because that's what I'm hearing."

Willa was startled. "No. I'm not saying that at all. I can't imagine being with another man. Bliss, do you see a man in your future?"

Bliss shook her head. "I can't imagine it either. Plus, I know everyone in town. And there's no one I'd be remotely interested in. It was always Hugh."

"Not to be crass," said Harriet, "but I'm at the age when the divorces are happening. The kids go to college and *sayonara, sweetheart*. You all have a few more years still, but get ready. You never know who might become available. Just sayin'."

Bliss and Willa stared at each other and shook their heads.

Bliss said, "Willa, you're going to make a whole new life for yourself. I am totally confident in that, my dear. I bet I get postcards from you from all over the world. Me? Return address: Wisconsin. And you know … I'm okay with that. I really am."

Willa believed her. But a new man in her future besides Jack? She couldn't begin to fathom it. She didn't want to. Instead, she arched back, arms over her head, and breathed in deeply, stretching her spine as far as she could. And then something gave way in her lower back. The pain felt like a labor contraction. "Oh. Ow. Oh. Oh. No. My back just went out."

She tried to roll to the side, but the pain was too great. She couldn't even move her neck.

Bliss swam over to Willa. "You're like a frozen claw," she said, trying to pry her open.

"No, don't!" screamed Willa. "This happens every so often. Since I broke my ribs. My back goes out. Just …" but she couldn't talk.

"Should we call 911?" asked Jane. "Could they even find us out here? Is there even cell service out here?"

"Just help me get out of the water," said Willa, breathing in shallow sips.

"How does a back go out floating in hot springs?" said Jane.

"You're not good in a crisis, are you, Jane?" grunted Harriet, trying to pull Willa up by her waist.

"This used to happen to Hugh," said Bliss, taking one of

Willa's arms. "Willa. Sweetheart. This is going to hurt, but it's the only way. Jane, you take her other arm, and, Harriet, you hold Willa's waist. On three. One … two … three."

Willa imagined her midwife whispering to her all those years ago. *Let it all go and just melt into the pain.* She let her body be hoisted out of the water, allowing the women to support her. She groaned. But she was standing.

"How are we going to get you out of here?" said Jane.

"We'll just have to go step by step. I don't know how I'm going to make it over those river crossings." Willa couldn't remember the last time she was physically dependent on anyone.

"This is going to hurt," said Bliss, drying her off with one of the towels and putting on her pants, leg by leg.

The pain was like a fireball, and she was silent while Bliss put on her shirt and jacket and then donned Willa's backpack. "Jane, you're probably the strongest. Why don't you take her right arm? Harriet, you're probably best to go on her left. I'll take up the rear just in case."

Willa's eyes begged Bliss. "I'm so sorry," she said. "I shouldn't have done that damn cartwheel."

"That's my fault," said Jane.

"It is absolutely no one's fault but my own. Please don't feel guilty."

"I do," said Jane, taking most of her weight.

"We're just going to do this one step at a time," whispered Harriet.

Slowly, Willa put one foot in front of the other, letting Jane and Harriet hold her.

"How much daylight do we have left?" said Bliss.

"Enough," said Willa. But she wasn't sure.

They were silent as they moved together. Willa fought against the urge to direct them. *Let them help you, Willa.* She was glad then that each of them had bear spray and weren't relying on her. Self-reliance. But together.

The first river crossing felt eternal. They didn't even try to step on the boulders. They just forded the water. There was no other way. "Thank God it's not deeper," said Bliss.

But it was slippery, and the current was strong enough to tug at Willa's ankles and cause her to trip. She screamed, a strange noise for her. She hadn't even screamed in childbirth.

"I need to stop," she said when they got to the other side.

"Is the movement helping at all?" said Jane. "They say it's good to move when your back goes out."

Willa shook her head.

"You poor thing," said Jane with such mothering eyes.

Willa looked at the sky. It was almost dusk. She thought of the potholes and the ride home. There was no way she could drive. But she'd worry about that later. For now, she had to keep going. The trail was hard to follow and she needed daylight to see the cairns. She saw one then, as if Jack was standing there, marking their way. But the bear had taken him. *Her* cairn now.

"Okay," she said, drawing in a deep breath. "We gotta keep going." She stepped onto the trail, accepting Jane's and Harriet's strong arms.

The women resumed their silence. The birds were making their dusk-time calls and a light breeze moved the treetops.

"Look at the moon!" said Bliss. "It's such a tiny sliver."

Willa knew that meant there would be less light soon. And the night would come on cold, especially for four women with wet hair, wet shoes, and jeans. They'd eaten the snacks. They'd drank most of the water. What had happened to her wilderness preparedness? She forced herself to make larger strides. "Ouch! Shit."

"Do you have a chiropractor who could make a house call?" said Jane. "Or a massage therapist?"

"In Willa, Montana?" said Harriet.

"Actually, we used to have both," said Willa. "No one could afford their services." She winced, willing herself up the steep embankment to the next cairn. "I'll be okay. I just need to get back home and ice it."

"One step at a time," said Harriet. "You're doing a great job."

Three more river crossings. Willa was making low moans now, exactly as she had when she'd delivered her boys. She wouldn't tell the boys about this. Or the bear. They'd think she was lost without their father. She hated that it might be true.

She stopped. "I was really strong before," she said. She closed her eyes and bit her lip against the pain. "I want you to know that."

"What do you mean, *was*?" said Harriet. "You're the ultimate Hard Ass, are you kidding me? Raising twin boys out here in the middle of nowhere? I wouldn't have made it through the first damn winter, let alone decades of this."

Willa shook with pain, like the vertebra was hitting more than a nerve. "I was good at it. Really good at it."

"We have absolutely no doubt about that, Willa," said Jane. "You're still good at it. You'll bring that with you wherever you go."

"Let's just get you home," said Bliss.

"Come on. One foot in front of the other," Jane said.

Willa bit down on her lip hard, until she tasted blood. *One foot in front of the other.* "Bliss, can I have those walking sticks? I think I can walk on my own."

Bliss passed them to her, but they weren't enough to carry her—not like the women.

"No. I need you," she said to Harriet and Jane. "We're getting closer. We just need to get down this hill and we'll be at the truck."

"I'm going to walk in front of you in case you fall," said Bliss.

"No, don't. I don't want to take you down."

"You won't." Bliss smiled and moved in front of her.

"I *never* get hurt," said Willa.

"You're human," said Harriet. "Getting hurt doesn't make you weak, Willa."

She didn't believe that one bit, and she was thankful for the fading light, so none of them could see the tears pouring down her cheeks.

The last cairn was ahead of them, marking the small trail that cut through the woods to the turnout where her truck waited. *You can do this.* But her back seized and clipped her steps in half. "I can't go any faster."

"You're doing great," said Bliss.

It took ten more minutes to go the last thirty yards.

"This is going to hurt," said Bliss, and Willa bore down as they hoisted her into the passenger seat of her truck. Bliss took the driver's seat. "That was the hard part. Now we're gonna get you through those potholes and over those washboards and back to your house, safe and sound."

"I'm sorry, everybody," said Willa.

"No *sorry*," they all said.

The potholes were excruciating, blast after blast of fiery pain burning through her body. Willa fell into a trance, letting the pain have its own conversation with her body. She looked out the window and stared at her world, from treetops to wide skies to open meadow to home. The pain even washed over the signs on every mile marker: PLEASE DON'T BUY OUR TOWN. PLEASE DON'T BUY OUR TOWN. And at the last one, just before the turn to her house, she had a moment when she couldn't have agreed with them more.

Propped up on ice packs, all Willa could think about was how glad she was to have made it to her bed. What the women couldn't have known is that she'd been sleeping on Jack's side ever since he'd died, and they'd put her back on hers.

"I'm just so glad you weren't alone this time!" said Jane, and then put her hand to her mouth. "Sorry. I didn't mean that to sound callous. I should just keep my mouth shut. Harriet's right. I'm worthless in a crisis. When things happen in our house, we call in reinforcements."

"Don't worry," said Willa. "We all have our gifts. You've given birth to four children!"

"Well, if you call a scheduled C-section *birth*, then okay. I was too chicken to do it the other way."

Bliss came in with ibuprofen. "Take four of these. I know that's a lot, but it'll do the trick."

"Four? I'm not much of a pill taker," said Willa.

"Just do it. We need our fearless leader up and moving."

"Maybe this is exactly what you need," said a low-glowing Harriet, so different from the woman who had fire-balled through Willa's door just days ago. "To be taken care of."

"You do realize that you're a fucking remarkable woman," said Willa.

"Because I hide in a beach shack and insult Jane and show you my thong and get you an ice pack?" balked Harriet.

"Exactly that," said Willa. "And that you want to be soft."

Tears filled Harriet's eyes and she turned away.

"I want to show you all something," said Willa. "There's a box of photos under the bed. I want to show you one of them in particular."

Harriet produced the box and set it on Willa's lap.

Willa found the photo and held it up to them. "This is my favorite photo. This is the four of us on the lawn where we were doing cartwheels today. Those are my little boys holding baskets of apples from our harvest. That's Jack holding the handle of his antique apple press. And that's me, of course, leaning my head on his shoulder."

The women peered at it, smiling.

"Look how young we were." She put down the photo and stared at the ceiling. "Do you mind if I tell you more? About this life I've led here? I feel like I need to tell *its* story, not just mine, in order to leave it."

"Please!" said Jane. "I could listen to you tell stories all day."

"Thank you. I need to do this. Maybe the only way I will is to be laid up with you three. Why don't you all sit down?"

Jane perched on the edge of the bed, hugging a pillow to her lap.

Harriet nestled into the window seat, her red hair lit by lamplight.

Bliss said, "I wouldn't mind stretching out. If I'm very careful, is that okay?"

Willa nodded gently, holding her breath as her friend took her husband's place in her bed. She looked at Bliss and used her sweet face as her guide. "What the photo doesn't show are the dozens of people—the whole town really—gathered around folding tables all over the yard, funneling fresh-made cider into jugs, a table of potluck dishes, a keg of Jack's local microbrew, bees buzzing on the pile of spent apples next to the barn, everybody toasting to the harvest. And then we'd take the too-big zucchini and the bad apples, and we'd spend the afternoon playing Zucchini Baseball. The zucchini were the bats. Apples were the balls. We mowed out a baseball diamond in the meadow. We played until dark. And then we all came back to the orchard and sat at tables made out of old doors or plywood slabs on top of sawhorses with pretty tablecloths over them, and Mason jars full of flowers, and white lights in the trees. And the band would play and we'd all sing and dance. It was heaven, and everyone looked forward to it all year long."

"I want to create a life like that," said Jane, hugging the pillow closer. "More please."

Willa smiled sadly. "Well, let's see … and then there was Salsa Day. We'd set up those same makeshift tables and everybody would come with a knife and a cutting board and that's all. There was a garlic table. A tomato table. An onion table. A pepper table. And a cilantro table. All from our garden which became the community garden, really, in those years before other people got the bug and started their own gardens. People would come, and Jack's band would play, and we'd go at it all day until we had mounds of chopped veggies. And then I would man the canning area with big pots of boiling water and Mason jars and ladles, and everyone would go home with canned salsa for the winter, and fresh cut salsa too." She closed her eyes and imagined herself canning and listening to Grin and Bear It. "It was a love story, this place."

"Like something out of a movie," said Jane.

It really was, thought Willa. What would it take for her to feel that way again? Where would she ever find that sort of belonging again in this life? It seemed impossible.

"Maybe getting hurt was a blessing in disguise," said Jane. "It got you to tell us the story of this place. Tell us more."

"The drugs should kick in pretty soon. Keep talking," said Harriet.

Willa looked at the photo again and then up at the window and the black outline of Bison Butte. "We had jobs, you know. Jack had his. I had mine." She looked back into the eyes of the woman in the photo, so happy and confident. "We did what came naturally to us. For me, that was to nurture and nourish, to clean and arrange, to garden and teach, to stage parties and activities and see them through."

"No wonder they're all so devastated that you're leaving," said Jane.

"Now I have all the jobs," Willa said, looking into her thirty-year-old eyes again. "Even if I wasn't broke, this place is too much for one person to handle."

Jane said, "I feel like this town is full of some of the most capable people I can imagine. Can't they help you? Do you really have to leave?"

Willa winced and Bliss helped her put a pillow under her shoulder. "Jane, I can't pay them. And I can't ask them to do it for free. And you can only barter for so much. They need someone else. And I need to get out of here. I can't go through another winter like this one, holed up in this house, alone. I was miserable. There are too many ghosts here." She pointed to the migration atlas on the bedside table next to Bliss. "Go to the index and find the Calliope hummingbird, would you, Bliss?"

"The one who migrates alone," murmured Jane. "In the jewelry box."

Bliss flipped through the atlas's pages. "It looks like it goes to Costa Rica in the winter. Or Belize. And then makes its way back up to Arizona and New Mexico. And along the Rocky Mountain front, to Montana. Pretty good life!"

"Yeah. Alone. The smallest bird. They're here. I saw one last night. Right now, they're making their nests out of moss and horsehair and twigs and bark, and then they spin it all together with spiderweb thread. And then they'll lay their eggs, have their babies, and head back south. One by one. If I could do whatever I wanted to do with my life right now … I think I'd follow their migration. Just to get myself moving again. And clear my head."

"You'd follow an *actual bird*?" said Harriet.

"No. That would be impossible. Just their approximate migration pattern and timing. And when I got to Central America,

I'd try every day to find one. They're hard to find and it would keep my mind focused and still."

"Talk about *mindfulness*. I love it. You could put up rows of feeders all along the way," said Jane, hugging the pillow.

"I think I'd rather go where they go. Following flowers," said Willa. The medicine was beginning to take effect and she let her neck soften.

"That's so romantic," said Jane. "I would love to do that. There's a Relais & Châteaux property in a jungle in Costa Rica that I've been trying to get Palmer to go to. But he's not into birds. And there's no golf course. Maybe I could meet you there and host a weekend. Maybe we could *all* meet there! My treat!"

"Ooo—I'd do that!" said Harriet. "I could split it with you!"

"I'm not sure I could leave Mother," said Bliss. "And I could never accept a gift like that."

"It's just a pipe dream," said Willa. "I can't really go through with it. The boys need stability. They can't have their mother taking off on them when they're only nineteen. Especially after their father has just died. And even if I could do it … I'd have to do it alone. But thank you, Jane and Harriet. You are too generous." Willa looked at Bliss, lying on Jack's side of the bed. "I'm so confused, Bliss. Am I making a mistake to leave here? Am I just running away? Is there some way to make it work here?"

They were silent.

Willa said, "Jack used to say, *When I kill a bird and eat it, I become that bird.* What does that even mean? He was always saying things like that. Can't you become the bird without killing it? Do I have to kill my Montana to move on?"

Harriet looked down over the orchard, as if she might find the answer in the dark.

Bliss put out her hand and held Willa's arm.

"I just have to get through Sunday and then I'll know more."

Her back went into spasm and she sucked air through her teeth. "God, this hurts like shit."

"Let's just focus on what we can control right now," said Bliss. "And that's getting you better. What's something that we can help you with right now?"

As much as Willa didn't want to say these words, she did anyway. "The closet. Jack's Cave. His stuff." And she pointed with her chin across the room.

Bliss groaned. "You haven't done it yet, darlin'?"

"No," Willa said. "I lied. I didn't want you all to take on my dirty work."

"I get it. I literally *just* went through this. When we got back from France, Hugh's stuff was still in the house. I finally told him that either he come over and clear it out, or I was going to have it all removed. I gave him a Sunday and I took Mother to Madison for lunch and shopping."

Willa tried to move onto her side, pain slicing through her lower back. She looked at her friend. "I'm so sorry, Bliss. All you did was raise that man up. You may have wanted those babies with all your heart, but you loved him and he knew it and he shouldn't have given up on you. He loved you too. I saw it in his eyes."

Bliss said, "What really flattened me was that when I came back from Madison, he'd still left a bunch of things. Like he was peeing on his once territory. I've tried to get rid of them but I don't have the guts. I still need them. I'm waiting for a day when I don't need them anymore."

"I've told myself the same thing. But do we?" asked Willa. "Do we *really* need them?" A bolt of pain shot up her spine. She winced, closed her eyes, and breathed through it.

"I love cleaning things out. I'm like a tornado," said Jane. "Closets are my specialty." She opened Jack's closet. "I can have us through this in an hour if you'll let me boss you all around. Not you, Willa. You read your bird book and let us go for it."

And just as Harriet opened her mouth, Willa stepped in. "You're absolutely right, Jane. Absolutely right. That closet has become a monster in my bedroom. I can't keep holding on to his stuff. I just need to give it all away. I would love your help more than anything right now, Jane." She wanted to take the words back the instant they came out of her mouth, but she knew this was the next step.

"Well, if you're broke, you could sell it all on eBay," insisted Harriet. "I'm a whiz at it. I got rid of my stuff that way, because frankly I had no idea if I'd ever make another dime again. It was the most freeing thing I've ever done! I could set you up an account tonight!"

"No. No, thank you," said Willa. "I want to give it all to Willa, Montana. It's the least I can do. And I want parts of Jack to live on here. I'd like to take it to the Merc and put out a sign that says FREE STUFF."

"And what they don't want, we'll pack up and drive over to Great Falls on our way out of town on Sunday, and give to the Salvation Army," said Bliss. "So you don't have to."

"What about the barn?" asked Jane. "Is it all packed up?"

"Thank God, I gave most of that away. But there's stuff in there too. Like the projector that we used for movie night all summer long."

"You had a movie night too?" said Jane. "I want *that* story!"

"Me too," said Harriet.

Willa knew what they were doing—they were teaching her to lullaby herself with her indelible memories, so she could do it anywhere and anytime. She took it as a gift. No point in resisting it. "It was my idea because I was starved for culture. It was so sweet. We'd show the movies up against the side of the barn on a huge screen I sewed together from sheets. And I'd make popcorn in the old-fashioned popcorn maker. And everyone would sit in the yard and watch. The people from town, our visitors, and people from all over the county."

She tightened her jaw. "You can give away the popcorn maker too. It's in the barn, in the tack room. And the apple press. But just not my saddle. Jack gave it to me as a wedding present. He bought it in Sheridan, Wyoming. It's gorgeous. I can't even look at it. I gave Nel my other saddle and tack. But not my King."

"We'll put all the things you want to keep in the tack room," said Bliss. "And then all you'll have to do is load it up from there. You won't even have to come back into the house."

"They say not to see it empty," said Jane.

"I think I'm going to sell it furnished. I'll just take the rockers and a few other things. I can't deal with it all."

"You really are brave," said Jane. "I could never do that."

"Never say never," said Harriet.

"I'm not brave. I'm scared shitless." Willa looked at each of them. "Before we do this, I'd just like for us ..."

"Say it, sweetheart," said Bliss, putting a hand on her shoulder.

"This is going to sound so ... Oh hell." Willa's voice split with tears. "Would you all just sit in bed with me? For a bit? Before we take it all apart."

Harriet moved toward Willa's bedside. "But even if we sit down gently, isn't it going to hurt?" she asked.

"It's the kind of pain I can handle," said Willa. "Please. I've missed having people in my bed. The boys used to come in on weekend mornings and they'd roll all over the place and we'd tickle them and hug them and laugh and laugh. Plus, I feel like we weren't quite done with our conversation in the hot springs. My back overshadowed it. We were telling each other dirty secrets."

"And not having to fix anything. I loved that part the most," said Harriet, stretching out on the bed.

Seated at Bliss's feet, Jane said, "Interesting way to put it: the kind of pain you can handle." Then she lay across the end of the bed and peered over the folds of the comforter and said, "Can I tell a quick story?"

"Please," said Willa.

Jane smiled, but not happily. "Well, I told you that I see a therapist. And she had me take a Rorschach test. Do you know what that is?"

"The ink blot test," said Harriet. "I believe in those. A lot of my psychologist friends use them."

"Well, they're all these images on cards, and they're like abstract art, so I liked this exercise. She passes a card to you and you have to say what you see. And you know I was an art history major, and I love nonrepresentational art, so I thought, *Oh I'm going to do really* well *at this. I'm going to come off really* smart *and deep and* secure *and just knock this out of the* park. So I really dug into each card and told her what I saw." Jane stretched closer to the center of the bed so Willa could see the spokes of blue in her eyes.

"Ready for this? The next week she showed me the results. She had this really serious look on her face. It turns out that I tested incredibly high on *coping mechanism*, but just as high on *pain*, so that on paper, if you just looked at the pain piece, she said that any professional in her field would ask, *Is this woman hospitalized?* But because of my off-the-charts coping abilities, she said it's like I've masked the pain so artfully that no one, not even me, can see it. It really rattled me." She put her cheek on the comforter and closed her eyes. *"Hospitalized!"*

"That doesn't surprise me about you," said Harriet. "I'm glad you took that test."

With her eyes still closed, Jane said, "I haven't told her about Charles. I'm afraid she'll take him away from me."

Harriet let out a large "Hah!"

"What? Don't judge," said Jane. She brought her knees up to her chest. "When I'm with Charles, I don't even think about my children. Or my life with Palmer. It's like that life doesn't exist. And I could walk out of that hotel room with my camera around my neck and be twenty again. And not need anyone in the world. And not have anyone in the world need me."

"Do you love him?" asked Bliss.

"Do I *love* him?" echoed Jane. "I don't know. I think I love *me* when I'm with him. I'm not waiting for someone to fill my cup with one little drop of *Thanks, Mom*, or *Perfectly done lamb chops, dear*, or *Looking lovely tonight, Jane*, or *Great job with the benefit, Mrs. Bradford*. Why do I base my whole life on those little drops? With Charles, my hands aren't cupped, waiting for them like they're my only nourishment. I just get what I want."

She rolled onto her side and stroked the comforter. "It's horrible. I know. And I don't really care. He's the same way. We just get what we want from each other. From the second we lay eyes on each other at the restaurant where we're meeting, to the art galleries, to the hotel, to the bed." She let out a long throaty sigh.

Willa looked at Bliss to see if she was struggling, but Bliss had her head cocked in curiosity, not judgment. "Sounds like you're in a place of *receiving* with Charles. Not always *giving*," said Bliss.

"That's another thing my therapist said. *Do you know how to receive without giving?* I honestly couldn't give her one good example. Receiving seems so *selfish* to me."

"That's the trick, isn't it," said Harriet. "Receiving without feeling selfish." She gave Jane a gamey grin. "I bet you don't feel selfish in bed, *receiving* from Charles."

Jane sighed. "Not in the least. I feel happy. It's like we're in a different world altogether where all the rules are different."

"Well then," said Bliss. "Maybe that's what Hugh is getting from this woman. Maybe he doesn't feel like he can give me what I want.

Since all I seem to want is a child. Maybe this other woman wants him … just for him."

And Willa thought, *Empathy for Hugh's mistress. Talk about walking the walk.*

Jane picked at her cuticles. "Well, maybe we should change the subject. I mean, let's be clear—what I'm doing is wrong and I know it. How screwed up that I can't find this in my own marriage."

"You're not getting out of it that easy," flared Harriet. "Just put morals aside for a moment and look at it for what it is. You are taking an active stand for yourself. An active, risky stand. And you're getting what you *want*. Expressing yourself the way you *want*. Just for *you*. And whether it's right or wrong, you need to look at that cold hard fact *precisely* so that you can bring it into your normal life. You deserve to have a life that you want, Jane."

Willa had forgotten her back pain and was thinking about what they'd said in the hot springs, about other men in her life. "What if we could feel that way all the time? Just freely give ourselves what we want. No shame."

"I keep waiting for that feeling," said Harriet. "You'd think that Big Sur would do it. But you have to know what you want. And it requires a playfulness. Jane, I bet those Art Hop Thursdays are full of playfulness. I don't think I ever learned to *play* as a child. The way a child does. Just doing what she wants. Not for the parents or the other kids or the teacher."

"Oh, I did," said Bliss. "And it was all because of my mother. She had a whole fantasy world that she served up for me. She insisted that the world was fluttering with fairies who only came out at night, and we'd make mud pies for them out of pine needles and dandelions and little stones and whatever we could find, and we'd put them out on the front stoop at night. They were always gone in the morning. I hope that before her mind is totally gone, she'll see fairies. Maybe I'll make mud pies with her when I get home." Bliss closed her eyes, and Willa could see tears in the corners of them.

Jane said, "My mother would have *never* done that with me. She didn't believe in imagination. I had a china animal collection that I loved, a whole imaginary world I used to play with in the garden. I wasn't supposed to actually *play* with them. They were too breakable. But I did anyway. Clandestinely. And I came back from boarding school for Christmas one year, and my bedroom had been turned into a guest room. All my china animals, everything—gone. I never asked where she put my things. I didn't want to hear that she'd given it all away to the needy. She was always giving our things to the needy."

"That's just horrible," said Bliss. "She should have asked you. That makes me want to hug you. Willa, would it hurt your back if I gave Jane a hug?"

"I don't care if it does," said Willa, watching Bliss give Jane the most motherly hug and then resting back on Jack's pillow.

Willa thought about her own mother. Alone in her book-thick apartment in Chicago. She really should call her and tell her that she was selling Willa, Montana. She hadn't wanted to hear the sigh of victory in her voice. She wondered then … had she been allowed to play? Or had she always been charged with vicarious playing, a book being placed firmly into her hands—someone else's story. Other little girls in faraway places.

"This is really beautiful, all of us lying here together," said Bliss. "I'm just sorry it took Willa hurting herself to get here. Women need this. Little girls do this. But then we have to go and grow up."

"Growing up sucks," said Willa, so happy to have them in her bed even if her back was knifing with pain.

Harriet stood like she was being called for showtime. "Let's do this thing. You ready, Willa?"

"No. But …" Willa nodded. "Yes. Please. Just take it all out of here. Load up the truck. There're big garbage bags in the garage.

And a bunch of half-packed boxes in the room down the hall—the one with the shut door. Bring it down to the Merc. Let them have it all." Willa gasped back tears. And then she wondered if maybe Jack had left some money in the closet. She hadn't thought of that. He'd always stayed away from the closet for his stashes. "Too obvious."

She wasn't sure how to say it, so she just said it. "Sometimes … Jack left money around. In odd places. So before you throw it all out … just make sure. Grandson of a homesteader and all that."

"Ooo—I love scavenger hunts," said Harriet.

Jane reached out her hand to touch her fingertips. "Willa. Are you sure? Are you sure you're not still in shock? Do you really want to do all of this? I mean, I could probably figure out a way to help you keep the house for a while. It would be my pleasure."

Willa's entire self hurt. Letting the tears flow, she said, "Thank you, Jane. But there really isn't anything here for me. The dream is over. Everything I wanted … I can't have anymore. I love this place. And its people. Everywhere I look, I see a memory of my family and town, so stitched together. And now it's all ripped apart and I can't imagine it being mended. It's over."

The women looked at her and she looked at each of them, good and hard.

"Okay, then," said Harriet. "Let's do this."

"I'll get garbage bags," said Bliss, rising from the bed carefully.

"Just leave the first floor the way it is." Willa thought of the twin Emerson books. "And if you find two *Self-Reliance* books, they're really special to me. They're identical and antique with this quote on the cover: *The love you give away is the only love you keep.* I somehow misplaced them, ironically trying to keep them safe, during a rough night this winter."

"Oh no! The books you were reading when you met on the train?" said Jane, frowning like she was going to cry. "That's horrible!"

"Where could they be?" asked Bliss.

"We are *totally* finding those books," said Harriet.

"Well," sighed Willa. "If you don't, you don't. I've looked everywhere. I was always going to give one to each son."

Willa opened the migration book and let it lie flat on her lap, looking instead into the stars, while the women pulled apart Jack's closet, shirt by shirt, coat by coat, like they were unraveling what was left of her husband.

Something deeply fond entered her periphery. "Not that one!" she shrieked, and her back sent shock waves through her ribs. "That's what he wore on our wedding day."

"He wore a checkered flannel shirt on your wedding day?" asked Jane. "How sweet."

"We got married on our horses. I wore his mother's dress, hiked up to my waist with jeans and boots underneath it. He had a purple aster in his buttonhole. A friend rode out with us, married us by a river, and then rode back and left us for a week in total wilderness. We were young and inexperienced, and I didn't have enough warm clothes. He didn't either. I wore that shirt at night when I was cold. He always was willing to suffer to keep me warm. And safe. And happy." Willa looked up at each of them. "Okay. Take the shirt." She pressed her lips tight to keep from crying.

"You sure you don't want to keep it for the boys?" asked Jane, with tears in her eyes.

"They took what they wanted," said Willa. "Let me just smell it."

Jane passed it to her and Willa held it to her nose, smelling pipe smoke and wood smoke and maybe gunshot. She pulled it close and wrapped it around her neck like a shawl. "I can't. I'm keeping it."

"Come on. Let's get this done. Quick like a Band-Aid," said Harriet, with tears in her eyes.

One by one, the piles grew. Whenever Willa got the guts to turn her head toward the closet, she saw more wall than clothes.

"What about this hat?" asked Bliss gently. "I remember him wearing this hat."

"It was his father's felt fedora. Save that. He saved it, so I should too. He worshipped his father. Put it in the boys' room on the bureau."

Finally, the closet was empty, the piles of clothes in their respective bags, and Jane said, "You can look now, Willa," as if she hadn't been watching all along.

"And we didn't find one dime," said Harriet.

"I didn't think you would," said Willa.

She dared to take a good long look. "Huh," she said. "It's just a closet. A closet in a house. Thank you. All of you. Now get those bags out of here before I dump them out and put everything back."

The women took the bags out to the hallway while Willa stared out the window. "Don't forget the Cave. And the barn. But not the saddle. And don't let me see anything. Please." She sobbed then and held his shirt to her chest, her back aching with every convulsion. "I'm so sorry, Jack," she whispered. Any anger she'd felt went out the door in garbage bags.

Willa must have dozed off because when she woke, the sliver of the moon was peeking through the window, and Harriet, Bliss, and Jane were standing by her bed. She realized she'd done nothing for dinner and tried to sit up but her back stabbed with pain.

"You can't move, remember?" said Harriet.

Bliss said, "I think sometimes our bodies give out so things can change in our world."

"Maybe," said Willa. "Are you all done?"

"The truck's all loaded," said Jane.

Willa said, "The Merc is closed at this hour. Bring it all to the Saloon. Tell them to take what they want. Tell them you'll bring the rest to the Salvation Army in Great Falls on Sunday. Tell them it's my olive branch." She put her hand out to Jane, who took it. "Just ... thank you."

Harriet put her hand on Willa's forehead. "You're very brave, you know."

"I don't feel brave. At all," said Willa, fading. "I'm sorry. I don't think I can make soup. And it was going to be my favorite tonight—white bean and elk meatballs."

She closed her eyes, and as she fell asleep she heard Bliss saying, "You rest now, Willa. We can take care of ourselves."

Willa mumbled, "Tell them I'm ill, otherwise I'd do it myself. But don't tell them that I hurt my back. That's no excuse around here. And tell Nel to come by on Sook. I want one more ride. When my back gets better."

Half in a dream, she heard one of them say, "She needs this town to know."

She tried to scream at them, *No!* But no matter how hard she tried, she couldn't. She was too far away. In a small house with a red door, somewhere new.

Day Five

Willa woke, not sure why her skin felt so smooth against her sheets. Then she remembered the hot springs. And then she remembered her back. She moved one hip a few inches. Then the other. No pain. She rolled over and let her body slide off the bed, feet on the floor, hands on her nightstand. Still no pain. Just stiffness. She stretched herself vertical, swayed from side to side. Somehow her back had corrected itself in the night, as if it knew she needed to be rendered immobile to finally shed Jack's things. But now it needed her to move. The auction was tomorrow.

She put on her robe and went down to the kitchen. The women were in the keeping room, talking and having coffee. Willa stood outside the doorway, not wanting to break their conversation.

"Maybe we could get the *Times* to write another article about this place," Jane was saying. "I think Charles knows someone in the Travel section."

"I think she just needs to move on and cut her losses," said Bliss. "Heartbreaking as it is. I'll miss this place. I've been my best self here over the years. I *know* myself here. I *trust* myself here."

"I think there's nothing like this place on *earth*," said Harriet. "It's gotten under my skin. And *nothing* gets under my skin. It's going to be like another death to her. She keeps saying she has to do everything alone. And believe me … I can relate. But do you think it's good for her to be alone? I think she should come live with me for a while. I could probably use the company too. The beast, even tamed, is a shitty roommate."

Bliss said, "I trust her instincts. If she says she needs to do this alone, I believe her."

Jane said, "Let's just not do *anything* hard today. Let's just have the most *beautiful* day together we can *possibly* have. And that will be the *best* send-off we can give her, even if no one comes to the party tomorrow. Especially after last night."

"*Especially* after last night," said Bliss.

Jane said, "We'll make soup and pie and bread today in good faith. And whatever we don't use, we'll freeze and donate to the town in Willa's name."

"So many olive branches," said Bliss.

Jane said, "I still wish she'd kept the best items to sell somewhere where people will pay top dollar. She needs the money."

"Not if this place sells the way so much of the West is selling these days. Montana is hot," said Harriet. "And she said the auction company has been advertising it all over. So it could be big."

"I wish she'd let us give her some help," said Jane. "I mean, Harriet, between you and me, we could probably help her get her start. Or help with the boys. Or just *some*thing."

"She wouldn't accept it. I can tell you that right now," said Bliss.

Willa couldn't take it any longer and rounded the corner.

"Willa!" swooned Jane. "You're standing!"

"I am. Sometimes it just goes out, and then back in, no

explanation. Thank God it did! Man, was that rough. Thank you so much for taking such good care of me. How did it go down at the Saloon last night?"

The women eyed each other.

"What?" asked Willa, pouring herself some coffee. Harriet was in Jack's chair, so she took another rocker. "What did you do?"

Harriet rocked, but with suspicious eyes. "Just like you said. We dropped it all off at the Saloon."

Bliss rocked. "We told them we'd take what they didn't want to Great Falls on Sunday."

"We got to talk to Nel. She's lovely," said Jane, rocking.

"We gave her the message about stopping by," said Bliss.

"Really?" Willa lit from within. "Was Marilyn there?"

"The alpha dog from the other night?" asked Harriet.

"Yeah. Nel's grandmother. The one who won't even look me in the eye."

"I think she was there with another older woman," said Bliss. "Both of them were sitting at the gaming machines. Shoulder-length gray hair?"

"Was she wearing a turtleneck?"

"She was, actually," said Jane.

"She's the one I'm most worried about. If this town was incorporated and we had a mayor, it would have of course been Jack. But Marilyn would have taken his place."

"Not *you*?" said Harriet.

"No way. The Inn is my gig. I'm the last one to be political. That's been the beauty of what we created—we all know our strengths. Like I said the other day, there's never really been an us versus them."

They all sipped their coffee.

Willa couldn't help herself. "What did Marilyn say? She's the person you least want to piss off in this town."

"She was definitely all about Jack. Like he was a knight in shining armor," said Jane.

"Listen!" Harriet clapped her hands. "Let's not bother away our last day together. We have a plan, Ms. Willa. We want you to teach us how to make your pie. And your bread. And your soup. And we want to make lots of it for the party."

Bliss added, "We were going to prop you up in a makeshift daybed and have you direct us. And we still can if you need to stay off your feet."

"I'm okay. That's very sweet, though. I'd love to teach you how to make those things, but I'd hate it to go to waste. What if it's just us at the party?" said Willa.

"Then we'll eat it all ourselves." Harriet smiled.

"Well, I guess we can drop it off at the Merc for them to sell," said Willa. "And I do need to use up the last of my rhubarb and strawberries." A warmth surged in her. "Frankly, there's nothing I'd rather do with this day than fill up my kitchen with you all and those old familiar smells."

"Oh goodie," said Jane. "I really want to learn to dry the morels and bring them back home to have a little griz in my cupboard the next time I want to look fear in the face." She was pink with excitement. "And I want to learn how to make the arnica salve too."

Willa directed the women to various ends of the house for ingredients, from pantry to root cellar, until the kitchen table was covered. Then she put on her MONTANA MAMA apron and took the stage where she'd been the star for years.

They started with the white bean soup. "This was Maria's that she passed down from her family in Tuscany. She taught it to Jack's father, who taught it to Jack, and he taught it to our boys and to me. I'm sure it's taken some variations along the way. I like to add elk meatballs in mine. It's my very favorite meat and not gamey."

Before long, Jane was chopping onions and garlic, and

Harriet was defrosting the ground elk meat in a plastic bag in a water bath. Bliss was chopping carrots and celery, and Willa was in her garden, harvesting more of the tenacious sage. She looked at Bison Butte, imagining Sook and Nel galloping around the bend, hoping that her gesture had been enough to bring Nel by for one more ride. She stopped for a moment to see if the Calliope might show itself. She needed every sign possible to get through this farewell. No Nel. No Calliope.

When she came back into the kitchen, Willa asked a shy, "What did they say to all of Jack's things? Did they seem at all grateful? Or curious? Did they say *anything*?"

"I think they were stunned," said Bliss.

"I'll bet they were," said Willa.

"I smelled guilt in that bar," said Harriet. "I know that wasn't your intention. But for what it's worth. The other day I smelled *fear*. And last night ... guilt."

"I don't want that for them," said Willa, taking the great northern beans from the boxes they'd stored them in last year. "These beans are the descendants of the originals that came from Vermont. They're the closest to the cannellini beans Maria's family would have used in Italy. There are all sorts of myths about how to cook dried beans—to soak or not to soak, to salt or not to salt, lid on, lid off. Here's the very best way to do it, and I have an Italian grandmother-in-law to thank for it."

"Wow," said Jane. "You grow and dry your own beans?"

"It's easy. You just leave them in the husk and they dry themselves and then you pop them out. My boys used to love to do that chore."

"I'll say it again: Can I be you when I grow up?" asked Jane.

Willa offered a weak smile. "I'll be a bean buyer just like most people, soon enough," she said. "The trick is to bring it to a slow boil, with a sprig of sage, garlic, and some salt, partially covered by the lid. Once the beans are tender, you can use the water for the soup. It takes a long time. Even with beans dried from your garden. *Pazienza*, was Maria's word."

She smiled as she put the beans on the stove and added the sage, thinking of Jack teaching her this very thing, how his eyes lit up when he spoke of his grandmother.

"Patience," said Jane. "Not my skill set."

Willa smiled at her and checked on the progress of the chopped vegetables. "We need about three more onions, Jane. And, Harriet, about ten more carrots. Bliss, one more stalk of celery. I think we'll make four big pots."

She went over to the warmest spot in her kitchen, atop the small shelf where she kept her spices, and reached for the one thing that she had not neglected all winter: her wild yeast.

"I have been feeding this old friend for years, twice a day. I learned this from Jack's mother who used to love to come visit when she was young and the boys were babies. I'm glad she didn't outlive her son. It would have completely crushed her."

"Oh ... oh ... oh." Jane's face was red and tears were running down her face. "I need to take a break from the onions."

"Phew," said Harriet. "Let's have this be a *fun* day. No more frigging tears!"

"I'll chop them," said Bliss. "I have an understanding with onions. They rarely make me cry." She giggled. "Willa has an understanding with deer. And then there's me and my onions."

"I'd love to learn how to make bread," said Jane. "I'd like to be the sort of mother who makes bread. But do I have to make my own yeast?"

"It's not hard at all. You just have to be willing to feed it and watch it like a hawk."

Jane looked at her sideways.

Harriet said, "Or you can buy dry yeast at the store, Jane.

No more trying to be perfect in absolutely everything you do. It's just bread."

"It's just bread. I'm just making bread. Got it," said Jane, throwing down her hands like a conductor. "I'm good at following directions."

Willa showed Jane how to marry the dry ingredients with the yeast, water, and oil, and how to knead it, but not too much. And how to set it in a bowl with a cotton cloth over it to rise. "Who wants to learn how to make meatballs?"

"Me," said Jane.

"Me too," said Harriet.

"You showed me a long time ago," said Bliss. "I'll finish up the veggies."

Willa laid the ground elk meat out on the counter. "This is lean meat. We need fat." She got a block of cheese from the refrigerator. "This is my *dirtiest* secret. We send away for Parmigiano Reggiano in the mail. This is the last of it." Willa unwrapped it and smelled it. "Who wants to grate?"

"I will," said Harriet.

Willa walked them through chopping the onion and parsley, mixing the eggs and cheese into the meat with a gentle hand, then adding the bread crumbs and the salt and pepper.

"I'd love to have these recipes," said Jane.

"I don't really have recipes," said Willa, pointing to her head. "It's all in here. It's a *feel* thing."

"Her boys always say that Willa's food is *made with love*," said Bliss.

Willa smiled, thinking about her boys, so happy in college, with new friends and city stories. They spoke on Sundays, but she'd have to skip this week. They'd wanted to be there for the auction, but she'd told them the flights were too expensive. Sooner or later she was going to have to tell them why. She started to feel that fretting grip around her neck. *What if they lost their scholarships somehow? They'd have to drop out. Their personal accounts didn't have anywhere near what it would take to put them through college. How could Jack have been so careless or generous or whatever he was? Delusional?* She thought of the empty closet and tried to empty her anger too.

"Willa, wherever you've gone, come back," said Bliss. "We're making meatballs."

Willa shook the thoughts away and smiled. "Ned and Sam both make excellent meatballs." Then she showed them how to roll three small meatballs at a time in each hand, laying them out on parchment-lined cookie sheets.

Jane tried it and so did Harriet.

Harriet made snakes instead of balls, smooshed them back together, tried again, failed, and gave up.

"You were the kid who put all the different colors of Play-Doh in one container at the end, weren't you, Harry?" asked Jane.

Harriet smirked. "Of course. Who had time to separate the colors? Plus it was much more interesting that way."

"Bliss, was Harriet just a total hellion as a kid?" said Jane, rolling three meatballs in one hand.

Bliss winked. "A *heavenly* hellion."

Harriet kissed Bliss on the cheek.

"You're a natural, Jane. It took me years to learn how to do that," said Willa, washing her hands, checking the temperature of the oven, checking on the slow simmer of the beans.

"You actually *love* doing this, don't you, Willa?" asked Jane. "It's no chore at *all* for you, is it?"

Willa just smiled.

"Maybe you should start a little restaurant of your own somewhere," said Harriet.

"Maybe," said Willa. "Let's get to the pie. The soup will be last, once the beans are cooked," she said, putting the meatballs in the oven. She turned to Jane. "Okay. Pie."

"Can I punch the bread dough yet?" asked Jane.

"See if it's doubled in size. Probably not yet."

"I'd like to learn how to make the pie too," said Harriet.

Willa cleaned off the counters and felt like she was running her hands over the skin of someone she loved.

Jane said, "I'm totally overwhelmed. How can you do this without recipes? And all at the same time?"

"Practice," said Willa, getting out her baking flour. "And patience."

"Like I said, I have never been patient," said Jane. "It's been practically impossible doing some of the things we've done this week. But I know it's been good for me. I'm trying. I really am."

"I know you are," said Willa. "Let's face it—we don't do anything unless there's a payoff. And cooking food from scratch and feeding it to people you love is an excellent payoff. You'll start to love it, if you give it a good try." Grief knocked and she forced it to stay on the other side.

"Do you know what I love about this?" asked Bliss. "Since the second we got into this kitchen, we haven't talked about anything deep or difficult. We're just making things together. Women used to do that. They gathered together day after day and helped each other with the mundane acts of life. And they talked. They didn't need a weeklong interlude to get it all out."

"We're like pressure cookers," said Harriet, sweeping the floor. "No wonder there's so much breast cancer and heart disease."

"This week has definitely been an explosion," said Jane. "By suburban Connecticut standards, it's been positively *nuclear*." She smiled, not at all demure. "But I didn't go Yellowstone. I just went … true. So far."

Harriet said, "*Brava*, Janey. *Brava*."

Bliss stood over the stove holding a wooden spoon in the air. "We need to change that, I think. I've often thought how much I'd just love for you to come over, Willa, and cook with me. Or how much I'd love to have a weekly trade-off with you—one week you come to my house and we do my laundry. And then the next, I come do yours. Or the same with cleaning the kitchen. Or tending the garden. The women in my prayer group would never do that. We save our pain for each other. I don't think they'd do pain and *dishes*."

"I'm telling you," said Harriet, leaning on the broom like it was a mic stand, "in all of my speeches and conferences and book signings and just being out there in the public and on the road, I must have heard from thousands of women who are fed up with their lives. Like we said on the first day—too many of us feel like islands. We need to start building bridges."

Bliss said, "We need to go back to the days when we had time for each other. When people took naps in the middle of the day instead of racing around. And paid visits to neighbors for no specific reason."

Jane said, "And women didn't have to be skinny. Or have good arms."

Harriet laughed. "Or have to hashtag motherfucking *gratitude* when, really, they are mad as hell, resentful as fuck, scared to death ... and just ... plain ... exhausted."

Jane peeked under the cloth at the dough. "It's ready to punch. Why don't you go for it, Harriet. Pretend it's your beast."

"Gladly," said Harriet, giving the dough a solid blow. "That felt remarkably good."

Jane smiled at her and leaned against the counter. "I feel like this is the *village* that you were talking about, Harriet. Here. This. I mean, I feel it at home sometimes too. I feel it at the school fundraiser. Or for a few weeks when someone gets cancer. Or right after someone dies. But in our daily lives? In the *quotidian*? No way. And believe me—as I've told Willa—I'm the *Queen* of Quotidian. But if I stopped by my neighbors' without being asked or without a specific reason, they'd think I was *rude*."

"I'm sorry to say, but I'm beginning to believe more and more, that the village you're talking about, is an illusion," said Bliss. "I mean, if we don't have it in small-town Wisconsin, then it doesn't exist. I used to believe in it. I really did."

"That can't be true! I don't *want* that to be true!" said Jane.

"Oh, it exists," said Willa. "The question is: Are you willing to make it happen? Because it starts with you."

Bliss looked away.

Jane laughed. "You mean I need to send people in my town an invitation to the rest of their lives? They'd think I was nuts." She put the cloth back over the dough like a blanket on a sleeping child. "I would like my life to be like it is here. In this kitchen. Why do we have to come all the way to Montana to have this?"

Willa couldn't take watching these women be so moved by this place she was about to leave. "Come on. We have pie to make. We'll need all of those jars to be opened. Who's feeling strong?"

"In what way?" said Jane.

Willa flexed her biceps.

Bliss raised her hand.

"You know the trick to loosening them, right?" Willa banged the side of the lid on the wooden chopping block and opened the jar with a suctioned pop. "That's the sound of true satisfaction," she said.

"That's the sound of summer being released," said Bliss as she banged the lids.

Willa looked at Jane. "You've got your mind on morels, don't you, love?"

Jane nodded. "And arnica salve, whatever that is."

"The morels are lying on mesh trays in the dry pantry. Bring them on in and you can sit at the kitchen table and pick out the larch needles and brush off the char." She opened a drawer and pulled out a dark pastry brush. "This is the brush I use to clean mushrooms. It takes a bit more work with morels."

"You don't wash them?" said Jane.

"I don't. They get waterlogged. But some people give them a quick rinse. A topic of debate down at the Merc," said Willa and watched Jane's face light up as she left the kitchen.

"She's having a religious experience this week," said Harriet. "It's so wonderful to watch her come alive. This is what she was like before she ran for Miss Connecticut Cookie Cutter. I hope she gets Montana forest fire char all over her white jeans."

Jane returned with the trays of morels and laid them down on the kitchen table.

Willa said, "At the end of the day, when the bread and pie and soup are made and the oven's warm but not hot, we'll put in those trays and let the morels dehydrate overnight. And each of you can bring home a nice bag of them. I like to rehydrate them in white wine instead of water, FYI."

Willa showed Harriet how to make the dough, fork-to-butter, add the dry ingredients, trickle in the ice-cold water. "Let the warmth from your hands form it into a ball. Don't overwork it." At the end, she put in a dash of apple cider vinegar. "There it is. You've seen it yourself. If you tell anyone, I'll have to kill you."

"Willa's *dirtiest* dirty secret." Harriet smiled. "Make me do the rest. I never learn anything unless I do it with my own hands."

Willa gave her the dough and sighed deeply. "My *dirtiest* of all dirty secrets ... is that my boys have no idea that we're broke. They think I'm leaving because I can't take the pain of staying. Which is part of it. But I didn't tell them about my fall. I faked it all through Christmas vacation. Told them that I gave away Sook because Nel would use her more. But I don't know how to tell them the truth about our financial situation. There is no way of laundering this mess their father left us in. I have to tell them the truth." She fought tears. "I don't want their papa to fall from grace. They loved him so."

The women were silent.

"Willa. You should call them," said Bliss. "I can be near, just in case. Like Jane was for me. It helped."

"I feel like I need to be with them so I can look them in the eye. God, I haven't even told my mother about our finances. I just can't bear any of them judging Jack."

Bliss picked up the lid and stirred the beans. "It seems to me that you need to tell all of them. Soon."

Willa groaned. "I'll wait until after the auction, so I know what I'm dealing with."

Harriet molded another pie crust. "If it sells for a lot, is there any chance you'd reconsider staying?"

"No," Willa said too loud and probably too angrily. "Sorry. I didn't mean it to come out like that. I just feel so heartbroken about all of this. And so ashamed."

"How did shame sneak back into this kitchen? Let's kick shame out once and for all," said Bliss, in the same hard tone.

"Fuck shame!" hollered Jane.

"Shame can kiss our motherfucking asses!" shouted Harriet.

Jane giggled and hummed while she brushed the forest floor from the morels.

Willa looked to Bliss. "I wonder when she's going to make up her mind. Did they give you a timeframe?"

"They said they needed a few days." Bliss had a way of making herself impermeable and she was doing it now, washing the meatball mixing bowl as if it was the only thing that mattered on earth.

"Bliss," said Willa.

Nothing.

"Bliss."

"I can't think about it."

Jane said, "Well, if you get that baby, I'm flying out to Wisconsin to throw you a baby shower!"

Harriet said, "And I can be there to help get you two settled."

Bliss spun around. "I must be crazy! Taking care of a mother *and* a baby?"

"You took care of a husband. This'll be a cinch." Jane winked.

Suddenly there was a hard knocking at the door.

Willa gasped. "Nel?" She wiped her hands on her apron and ran for the front door. "Check on the beans, Bliss," she called behind her. "Don't let them boil. And take the meatballs out of the oven."

She swung open the door, hoping to see her horse and the lovely young woman she'd given her to standing there.

But it wasn't Nel. It was Marilyn.

She wore a white turtleneck, an old Carhartt coat, and her signature Wrangler jeans. "I have something I need to tell you, Willa. It won't take long."

Willa looked over Marilyn's shoulder for Nel and Sook, or Marilyn's truck, but she must have walked. "Do you want to come in?"

"No. I know you have guests. We can do this on the porch. Nice to smell your kitchen again, though," she said, but not really smiling.

"What's going on, Marilyn?" she asked, suspecting that this had something to do with the women going to the Saloon last night. Her stomach rolled in fear.

Marilyn put her hands in her coat pockets and rocked a bit. "I'm not one for chitchat. As you know."

"Lay it on me, Marilyn. Nothing can hurt my feelings at this point."

"Well, your friends were at the Saloon last night. You probably know that."

"I do." Willa knew that Marilyn wasn't mean. So she tried to help her. "I want you to know, Marilyn, that I never wanted to leave here. I just don't know how to stay." *Don't cry, Willa. Do* not *cry.* "It's too hard for me here. In too many ways."

Marilyn looked at Willa's feet, which were bare as usual. She cleared her throat. "I won't lie. I've been real mad at you. I know what this place was to Jack and I thought it meant the same to you. And I've judged you."

Willa stared up at Bison Butte for strength.

"And when your friends told us what they told us, I didn't believe them. *You?* Broke? I never would have believed that, being from back East and all."

Panic rose in Willa's throat. What had the women told the town?

"And I went back home. And I told Vic what they said. And he says … it's true. Jack was helping us out. He says it started when he got his emphysema. Jack found out we didn't have insurance. How was I supposed to know Jack was paying for all of his oxygen? And his doctors' appointments. And not charging us rent for months at a time." She looked at the ground in undeniable guilt. "With Vic's Social Security and Medicaid, and my job at the post office, I thought we had enough on our own. Vic takes care of all the bills. He didn't tell me what Jack was doing. A man has his pride, I guess."

Marilyn pursed her lips. "And after your friends left, the whole bar fessed up. Turns out it wasn't just us. It was pretty much everybody, in one way or another. And he had them all swearing to secrecy. And people took his help, because … you know … everyone just assumed you had plenty of money to spare."

Where was there to go from here?

Marilyn took her hands out of her jacket and put them on Willa's shoulders. "I owe you an apology. What your husband did for us … Well, I'm sorry. These shoulders of yours have enough on them for one girl."

Marilyn put her hands back into her pockets. "You probably didn't sign up to marry a saint."

"Who knows?" said Willa.

"Everybody," said Marilyn.

Willa looked into Marilyn's eyes, cloudy with cataracts. "Was there some sort of an *agreement* Jack had with them, Marilyn?"

"Vic just said that Jack told him your family had enough. And not to tell anyone. Even me. It's not fair what happened to you, Willa. He was a dreamer. And dreamers aren't any good with money."

Her wrinkled lips and cheeks almost smiled. "But fair or not, you're always going to be the reason we lost our town, and likely our homes, to some outsider. And we won't be able to forget that. So when you come down for that auction tomorrow, you won't see me smiling at you or even looking at you, because I can't. Nobody can. You're leaving. We're here to stay. *Somehow* ... we're here to stay. This is home."

And then it settled in even worse than before. If everybody knew she was broke now, and had a good inkling why, and they were *still* so angry with her, then well—it was the same reason she was mad at herself: she was giving up.

Willa couldn't think what to say. Only, "I'm not sure what else my friends said at the Saloon. They're not from around here. But they mean well."

"They had your back. That's all I'm going to say." And Marilyn, who had never been prone to hugging, grabbed both of Willa's hands, gave them a quick squeeze, and walked off into the hay-colored light exclusive to a Montana May early afternoon.

Over her shoulder she called, "Maybe give Billings a try."

But Willa knew she needed to go much further than that.

"So I guess I won't be seeing Sook," whispered Willa, because at that moment, that's all she wanted. Not even Jack or her boys. She wanted her horse.

"Hey! Hey, Marilyn!" She ran to her. "Hey!"

Marilyn turned.

"Tell Nel to come by on Sook. I have something I want to give her."

One last ride was worth her wedding gift.

Marilyn nodded and went on her way.

Willa stood there, staring at Bison Butte, which no longer looked like a mountain to her but a living, breathing creature summoning her. *Tomorrow all this will belong to someone else. It's time to spread the ashes, Willa.*

Back inside the house, the women were silent as Willa crossed her arms and shook her head. "You don't understand small-town living. Clearly."

Harriet leaned against the refrigerator, her shirt dusted in flour. "It's my fault. I don't know what came over me. I went into motivational-speak-ese." Her face turned as red as her hair, her green eyes pulsing. "But, Willa, someone had to do something! You can't just give this place your *life* and leave without anyone understanding."

Willa all but glared at her. "What did you tell them?"

Harriet's eye twitched. "I might have told them that you're broke. And that … rumor is that Jack spent all your money being a do-gooder. And they might have put two and two together."

"Shit," said Willa.

"And we might have told them that there's still going to be a party whether they come or not," said Jane.

"Willa, they should know the truth," said Bliss. "You've lived here your whole adult life. You've given them a *town*. They should know that it's breaking your heart to leave."

Willa felt steamrolled. "Is that really the truth anymore? Because I'm not so sure. And maybe I don't even want to throw the party. Maybe we'll just bring the soup and bread and pie to the Merc on our way out of town."

"Listen, Willa. I know you are deeply attached to this place and these people. And they're just as attached to you, otherwise they wouldn't be throwing this inane hissy fit," said Harriet. "But you don't owe them anything more than you've already given them. And you've given them so much."

Bliss said, "Willa, I know you. And you'll feel better if you give them your best *goodbye*. And if they don't want to come, that's their problem."

"Yeah. Maybe," said Willa, tasting the beans. "They're done."

Harriet whispered, "Can I help?"

Willa got out her largest stock pot and said, "Yes. Put in enough oil to coat the pan. Then sauté the onions until they're translucent. Then the garlic. Don't let it brown. Then the carrots. Let them get just a little brown, but not burned, to let their sugars out, and then add the celery."

Harriet went to work.

"Bliss, strain the beans, reserve the broth. We'll use that pot too. Jane, there's a copper pot hanging over the stove. You just need about two bars of the beeswax for the arnica salve. It's in the pantry, along with the flowers. We're going to heat the arnica in olive oil to extract its properties. You can grab the olive oil in the pantry too."

None of them spoke.

"You know ... this is my decision," said Willa. "And as much as I love how you women have taken on my problems ... they're *my* problems. Right now, I need some time and space to think about it. And, Jane—"

Jane looked like a little girl getting scolded. "Jane. All you do is heat up the oil, mash up the flowers a bit, throw them in the oil, let them simmer a few minutes, and ... Oh shit. Google it with that cell phone of yours. I've got something I need to do. Bliss, keep them in line."

Willa took off her apron and went to the keeping room, took Jack's ashes from the shelf, and Dash's too, put on her parka—not for warmth but for its deep pockets—felt the thank-you note, threw it in the woodstove, and ran out the front door. She stopped short, staring at Bison Butte, which all but stood on her front porch, tapping its thundering fingers.

Now she needed to hear the cries too. She walked and ran and walked and ran until she stood at its base. She stopped and listened. Nothing. She felt Jack's ashes in her pocket. *How can this be what's left of his giant mind and heart and body?* she thought, and then started her ascent.

She was out of shape from the winter of dormancy and her lungs burned. Jack would be waiting for her to catch up, always in excellent shape, Dash yards ahead of them. There were huckleberry bushes on the way up, and she saw her boys with purple hands and buckets, on their knees in the bushes. She saw her pie cooling on the rack. She saw them at dinner, all of them so full in every way.

You can do this, she heard, in her sons' young man voices. *You can do this, Mama.* Her boys hadn't wanted to be there to spread his ashes. She'd tried to get them up Bison Butte after the memorial, and again on New Year's Eve, but they wouldn't budge. They'd said to her, "You two came here together. You should be the one to send him off." As much as she wanted to make them change their minds, in her heart she knew it was true.

She walked on, past the huckleberry bushes, just now beginning to leaf. The butte was mostly bald, dotted by ponderosa pines. She stopped at the one they called the Grandfather Tree and put her nose in its bark's amber, just as Jack had taught her long ago. *Vanilla.*

Her heart raced and she gripped the heavy boxes in her pockets and trudged up the hill taking long steps, avoiding the betrayal of every bison ghost that was herded up this hill to its death. "I am invited to the rest of my life," she huffed, short of breath.

Willa forced herself to keep going at this pace, even though her calves stung and her pockets were heavy, imagining the bison charging up this butte, thinking they were running toward freedom. "I can do this," she said in rasps of breath.

Three more long strides and she was at the top, at the two flat and forgiving rocks that they had sunned upon and reflected upon and picnicked upon over the years. She pictured the bison losing their ground as they soared at first, and then dropped. She stood at the edge and looked down over their land, the Homestead so tiny for all that it had been to her.

Willa took Jack's box of ashes from her pocket and set it on the largest rock. Then she took Dash's box and put it next to it. Why hadn't they ever had this discussion? Because they'd so believed in their lives being long? Because they didn't want to give it the time of day? She was proud of all that faith. Jack wouldn't be attached to his ashes anyway. She needed to think like Jack for this. He'd be content with this place, she was sure.

Pause, Willa. This moment needs you to pause. So she sat on the rock next to the boxes of their ashes and took one last look at what had been theirs.

The day was still and the distant hills were greening with larch trees, backlit slopes of yellow balsam root and the lavender beginnings of lupine. Willa looked down on the house and the orchard and marsh, over the ponds and meadow. And then it was all too much. So she lay on the rock, her knees pointing to the endless, cloudless sky.

"Where *are* you? Why did you leave me? I don't want to be alone!" Tears spilled down her temples and into her ears and she let them pool there, deafening the sound of a shrieking hawk, replacing it with the thump of her heartbeat.

She watched the hawk riding thermals and remembered the time they'd seen the eagles mating in the sky, careening toward each other, clasping talons, spinning toward the ground—as if they would die for their union and their offspring—then releasing and soaring again into the ponderosas. "That's where they'll make their nest," he'd said. And she'd known they were those birds.

Staring at the sky, Willa said, "I've let everything of yours go now. Except you. You're gone. I know it. You left me in the forest with the sow and her cub. I just have to let what's left of you … go." She hit the rock hard. "And Dash? Why'd you have to go and get cancer? I need you here."

Willa felt the bison thundering behind her then, charging and snorting and keening, and she sat up, suddenly dizzy, spinning with images of flinging her body over the butte, boxes open, all of them falling … falling together. And she held onto the rock while the vertigo swirled over her and charged past her. She held onto the rock because there were two boys who needed their mother, and for that reason alone Willa took Jack's box and Dash's box, stuffed them back in her pockets, and ran home as fast as she could, like she was being chased by the sow griz she'd locked eyes with, who would wrangle her back up the butte like a doomed bison. And if it did, she might just jump this time.

Breathing in heaves, she ran through the meadow and past the pond, up the glen and through the orchard, until she leapt onto her front porch, grabbed the door, and slammed it behind her, panting. She leaned against it, trying to catch her breath. She tempered herself until the room was steady. "What was *that*?" she whispered. Yes, she'd lain in bed holding her breath, thinking she could just go to sleep and not wake up. But the next breath always came.

And as her heart slowed against the sturdy door at her back, she knew: What happened on Bison Butte wasn't suicidal. It was vision. It was future. It was a claiming of life over death. This time, it was not up to the bear, or anyone else. This was all her.

A relief that she hadn't felt in so long poured over her. It grounded her feet into the old worn wood they had laid themselves decades ago, scarred by dog claws and boys and boots.

She heard the women talking in the kitchen. She didn't want to go in yet. Maybe she'd go to Nel. Maybe she was brave enough to walk, as Marilyn had, to the renters. She'd bring them the last of whatever was in the freezer as an offering. She'd personally invite them to the party tomorrow after the auction. And maybe they'd forgive her.

Keeping the ashes in her pockets, she went around the house to the garage. It smelled like gasoline and garbage and the forever-scent of rotting apples. The freezer stood in the corner, holding the last of the kill. She prepared herself and opened it, knowing how empty it would be. The light was out, and it made it easier in the dim garage to accept its emptiness.

She reached in for a few packages of sausage links. *One ... two ... three* was all. Five trout fillets. Some venison steaks—the tougher cuts. Two whole chickens from some old laying hens Jack had finally retired. And then, in the very back of the freezer, a large mass presented itself, wrapped in brown paper.

Willa reached in for it, the freezer breath cool in her face. It was heavy, whatever it was. She peeled back the brown paper from its masking tape stitches. And in the glint of the May sun streaming through the garage window, she saw an eye. A yellow eye. Lined in black.

The Montanan in her thought, *Easy. Calm and easy.*

She pulled back more of the paper and saw the whole mask. The furry spiked ears. The point of a beak.

"My God. It's a great horned owl," she whispered, pulling it out of the freezer.

She cradled it in one arm, grabbed a flashlight off the shop table, and shined it down its breast. Like the hummingbird, it was perfectly preserved.

She said the words aloud. "To hold something this mighty, this beautiful and brave, that we were never meant to … in the palms of our hands."

Willa paused to honor this creature. "You radiant being," she said, for the owl. For Jack.

She unwrapped the rest of it. It didn't feel dead. More like if she kept it out of the freezer for long enough, it might thaw, blink, spread its massive wings, and fly away. "Lord," she said. "You absolutely gorgeous creature." Her mind flashed for an instant on the cruel yet elegant truth that if she hadn't come to Montana and lived this life with Jack, she might be entirely unable to glory in this moment.

As if in direct response, she saw an envelope with *Willa* written in Jack's spidery script. It was taped to the back of the freezer.

She put her hand to her heart. She set the owl back in the freezer with the door open, as if it really were still alive, and took the letter out of the envelope. There was his typewriter ink, the periods stars in a constellation.

My dear Willa,

If you are finding this, you are likely sad and cold, because you never wear slippers and the garage floor is always cold. And if you are standing at the freezer and finding this note, that means you are almost at the end of the meat. And that you are hungry. And ready to know my truth. I'm sorry that I can't bring you home food anymore. I wish I could. I wish I was there, standing next to you, talking about what's for dinner. You told me once that this freezer was a symbol of my care for you. Hopefully the boys will know better than to let it go completely empty.

Willa, I put this owl here for you. Last year, when I found out that I had a heart condition, I decided not to tell you. I wanted to take my life before my heart did. They told me I could drop dead at any moment. I didn't want to put you and the boys through the hell of that. Not on top of what I've done to our savings. I thought I'd have plenty of years to make it back in different ways. I wasn't so lucky. I have totally failed you all. The loves of my life. I put Willa, Montana, and my damn self-reliance before my family. I was, and am, so deeply sorry.

So I wrote you a note, not unlike this one, took my rifle, and went for a walk up to Bison Butte, where I always pictured myself dying, or at least where my soul would go before it stepped off into the Great Beyond. And on the way, crossing the logging road, in the ditch, I saw this great horned owl. I figured it must have been hit by something. Odd but possible. But it was perfectly intact. Like it had fallen dead from the sky.

I knew in that moment that the owl was for both of us, and I went home and burned my letter and loved you until

my body wouldn't let me any longer, which I suspect wasn't
long enough to make back our nest egg, though I tried. I
am so sorry, my love. So sorry. I failed you.

   Willa, my dear beloved beautiful Willa. Take a feather
from its wing and bring it with you to our bed. Put it
under your pillow. Let it help you. You don't have to do
this alone. Owl will help you. If I haven't come to you
yet in dreams, I am sorry. Believe me, wherever I am, I am
trying. I love you so. I want to tell you: It's time to
dream your own life now, my love. You have a life ahead of
you that is calling you to live it. It's time for you to
fly now.

                         Eternally,
                         Your Jack

Now: one more thing. Go to our *Self-Reliance* books in the
keeping room and you will find some help moving forward.
It's all I could put together, considering. I thought I'd
have years ahead of me. Not months or days. I hope it was
at least months.

            "How do you know but ev'ry bird that
                cuts the airy way,
         Is an immense world of delight,
                clos'd by your senses five?"
                         —William Blake

And remember: "The love you give away is the only love
you keep."

PS: Go inside and put on some slippers.

He'd dated it. Six months ago. Right before he'd died. Weeks. Not months.

Willa erupted into tears, loud and gasping and staccato. She wanted to scream, but her voice fell away. And she took the owl and the note and held them and cried until she was sitting on the garage floor, rocking forward and backward.

Then Willa held the note up to the window, and yes, there they were, the little period stars—the constellation that was their night sky. She would find him there. And it looked remarkably close to, yes, Delphinus. The end of his inky sentences, but not the end of their love.

You don't have to do this alone. The exact words she'd used in the invitation. Was he somehow behind all of this? It didn't matter. She couldn't get him back.

Time for her to fly? Did that mean leave Montana? She put her fingers around one wing feather. If it was a struggle, she'd find a way to stay. If it pulled easily, she'd leave.

She pulled.

It gave way.

Low and open-toned, she said, "Thank you, owl." She breathed deeply. "For giving him back to me, for whatever time he had left."

She wrapped the owl back in the paper and put it in the freezer where Jack had perched it, took the flashlight, found her slippers in the boot closet, and went through the house, past the women, and into the keeping room, where she put Jack's ashes, and Dash's, back on the shelf.

Oh God, what the hell did I do with our Emersons?

She eyed the spaces where the twin books used to be. Where would she have put them? Had she gone in his Cave in her grief-driven stupor and put them in his desk drawer? As much as it pained her, she went down the steps to his little room and hunted for the books. Not in the desk drawer. Not on his shelf of favorite books. She went to the barn. Maybe she'd put them in the tack room with her treasured saddle. But they weren't there either. She could only think that they must be somewhere safe. And that she would find them. And that there would be something there to help her soar.

"I shouldn't have doubted you, my love."

Then she wound her hair in a long braid, put the owl feather in it, and went into the kitchen. She didn't feel happy, or any other recognizable emotion. She was like an owl on a field mouse, wings fully spanned. She had to decide what to do with the rest of her life. Now. And the women did too. And she forgave them for loving her in the way she hadn't known how to love herself. She knew exactly where they needed to go.

The soup was made, the arnica and beeswax salve setting in jars, the pie and bread cooling on racks, the morels drying in the oven, the women standing on a wide footbridge that Jack had made years ago out of felled larch, thirty feet above Emilio Creek.

They looked down at the springtime runoff crashing over boulders, sparkling and swirling in pools of deep greens and cerulean blues. The spray from the creek rinsed Willa's face and she smiled into it.

"So here we are," said Willa. "Our last afternoon, just us." She stared down at the creek and fingered the feather in her braid. "This is something that Jack and I did every spring and every fall. I have to believe it will help us find our So Now What."

She leaned over the railing and looked into the rushing water, which not long ago was snowpack. "You are invited to the rest of your life," she said, feeling she was part of a tapestry of women that spanned the ages. "This bridge over this rushing springtime creek is a symbol of what we have been to one another this week."

They were silent, looking into the creek.

"We're no longer islands," said Bliss. "We're bridges. To each other."

Willa thought of the phone call that had inspired all of this. "And I have to believe that we're bridges back to our lives."

Bliss smiled and nodded at her, and Harriet and Jane nodded too, all three of them holding their walking sticks.

Willa continued, as sure and as strong as she'd been in months. Maybe ever. "Let's ask ourselves: *What do I want to leave behind, and what do I want to receive?* What do you want to leave behind when you leave Montana ... and what do you want to receive, moving forward in your life?"

She produced eight notecards—the same handmade paper she had used to write the invitations—and four pens, passing them to Bliss, Harriet, and Jane. Then she took her own.

"Let's sit here and write down what it is that we want to let go of on the first notecard. And what it is that we want to receive on the second one."

They each sat, the water swirling and rushing beneath them, writing on the fine paper. Jane lay on her stomach, her feet scissoring lightly in the air. Harriet sat cross-legged, hunched over her piece of paper. Bliss and Willa sat at either end of the bridge, both with their knees up, writing against them for support.

Harriet

What to leave behind:
    I want to leave behind my hardness. I want to leave behind my hermitage. I want to leave behind the delusion, the dance, the red and shiny and witty and fake-fabulous. And the torture. I want to leave behind the tortured push-

*push-push toward taking that one ... supreme ... stage ... of
my life. I want to let go of everybody else's idea of who I am
and who I'm supposed to be. I want to let go of self-violence.
I want to let go of fear.*

Harriet lifted her pen and took the next card.

What to receive:
    *I want to receive my quiet self. I want to receive my
gentle soft self. My plain self. My cool green jade self. I want
to receive love from myself. And from people. I want to be in
the audience. I want to receive the applause that comes from
my hands.*

She looked down at the rapids, crashing against the rocks,
shaping them for hundreds of years into smooth undulations.
And held her hands in the air, slowly clapping.

Bliss

What to leave:
    *I hereby leave behind my religion as I've known it. I
hereby leave behind my anger at Hugh. My hurt. The family
that we never were.*

She bit down hard against tears and pushed down harder on
her pen.

*I hereby leave behind those babies. And the mother I would
have been to them. And the father Hugh would have been.
And the Christmases we never had. And the birthday parties.*

And the vacations. And the Easter egg hunts. And the Sunday bacon and eggs. And the baptisms and confirmations and … weddings. I hereby leave it all behind.

Bliss was holding her breath. She let it out and drew in a deep one, putting her pen back to the notecard quickly.

And I hereby leave behind my shame. I am sorry. And that has got to be enough.

Then she took the next card.

What to receive:
   I hereby receive this child. If they will have me.

Bliss sniffed and looked down at the rushing water. And wrote,

If not … I'm moving on. It'll be just me. And I give myself permission for that to be enough.

Resolve felt firm, the way she liked to feel, the way she used to feel. She whispered, "And I will find a love for you, God, that is real. For now, here is my prayer: show me what it is to love … and be loved." She cast the long slog of her loss into the river's rush, and said, "It all starts now."

Jane

Jane dizzied when she looked down. So she looked up.

> *What to let go of:*
> *I need to let go of this race I'm in. There is no finish line.*
> *I know that now. I've always known it. I just didn't want to*
> *stop long enough to see it. Life isn't a list to cross off and call*
> *complete. There is no complete, just like there is no perfect.*

She dared to look down for just a second, trying to learn from the river.

She thought, *That water is racing to the sea. But when it gets there, it doesn't stop. It becomes part of the tide. I don't have to stop. I just have to become part of the tide.*

She peered over the bridge again, this time a bit longer.

I need to go back to scratch. Flour. Butter. Leavening. No. To heck with leavening. I'm going to find wild yeast.

Jane looked down at the crashing, churning water and felt dizzy again, but she welcomed it. A little dizzy seemed like a good place to start. She held her pen tighter, took the next notecard, and wrote:

> *What I'd like to let in:*
> *What I'd like to let in is a new Jane. I'd like to let delight*
> *in, and laughter, and cartwheels. And saying what I really*
> *want to say. And love letters to myself. I want to swim naked*
> *in the river behind my house and not care if anyone sees me.*

She put her head down on the cold wood and whispered, "I'm just so afraid I'm going to go back and life will be exactly the same. And worse, I'll settle for it."

She bore down and forced herself to put her pen to the paper.

What do I want to receive? Change. Change for the better. I want to find my way back to my children. And maybe even to Palmer.

Jane took in a deep hit of Montana river ozone. Then she wrote,

I'll give it six months. Six months of saying what I want to say. Being who I want to be. Giving, but also receiving. To Palmer and to my kids. And I guess I have to let go of Charles to do it.

She clenched her jaw. *Six months. And then we'll see.* She took her phone from her pocket, snapped a photo of the piece of paper, and added,

And there will be as many Stolen Moments as I can possibly find.

Jane looked down and forced herself to keep looking. *I wish I could make the water stop,* she thought. *Just for a moment.* She blinked. And blinked again. Freeze-framing the coursing water like she was stopping it, even though she knew she wasn't. Like the shutter of a camera, she could close her eyes and try to learn to pause.

Willa

Willa thought a long time before she committed pen to paper. She wanted it to be simple. Jack always said that rain was the best raincoat.

To leave behind:
    Jack. Jack as my leader. Jack as my charge.
    The twins. The twins as my charge. The twins as my sustenance. The twins as my future.
    My family. My family as my life force. My family as my promise. My family as my security. My family as my story.

She looked at her hands. *Getting older*, she thought. *Hopefully wiser.*

Then she added: *And this place. I have to let go of this beautiful place.* She held back tears.

She took the next notecard and wrote,

I receive a whole self. I receive a whole future. I receive a whole happiness. I receive a whole world of possibility.

Willa stood. She touched the owl's wing feather in her braid and breathed the water's cool wind as deeply as she could, like a shawl. She felt like the vertigo had released something in her. The bison had charged over her. She had held strong to the rock. She hadn't heard the cries. She didn't need to.

She looked down at the river rocks, holding their place too.

The others did the same.

"Okay. Let's stand on the downriver side. And let's send off what we're shedding and let the water carry it away. The first night we shared what was supposed to happen. We're letting go of what we need to shed now. Allow yourself to give it over. Ready?"

The women nodded, supplicant.

"Drop the first notecard into the water. Watch as the rapids take it. And bring it away. To lakes and rivers and eventually to the sea."

The women stood at the railing of the bridge, holding their cards in the air. One by one they dropped them and watched as they floated down the roiling river and rounded the bend. Then they waited, watching. Silent.

When it felt like time, Willa said, "Now, let's stand upriver." She felt powerful. She felt sow. Doe. Calliope. Goose. Piegan. Owl.

The women went to the upriver side of the bridge and held out their second notecards.

"Just hours ago, this water was snow. It melted and freed itself to become water that goes to the sea and nourishes the land for thousands of miles. Receive it as the gift of life that it is. And now, receive the So Now What. Whatever it is. However it comes, listen and know: you are invited to the rest of your life."

The women held their cards over the river, the spray in their faces.

Jane dropped hers in first. Then Harriet. And then Willa. Bliss looked to the sky, then tore her card into six pieces and dropped them one by one, closing her eyes and whispering something, and Willa knew that this was the ceremony she had longed for.

Then all of them watched as the air currents floated them riverward, the sun illuminating them like falling wings. When they touched the water, they swelled with the current over boulders, sucking into the rock cleavage, and snagging on sticks, and something in Willa wished they'd all get torn and sucked under, right before them. But they released, and flowed under the bridge, soon to come apart altogether.

Without Willa's prompting, they went to the other side of the bridge, all watching as the river took their future words into its flow.

Then there was a moaning, like a dying animal, and Willa looked into the woods. It got louder and higher until it was a level but cutting shriek. And she realized it was Bliss.

She looked at the other women, all realizing the same thing. Willa looked closer. Bliss was leaning into the railing with all her weight, rocking against it, like she was forcing the noise from her in fits of moans and more shrieks and fast panting.

"Bliss?" she said. "Are you okay?"

Bliss was lost in her body, writhing against the railing. And then she stopped. And her head fell back, and she trumpeted into the sky, bravado: "You don't deserve my pain! You don't deserve me! Get ... thee ... OUT!"

And Harriet whispered loud, "Let that shit go, Blissful. Let that shit *goooooo*."

Jane's eyes darted from woman to woman like the birdsongs she could finally hear. And then she said, "Yes. Let ... it ... all ... go."

And Bliss turned to her, her face awash in springtime runoff spray. "I know what my So Now What is." She opened her chest wide. Willa would have gone to hug her, if Bliss wasn't already in her own embrace with the Montana sky. Then she looked at Willa. "I'm going to be a mother. I know it. I ... just ... *know*."

"You have everything you need," said Willa, low.

Then Harriet took her walking stick, held it to the sky, and screamed, "Take it!" throwing it over into the water. And she screamed so loud her voice cracked. "I'm walking straight and real and true from here on out! Even if it means I'm a nobody from nowhere. I am NOT going BACK!"

Jane looked at Willa with wide eyes and Willa knew she was wishing she had something big to say or do or think or feel. "I've loved being in nature. So much. What am I going to do when I get back home?"

Willa nodded at her. "Jane. You *are* nature. Even in New York City. Just remember the aspen grove."

She looked at Willa and said, "What if I can't feel it there? What if I can't feel *this* there? I'll be back to running around. And all those screens. And appointments. And calendars. And lists. And the trees in my yard all look like they're dressed up for a party. The rivers aren't anything like this. The one that runs through the backyard looks like it's just ... given up." She looked off into the cascading water. "But I can't leave my life. I have to stay. Until I know for sure that I have to go."

"That's its own kind of pilgrimage," said Willa. "Staying."

"I guess," said Jane, opening her eyes wide to Willa. "I'm going to have to make *staying* into something wondrous. It can't feel like it's a concession. I have to make my quotidian into the most exotic role of my life." She smiled into the sky, like she was letting rain fall on her face. "I have to start living like every moment is the most *important* one there is."

Jane's eyes danced. "Maybe I'll start leading gatherings for women who need to do what we've done here. But who can't leave their lives for a week. Screw book club!" She held out her hands to the river. "I'll call it Stolen Moments, and we'll help each other live like this, pausing, watching, paying attention, taking photos. And then once a month, we'll come together and share our photos and stories about *stopping*! And then say what we really want to say about it all. I love it!"

She took a photo of each of the women, rapid-fire. Then she held her camera to the sky and took a photo. "You will all be receiving something very special in the mail in a few weeks." Her eyes stopped dancing. "Only, Willa ... Well ... I'll send it to your post office box. They'll forward it to ... wherever."

"To ... wherever ..." Willa felt for the owl feather in her braid and slipped it out like a bow from a quiver. She held it in front of

her, striped in brown and cream—woven like her and Jack. She let
the air currents turn it in her fingers and she held on tightly, until
she felt her thumb and forefinger gentle and part. The feather floated
away in the current of sky and spray for a long time before it touched
water and rounded the bend.

Fly now, Willa, she heard. It didn't matter whose voice it was.
They all stood there watching the water.

"I'm scared to go back," said Jane.

"I am too," said Harriet.

"We *should* be," said Bliss. "Our lives are in tangles. But we're
changing that. Aren't we."

"Yes. We are changing that." Willa looked for birds but instead
found herself in the company of conifers and very good friends.

"Just remember, wherever we go, we have everything we need,"
she said.

It was dusk when they pulled into the Homestead. Sook was
grazing in the orchard, and Nel was lying next to her in the grass.
Willa's heart rolled and leapt. "Stay calm," she whispered.

The women went to her horse.

She forced herself to go to Nel first.

"I guess you know now," she said to Nel, who jumped up and
backed away a few steps.

"My grandfather told us," she said. "We didn't know how
much you and Jack were helping us. We thought you were just
leaving because you didn't care. It's got everyone talking but no
one has any answers."

Willa started to say *we* and changed it: "You'll find your way,"
she said, opening her arms to Nel, but the girl pulled back, and
Willa remembered what Marilyn had said at the Saloon. "I'm

sorry that I'm leaving, Nel. I will miss you. You're a fine young woman." Tears gripped at her throat and she pushed past them. "I want you to know, Nel, that you can be anything you want to be."

Nel looked at Sook. "Wink came over yesterday and did her feet. She'd probably love a ride up the butte." Then she reached into her coat pocket and pulled out a bundle of wild white sage and put it into Willa's hand. "To clear out the old. For the new."

Willa smiled with tears in her eyes and brought the bundle to her nose.

"I don't have much to give you," said Nel looking at the ground.

"You have given me so much, Nel." But she didn't dare touch Nel who would surely cower. "My garden sage wintered over this year. Of all years."

Nel smiled, but with severity. "Burn both. When it's time." It was as if she knew about Willa's first trip up Bison Butte today.

Then Nel handed her a small book of matches, "You should do it sooner than later." Willa couldn't help but think about her Piegan father that no one had met, and how this girl had kept her roots. All of her roots. Was Willa any better? No. She slipped the sage bundle and matches into her pocket.

"Nel. What is hummingbird medicine?"

Nel's freckles seemed to come together into one continent. "Hummingbird is an invitation. To the sweetness of life."

"An invitation to the sweetness of life." Willa's heart pounded. "Thank you. I just need to get something." She looked at the women fondling Sook, and Sook craning her neck around, muzzling Jane's palm like she knew she'd be the type to carry carrots. "Why don't you take her for a ride down in the meadow, Jane. She has a rocking-horse lope."

Jane's face rounded and opened. "*Seriously?*"

Willa nodded. "Just don't pull on her face. She's very sensitive to the bit. Give Jane a leg up, Nel, and show her how to neck rein. Maybe give her a look before you turn her out alone. But she knows how to ride."

Jane didn't blink. "Well, I suppose these boots better be good for something." And she reached up for the pommel and stepped into Nel's clasped hands.

Willa went into the house, smiling at the almost maternal sounds she heard from Jane. If you could take Bliss's moaning from the bridge and put pure joy in it, that was what was coming from Jane.

Willa took down the ashes from the keeping room shelf—both boxes. Then she crossed the orchard, smiling at Jane and Sook in a graceful lope in the grass, went into the barn, and put the boxes in her saddlebags. She peeled back the saddle cover and ran her hand over the intricate designs, taking a strong hit of the leather.

I can do this.

When Willa heard Sook's loping hooves and Jane's high-pitched "Yippee," she knew it was time.

Out in the orchard, Jane was standing with her head on Sook's shoulder. She looked up at Willa. "You have no idea," she said, tears rolling down her cheeks.

"I actually do," said Willa.

And Jane hugged Sook like this horse now held whatever the river hadn't taken. Then she let go and said, "What a beauty. She's all yours. I'm going to start riding again. No matter what. Thank you." Jane brushed Willa's cheek with a kiss as she joined the women, standing under an apple tree.

Willa took off Nel's saddle and put her King on Sook, who blew out with the heft of the leather, but accepted it like an old burden she understood. Willa didn't need a bit with this horse, so she pulled off Nel's bridle and fit her hackamore over Sook's nose, holding the end of the reins, and hoisted herself up.

Jane said, "Oh, let me take a photo of you. You can bring this with you on your journeys. You look so beautiful. And happy."

Willa held her head high, with one hand in Sook's black mane and the other on her waist, smiling, so proud, the way *goodbye* smiles so often are.

Sook sidestepped, knowing where they were going, and Willa barely needed to press her leg into her barrel for Sook to break into her rocking-horse lope through the orchard, until they got to open trail, Willa leaning forward and Sook breaking into a wide-open run through the field, and then up the butte, slowing with the incline into a perfect stride. Willa breathed hard as if she were running herself, keeping the saddlebags tight on the pommel.

They went past the huckleberry bushes and ponderosas, the lavender patch of lupine and golden balsam root that she'd eyed in vertigo on her way down earlier in the day. She didn't feel dizzy anymore. Sook was the one creature on this planet that knew what she knew. Even more than her boys, and in a way, Jack too. Sook had known her body and how it held her thoughts and feelings. Sometimes all she had to do was think of a direction, and Sook would take it.

She thought her direction now. *Up.* And Sook followed.

Willa stopped Sook at the place where she'd imagined the bison knew their fate and turned into their own, pummeled by the lie of safety. She stood there, breathing hard, feeling Sook's body rise and fall with her own deep breaths. "I will become the bird," said Willa, pressing just a bit with her legs so that they walked slowly, ceremoniously, to the ridge.

"I wish I could take you with me." Willa felt every inch of Sook's four feet take this terrain—steps she would remember when she needed the courage to dream her future alive. Sook had known Willa when she wasn't sure of her own feet on this terrain. And Sook had taught her so much about how to be in this place and call it home.

And that was why, when they got to the top, Willa knew she had to put her feet on this ground for the second time that day.

She stopped, dismounted, and took the two boxes of ash from her saddlebags. Then she set them on the rock.

It was silent now. No charging bison. No vertigo. No cries.

She opened the boxes, put her finger into Dash's remains and stirred, working the ashes between her fingers. Then she rubbed them into her sternum and dipped her fingers into the next box. Jack's. She stirred her fingers in them, small bones interrupting the circles. She took one and grasped it to her heart. She wanted to keep it. But knew she needed to let him go.

She walked to the edge of the butte with both boxes, Sook standing behind her, looking around like a guard.

Willa held the open boxes up to the Montana sky, and said, "Go now, dear ones." And she flung the ashes, boxes and all, into the sky. Closing her eyes as they became sky.

Then she took the sage bundle from her pocket, lit a match, and watched the bundle ignite until the tip was in full flame. And without knowing how to use this sage in the Piegan way, still, she felt it deep inside her. Because of Nel. Because of Montana and Bison Butte and Jack and her boys and all who came before her. Emilio, Maria, and far before that. And she held it to the sky. And let it burn. And then circled it around her, smelling its sweet bitterness.

Then she laid it on the rock and watched until it burned to its stems. And out.

And then Willa said, "Thank you."

And as she turned to go home, she thought, *I know what he meant now. When I kill a bird, and I eat it ... I become that bird.*

Willa took off the hackamore and left Sook to graze. And she went into the garage again, to the freezer, and took the raptor that had given her more days with her beloved, and cradled it once again in her arms. *Take a feather from its wing.* She had. And she'd let it go down river. Now she took another. This time for her future. It gave way with ease, like the other. Then she pulled out the rest of the frozen meat and brought it out to Sook, filling the saddle bags until they bulged.

She looked into the brown globe of Sook's eye, which had always known so much, much more than Willa. "You take care of them all, girl. You take care." Willa kissed her nose one last time. "You take care."

And Willa left her horse, which meant, coupled with the ashes, that she could leave this town. She walked tall and slow through the orchard, she guessed like Harriet had said—like a horse in snow.

Inside, the women were having tea with Nel, and when she walked in, they stopped abruptly. Bliss got up and hugged Willa. Then Harriet and Jane joined her so that they all held her, together.

Willa did not cry. She allowed herself to be hugged. "I did it," she said.

"Good," said Bliss.

Nel tried to slip out the front door unnoticed, but Willa went after her. "That's your saddle now, Nel. And hackamore. I'll drop your tack off down at the Merc tomorrow. And don't you say one thing. You deserve it. You ride home and you tell your family and your neighbors that whatever Jack did for them … he meant it with all his heart. And you tell them all that sometimes people do things for each other. Just because they can't do it any other way. Even if it doesn't make sense." Her voice cracked. "Okay?"

Nel looked up at her for just a second, with something like a smile in her raven eyes. "Okay." She nodded and walked out into the orchard.

Willa called after her, "Don't forget to check the saddlebags!" Then she shut the door and went to the window and watched Nel in the last light, looking at Sook.

Nel stopped. She backed up, her eyes fixed on Sook. Then Nel looked over her shoulder at the house. And walked forward with her hands out like she was about to touch kindness itself. First her fingertips on the leather. And then her face against it. She slipped on the hackamore, put her boot into the stirrup and hoisted herself up, pausing in the saddle with the smallest but truest smile. And the two of them moved off together into the last light, the North Star on the horizon.

Willa smiled and leaned against the windowpane, glad for its cold on her cheek.

Back in the kitchen, the women had the pot of soup on the stove, the smell of bread drifting from the oven. "Dinner?" asked Jane, ladle in hand.

"I would love nothing more than that exact soup," said Willa.

Harriet said, "Talk about baptism-by-fire. I learned more today than I have maybe ever, about what it is to make things. Honest things. Thank you, Willa, for making a girl honest."

Bliss said, "I'm sorry if you feel that we betrayed you last night. At the Saloon."

"You did exactly what needed to happen," said Willa. "Thank you."

They ate the soup without much talk, thoroughly hungry.

Bliss stared at her empty bowl, wiped her mouth with her napkin, and said, "I spoke with them. They said *yes*."

"*WHAT?*" shrieked Harriet. "Oh my God, oh my God!" She leapt from her chair and poured herself over Bliss with hugs and kisses, then came up for air. "Oh my GOD! You're going to be a *mother!*"

Jane clapped and cried, "The stork has landed!" raising her hands over her head and clapping some more.

Bliss looked shell-shocked.

"Are you okay, Bliss?" asked Willa, knowing to keep things calm and stay seated.

"June twenty-fifth," said Bliss. "Not even two months." She held the sides of her head like she had a migraine.

"Bliss. This is your *dream*. This is *incredible*!" said Willa, but Bliss looked so sad. "You can do this, my friend. Out of all the people I know, you can do this."

Bliss shook her head slowly. "Willa. I don't know. I asked Nel a question just now." She closed her eyes and tightened her lips. "I asked her what it was like to be raised by her grandparents. You know. An untraditional family in a small town."

Willa pictured Nel's face. She probably hadn't known what to say. She probably had thought it was some sort of judgment of her own mother's addiction and abandonment and unknown native father. "What did she say?"

Bliss opened her eyes, then folded her napkin and put it on the table, patting it. "She said she wouldn't wish it on her worst enemy."

"Oh, she's just a *teen*!" said Jane. "That's how they *talk*. It's their *power*, giving everything the proverbial eye roll. I'm sure she *loves* her grandparents. And I'm sure she's grateful too," she added, like she was trying to convince herself.

"She looked pretty serious to me," said Bliss. "I mean, is it even *fair* of me? I've been thinking of myself and my needs. But what if my child is ostracized? I know how that feels. And I wouldn't wish *that* on my worst enemy." Bliss shook her head. "And what if something happens to me? She wouldn't have a grandmother or grandfather to raise her. Or aunts or uncles. Or cousins. I mean, what am I *thinking*? And I'm not young either. I'll be the oldest mother."

Harriet slapped her hand on the table. "Well, that child would have *me*! Whether or not that's a good thing."

"And it would have *me*," said Willa. "And my boys. They consider you their aunt."

"And it would have me too," said Jane. "If you'll have me."

Bliss just shook her head. "She said, *I know my baby will be safe with you.*" Then she looked up. "It's a girl." And her smile overwhelmed the fear in her eyes.

Harriet jumped up again, Jane clapped, and Willa's eyes swelled with tears.

"What did you tell her?" asked Willa.

"I told her *yes.*" The smallest smile rounded out her staunch Midwestern face, framed by those sensible bangs. "What was I supposed to say? She picked me out of the others. And she's sticking with me. She told me that her parents are leaving it up to her. But that they're concerned."

"Fuck 'em," said Harriet.

"If she was my child, I don't know that I'd want her to give me her baby either," said Bliss. "But you know, I've been thinking. It's not really about me. It's about what's best for this child. I want to be what's best for her. I *think* I can be what's best for her."

Willa said, "Bliss. You don't have to be a mother tomorrow. You're here for another day. Let it come. Let it come."

"No," said Bliss, holding on to the side of the table, the look of utter faith sweeping her face. "I know. I am going to be a mother to this little girl." And she produced a stalwart smile. "I *am.*"

"Yes, you are," said Willa, and she got up and went to Bliss and hugged her hard from behind as Bliss leaned into her. "Yes, you are."

"I think if I had to give a name to this week, it would be the Grove," said Willa. "One organism. Each of us standing in what feels like our own shoes, yet connected."

"I'd call us the So-Now-What Sisterhood," smirked Harriet.

"Ah yes, the big question ..." said Bliss. "I guess I have my answer. What about everyone else?"

"I think I do," said Jane. "I'm giving my best self to my family and Palmer for the next six months. Which means ... no Charles. And I love my Stolen Moments idea. I can't wait to get back to start it. I have no idea who will join, but I'm going to try. What about you, Harriet?"

"I don't know yet," said Harriet. "But I'm not going back in the game. Sorry, Jane."

Jane smiled at her. "No *sorry.*"

They all looked at Willa.

"Mine will be determined by tomorrow," she said. "But I know I have to fly."

Harriet looked up, her hair and her eyes wild. The other three women met her gaze and their eyes grew wild too. With the soberest stare, she said, "We have to *fight* for this. The four of us. We have to keep this *alive.*"

They all nodded slowly, as if in time with the beating of their hearts.

"Yes," said Bliss. "We have to fight for this."

"We *will,*" said Jane.

Then Willa said, "I love you women," like she was saying it for all of them.

They all stood and linked arms and hugged in an organism of arms and hands and hearts, and went to the Inn, lingering at their doors. "Good night," said Willa. "The auction is at three o'clock. Let's sleep in."

The others agreed, yawning, all but limping into their rooms.

Willa stood on the front porch. She couldn't remember a day like this, with so much emotion and so many firsts and lasts. "So Now What?" she said and looked up at the night sky. And it looked down at her, so clear, the sliver smile of the moon so oblique and charming, like it was nodding at her, promising to watch over her wherever she went.

She dropped her head back. "Oh God, if you are out there, please ... take care of him!" she beseeched. "Please."

Then one meteor sliced through the sky, leaving a streak of

dust. Of course, he could give her a private firework display, if just for one moment. This moment.

Then nothing. And then only the sound of a faraway bird.

When I kill a bird, and I eat it ... I become that bird.

The Last Day

Willa woke knowing what was ahead of her. It required getting up, and facing it—and a good long, hot shower. Her breaths were shallow and she didn't care. Deep breathing was overrated when you wondered if you were going to be able to breathe at all.

She got dressed in her most simple pair of jeans and an old sweater. She needed comfort and wasn't going to deprive herself of it, especially today. She hoped the meat had made it to Marilyn's freezer. She hoped that Nel had been easy in the saddle. But it was no longer her role to hope for these people. She'd still do it—but she'd do it from afar.

Yesterday had been so full: cooking and making things, and spreading the ashes, and the women at the bridge, and her horse. Today she just wanted the day to speak for itself. She'd go along with it, no matter where it took her.

Willa went downstairs, expecting at least Jane up, making coffee. Instead, silence.

She put the teakettle on and a log in the keeping room stove, even though it was warm out this morning.

The gardenias were still beautiful. She'd gotten used to their heady smell. She'd never be able to smell a gardenia the same way again. She took one and put it in her braid.

What was for breakfast? She didn't have the energy, nor the stomach, for more than toast and tea this morning. She couldn't think about anything other than just getting through this day.

So she sat in Jack's chair and rocked. She'd have to keep these chairs, or at least this one. And the gate-legged table. And the Blue Willow platter. She pictured all of Jack's things in the Saloon, by now in the homes of the denizens of Willa, absorbed into their lives. It made her happy. But where were the Emerson books?

Stand strong today, Willa. She resolved not to fall into emotion. Or fear. She'd use the women as her fortress against who knew what.

Ten o'clock rolled around and there wasn't any stirring, so she wandered into the Inn to see if maybe they were sitting there with their own coffee in the great room, chatting, poring over their time together.

Nothing could have prepared her for what she saw.

The rafters were wrapped in long swags of aspen branches dripping in white lights. On every surface there were bunches of balsam root and lupine in Mason jars.

She walked out the front door, and the orchard was full of makeshift tables of sawhorses and plywood, covered in blue-and-white checkered tablecloths with more Mason jars of lupine and balsam root, gardenias woven in. Her eyes rested on the old Inn journals, one on every table. She smiled at them like old friends, too emotional to open one up now. She looked up at the Chinese lanterns that hung from the apple trees, in every color. Kegs of beer stood in rows, galvanized tubs ready for something—ice or lemonade or whatever these women had thought up and brought to life. Just like she'd done it herself. Just like it.

Where in the world had they gotten all of this, and when had they worked this magic?

She went back into the Inn and noticed a table with a fresh journal on it, and an ink pen with a sign in Jane's handwriting: *WRITE DOWN A MEMORY OF THE HOMESTEAD.*

And then in Bliss's script:

Willa,

I found this quote in a book in the keeping room. It was underlined by Jack with a note in the margin that said, 'Willa.' The author wasn't a bird, but as a pilot, she flew through the sky. Like you are about to do. I believe in your migration, wherever it takes you, my friend Willa. And I'm sure Jack does too.

Your old friend,
Bliss

"I have learned that if you must leave a place that you have lived in and loved and where all your yesteryears are buried deep, leave it any way except a slow way, leave it the fastest way you can. Never turn back and never believe that an hour you remember is a better hour, because it is dead. Passed years seem safe ones, vanquished ones, while the future lives in a cloud, formidable from a distance. The cloud clears as you enter it. I have learned this, but like everyone, I learned it late."—Beryl Markham

And next to the journal, another note, this time in Jane's handwriting, *I found these tucked behind the journals,* with a giant pink heart.

The Emerson books.

Willa's heart pounded as she opened Jack's copy, just a bit more worn than hers. Her hands shook as she turned the page. There was a hundred-dollar bill. And she turned the next page. Another one. She turned the next page. Another one. His hands had been in these pages and she didn't want to get to the end, never mind the money. But she kept turning, leaving the bills in place. Fifty-nine pages. Thirty hundred-dollar bills. Some of them crisp. Some of them wrinkled. She shut the book and opened hers.

The same.

Then she held the books to her heart and closed her eyes, picturing him knowing he was leaving her, doing whatever he had done to get her this money. Maybe he'd even been desperate enough to take from the town coffer—finally given himself a paycheck. She wished she didn't need this money. She wished she could give it to the town. But if Willa, Montana, sold well, in good conscience, she'd have to keep it in the family. As he had intended. How would she ever tell her boys what their father had done to their savings? He had not written, *Don't tell the boys*. He knew she would have to.

But she couldn't afford to be romantic. Carefully, she took each of the bills and counted them. Six thousand dollars: what their *self-reliance* had added up to, outside the value of Willa, Montana. She felt ashamed and she felt grateful. Because they had done it their way. They *hadn't* chased mainstream ways. And for so long, it had been such a dream come true. And nothing could take that away. She'd keep the money for herself, as Jack had meant, and put the books in the mail to her sons next week, not as a cautionary tale, as much as a vote for their futures.

And then she saw Harriet lying on the window seat, stirring, still in her clothes from the night before.

"Busted," Harriet said, yawning. "Oh good. You saw the Emerson books. Jane was so excited I swear she *peed* in her *pants*."

"Harriet, what is all this?" Willa said, stuffing the money into her pocket. She wondered if Jane had opened the books. She didn't want to tell the women that all she had to her name was more or less, six thousand dollars.

"Well shit. Blame it on women. This is apparently what women *do*. When Jane's in charge. She went a little *nuts* a few days ago with some party store in Helena that delivers." Harriet yawned again. "You should see what those two women *do* when they're on a mission." She observed the rafters and smiled. "They make things *beautiful*."

"I'll say." Willa looked at the corner window seats and saw her friends now, sleeping under throw blankets, mouths open.

"It was fun. Trust me. You should have *seen* Jane and Bliss gathering fallen aspen branches in the dark with headlamps. I must have heard Bliss say the word *golly* four hundred times. I *swear*, that woman's gonna single-handedly bring *golly* back."

Willa smiled at the image of Jane and Bliss gathering branches in the dark. She looked up at the ceiling. "This is as beautiful as this place has ever looked."

Harriet yawned again and said, "Big day, huh."

"Yeah. Big day."

Harriet came over to her with wide wild eyes. She reached into the pockets of her pajamas and pulled out a tight fist. "I went to the buffalo jump early this morning. Not to the top. That's your place. But I went to the bottom. Where your boys went. And the bison landed. And I was scared. But I forced myself to stay. I imagined those beasts careening off that cliff. Dying at my feet. And I swear ... I felt them, Willa. I *felt* them."

She turned over her fist and slowly unfolded her fingers. "And I found these." Four bones. "I hope it's okay," she said, pressing a bison bone into Willa's palm.

Willa wasn't sure what was okay and not okay anymore, and it didn't matter. She gripped the bone and hugged Harriet and said, "It's time to start giving yourself a break."

"I'm trying to. I think that maybe ... my beast can live there.

At the bottom of the buffalo jump. For a while. Instead of in here." She pointed to her mind, and hugged Willa back hard. "I really love you, Willa."

"I really love you, Harriet," said Willa, slipping the bone into her bra, close to her heart.

"I have something I want you to see, Willa." Harriet took her hand and led her into the yard, past the tables poised for a party that had no promise of happening.

Just ... get ... through ... this ... day. It wasn't one of their parties and it wasn't Jack's memorial. Willa wished he could see it now. She wondered who would be there to see it. Usually everyone from Willa, Montana, and the whole county came to her events. Today, who knew?

Harriet walked across the yard like she owned the place. And she slid back the stubborn barn door like she'd done it a thousand times.

"You can hate me and never speak to me again and bring on my early demise. But this is what the last plane from Great Falls brought in."

Willa's eyes settled first on the windows above, which sent shafts of light down to the floor. Where she saw two sleeping bags in the straw.

She looked at Harriet.

"They know everything. I'll leave you alone."

Willa stood there.

Ned. Sam.

She looked up at the rope swing. They'd clearly been swinging on it. She'd laid it dormant, tied to the stall. Now it hung in the center. What a *meteor* brought in ...

She didn't want to wake them. Everything would have to be spoken once she did. She leaned against the barn wall, old nails poking at her back. She didn't care.

She knew this sleep of theirs. They had been up all night.

Nothing woke them when they were like this. So she went to the swing, dripping in morning barn light, and took the rope. She looked up at the top of the ladder. Why not. She held the rope as she climbed the ladder, rung by rung, up to the top window, until she sat on the platform that Jack had built years ago.

She looked down at the barn, at her sleeping boys, and at the day ahead of her. She leaned her head back as she had to the meteor last night. And she put her feet on the top, tight worn burl of a knot where they'd steadied their feet for years. *Jump, Mama*, she heard her little boys say, long ago now. "Jump," she said. "You are not going to fall."

She grabbed the rope like the rock on Bison Butte, and she flung herself out into the grainy filtering of light that was the world above her children's heads. It careened her out into the barn and she squealed and smiled and held on, until she was on the other side, almost to the platform, but just missing. And the rope brought her back, all the way, over her sons and all the years of horses and life and lovemaking and movie nights to the other side. And she dipped back her head and held on hard but let her arms go long. Not caring. Not … caring.

"Mama!"

She opened her eyes and looked down.

"Mama!"

Her boys were laughing and jumping like they could catch her. Like she was a bird they needed to release back into the wild.

"Hi!" she screamed, laughing. "How do I get off!"

"You just have to let it do its thing!" said Ned. "And then slide down. Or jump!"

"Here. I'll catch you," said Sam.

I'll catch you … She felt utter relief.

"Hi, boys!"

When the swing slowed its pendulum, she jumped down and

they both swept her up into their arms. And they hugged, rocking, as she had rocked them so many times. No words. They knew the truth. The women had done her work for her. The family hug forgave everything.

Then she pulled back and with her hands on their shoulders she said, "I'm sorry."

They looked at her, loose-jawed.

"I can't do this life alone, boys. Even if I had the money."

They were silent, both of them with tears in their eyes, squinting them away just like their father.

"Maybe you don't *want* to," Ned said, stone-faced.

"We don't expect you to," said Sam, eyeing his brother. "We've been thinking … maybe we can come back and take care of it."

Willa pulled them both in tight. "Listen to me, boys. You are *not* dropping out of college. Your father would never allow it, and I won't either. We've had a pretty good run here. And memories live even when people need to move on. Nothing … *nothing* can ever take your memories away from you."

She held them close and they held her back.

"But we want the Homestead, Mama," said Ned. "We can't let it go! Pops would never want that!"

Sam burst into tears and swiped them away. "He really didn't leave us with anything? I just can't believe that."

It was shattering to look at her sons' hero falling from his pillar.

"Don't worry. We saved a little bit for each of you. And he left me with a little something too. Enough to get started. He just had no idea that he was sick. He was so strong all his life, and … such a man of duty. Willa, Montana, was like his family too. They're hurting. I gave all the stuff that you boys didn't claim to them. I thought it was the right thing to do."

"There's got to be a way to save this place!" said Ned.

Willa thought of the owl and Jack's note for courage, and

translated it best as she could for her boys. "We have to let it go, Neddy and Sammy. There's a whole world out there. We have a new life in front of us. We have to live it. Pops told me that if anything ever happened to him ... I should go." Willa couldn't hold back her tears anymore, and she put her head into their shoulders and let them spill.

They held her tight and they wept in the crippled missing of their fourth person.

"Where *are* you going to go, Mama?" asked Sam, holding her tighter. "The ladies wouldn't really tell us. They said it's for you to say."

Willa pulled back and looked at her boys. "Well, up until yesterday, I didn't know. But I think your Pops has been talking to me through animals. He *would*, wouldn't he?"

They nodded.

"I have two ideas. It depends on how the auction goes. Either I move somewhere near you boys and find a job. That would be the practical thing. And if there's some money from the auction, I'll of course invest it for your futures. But first, I might do something that your Pops and I spoke of doing when you went off to college. It sounds a little wild. But we were a little wild, weren't we?"

They both nodded and smiled.

"Well ... I feel like I need something between my chapters." She paused and looked up to the rafters. "If I have a little extra windfall from the auction, I'd like to follow a bird migration for six months. Just to clear my head. It wouldn't cost much, and you know I could hop on a plane at any time if you needed me. We'll see. Plan A is more practical."

Sam patted her hard on the back. "Mama. We like Plan B. Don't we, Ned? And then Plan A."

Ned nodded, with just a blush of worry.

"Well, we'll see later today. In any case, hopefully whoever buys Willa, Montana, will pay top dollar. Who knows … we might even make some real money off of it."

They both gave half smiles.

"I spread his ashes. I know you didn't want to be there for it. And you were right. It was good for me to do it alone. I spread Dash's too. I watched them become one in the wind."

"Bison Butte?" Sam asked.

"Of course," Willa said.

All three of them looked up toward the butte, and Willa put her hand over her heart, feeling the bison bone.

"We'll get through this, Mama," said Ned.

"Wherever they are, Pops and Dash are doing deals for us, I bet," said Sam.

And Ned said, "Pops said something strange to me, just before he died. He said, *Tell your mother that she needs the book that brought us here. But don't tell her just yet.* I wasn't sure if I should tell you because I didn't want it to upset you. But I bet now's the time."

Willa took him in her arms. And Sam too. "You don't need to do this life alone, boys. That's what he was saying. Trust family. And always have friends. It's important to rely on yourself. But we need each other."

AUCTION. THREE O'CLOCK.
WILLA, MONTANA

The auctioneer, who was distinctly Not Local, stood on the back of a flatbed truck with a mic and a ten-gallon hat and a look of piqued hunger. No one wore a ten-gallon hat in Willa, Montana.

Willa and the women and her two boys were crammed into

her truck, parked just outside of the Merc parking lot, watching it from the back.

"Where is everyone?" asked Jane.

"In the Saloon," said Willa.

"What's all that *stuff* everywhere?" asked Bliss.

Willa looked closely at the scene. Closer than she wanted to. But couldn't read it.

"Ma, we're going to go see what's up," said Sam, opening the truck door. Ned was fast behind him.

"Boys," Willa called after them, but they were long gone.

"They're incredible," said Bliss. "Always have been."

"Yes," said Willa.

They were all silent.

"Listen, you three. I know that you have been doing things. On my behalf. And I'm embarrassed. Or maybe I'm pissed. Or maybe I'm ungrateful. Or maybe I've never had friends like this."

"Willa," said Bliss. "You don't have to say a word."

"Especially if you hate us," said Harriet.

"We overstepped," said Jane. "But did you see that I found something you were missing?"

"I did," said Willa. "Thank you." She looked at Jane and said, "Did you happen to read any of what was *in* the books?" And she waited. Six thousand dollars would be minuscule to a woman like Jane. Willa was good at stretching money and she did *not* want to be anyone's charity case.

Without blinking, Jane said, "I didn't feel like it was my place to do anything other than deliver you the books. They're so special and so personal. Plus I read *Self-Reliance* in prep school and that was enough. I'm pretty much everything it warns *not* to be. I'm the definition of *A foolish consistency is the hobgoblin of little minds.*"

"*Were*," said Harriet.

"Were," said Jane. With a residual question mark.

And because Jane was so honest, so respectful, Willa felt that she could speak. "That's where Jack hid the money. Okay? In the books. Of course. We never look in the obvious places for what we need. Do we."

Bliss said, "Well, let's hereby declare the four of us our *obvious place*. Going forward. We'll need each other."

"Done," said Harriet.

"Absolutely," said Jane.

"Was it substantial?" asked Bliss.

"Yes," said Willa. Then she smiled and nodded at them. "I can't thank you enough for saying *yes* to the invitation."

Then Bliss got out of the truck and opened Willa's door. "We got you."

Willa looked into her friend's eyes, nodding. Then she looked at Jane, who blew her a kiss. And then at Harriet, who gave her a sturdy thumbs-up and said, "Let's do this."

They walked toward the Mercantile parking lot to the bass-booming sounds of auction music that no one in Willa, Montana, was used to. It was the sound of greed. Willa wanted to rip the speaker wires out of the sound system.

The auctioneer stood on the back of a flatbed in a crisp white shirt, bolo tie, cowboy boots, and his enormous cowboy hat. It was hard not to look at him like the enemy. And yet she was the one who had hired him.

He's just doing his job. This is not in my control anymore.

The women walked with her around the flatbed. She put out her hand to the auctioneer, whose skin was Ivory-soap clean.

He smiled at her and said, "We stand a good chance, Mrs. Silvester. We have a lot of value here. And we've been spreading the word. Flyers. Radio ads." He tipped his hat. "Do you think we have at least two bidders? Takes two to tango."

She nodded and tried to smile with some level of confidence

where there was none. Then she took her hand back as fast as she could, looking for her boys.

Instead, she saw something entirely different. "Oh ... my ..." Willa couldn't finish her sentence.

Harriet put her arm around her and pushed her forward. "I don't know what this is, but I think it's *good*, Willa. I've seen bad, and *this* is good."

In the parking lot, on makeshift tables, against the Merc and the Saloon, the gas pumps, everywhere ... were things. Things that Willa knew.

She looked at Bliss.

Bliss walked on.

And then she saw Jack's hammer. Glinting in the sun, because he would never put it away unless it was cleaned and oiled and perfect. And his handmade bow. And all of his hand-fashioned arrows. And his quiver. Rack after rack of antlers, many of them twelve-point. His guns and his ammunition in boxes, all placed in careful rows. His fly-tying supplies. His river maps. The popcorn maker. The movie projector. The apple press. The typewriter.

"Bliss?" Willa whispered loudly.

"I don't know what this *is*," Bliss said.

Willa walked among the tables. This was her *life*.

Please not my saddle, she thought. "I need a beer," she said, walking into the Saloon, forgetting the last weeks.

The place was packed.

Willa went straight to Earl. "What's all that out there for?" she asked. "I gave all that away."

Earl shrugged and the auction bell rang. The Saloon emptied into the parking lot. Earl, Wink, Vic, Syd, Poe, Adele, Tally, Marilyn, Nel. Jane, Harriet, Bliss. Her boys. Everybody.

And it wasn't just the denizens of Willa, Montana. Willa looked around her. It was people from all over the area, up and down the highway, and deep into the woods. And some she'd never seen before, maybe even from Great Falls or Helena. A parking lot full of people with nothing else to do on a weekend afternoon in May but watch her town get eaten alive.

She reminded herself: *That's the point. I'm selling. This is what I want.* She scoured the crowd for the *two to tango* the auctioneer prescribed. Or the developers that had stood at their door in new jeans and cowboy hats over the years. She didn't recognize any of the Not Locals.

The auctioneer came in loud and thunderous like a rodeo announcer. "*Here* is the town of Willa, Montana. One square mile and that's six *hundred* and forty acres, folks! Let's bring the auction to start. One farmhouse, an inn, a barn, a mercantile, post office, a gas pump, a saloon, *and* its very own zip code in one of the most *beautiful* parts of *big* sky country." He pointed to the tables. "*And* some odd lots, looks like. Let's start the bidding at fifty *thousand* dollars." The auctioneer tipped his ten-gallon hat and leaned in, chanting, "*HABUDADABUD-HABUDADABUD-A-FIFTY-A-BUDA-CANWEGETA-HABUDADABUDA.*"

Fifty thousand dollars? Willa thought. She'd put the reserve at two hundred and fifty thousand dollars. Which was still low. *Fifty thousand dollars?* That wasn't anywhere near what this sacred place was worth.

Willa thought of Emilio and Maria standing there. The ones who'd known it was priceless. And she couldn't stand to imagine the ones who had come before them, the natives.

She looked at Nel and wanted to get on her knees and beg for a world of forgiveness. But Nel looked past her at the auctioneer.

"This is *not* how they do it at Sotheby's," said Jane.

"No *kidding*," Harriet replied, putting her arm around Jane.

The auctioneer continued, looking around for his heat, "Can I get fifty thousand dollars? Fifty thousand dollars for an *entire* town of *prime* Montana real estate, folks. Your slice of the *biiiiiig* sky."

Then Willa remembered what he'd said. "We like to get the bidding started somewhere lower than the reserve. We'll let the auction work, to drive the price high enough to be acceptable to you, Mrs. Silvester."

Acceptable. What was acceptable? She shook her head. She couldn't help it. Maybe they would see her utter shame.

No one said a thing.

The auctioneer looked over at Willa as if she had answers.

She looked off into the crowd. *Where are they all?*

The auctioneer changed his tone to a low and somber baritone, "Folks, there will be a reserve on this property and it's going to be reasonable, so don't be shy."

Willa's heart raced, her mind flipping from the million-dollar offers to her reserve, wondering if she'd been foolish. She remembered his words, "We want to get your town sold. And we don't want to waste your time or ours." Why was she worrying about the auctioneer?

He mopped his forehead with a bright white handkerchief. "Folks, this land has everything you want: Rivers, creeks, mountains, meadows, trees … all under the *big* big sky. This is a *very* desirable, highly sought-after piece of Montana property." He almost sounded insulted.

Willa couldn't help but agree. She scanned the crowd, looking at each denizen of Willa, Montana. And the rest of the Not Locals. No one met her gaze. Was this all just going to be *entertainment* for them? Were there no real *bidders*?

She watched her sons, wanting to protect them as they looked around too.

She looked for Nel. She was leaning against Marilyn, both of them stone-faced.

Then she looked for Sook, tied up at the hitching post.

How had her life come to this?

The auctioneer boomed from the flatbed. "Folks, can I have *fifty* thousand dollars for one square mile of Montana land and all of this *knock-your-socks-off* beauty in *the* last best place in the *United* States of America? Can I have fifty thousand *dollars*?"

"Maybe they'll call in," said Jane. "That's often done."

Everyone stood in the parking lot, most of them with their backs to the Saloon or the Merc. Holding beers. No one spoke.

Willa looked at the tables. Certain items seemed to beat like hearts: Jack's hammer. Jack's bow. His typewriter. Rows of tools and boxes of odds and ends from all corners of the Homestead. *It's a gut pile of my life.*

"Folks … this is a *steal* at fifty thousand dollars!"

Nothing.

The auctioneer shook his head, mopped his brow with his handkerchief again, and called out loud with his baritone, "One square mile. One homestead, an inn, a saloon, a mercantile, a gas pump, a post office, *and* its very own zip code. Fifty thousand *dollars*, folks. What a steal!"

No one.

Willa shrunk. And she thought of something the auctioneer had said to her on the phone. "It doesn't matter where you start, it's where you end." Just where was that going to be if no one bid on Willa, Montana?

Bliss stood sentry next to her.

The auctioneer leaned into his mic.

Harriet whispered, "Come *on*, people!"

Jane tore at her pink nails.

"I'll bid on the hammer," yelled Earl. "Five hundred dollars."

"The hammer. We've had a bid of five hundred dollars." The auctioneer held on to his ten-gallon hat.

"*FIVE ... HABUDADABUD-HABUDADABUDA-FIVE-ABUD-ACAN-WEGET-AHABUDADABUDA.*"

Willa looked at Earl.

Syd stepped forward. "Five-fifty," he said.

The auctioneer all but spat on his mic.

Then Nel. "Five seventy-five," she said.

"Nel!" Willa couldn't help but shout.

The auctioneer took it and ran. "Five seventy-five for a hammer. A *hammer*! Folks, can I get six hundred dollars for this apparently *very* special hammer? Anyone? Anyone?"

No one spoke.

"Fair warning." He looked around. Then he screamed, "Sold! To the woman in the front here. Congratulations! You got yourself a five-hundred-and-seventy-five-dollar hammer!"

Nel looked at Marilyn and Marilyn looked away.

Then it was the ammo. Fifteen hundred dollars. And the bow. Six hundred dollars. And the elk bugles. Three hundred and fifty dollars. All locals doing the bidding.

Willa stared agape at every citizen of Willa, Montana. They didn't look at her at all.

"Next lot," said the auctioneer. "A bunch of frozen meat, it looks like. Let's start the bidding at two hundred dollars. Can I get *HABUDADABUD-HABUDADABUDA-TWOHUNDRED-BABDBABDBAD-BABDABDABDBA ...*"

Willa looked at Nel, who looked at the ground.

Vic stepped forward, his oxygen tank not far behind. "Five hundred twenty-five for the meat."

"What the *hell*?" said Willa. *That was a gift!*

Lot by lot, Jack's things were sold. The popcorn machine. The apple press. His Remington.

But not the town. No one bid on the town.

"Well, folks, we have over five thousand dollars for odd

lots, but *zero*, that's *zeeee*-roe for the town of Willa, Montana."
The auctioneer seemed like he'd seen this more times than he
hadn't.

Willa stared at her boys who shrugged with their hands in
their pockets.

The auctioneer went on, drunk on it all. "What do we have
next?" He hooted and leaned into the mic. "Looks like we have a
nut bucket, folks! And that's the last lot. Even if I can't get a buyer
for Willa, Montana, can I get three hundred dollars for a pretty
darn good nut bucket? Start the bidding at *CANIGET-CANIGET* ..."

One of the Saloon assholes she'd overheard days before raised
his hand. "Three hundred."

"Three hundred," called the auctioneer. "Can I get three-fifty?
Three-fifty ... three-fifty."

No takers.

"Hold on!" yelled a young voice. That's when Nel walked
forward into the parking lot, stepped up onto the flatbed, put her
mouth to the microphone, and asked, "Is that enough, Willa? Is
fifty-three hundred dollars enough?"

"Fair warning on the nut bucket!" called the auctioneer.

And Willa understood. They were doing what they could
to pay her back for what Jack had freely given them. And what
she had freely given them via the women, the other night at the
Saloon. She looked at Nel and then at her boys. She knew these
people. Refusing the money would be the worst insult of all. Willa
gave Nel a faint but clear nod.

Nel stepped aside.

"Can I get three-fifty ... three-*fifty*, folks?"

No takers.

"And, sold! A nut bucket for three *hundred* dollars, folks! *Now*
I've seen *every*thing!" The auctioneer mopped his forehead with
his handkerchief. "Folks. We're at an impasse here. We don't have

the buying power to satisfy the seller's reserve bid. So we're gonna No-Sale the property."

Everyone clapped and hooted and a few did little jigs.

Except for Willa.

"And that marks the end of the auction. Thanks for coming out, folks. You can spend your money over at the table here where this lovely lady will gladly take it." He pointed to an unfamiliar old woman in a violet pantsuit, wearing a large rhinestone broach that said JESUS.

Bliss turned to Willa and said, "Now *I've* seen everything."

The auctioneer was sweating through his shirt, and he went over to Willa. "I'm sorry, Mrs. Silvester. But you still own yourself a town. Small towns out here in rural Montana stick around like crumbs in a bed."

"But we've had so many developers over the years want to buy us out. I don't understand."

The auctioneer shook his head. "Blame it on the missile silos. Blame it on winter. Blame it on Washington, DC. But you've still got yourself a town, ma'am."

Her boys came up to her. "Mama—we still own our town!"

"Yes," she said, not knowing what else to say.

Bliss took them under her wing. "Sam and Ned, maybe if you announce the party, people will come. You wrangle the troops back home, why don't you?"

Willa tried to say, *I don't want people to come anymore*, but that was as true as it wasn't.

The boys stepped up on the flatbed and took the mic. Sam said, "In true Willa, Montana, form, as a thank-you, we'd like you all to come up to the Homestead for soup and pie and our Pops's homebrew. You know no one can throw a party like our Mama." Sam added, "And bring your instruments!"

Willa couldn't bear to look one person in the eye. Not even

her boys, who were being circled like heroes by all of the locals.

She got in the truck as fast as she could. Jane jumped in, followed by Harriet and Bliss.

Willa jammed it in reverse and pulled out toward the road. "What. Just. *Happened?*"

"You still own the town," said Jane. "And you made some money. They're trying to say they care about you. That was their olive branch."

"Are you sure?" said Willa. "I mean, maybe I was supposed to refuse the money. Maybe it was some sort of *gesture* after what Jack did for them. But maybe it was a final test. Like we got them into this mess to begin with by creating a town that we couldn't keep. And I was supposed to say *no*, and give it back to them so that *they* could buy the town? Was that what was going on, do you think? Do they even *have* fifty thousand dollars amongst them?"

"Willa. That makes no sense. Nobody buys a town for fifty thousand dollars," said Jane. "Take a deep breath. You're in shock. Nobody bought the town. They're just giving you a gift in the only way they know how."

Willa went on, "What did Nel mean by was it *enough*? Enough to live off of? Enough to stay here? Enough to pay me back? I'm so confused!"

"You heard Nel," said Bliss. "I think she was speaking for them all. That money is for *you*."

"But is it for me to stay and not *leave*? I don't *want* to own this town! And I already feel bad enough. I can't take their money and leave!"

"We had nothing to do with any of that, just so you know," said Harriet. "But holy fuck was that powerful!"

Willa put her hand to her breast and pushed on the bison bone until it was sharp against her flesh. She pulled over to the side of the road and looked them all square in the eye.

"I don't *want* powerful. I want *release*. I'm *leaving* here. That's what I felt at the river yesterday. And on Bison Butte. I need to get *out*, Harriet. Everything I know of Montana gave itself to me yesterday." She heaved a shallow breath. "And I have to listen."

"Everything. And today ... every*one*," said Bliss.

Harriet held up an imaginary drink. "Cheers to that."

Willa's head felt like it was doing 360s. "It didn't sell! I never thought in my wildest dreams that it wouldn't sell at *all*. I'm stuck here." *I'm stuck here*, she thought.

She jammed the truck into gear and they were silent as she drove them back to this land that wouldn't let her go, and this town that wouldn't either. She shook her head past every mile marker sign. PLEASE DON'T BUY OUR TOWN. "Well, their wish came true." She had never felt more like a betrayer.

The Homestead was waiting. It was more beautiful than Willa had ever known it could be. The lanterns, the flowers, the tablecloths, the white lights, and tree boughs. Willa looked at it all. She didn't feel sad. She didn't feel anything. Willa, Montana, was still hers. Not only that ... no one wanted it. And the people who did couldn't afford it.

Jane, Bliss, and Harriet went to work, bringing out the loaves of bread, setting up the hot plates with two giant pots of soup, lining up the pies. So hopeful. The boys would be here soon, likely having a beer with old buddies at the Saloon.

Willa couldn't take it. She didn't want the whole town in her yard. She didn't know what she wanted. But she *did* have a deep knowing that she had to call her mother. And the best place for that was in her bed.

She answered, like clockwork, just after the second ring—never wanting to come across too eager. "Hello?"

"Hi, Mom. It's Willa. Sorry I haven't called for a while." She was past tears. "I just wanted to say that I tried to leave Montana.

I put the town up for auction. And no one bought it. So I have to stay. And I'm scared. I can't do it without Jack. And I'm sorry that I didn't do what you wanted me to do with my life."

Her mother was silent. And then she said, "Of course you can do it without Jack, Willa. You're the strongest woman I know." And she added, "And your father thought so too."

And Willa sat there at the edge of her bed, staring at her hands, so rough and weathered, and thought of her mother's hands, so soft and pink. "The boys are home. And there's a party in the orchard."

"Tell them *hello*," she said. "And come back for a visit one of these days."

Willa nodded. "I will, Mom. Thank you. I love you. I'll call when I have more time."

She hung up and got into bed, drew the bison bone from her breast, stuffed it under her pillow next to the owl feather, and pulled the covers up over her head until strains of familiar music played in her dreams.

Fiddle tunes and still-sunny evenings and little boys running through sprinklers and bees and hummingbirds sipping apple-blossom nectar. She lay there with her eyes closed. She needed to get down there and do her thing. Serve food. Make the rounds. Take the pulse of Willa, Montana, where she was the mother of it all. Jack would be down there already, sitting on his grandfather's old stool with his mandolin, making Syd's fiddle-playing better than it was, and making Earl think he could sing. They were playing "Shenandoah." Maybe she'd join in on the harmony. Grab her guitar and play along.

Oh, Shenandoah,
I long to hear you
Away, you rollin' river

Oh, Shenandoah,
I long to hear you
Away, I'm bound away
'Cross the wide Missouri

Willa listened, soothed by the mandolin, which always meant her love was nearby.

She sat up, breaking the dream.

Who was playing the mandolin?

She looked out the window, but she couldn't quite see.

She saw Bliss and Jane standing under an apple tree, holding beers. She saw Harriet and Nel by the barn in close conversation, especially for Nel, who was letting Sook graze next to her. She saw an empty yard. And her old truck parked where they used to position it for parties, expecting bumper-to-bumper trucks in the side-yard by the aspen grove.

She went to the mirror and practiced saying it into her tired eyes. "I'm not staying. I'm giving the money back. There's no way I can keep it."

She slipped on an old sundress and brushed her braid out. Found her old straw hat and a cotton shawl she'd crocheted before she'd even had the boys. Barefoot, she pushed herself out of her room, down the stairs, and out the front door to the stoop, part of her believing she'd find Jack there with his mandolin.

It was almost Jack. Almost. She smiled.

Ned looked up at her and smiled back, picking out a lick for her on Jack's mandolin, smiling at his brother who sat on a log, playing her guitar. Her boys were fiddle players. When had they learned to play their parents' instruments? She smiled at Earl and Wink who gave her shy nods. And then at Syd who blushed, always better around dogs than people.

They played the first stanza again, and she went over behind her boys and sang the harmony with Syd. *"Away. We're bound away. 'Cross the wide Missouri."*

"Put your hands together for Grin and Bear It!" Ned shouted.

Jane and Bliss clapped, holding their beers in the air, Harriet and Nel joining them.

"Well, this is a party, just us, isn't it?" said Willa, trying to smile, pouring herself a beer, smelling the old familiar malty hoppy brew that her husband treated as well as anything in his life.

Jane came to her and held both of her hands. She pulled her in and whispered, "Willa. Like you said to us. You have everything you need." And she slipped a gardenia into Willa's straw hat. "You deserve to be festooned in beauty, my dear friend."

Willa was about to say *thank you*, as the first truck crested the hill. Marilyn.

And then the Petersons. Halls. Andersens. Ploumes. Rasmussens. O'Briens. Hansens. Carlsons. Fitzpatricks. Pillens.

All of them parked near the aspen grove, and all of them walked toward her, holding something in their hands.

Antler racks, a bow and arrow and quiver, guns and ammo, a shiny hammer, and even a nut bucket. They brought them the way a country town does, with purpose and no nonsense.

Marilyn shouted, "You'll be needing these things up here, Willa!" and led the way to the barn, where she slid the door open with her foot and went inside, the rest of them following her.

Willa stood there like she was watching it all from atop the butte.

Then they filed out of the barn and came to her, Marilyn at the lead. She presented Willa with a sheet of paper with a long list of what looked like signatures.

Willa looked closer. They *were* signatures. And next to the signatures, there were words: *Fence-mending, Haying, Pruning, Gardening, Cleaning, Canning, Soup, Pie, Bread*. She recognized every single signature and she looked up at each of the humans they belonged to, wishing she could say something or show something other than this utter overwhelm.

Marilyn said, "You'll need help."

Then Harriet stepped forward holding Nel's hand. "Willa. I've decided … we've decided … if you'll allow it … that I'm going to move here for a while. And run the Homestead. So you can take a rest. Get out of Dodge. Spread your wings." She winked at Willa. "That's my So Now What. I hope that solves yours too."

Willa choked out these words: "But … there's no money to run the Merc. Or the Saloon. Or to take care of the rentals."

Marilyn looked her dead in the eye. "We're going to keep doing what we've been doing down in town." She eyed the two young men who had said such hurtful things. "There's plenty of able-bodied young people around here who can help out." Then Marilyn eyed Jane, paused, and smiled wider than Willa knew she could. "And your friend Jane here is going to help us get on our feet. She says Montana has given her something she'd never be able to receive back East. And she wants to help us keep things the same around here. And we respect that."

Jane clapped and jumped up and down.

Willa looked at Jane and then Bliss, who smiled and nodded. She didn't know what to say or do or think.

And with all of these people in her yard, everyone she truly loved, except for her beloved, she realized that she didn't have to say or do or think anything. They were doing it for her. And it felt so good.

"Okay," Willa whispered, tears streaming down her cheeks. "Okay." She paused. "Thank you."

"Thank *you*!" said all of them.

"Any requests, Willa?" asked Earl.

Willa thought. "Well. Yeah. Actually, I do have a tune I'd love to hear if I'm really going away for a while." She smiled at the band, and then her boys, and then the women, and then the town. She was really going to do this.

"'I'll Fly Away.' The way Jack used to play it. Slow and sad." She looked down at her bare feet and up again. "Like I'll be."

And that was that. The music started up. They all got beers and served themselves soup and tore off pieces of bread and sat down, and some of them danced, and some of them sang along.

> *I'll fly away ... fly away, oh glory*
> *I'll fly away in the morning*
> *When I die, Hallelujah by and by*
> *I'll fly away.*

And they all folded into each other, there in the orchard. Like they always did.

The Invitation

Willa stopped at the corner of Main and the highway. She looked at the Mercantile, with its freshly painted sign. No cars yet, so early on this June morning.

She took a deep jittery breath and eyed the envelope the women had given her as they'd disbanded two weeks before—Bliss and Jane to the Great Falls airport, walking sticks in hand. She and Harriet standing on the front porch, waving, as the mud-encrusted rental bumped down the drive.

"Don't open it until you miss us," they'd said.

"Which might not happen until Belize," said Jane.

"Or at all," said Bliss.

And she thought of Harriet, just this morning, standing in the orchard, wearing her MONTANA MAMA apron, looking more like she belonged there than Willa had in months. She'd held Willa by the shoulders, green eyes to green eyes. And she'd given her a bundle of the wintered-over sage from the garden, wrapped in twine. "Take this with you. It's from Nel. She says to burn it when you get lost in the past."

Willa put it in her pocket, thinking about Nel in her garden, maybe by moonlight.

And then Harriet gave her the last journal from the Homestead party and said, "You have everything you need, Willa," and pushed down on her shoulders, steadying her.

Willa allowed herself to feel the Montana ground she loved underneath her, holding her. "I have no idea what that means, but every reason to believe that I'll find out."

Willa needed to open the envelope now. She needed the courage. Or whatever it was that brought open hearts into open lives.

She picked it up and turned it over, smiling at the familiar sage green wax seal. She slid her finger under the wax and pulled out a pressed gardenia. She smiled and held its creamy remembrance to her nose. Four feathers fell out then. White with black tips.

Next, she pulled out a photograph. It was of all four of them, standing in the orchard, arm in arm, with the whole town behind them, her boys perched below her, all of them holding up a glass, smiling vigorously, and only a little sadly.

Then she pulled out a notecard in her handmade stationery. Written on an old typewriter, the card read:

Willa,

you are invited to the rest of your life.

We believe in your migration.
One year from today,
all four of us are invited to migrate back,
for another week together
in honor of our ever-growing So Now What.

Thank you, for beginning this grove.

Love,

Bliss, Harriet, and Jane

At the bottom, three signatures:

An elegant slanted *Bliss*, a wide-looped *Harriet*, and a neat-but-not-too-neat *Jane*.

Willa put the invitation to her heart, smiling, and gasped back a few tears. Then she tucked it all behind the sun visor where she'd keep it for when she needed those words, those feathers, and that photo ... along the way.

Tears streamed from her eyes and she let them. She tasted them. She swallowed them.

Then Willa looked at the Homestead journal—she'd save it for later—and then at the owl feather hanging from the rearview mirror, bundled together in a braid of Sook's tail hair, the sow's bone and the bison bone woven into the braid. She pressed the bison bone between her thumb and forefinger until it hurt. Then she released it and brought her thumb to her face and stared at the imprint. In the center of that imprint was the circle of her finger's map, and all around it, circles.

She smiled. Put her hand in the pocket of her flannel shirt, took out another bone. Held it hard. Looked at the atlas on the passenger seat. And headed south.

*"You know … we're all fluent in this language.
In the language of community. And yet we so rarely
speak it. It really is our mother tongue."*

Dear Reader,

I have learned something that might just be the most important lesson of my life, and I would like to share it with you. There is a language that we crave. A language of the heart that grows from our worry and our wonder and our stories, rooted in our experience of this beautiful and heartbreaking thing called life. Too many of us have trained ourselves out of speaking that language. We were all fluent in it when we were children. But somewhere along the way we were taught or conditioned to forget it. To not be honest when we are asked, "How are you?" And to not really listen to the answer when we ask others the same question.

So many of us have lost our authentic voices and reduced our conversations to grocery store talk and texts with an emoji at the end. The truth is, we long to be seen and heard and accepted, *especially* when we are in pain—yet out of fear of judgment or rejection, we too often draw in and become islands, rather than bridging to our family and friends. I know this because, at times, I've made that choice. And the fallout from that led me to devote a major piece of my life to bringing people together in safe, intimate circles of self-expression. Which led me to write this book.

I wrote *Willa's Grove* to capture the power of people stepping out of the isolation and self-doubt that so many of us feel in times of transition, and instead, gathering together. These women show us that we don't have to endure hardship alone, nor should we. We have choices. If, for whatever reason, connecting with our usual community is too fraught, we can instead create temporary circles, friend to friend to friend to friend, carving out small interludes from our daily lives in order to focus on what comes next. To have those conversations we need to be having but aren't. To move boldly outside of gossip, small talk, pretending ... and into the connection we so deeply need.

I hope that in reading this book, and in the spirit of Willa, Bliss, Harriet, and Jane ... you will be inspired to reach out to your own dear friends, whether close by or far away. And that you will invite them to come together for short respites to support one another in the powerful way that people can when they give themselves permission to say *yes* to the profound invitations of their lives.

My mission is this: We will start a movement of weeklong interludes from the stresses and pain of our crossroads moments, and in radical and real communication, we will provide ourselves, and our kindreds, with a map for our next steps.

Our voices deserve to be honored and heard. No one has your voice. No one. However we speak, now is the time for truth.

And yes, we don't have to do it alone.

Yours,
Laura

Acknowledgments

I would like to thank:

All the folks at Blackstone for making a very old dream come true. When I saw that you started in a garage in Oregon ... I knew I'd found the right stewards for this novel.

My stalwart and abiding agent, Beth Davey, who has held my hand and heart for a long time now with her stunning love, grace, and excellence.

My editor, Madeline Hopkins, for seeing with my eyes and heart and delivering my blind spots with such acumen and aplomb.

My early readers, especially: Anna Gellar, Christina Henry de Tessan, Lee Woodruff, Christine Pride, Molly Caro May, Caroline Hemphill, Kassidy Harris, and Kylanne Sandelin. Sharing the early drafts of a novel requires a specific sort of trust. You all truly saw this book. And me.

The angels at my table, especially: My personal cyber slather guru, Susie Stangland, who knows how to make the internet a friendly and generous place, especially for writers. And Connie Cermak, who took my vision for this book and its ripples and ran.

David Rasmussen who stood by every step of this book until the end and held my heart as I went. And who listened in the way the women of *Willa's Grove* listen to each other. Endless gratitude.

Bobbi Hall, Helen Pilling, and Sarah Jane Anderson who have taught me much about being a woman in Montana, self-reliance, and community. Willa would be dear friends with you all.

Stephanie Winchester and Kari Pricher who held and inspired my early thoughts about this endeavor and who speak Grove language fluently.

The Black Sheep Masterminds who keep me on track every Tuesday at 11:00 on the dot. AF.

The real Grin and Bear It for teaching me that when you sing about dancing with bears, the forest opens its heart to you.

J. J. Elliott for being there exactly when I need her and who also loves an ensemble cast of women characters. Now it's your turn!

Every single alum of my Haven Writing programs for showing me the power of temporary community and that sometimes, it's the only way to become aware of old patterns, shed them, and move forward in our lives.

The Walking Lightly Ranch and the Dancing Spirit Ranch for holding me, as I hold my retreaters.

The beautiful and powerful yogi, Arlisa Houston, who taught Haven Writing Retreat how to breathe. Your memory will live on in all of us.

Dani Shapiro, Linda Sivertsen, and Jennifer Schelter (who is my personal and movable Grove. *Ti amo sempre.*), for telling me that I would be a natural at leading writing retreats … Thank GOD I believed you.

Lee Woodruff. Sister in words and spirit. Thank you for being exactly you.

My literary hero, Jim Harrison, who promised he'd blurb a novel if I could pull off getting one in print. You are the reason I knew at eighteen that I wanted to write fiction. Rest in peace and birdsong.

My mother and my sister who pray for me faithfully and have listened to my dream of publishing a novel for many, many years. Deep and forever bows.

Dad, Mimi, Chet, Gogo, Fafa ... I feel you watching over me. I took your bedtime blessings to heart: "There are more eyes watching over you than you'll ever know." "In this world of darkness, we must shine. You in your small corner, and I in mine." "People are the same everywhere."

Montana, and all of the Montanans who have touched my heart in this twenty-seven-year surprise chapter of my life. You serve up undying inspiration every day.

And of course, my children, who have had faith in my ability to write a novel and who have been exceptional troubleshooters and brainstormers from the start. You have my whole heart.

I also want to thank my muse. You've never left me. And you never will. I know that with every fiber of my being. Thank you for being so true.